ORIANA'S EYES

ORIANA'S EYES

BOOK ONE OF THE GREAT OAK TRILOGY

Celeste Simone

iUniverse, Inc.
New York　Bloomington

Copyright © 2009 by Celeste Simone

All rights reserved. No part of this book may be used or reproduced by any means, graphic, electronic, or mechanical, including photocopying, recording, taping or by any information storage retrieval system without the written permission of the publisher except in the case of brief quotations embodied in critical articles and reviews.

This is a work of fiction. All of the characters, names, incidents, organizations, and dialogue in this novel are either the products of the author's imagination or are used fictitiously.

iUniverse books may be ordered through booksellers or by contacting:

iUniverse
1663 Liberty Drive
Bloomington, IN 47403
www.iuniverse.com
1-800-Authors (1-800-288-4677)

Because of the dynamic nature of the Internet, any Web addresses or links contained in this book may have changed since publication and may no longer be valid. The views expressed in this work are solely those of the author and do not necessarily reflect the views of the publisher, and the publisher hereby disclaims any responsibility for them.

ISBN: 978-1-4401-8724-7 (sc)
ISBN: 978-1-4401-8722-3 (dj)
ISBN: 978-1-4401-8723-0 (ebook)

Printed in the United States of America

iUniverse rev. date: 02/17/2010

For Carolina and Natalie.

CHAPTER ONE

The bleached ceilings, walls, and floors gleam in perfection. Drained of color, wiped of contamination, forever untainted they exist; a cold reminder of my purity.

I walk down a blank hallway lit by a series of white lights from above. Each one is a half orb, emerging from the ceiling like an unblinking eye. They're practically blinding as their glow reflects off the stark white walls. There are no openings for us to see out of—only for Odon to see in.

A clump of books rests on my hip while my arms cradle them close: *The History, The Faith*. They're practically attached to me. I can't remember a time when they weren't close by. I've read them over and over for class, but no matter how many times I read them, I still can't find the answers I'm looking for.

The History, which takes up two of the volumes, speaks of how Odon created us and rescued our race from our own ignorance. At first the Rebirth did not exist, and we were of many races that thrived on violence. We battled constantly for anything we could contrive to fight for. Then Odon arrived and divided us into our purest forms, the Winglets and Finlets. The Winglets have a light complexion, while the Finlets are a darker people.

He taught us that being pure made us stronger and brought us peace. Of course some didn't agree with this, because they were not pure, and they started to rebel. Odon decided the only way to stop this was by separating the races so that we were only in contact with our own.

My other two books, held tightly, tell of our Faith: how to follow Odon, how to live life in accordance with his standards. I know all his rules well. I must not question them. It would not be approved of. It would cause suspicion among my peers, regardless of my pureblood. In this place everyone has the potential to disappear.

I try to avoid the gazes of other purebloods. Some are male Winglets, searching for some meaningless connection with the opposite sex. Their interest in me doesn't go beyond my golden hair and blue eyes, both Winglet features. The purest Winglets achieve both traits with the palest skin to match these hallways. I am no exception in that regard either.

Some show the darkness of the Finlets in their eyes or hair. They are called part-bloods. Finlets can be part-blood too if they have Winglet in their blood, but these combinations of races hardly ever happen anymore. Odon makes sure of that.

It's the half-bloods that are the least respected. They're barely thought of as Odon's children. They are neither Winglet nor Finlet, yet equally both. They're rarely seen in the University. Following the Rebirth there are said to be none at all. They have a habit of simply disappearing, never to be seen again, but no one cares.

I head to the library. I have a test tomorrow, and I've decided to study a bit more before I go to sleep. Another male Winglet passes, and I avoid his eyes completely. The effect is the same as if I had made eye contact: a dull pain in my stomach.

I notice immediately a passing half-blood. His combination of black hair and blue eyes upon darker skin are a beacon in the crowd of identical features. Something urges me to look straight at him, maybe to test him. He is expected to look away. It is unheard of for a half-blood to meet the gaze of a pureblood. Our history says that his race doesn't deserve to exist, much less live with us. It's because of what he is. He is the offspring of two purebloods, the ultimate defiance of Odon.

It frightens me to even think of going against Odon. All the books tell of his limitless power, endless knowledge, forgiveness and insatiable wrath. I have no doubt he would find me, persecute me if I ever—the half-blood continues toward me. He is the representation of two fallen servants of Odon, and yet my eyes will not turn away. Something leaps inside me when his eyes meet mine. I have a moment's thought—*Doesn't he know I'm a pureblood?*—but he doesn't seem to notice at all.

I'm surprised by my initial dislike that fades into an aching fear. He continues to meet my gaze. I wonder what expression has formed on my face, although there should be none at all. When we pass on opposite sides of the hallway, an unmistakable smile forms on his face. I gasp and drop my books. He is nowhere in sight as purebloods help me gather them back up.

The thought of him follows me into the library and festers at the back of my mind among other open sores. The question whether I should report him continues to resurface in my thoughts. I've only told on a student once before.

She was a part-blood, and we were eleven years old. I remember her brown eyes and wavy blond hair. The Finlet in her had given her the darker eyes, but they were not as black as a pureblood Finlet's would have been. She had fair skin that wasn't quite fair enough to be pure. It was obvious she was a part-blood.

We were waiting in line for lunch. A part-blood is always expected to sacrifice their spot in line to a pureblood, another privilege we are taught to uphold. But when I asked this girl to let me take her spot, she wholeheartedly refused. Her mouth twisted into a pout and her eyes narrowed into a stubborn glare. Even after I politely explained that I was pure and showed her my eyes and pointed at my hair, she just shook her head.

I was surprised, but pressed no further. Instead I did what I was told to do, being too young and ignorant to fully understand. I approached a nearby teacher and explained what had happened. I was told I had done the responsible thing, I was told I was a good little Winglet—and I never saw that girl again.

The memory makes my stomach cringe. Despite the time that has passed, it remains vivid. I try to keep it hidden, to save myself from the wave of anxiety that overcomes me each time I recall her face. Do the others suffer in silence like me? If they do, it never reaches their eyes.

CHAPTER TWO

I consider for a moment asking Lenora what to do. Should I report the half-blood for his curious behavior? After all, he not only met my gaze, but defied mine with a smile. But I already know what she will say. She will tell me the only honorable thing to do is to tell one of the professors and let the faculty deal with him. I decide I'd better not tell her.

The softer light of the library is a relief to my eyes. I enter between rows of square desks. At the back of the room a single bookcase holds two shelves worth of the four different books that each student already has: the two of History and two of Faith. Looking at them now, I can't understand their purpose. A student would *never* lose their own copies, not if they wanted to remain at the University.

From here I can see plainly that the library's books have never been opened. Their bindings were never creased; the pages have never seen the light of the room. When I start to covet them, I turn away to quickly take a seat at the side of the room that is furthest from the Odon's Eyes.

The only way to describe Odon's Eyes are as large oval mirrors that sit on at least one wall of every classroom at the University. Hideous in their enormity, they are unbearably blinding when they reflect one of the many lights ranged in rows above the students. When one happens to align, it's impossible to ignore. The beam bores into my eyes, practically burning through them.

What's worse is that, no matter where I sit in a classroom, they seem to reflect my pale image, a hollow ghost. When my eyes meet the look of indifference on my face, it frightens me—the lack of affect even more so. Other times it doesn't seem to be me at all, but another being staring out of the blue eyes. Sometimes she's screaming.

The Eyes are meant to keep us from disobeying and maintain our focus, but I can never fully concentrate around them. I feel their presence penetrating through my mind, glaring into me as if I'm transparent, as if I'm a blank board with my thoughts scribbled out for them to read. I fear glancing in their reflection, afraid I might find some grotesque embodiment of myself staring back from another plane, or worse: I'm afraid I might see Odon, a knowing look in his eye.

I steal a glance at their imitation of our white world. For a moment I attempt to find a flaw in its interpretation, but see only the infinite glow of perfection.

My white robe moves with my body, falling lightly around me as I shift to an upright position and prepare to focus. With an inaudible sigh, I pull my books onto the desk. Placing my bare elbows on the smooth frozen surface, I open a book and attempt to study.

The silence is heavy now that I've settled. The other students around me don't seem to notice. They gaze solemnly into their books as if they are staring forlornly at their own reflections. I turn back to my own, the words looking like a foreign language of absurd symbols and spaces. I suddenly see the half-blood's smile ... the forbidden connection he dared to share with me. It remains so solid in my mind. The way his eyes showed the smile with an unspoken depth that I had never seen before. I try to describe it to myself but fall flat. There was life there that went beyond movement.

I try to control myself, narrowing my eyes to focus them on the page. I steal a moment to glance at the Eye. I see my own haunting twin, reflecting back a side of me I thought I left behind. I stifle a shiver.

"*Odon is everything. Life is lived for the sole purpose of pleasing him.*" I finally manage to begin reading a paragraph. "*Was it not his hand that placed life on this earth? Was it not his hand that gave the people such a privilege?*"

Then why does my mind formulate these thoughts against him? I shut the book in frustration. A few students look up from reading, their eyes in a glazed shock.

I gather my things and, face averted, hurry out. I let my hair fall from behind my ears, trying to hide behind it. It's what makes me like them. I wonder if it even matters. Is my face recognizable anymore? Does my name even matter? Or is the title *pureblood* enough?

I walk outside past a few pureblood girls from another sector. They smile at me and nod. I notice now more than ever that their smiles don't reach their eyes, not like him.

I return the gesture. They go inside, probably only out to prove their superiority. I start across the grass toward the garden. It's hardly ever used and never spoken of. I'm not even sure I could explain why it exists. Yet it has become a place more inviting than my own bedroom that I share with Lenora.

Square-cut plants surround the garden on four sides. The walls of shrubbery reach well above my head, so it's hidden from outside observers. On one wall, the hedges break briefly to form an entrance.

My pace quickens as I stride down the dip of grassy earth to the small valley where the garden sits. I don't bother to look back at the University looming behind me. I know what I would see: the many Odon's Eyes watching me leave, glowing red in the dying rays of the sun.

I allow my mind to drift. The smells are strong outside, though I cannot identify them. Nothing like that is described in Odon's history books. The grass surrounding the University is freshly cropped to a uniform height. I feel no remorse in tramping through it; the sole of my sandal leaves no trace of my passing.

I arrive and set my books outside the garden entrance. I feel uncomfortable walking without the weight of them in my hands. This is the only time I part with them. It never seems proper to bring them in. They don't belong, I don't see any reason for them inside, and no one is around to judge. I enter devoid of any supplies and follow the pathway to take a seat on the hard stone. It has become a welcomed seat, in a way more comfortable than the metal chairs of the University that never seem to warm beneath me. My robe settles around me in a white pool. I feel the bottom hem wet upon my ankles from the damp grass.

Around my feet small clusters of yellow flowers smile up at me. There is strange company in their faces, and I find myself wishing there were more. I stare down at my sandaled feet planted straight in front of me on the smooth stone surface of the pathway. I have unknowingly placed them that way; I seem to always situate them in neat parallel lines. I slide my right foot slowly out of place. It looks awkward, at an angle next to my other foot. I move it again, seeing how long I can withstand the oddness of it, and then bring it straight again. I smile at the new effect it has over me. My reaction to such a simple adjustment is alarming. How else have I been unknowingly trained? Will I ever learn to resist it?

I blink hard, trying to focus in the dimming light, and it jolts me from my suspended reality. For a moment I was a separate being, testing my limits, challenging my surroundings. Now I must return to my room and get some rest; the guards will be making their rounds soon.

I stand to leave and notice a shadow at the far corner of the garden. I haven't heard anyone enter, and I gasp with a fear that is more exciting than it is paralyzing. The shadow surrenders to the last dying rays of sunlight, and I recognize him. *Has he been watching me the entire time?* It is the half-blood.

"Stay away!" I am surprised by the sternness in my voice. I hope it has overshadowed all the fear at the back of my throat. I look around to see if anyone has seen us together, though it seems unlikely in the fading daylight. I'm not sure what I would be hiding from.

"You remember me?" A flicker of nervousness causes him to fidget in his beige long-sleeved tunic and plain loose pants. They are not the silky white of my own clothing, but a rough woven cloth material. His hesitation passes quickly, and he stands tall, brave and unmoving. I note his courage and admire it before pushing the idea far from my mind.

"Yes. I should report you!" I try to be threatening, try to bargain my way out of the situation.

He only laughs. "Should? You won't then, will you?" He gives me an odd look. "You're curious."

I hold my lips tense to hold back an answering smile of embarrassment. He should not have that effect on me. He is a half-blood; his existence is wrong.

"I'm not curious. Please, just leave." I speak calmly, assertively. I think he will listen, I think he will obey and leave, but—he remains.

"Dorian." He offers his hand in greeting. I'm intrigued as I place my own in his gently. He looks up, and his face is barely visible in the dying light; only in memory of the bright hallway do I see him. Still, it is hard to focus in the faint light of the University, and I wish to see his face properly. The surrounding greenery casts shadows on his face, and give him the look of some wild animal.

I stare in fascination and find the words trailing from my lips, "My name is—"

"Oriana!—Get away from her, you trash!" Aurek shouts, rushing toward us. He is a pureblood. I can imagine the pride that plays upon his face. I need no light to tell me it's there behind his brief severity. I don't understand why he finds it necessary to come to my rescue. It's his nature to play the hero.

He certainly looks it. His broad shoulders, fierce height, and a masculine face complete with chiseled jawline and prominent nose, perpendicular to two impressively blue eyes. He wears the clothes of a pureblood, long-sleeve shirt and loose pants, similar to Dorian's though made of the same smooth material as the gown I wear.

He is well respected at the University. The females admire him, and the males have good cause to fear him. Everyone knows him, but not everyone likes him, if I alone am proof. Despite obvious efforts on my part, his feelings for me will forever linger.

He dashes to my side, with his part-blood devotee, Fisk, not far behind him. Fisk is an odd creature. His skinny limbs must struggle to keep up with Aurek's long strides. His face resembles that of a rodent, with a narrow, crooked nose and two hazel eyes deeply hidden within a forest of brown eyebrows and bangs. His upper lip always seems to be in a snivel, curling atop two large front teeth. I wonder for a moment why he is out so late, but presume it is Aurek's doing.

I look for Dorian. He has left.

"Did he hurt you at all? Touch you?" He searches my eyes like a false hero.

"No, of course not. He's just a half-blood," I reply with a shrug, partly to nudge his hands off my shoulders.

"I can't believe he'd actually talk to you, much less touch you," Aurek says with distaste.

"Yeah, that's sick!" Fisk chimes in.

"Shut up, part-blood, you're no better!" Aurek gives him a glare that silences the emaciated figure and leaves him shivering in the garments draping his slight form. I now notice that the part-blood wears a material of a coarser substance than my own, yet of better quality than Dorian's. Every detail of our lives seems to be a matter of ranking.

Aurek turns his back to me. "I promise you, Oriana, next time I see that scum, I'm going to teach him a lesson. Half-bloods need to know a little discipline," he states matter-of-factly. "Trust me, you won't have to worry about him bothering you anymore."

I wince at Aurek's demeaning tone, and he puts his arm around my shoulders. He believes he is consoling my disgust at what has happened with Dorian. He is wasting his time. I walk away from his arm heading for the exit. "Please, Aurek, just leave him alone."

"And what will I get in return?"

I turn and glare at him. "What did you say?"

"What will I receive in return for my favor to you?" he asks again. The white of his teeth is visible in the glow of the setting sun as he smiles at his own cleverness. I know Fisk wastes no time imitating his grin, but my patience is waning too quickly to investigate. I wish to escape that impudent smile.

"Maybe some salvation from Odon. He's the only one who can help you now!" He won't apologize, only beg for my attention tomorrow. *What a heartless, self-absorbed, arrogant ...* I try to control the words coursing through my mind as I turn to grab my books. I almost storm away without seeing the slip of paper float from the inside cover of a textbook. I stop and pick it up; it has grown too dark to read, so I wait until I've reached the inside of the University.

There I unfold it delicately with anxious fingers.

The garden. Meet me tomorrow night.
Dorian.

CHAPTER THREE

I grow dizzy and unsteady on my feet. I know I want to go, but should I? Lenora will tell me not to, she is a smart Winglet, always getting good grades, always staying in line, never acting against Odon. If I go, it will be wrong—yet I want to find out what is waiting for me there. In the back of my mind I know I have already decided to accept his invitation. My conscious is still denying it.

I walk blindly through the corridors and stop in front of my room automatically. I open the door carefully and step inside. It is a small room with two sets of identical furniture and white walls to match the ones throughout the University. Two beds are pressed against the wall to the right of the door so that their ends lead out to the center of the room. Pearly soft bed coverings neatly adorn both. On the opposite wall, two square white desks sit, without a single item on either one. Each lines up with the corresponding bed to form a T, broken at the top for a walkway.

Luckily no wall possesses an Odon's Eye, or I wouldn't be able to sleep. It's difficult enough with the furnishings consisting only of white. The first desk and bed are my own, and I mechanically slip the books in my hand into the top left drawer. My way is lit by the familiar spherical light fixture from the hall. Its brightness follows the stages of the sun, slowly dimming throughout the evening until it is completely off at night. The process reverts for sunrise and then begins to darken again at midday. Now it is a dull glow, almost completely out but with just enough light reflecting off the white of everything so I am able to see.

I notice Lenora in her bed. She is beneath the sheets, though I wonder if she has been sleeping or waiting for my arrival. My mind wanders inward. Dorian's note feels heavy in my hand, and its message replays over and over in my head. "… *Meet me tomorrow night …*" I mouth the words in a trance of uncertainty.

What can this all mean for me? A story has begun unraveling itself, and no one must find out. Powerful risks lie ahead if I continue down this path, and yet I feel compelled to discover what destiny waits in the garden tomorrow night. The need seems to overpower any fear of defying my faith—a faith where one is born into a respect based on blood, where those below do not deserve an equal love. Do I believe such a faith? Do I dare go against it?

Lenora startles me from my thoughts. "Where were you? You know we have a test tomorrow." She sounds angry. She doesn't shout, just furrows her eyebrows at me, an expression I know well. Even when she is angry, Lenora's face seems unthreatening, with large blue eyes and a delicately upturned nose. She has the pale skin of a pureblood and long flaxen hair falling in a slight wave down her back. Her lips squeeze together, turning them a bright red as she tries to look intimidating with disapproval

"I know, it's just that I got caught up at the garden—" I look away from her gaze, certain she knows something has happened.

"Got caught up?" Lenora smiles cleverly. She is hinting for me to explain.

I hesitantly toss the note on the space next to her on the bed. I feel as though a large burden has been released from my grasp, although a heavier one remains. She unfolds it quickly, and I watch her face turn grim after reading it.

She looks up at me and speaks slowly. "Dorian … isn't he a … a half-blood?" She spits the words out disgustedly.

I nod solemnly but say nothing.

"Oriana, what happened? What did you do?" She is furious now, and her voice is rising. She stands up from her bed and looks me straight in the eyes; we are the same height. I respond by averting them quickly. "Oriana! Don't tell me you actually like—"

Now I look at her, astonished that she would think such a thing.

"Of course not! *Nothing* happened. He just—we just met each other, but then Aurek came, and Dorian disappeared."

"Aurek? Good, you should be spending more time with him anyway; he's a good influence, you know."

Lenora sinks back onto her bed, satisfied with the advice she has given.

"Lenora, you sound like our professors! Telling me who to hang out with …" I laugh a little without thinking.

But Lenora answers back very coldly, "What's wrong with that?" She raises an eyebrow at me suspiciously.

"Oh calm down, I was just joking—"

She cuts me off, but I have nothing more to say anyway. I've said too much.

"Joking does not suit a pureblood. Honestly, Oriana, sometimes I just don't understand you." Lenora lies down in her bed and faces away from me, saying nothing more.

I glance at her still form once more, and it brings back a memory. We were only nine at the time, still learning the rules and regulations. We enjoyed the freedom of the playground outside the University. Segregation wasn't as strict when we were younger, so part- and half-bloods were allowed to play alongside the purebloods.

Lenora had her eye on a particular part-blood. He was certainly a handsome boy, with dirty-blond hair and hazel eyes. She was positively smitten. On one occasion when they were sitting beside one another on the swings, Lenora leaned over and kissed him on the cheek. Being at such an age of innocence, the two couldn't help giggling over it.

Unfortunately, a nearby professor had witnessed the event and immediately took them both by the arm and dragged them away. The part-blood boy vanished, and Lenora returned forever changed. Now she never relates to Winglets other than purebloods. And she never thinks of much besides her studies. She acts as though she wants me to be more like her. But sometimes I feel that it's more the other way around. There is a fear that goes deep inside her. Something they did to her put it there, a fear that ensures she will never defy the faith again. But I may never know what took place that day, so many years ago. She does not speak of it. Any scars are embedded far below the skin, never to surface.

A shiver goes through my body as I slip into the softness of the sheets and place my head upon my pillow. The warmth is a temporary distraction from my thoughts, but my mind pushes through my comfort. Who can I trust? A friend who follows the teachings? A friend who is only a friend when it suits the University? No, I can't settle for ignorance. Whatever rules are broken, whatever risks will be taken, I need to go.

My stomach turns over as my decision is finally made. I feel exposed with the thoughts in the forefront of my mind. As if they are visible to the outside world. I roll onto my stomach and push my forehead into the pillow, hoping the fabric will absorb my memories and allow me to sleep peacefully. Time is passing as I lie awake, Odon knows how long. I turn onto my side and then onto my back. After a few more positions, I end up on my side again and finally fall asleep. I wake with the coming of morning less than refreshed.

I'm moving through school today, but I'm barely remembering what is happening. As I sit in history class, my professor sees I am not paying attention. My mind is wandering and tossing over decisions back and forth. I can't accept what I've decided to do. Should I trust myself? I want to see that boy again, but I know it is wrong, unheard of, frowned upon—*no … worse.*

The professor calls upon me. "Oriana please, what have you to say?"

I jolt straight up in my seat. "I'm sorry, sir, what was the question?"

He looks at me curiously. The students around me whisper to each other and shake their heads. Lenora does the same.

"Silence!" he says sternly, and the whispering stops. "Why were you not listening, Oriana?"

I try to swallow the lump in my throat. I shouldn't have let this half-blood control me, I shouldn't have taken interest, but it is too late. "I was thinking, sir." The words get caught in my throat, but they are still spoken, and I regret them as soon as they come out.

"Oriana, you should be concentrating on classes. Do you need to go to the Odonian?"

The word stabs at me, deep into the open wound of fear.

The Odonians are an elite rank of professors, all pureblood. They are appointed directly by Odon himself and assure that all students follow the teachings of Odon exactly. There is one at our University for each race and rank. I must not get sent. I would have no choice but to attend. And then? Dangers beyond my imagination lie in the office of an Odonian, that even my terror cannot conjure up.

"No, sir." I look down at my desk, willing my release from further interrogation.

"Are you certain?" The professor raises a thick and wiry eyebrow, a peppered gray and light brown. Such an act, however minuscule, leads me to hate him immediately. He is a part-blood; all the professors are, except the Odonians. In fact, I've never seen a grown pureblood. They leave after the Rebirth. This particular part-blood is well liked, a devoted servant to Odon, but he will always be a part-blood, no matter how impeccable his record is. And for that reason his students will never respect him. An anger such as I've never felt before consumes me. I want to yell and push him down! He is below *me*! He has no right to speak as though he is better. He is worthless, middle-class, impure!

My hatred is growing now. I struggle to nod in answer to his question. I dare not speak and reveal the anger in my voice. He turns his back to the class. I calm down, but I am trembling with chills of pent-up spite. It's all I can do to maintain my composure. I breathe. In, then out, control, steady pace, in, then out. The air rushing through my lungs cools my nerves. Eyes straight ahead. I cannot be sent to the Odonian; survival depends on that. I keep myself from looking at his face. Just listen to his words. I must protect myself. I must not show these changes these … emotions.

CHAPTER FOUR

The school day becomes a mindless glaze of incoherent white, so bright that it erases any functions of the mind. I choose not to fight it. *Do not think; ease the pain, trust in Odon. Your destiny lies in your success as a pureblood. Write, listen, repeat their information; this is what matters. History class, then Faith, then test*—the test that was so important only hours ago.

The teacher walks down the aisle, handing out a packet, neatly clipped together. She passes me, and one finds itself on my desk. I grip the metal pen in my burning palm. My other hand drags the test in front of me. I must not make a mistake, a single mistake, and they would know. They would send me to the Odonian, and then there would be no hope. I would return forever changed, scarred by the same unknown infliction that laid its injury upon Lenora.

I turn the first page over. Have I finished it already? My mind is somewhere else, and I can't remember the questions. I scan it; yes, it is complete. I begin the next page. Concentrate; I must not make a mistake. Haven't I studied? Didn't I prepare? And yet my memories grasp nothing except the fear of not remembering. After I've read and answered the last question, I turn it over. But relief at the test's completion does not wash over me. I am caught in time, trapped in the moment when the packet was placed beside me.

Why couldn't I have pushed it to the floor? But it's done; nothing in the past will change. Somehow I muster the strength to rise from my seat and approach the desk at the front of the room, where the professor sits reading the *History* book.

I reach the desk and place a hand on it to gain balance. The test is squirming in my hand, all but leaping onto the blank silver surface of the desk. Did I finish first? There are no other tests; mine sits by itself, a white rectangle on the metal. It looks so blatant lying there alone. But it has left my hand, and there is no way to retrieve it from its solitude. I stare at it, wanting to take it back. The professor doesn't notice me but continues to read, unaware of the crisis that is occurring before her. Her light brown hair is tucked below her neck, a part-blood. My eyes are still upon the abandoned test, as if I am holding it in time or willing it to disappear.

How long I stand there, I can't tell, but it isn't until a second student approaches from behind to lay his test over mine that I leave to take a seat. All that waits for me is my metal ink pen on my desk, the pile of books visibly tucked beneath it. Once seated, I take some comfort in the absence of that foreign test and gather the familiar items close. My fingers wrap tightly around the pen, and my arms find safety in hugging the books. Is this the extent of my faith, the need to seek comfort in something known? *Odon protect me, keep me safe, and I will love you forever.*

Later I'm walking to my locker across the school. I stride quickly; I have to get out of this place before someone stops me. My head is whirring, and I run into someone, apologize, and then collide with someone else; "Sorry" again. They know. *I know they know.* They are wishing to see me fail, mess up, lose control of myself for just an instant. The lights are burning my eyes, scorching my brain. But the thoughts are still there, eroding my composure. The blank look I've always managed to maintain, until now.

A hand clamps down on my shoulder, fastening itself and stopping me from moving. I gasp, and my eyes flicker out of focus. I don't scream, just draw a breath, but in my ears it's as loud as a scream. I stare wide-eyed into a face, too bright to see.

"Oriana, what's the matter with you? You're paler than pale!" Aurek has me unwillingly gripped by the shoulders. He wraps his arms around me, and I sink into his body trying to hang onto a fading consciousness. I am frozen, hidden in Aurek's shadow, the world shifting out of view. He strokes my hair. "You're ice cold. What's happened to you?"

I shiver but do not respond. I only answer within myself as my stomach lurches. *Fear,* I speak without my voice. *Fear is what has happened.* I fall backward as Aurek's face disappears into the pinpoint of a black tunnel.

All I can hear is a buzzing interrupted by a steady heartbeat. I sit in the darkness. My body floats above me. I'm headed straight for it. We will connect soon. I feel myself return, and now I can control my eyes. I open them to get out of the darkness—to get out of the black and then white: white walls and light and sheet and face.

I blink to organize things. Everything is blurry except the face. My eyes remain there. I sit up, my eyes still fixed. My hand reaches for the skin. I see it is slightly darker than my own. I pull back as soon as my wits return. I do not touch it, him, Dorian.

"What are you doing here?" I ask. My voice is raspy and I reach for the glass of clear liquid in his hand. He raises it to my lips concentrating on allowing me to drink.

Once I have finished he answers. "I work here."

"The medical ward? They allow half-bloods to treat patients?"

"Well, I mostly clean the rooms. I'm not really supposed to be talking to you."

I stare at him in shock before gaining back my voice. "Since when?"

"Since awhile … I don't know; last year maybe." He shrugs.

I suppose it is a credible answer. Those who are not pureblood are often required to volunteer in the school's facilities in exchange for classes. Half-bloods are usually assigned to the monotonous work of sorting files and cleaning.

My questions take a new route. "Have you heard what's wrong with me?" I stare at the ceiling, as if I'm not worried, but I listen intently.

"Nothing."

I look at him strangely, "Nothing? Then what am I doing here? Why did I faint?"

"They don't know," he answers frankly. "They don't have a clue."

"They?"

"The doctors, examiners … whatever you want to call them." His voice gets significantly lower, and he looks down at his hands, "I know."

For a moment I think I have misjudged his meaning. Yet his confident expression of a well-kept secret confirms otherwise.

"Are you insane? What do you mean, you know?"

He grins at me slyly and brings his face closer to mine, "I know what's happened to you, and you know too." He draws back and shrugs again.

I avert my eyes. "I don't know what you're talking about—"

"Then what happened?"

"I don't know! And you don't either, so stay out of my life!"

It seems so simple just to admit that there is something different about me, something that I had control of before but no longer. Still, I can't, and in a final defiance I lash out, "I could get rid of you, you know—" I stop myself knowing I shouldn't have said that. I look him in the eyes. He sits on the edge of my bed, close enough to touch my legs beneath the sheets. Why is it that I notice every detail when he is near, every expression, every moment?

His mouth flickers with a smile.

"You're not afraid …," I say. It isn't a question because the answer is obvious. His eyes are unblinking without a trace of fear. Something inside me sinks.

"No, but you are."

Dorian rises from beside me and begins to leave the room through a thick white door that I am hoping has blocked out our conversation. Before he reaches for the handle, he adds, "Get used to it, it doesn't just go away."

My stomach twists, and I gasp. He is right; I'm afraid, terrified. I've known all along; I never needed his simple diagnosis. The fear has consumed me, and I had collapsed in a horrified heap.

But why can't I control it as I have before? I already know the answer to this as well. The danger is closer, breathing down my back. I can feel it even in this moment alone, unwatched, inside the medical center. I don't need the stare of an Odon's Eye or a professor's warning. Odon is everywhere, and he is watching. No fear could be greater.

CHAPTER FIVE

I'm sitting up in my bed, unable to sleep. They released me from the medical center, telling me I'm not sick, that I'm fine, but I'm not fine. Lenora is asleep in her bed. She has not asked me how I feel; she will not even speak to me.

I want to leave this room. I want to go to the garden and think. Not about school or part-bloods or purebloods or Finlets or Winglets. I don't care anymore. I don't care; they don't matter. Not even school or tests. I know what I want. But I can't even admit it to myself. In the garden, I must go there … he'll be there. I know it. Only he can answer the questions burning inside me.

I slowly turn back the covers. My feet touch the cold floor, and I pad silently to where my sandals lie, side by side. One foot slides in with care and then the other.

My breath is hushed. Lenora remains still in her bed, her breathing consistent and calm. I pray she will stay asleep as I approach the door. I turn the handle like ice in my hand, and it releases the door to glide open without a sound. I only open it enough for my body to slip through, afraid the light from the hallway will cause Lenora to wake. Her personality tells me she is a light sleeper. The door closes behind me with no more than a click.

Once in the brightness of the hallway, I close my eyes to give them a chance to adjust. Slowly I unclench them as my sight improves.

My obstacles now become far more risky. If I am to make it to the garden I will need to completely avoid the guards. Yet the idea of that happening seems near impossible. Never have I been out wandering past curfew. I have no idea where the guards patrol or for how long. I'm fighting the impulse to sneak back inside my room and return to bed, but the curiosity I've been denying all along is impairing my judgment. I must try to reach the garden; there must be some way.

I hear footsteps echoing down the hallway to my left. I push myself into the indent of the doorway. My eyes peer around the frame. My face presses against the cool metal and my breathing ceases.

It is a guard. A tall man, broadly built and clad in a button-down white tunic and stiff matching pants, a small-brimmed hat stately upon his head. Whether he is part- or pureblood I cannot determine; he is still a fair distance away and I don't try to crane my neck for a better look. In fact my eyes concentrate solely on the long metal rod that he swings deftly in his fist. The rush of air follows in its wake along with the obvious strength in the man's trunk of an arm. I try not to further imagine the pain inflicted by a blow from such a weapon and arm. I must concentrate on my goal. *I can do this; I can figure it out.*

The guard continues down his hallway, never glancing down the aisle of dormitories that I stand in. He is most likely accustomed to empty halls. Who would even try to leave? If someone was caught, no matter how pureblooded, their name would be scarred, their body banished, and their soul forever damned by Odon himself. *Push the thoughts away; don't think about what might happen. I can't let that happen.*

He passes out of view. All this took only a moment, yet the gleam of the metal object is still blinding. Now the guard is out of view, and I allow myself the slightest gasp of air before releasing a sigh of relief. I am once again alone. I must begin to make decisions.

I wait a few minutes longer. Perhaps I will hear another guard at the hallway to my right. This may give me an idea of where they are patrolling. I will be able to take either hallway to reach the garden. Which one will be the safest?

The sound of footsteps reverberates to my right. So there is another guard … My assumption is confirmed as the man walks past the end of this aisle. My breath is silent once again, and the earlier apprehension is back at the sight of an identical weapon in his hand.

In fact, overall the guards look very similar. They wear identical uniforms and are both wide in body structure. This man must be different though, as he walks from the side of the wall that I am pressed against to pass behind the opposite end. This is not the same direction the previous guard took, and it would be impossible for the guard to arrive on this end walking in that direction without passing back through the opening. Basically, I would have seen him.

Two guards, two hallways, but their timing is slightly different, a minute, maybe less. *How can I do this?* My thoughts are so calmly spoken, but my heart is racing.

Go back to bed, Oriana. It's late, it's dangerous, you're not thinking straight. Dorian will not wait for you. How could he get past the guards himself? You are trapped. Give up.

"No ...," I whisper and then freeze in strained silence. I have to go through with this. I feel its importance. *He will wait; he has to.*

The silence remains. I gather a courage I thought did not exist and fly to the next doorway down to my right. My sandals tap lightly on the hard floors, but it seems loud in the heavy air. Then comes the expected sound of footsteps to my left; the guard is returning down the opposite direction. I am still, quiet, holding my breath. *Don't move, not a sound.* He passes; I do not watch.

Now I rush, tapping louder than I'd like, to the end of the hallway where the second guard passed not long ago. I peer down the hallway and see him walking, his back to me. He will reach the end of the hallway very soon, too soon. Then he'll turn and see me, he will look right at me, and then the metal baton will rise to come crashing down upon its victim like a diving bird. I shudder.

Stay focused; there's not much time! Go ... I glance down the other end of the hall. *Empty! Run!* I dash out into the hall, on my toes, moving toward the guard. There's no turning back. I'm almost to the doorway, the garden. My feet patter. My heart pounds. *Almost there!*

But the guard has almost reached his destination as well, and he will turn around. No, he *is* turning around. About to head back down the hall, about to see me, the cornered prey, standing in all this whiteness, my hair a golden beacon.

I fall into a nearby doorway. Try the handle; it is locked. I remain in the frame. This one leads to a classroom. I have passed this way before. I picture myself walking here, the hallways filled. I pass this doorway, and I see me. A pathetic little girl tucked in panic against the white doorway, waiting to be found. This is how I will look when the guard passes, when he sees me, when his hand grips the metal tightly, when it rises above his head.

I tremble with each approaching footstep, closer, closer, with each thud on the porcelain floor. *Why didn't I listen to that other voice, the sensible one that would have led me safely into my bed, hidden in the darkness?* But I am far from the dark, and only hidden by the slight impression of a flimsy entrance. The present safety will last for only so long before I am discovered.

The pounding of my heart in my ears is drowning out the footsteps. *How long have I waited? How much longer will I have to?* I peer slowly down the hallway. My forehead, beaded with sweat is relieved against the cool frame. *Empty?* The guard is nowhere in sight. I look the other way. No, there is no one in sight.

The guard has turned down a hallway, one further down that connects to the opposite side. His patrol is more complicated than I assumed. He will not be there long. I already hear his steps growing louder. He has already surveyed the area and is heading to the main hall.

There is not much time. If I don't leave, I will definitely be trapped. There is no other chance. *Move, feet!* I flee from my place of hiding and reach the door, the one that will lead outside, to the garden, to freedom.

My hand grasps the knob. I see the night sky in a small window above the door. *Let me out!* I shove against the heavy metal door. The air rushes around me. I gasp for breath. The door, now wide open, is caught by the wind and torn from my hand. The hinges hyperextend, and the door slams into the side of the building. But the sound isn't half as deafening as the blaring siren that has me frozen like a stone statue in the night air—an alarm.

CHAPTER SIX

Of course, why didn't I think of this? Why did I think it would be so easy? That I could just rush out into the dark completely unharmed and then return as swiftly as I came, completely undetected, and that everything would be okay?

It isn't so easy, and the resounding horn endlessly piercing the silence is enough proof of that. I stand waiting to be captured. Waiting for the cold metal to come crashing down on my skull and bring me into a darkness of peace far from the white lights. Let it just be over with.

I feel the warmth of a hand clasp my wrist firmly. They're taking me, bringing me to the Odonian, to the punishment. Why did I go through with it? Why couldn't I be happy with how things were? Then the unexpected happens. My arm is tugged sharply, and I'm half thrown into a shadow cast by the line of square bushes hugging the University walls.

Now hidden from the light, I release a pent-up breath and appear to deflate. An arm grasps me tightly, and a hand fastens over my mouth. Somehow whatever danger I currently face seems to be less threatening now that I've escaped the white, now that the guards will not find me.

They will not expect me to hide. Who would have thought to anyway? The idea of rebelling against a just punishment is unthinkable. I myself would have submitted willingly if I hadn't been forced into hiding. I realize I'm a criminal against my own way of life, my only home.

The guards arrive at the door somewhat dumbfounded. If their pale, lifeless faces could actually express the emotion. I watch silently through the shadows, through the leaves and branches. It is not hard to see them in the bright light, dressed in the white uniform. I myself stood out in the night only seconds ago. But now my robes have been cloaked by the darkness, welcomed into the black so that I've become one of her children.

Beneath me a chest rises and falls. Hot breath brushes the nape of my neck and I can feel the warmth of a living body. The dark conceals this being as well, and now this dark becomes a thing to fear. I no longer wish to hide, to be sightless; now I am suddenly aware of this new danger.

The guards have not ventured far from the light, and like moths they hurry back to it in hunger. Have the other students awakened? Did Lenora open her eyes to find me missing? There is no time to wonder. No sooner does the door shut than I have slipped quickly from the arm that binds me. The hand still holds my wrist, and I wrench fiercely as if it is on fire.

"Oriana," come the hissing words, "it's me!"

I stop and then squint my eyes as if it might help me see through the darkness. "Dorian?" A whisper, but it sounds so loud, and it feels like ages since I've heard my own voice.

In the darkness it is impossible to see his face, but the voice is recognizable, and the familiar smell that I realize had always been lingering leads me to identify him.

"How did you find me?" I ask, keeping my voice low.

"I was about to go inside, lucky for you," he answers smartly.

A silence follows as we slip through the line of bushes. With no sign of wind, the rustle of our feet and bodies against the leaves becomes the only sound. We escape the cover of foliage and pad down the hillside of damp grass. He leads me to the garden, his hand still clutching my wrist, but I do not fight its hold. A sense of calm settles over me, even more so than during my usual walks to the garden.

I know this trip is far more dangerous, yet I am relieved to feel the lack of eyes upon me. The night encloses my face, my body, everything that shows my identity. I am someone else, a nameless shadow.

The walls of the garden loom above us before I realize we've come this far. Now that I've reached it, now that I have accomplished my goal and I am with him—what comes next? I've merely wondered how

I might escape the University, how to reach this very spot. When I finally place my feet upon the soft ground and face the entrance to a night much darker than I thought possible, I hesitate. The garden walls seem less inviting in the dark, resembling a square jaw awaiting my entrance before snapping shut on me. Is this what I wanted? Would I have come, knowing it would lead to this?

Dorian feels a tug on our linked hands when he tries to move onward into the garden. It is hard to determine clearly, but by the faint moonlight I can see his head turn to glance behind. I recover and follow, knowing nothing worthwhile waits for me back in my dormitory. Knowing that turning back can only mean digression, returning to a life that will leave me unsatisfied.

I pass through the shadows of the foliage and emerge once again beneath the night sky. I realize now that the garden is no darker than the outside air; that considerable blackness grips only the entrance. In fact the slate pathway catches the glint of the moon, which gives the rocks a soft glow that brightens the entire garden.

Dorian steps on the first slate, and the slab goes dark in his shadow. I wriggle my wrist in earnest, as it is awkward to follow from behind. He drops it quickly as if just now realizing that he is still holding it.

A deep intake of breath greets me with the smell of those sweet golden flowers, in neat rows with their constant shining smiles. I want to be those flowers, always happy, always carefree: a race of beautiful perfection.

We reach the familiar stone seat, and I lower myself upon it. The rock is cold, much colder than the night, and I hug myself, waiting for it to absorb my body heat.

Dorian stands beside me watching, his blue eyes glowing like two moons in the night of his black hair. At last he speaks. "Why are you up so late? And sneaking around the school like a felon?" He grins when I give him a glare.

"You invited me; don't you remember?" I look down at my feet; the thought encourages a blush upon my cheeks. I have admitted to arriving at his bidding alone. But it wasn't just the letter, "What you said … before. Tell me what you know."

He sits down next to the flowers and leans back, propping himself on his elbows, "You want to know? About what?"

"About what's happening to me …"

He thinks about this for a moment and then gets up and sits beside me on the bench, "About your feelings?" he asks, his face close to mine.

He kisses me and then pulls back slightly. "What do you feel?"

"I don't—"

He kisses me again, and I sink into the bench.

"Oriana ..."

"Yes?" I barely respond, but he hears me, we are so close.

"Tell me."

He attempts to kiss me again, but I pull back.

"What—what are you doing?" I gather my thoughts. "What are you trying to prove?"

He looks at me, his eyes showing an emotion that I have never witnessed before, and yet I know what it represents. I am shocked into a memory.

I'm sitting, a young girl, too young to determine what's right, a young girl not yet understanding womanhood. We are alone hidden in an alcove of a hallway. I can't remember the day, time or reason for us meeting. Aurek smiles broadly, like a glutton, like a greedy glutton. His hand is bound tightly around my arm. It hurts a little, it's uncomfortable, but I don't move or try to pull away. I'm thinking this is right, that this should be happening, but my own mind is telling me it is wrong.

I remember pulling away from that kiss and seeing his eyes. Blue eyes, filled with victory, filled with triumph and my own I know are filled with nothing.

Dorian looks at me, concern embedded deeply in his features, and the bitter memory has etched itself upon my own. His eyes are the same color as Aurek's, but they are so different.

"What's wrong?"

Then my tears are streaming in an endless blinding flood. Has it ever happened before? I can't remember the last time I cried, and it feels so good. Dorian's arms encircle me and I try not to feel ashamed, the touch is so unusual. I discover soon that any efforts to hold back the tears are useless. Yet although I can't end them, I make sure not a sound escapes my lips. It seems I can lose no more of myself. I am no longer the Oriana I have known. Or has she always been lying just below the surface?

CHAPTER SEVEN

It is time to leave. Leave the moment, return to the past, the previous state of blind obedience in a world that will never care for me: who I am, what I want. Am I selfish? I don't know, and it makes no difference. I must return to my other life, but I can never be that other Oriana again.

Dorian's hand is warm in my own. His touch is that of a half-blood. But it is the most wholesome contact I have ever shared with a person. And that means more than his blood ever will.

We've been silent for a while. It has been too long already; we allowed ourselves more time than the crime permitted. Now I feel the anxiety return, pulling at me harder than Dorian can compensate for. I stand, the movement taking every bit of will.

"Dorian, I have to leave, I have to go back." I avoid his eyes. Nothing is farther from what I want at this moment. How can I explain what I am feeling? However much I own this anxiety, this regret, it is he who causes it. My choices are to stay and be caught or return and be safe yet miserable. Maybe it is the fear—the fear they bred in me at birth—that forces me to obey and return to the University.

Dorian doesn't respond with words. He faces me, staring into my eyes and telling me everything he can't speak. Standing close, I realize his height is perfect, and I fit myself inside his arms, my head reaching just below his chin. If I don't speak, we will be stuck like this forever.

"Dorian?"

"Yes?"

"How will I get back inside? I'll be caught."

He pulls away to hold me by the shoulders. I know by the look in his eyes that my words have ruined the moment. "I know how. I'll bring you back." He speaks with a sigh, and yet his jaw is tight.

He stares at me for a minute longer. His eyes flicker from my eyes to my mouth, and he bites his own lower lip. If we embrace in such a way, there would be no escape for me. He seems to realize this and turns away, his arms dropping helplessly at his sides like limp ropes. As a noose, his hand tightens around my wrist. He does not look behind as he sluggishly leads me out of the garden and back into that other night, different from the night inside these walls of foliage.

He takes one stubborn step after another, restraining the urge to boil over. I can feel his rage simmering beneath the surface.

We reach the side of the building and crouch in the bushes, motionless, in the exact spot where we met last night.

The sun is already rising and the sky turns a sullen gray that brightens to a bleached blue on the eastern horizon. We remain inside the bushes, listening to each other breathe.

"Now what?" I whisper through clenched teeth.

"Now we get inside," he says, still cross over bringing me back. He gets up from behind the bushes and leaves our hiding place to stand in the open daylight. He reaches into a fold of his clothing and slides out a thin piece of slate. I hold my breath as he approaches the door slowly.

I imagine the door waiting for him to release it from silence and allow its screeching voice to carry throughout the walls. I presume the door will enjoy its moment of recognition; it doesn't happen often. It stands expectantly, awaiting salvation.

Dorian slowly slips the slate into the upper part of a gap on the side of the door. He slides it downward, head tilted intently. I hear a click and release my breath.

He reaches for the handle, and the door glides open soundlessly. Dorian motions for me to approach, and I warily leave the cover to join him in the doorway. His foot keeps the door open while his hand holds the slate against the frame. He must be pushing back a small mechanism that otherwise would have tripped the alarm.

There is a moment, while we both regard each other, when we share a spot between two worlds.

"The guards have switched patrols by now," Dorian whispers directly into my ear. "Just listen for his approach and count the first three steps. Then run straight to your room." His free hand comes to the side of my neck. He roughly kisses me before guiding me through the door. I look back at him briefly and catch one glimpse of him in the growing daylight. Then he has closed the door and is away. The good-bye was fleeting, but I don't waste time wishing it were longer.

I listen for steps, nothing, and then one, two, three …

I run to my room, through the door, and to bed, falling into a sleep forced by exhaustion.

CHAPTER EIGHT

In the University I can't help but constantly wonder, does anyone know where I was last night? Is it written all over my face? I feel as though everyone around me is watching the events replay themselves over and over in my mind. The chore of withholding my thoughts is a heavy burden, laid in my arms, at the back of my throat, strapped to my knees. I don't know how I can even walk around.

I haven't confronted Lenora yet. She had already left the room when I awoke for classes. She knows me so well, she would definitely notice any change in me.

A bell rings, and I head for the cafeteria. My hunger is powerful now, and I rush through the double doors. I missed my afternoon meal yesterday while at the medical center. Now my appetite takes control, and I grab a tray to start piling it as high as possible. I falter, realizing I must avoid attracting attention, and instead slowly take my normal portions.

The meals are laid out in silver trays that sit in rectangular cutouts in the counter's surface. Bright lights shine above the food, keeping the grainy substances warm while the students file past, scooping out servings with metal ladles. The gritty food is filled with the best nutrients to keep students healthy and active, or at least that's what they tell us.

The line exits from the serving counter back into a domed arena, all white, holding scattered round tables surrounded by cold metal seats and a listless student in each. It is hard to tell they are even hungry.

I follow the line out the door into the coolness of the large cafeteria. It takes a few seconds for my eyes to adjust; it is brighter out here than in the kitchen.

There is a monotone hum of conversing students around the tables. My group nods in recognition as I place my tray on the table and sit beside Lenora. There is a glint of something in her eye as she acknowledges me, but it is gone almost before I see it, and I soon forget it even transpired.

Aurek looks me square in the eye from across the table. "So how are you feeling? Did they treat you well?"

I nod solemnly. The mention of it brings back memories of Dorian as well as an underlying knot in my throat.

"What did they say was the matter?" he presses halfheartedly.

A reasonable question, yet I am stupidly not expecting it.

For a minute I am frozen, jaw clenched. There is general attention on me for what seems like forever.

Then I breathe. I shrug and say, "Dehydration ..." It's a reasonable explanation for passing out, and the topic turns to something about a group of part-bloods disappearing.

"Where did you go last night?"

The words cause me to nearly choke on my food, and I cough awkwardly. After pressing a napkin to my lips, I look up at Lenora. She is watching me, waiting.

"What are ...?" My voice is hoarse, and I cough again. "What are you talking about? I didn't go anywhere." I put on what I hope is a believable smile to ease tensions.

"I saw you leave the room," she says evenly.

"Oh yes, well, I did go to the bathroom that one time ...," I answer, hoping the explanation will suffice. The bathroom is right next door, however, so that excuse is risky, given the amount of time I was gone.

"And that took you the rest of the night?" She looks down at her plate, and I glance around the table to see if anyone is listening. They seem too involved in their discussion to have overheard, and I relax a little.

Still, whatever words I might respond with are caught in my throat. There is a silence, and I still can't think up anything worth saying. Lenora's gaze flits back to me, and I gape at her with the helplessness of a prey caught beneath the claws of a toying predator. Lenora's wide eyes are lit with triumph that makes my insides boil.

"You're always accusing me of losing faith," I say spitefully. "As if *you're* the perfect one, and Odon loves you more. Ever think that maybe you're just jealous of me? *I've* never been brought to the Odonian."

She blinks in surprise. Did I strike that deep? I get up and leave, hoping my words have done their worst. Wasn't she deserving of every second? And then I realize I should have said more; I should have gone for the core. Lenora never has any compassion for anyone, especially me. She doesn't know the meaning of the word. She loathes me, and I unwillingly put up with her.

My anger dies down, and I realize something that I forgot in the heat of my hatred. *Lenora knows*, and whatever she knows, it is enough to cause considerable damage to my life. There's no question that she would jump at the chance to set my downfall in motion. I stop in midstep and hold my breath. The panic is building within. I have to leave, and the sooner the better. Admitting this lets me continue walking, and I assure myself that it will happen soon. I will leave, and then Lenora, the professors, the Odonian, will all be behind me.

I wander through halls, getting lost in my mind and losing connection with the contact of feet and floor, eyes and vision, or lungs and breath. Living takes on a new and unimportant meaning. Maybe when I was with Dorian it all had purpose, but this place has stolen it away. I am a faceless mask of order and routine.

A bell rings overhead, signaling the end of mealtime, and I start toward class.

I scribble away in my notebook, more useless information. But I listen to all that is said, and I answer all that is asked. There is no need to think in class; it is done for you. No need to feel, because there is no use for emotions. Yet here I am, thinking and feeling. I want to stop the frustration, the temper welling up within. I grip my moving pen until my knuckles shine white.

An announcement reverberates from somewhere within the room. I almost jump from my seat but luckily catch myself.

"Students who are invited or involved in the Rebirth will attend it a month from now, at which time they will follow their Odonians accordingly. That is all; good day." The voice cuts off, and we are left to wait in silence for the bell to send us to our next class.

It seems odd to me that after so many years I still have no concept of the Rebirth. What could it be? Is it simply a graduation into a new life? What lies ahead in such a life? My peers around me seem uncaring about the subject, and I dismiss it with a sense of useless questioning. I'll be far away long before it happens anyway.

The bell rings, and we all mechanically head for the door. It's strange, but I look for the first time at the others' faces. They look so similar: pale skin, blue eyes, blond …

"Oriana." It is my professor. She smiles as I approach her warily. Her hazel eyes are empty of any greeting.

"Yes, Miss?"

"Oriana, your grades are beginning to concern me. On this past test you've scored below your usual quota. Has something affected your studies?"

The thought of Dorian flashes before my eyes. A drop of sweat rolls down my back.

I swallow, my mouth completely dry and answer blankly. "No, Miss, I suppose I was a bit confused … I will straighten it up. Don't worry."

"I'm sorry, Oriana, but I have already signed you up with the Odonian. He wishes to meet with you today after school."

The words ring in my ears, and I swallow again. The thought sends a wave of pain through my body. I know how people return from a meeting with an Odonian: they are changed, forever.

I nod and turn to leave.

"If you do not attend," my professor remarks, "I will find out and I will report you."

"I'll attend."

"Of course you will, Oriana."

I clench my teeth, tighten my fists, and walk out. The realization of danger digs its heels deeper into my stomach. I am in trouble now, and there's no way out. I'll have to be strong. Show no signs of my changes, my anger, and any others.

I find motivation. Somewhere inside of my panicking form is the strength that keeps me sane. The courage to remain in my seat and be the student I was not long ago.

CHAPTER NINE

The last bell of the school day rings, and I gather my books. I'm heading to the Odonian's office. My feet are heavy, and my pace is deathly slow, but somehow I make it there quickly.

Before I can knock on his door, he answers it with a beaming smile. "Oriana, I'm so happy you made it. Please take a seat."

His gold hair sweeps down in a crescent moon around his head. His upper scalp is pale and dotted with unsightly marks that continue to his forehead. Two near invisible eyebrows, so blond they blend into white skin, sit above vibrantly blue eyes. He is still smiling, white teeth gleaming unnaturally beneath fluorescent lights.

He reaches beneath his desk into some neatly filed papers and pulls out a folder. He leafs through its contents as he speaks. "Oriana, your professor tells me she is concerned about you, says something seems to have interfered with your academic performance."

I shrug and smile sweetly. "I was as surprised as she was at my grade on the last test. I guess I've become slightly anxious about the Rebirth. It's just a month away, you know." I hope my statement is believable and hide all doubt with a smile.

He chuckles. "Ha ha. Yes, of course, I know. But school is always a priority … Would you like a glass of water?"

I start to refuse but then decide against it after he looks at me dejectedly. I nod. He hands me a paper cup and then fills it from a small pitcher.

"This is special mineral water with vitamins, perfect for a young Winglet like yourself."

I drink it down. It's sweet and cool, and I enjoy the way it glides down my throat.

I feel exhilarated, with a new energy and strength. What was causing so much fear? The feeling seems to vanish from my memory.

"Oriana."

I hear my name and realize I am still sitting in the office of an Odonian.

"I trust you'll try harder in school, no more stress or anxiety. Just keep praying to Odon, and continue to drink this." He hands me a jar of the water. "It'll keep you healthy and alert."

"Thank you." I smile. I've tricked him, outsmarted Odon himself. His system is oblivious to the complete fraud sitting before him—me. "I feel better already."

I leave his office with a gentle numbness. I've forgotten why I was even nervous about coming here in the first place. I will return to my room and study with Lenora. Then I will get a good night's sleep. It will be the right thing to do, and shouldn't I do what is right? There is no pain in following the rules. No constant breath upon my back. My palms are dry, my step more sure. I am a new person. There is a new Oriana looking out through my eyes. She protects me. Don't fight it; fall into the embrace, cool and comforting.

That night I wake from sleep shaking in a cold sweat. I feel sick and my head is reeling.

"Lenora, Lenora! Wake up, I feel *terrible!*"

She is already awake, holding a glass of water close to my face.

"Drink this," she says solemnly.

I don't think, I don't ask—I just drink. The headache, the pain, and the spinning are gone. I fall back to sleep.

The morning arrives politely, like an old friend. There is nothing beyond this simple morning. There is nothing to concentrate on, no tangle of emotions to sort through. I can't even recall their presence. Why did I want them so much? It is beyond me now, and something in this knowledge encourages me to smile at Lenora, my friend, my savior from last night's trauma.

I know where I belong in this society. I was not cut out for rebellion. I realize my one and only calling. It is to follow Odon. He is my only love. He will save me in the end. He will free me from the darkness of the night. It brings a pang of devotion to my chest.

Lenora smiles back, and I know all is well once again.

We leave the comfort of our beds to dress. We gather supplies from our desks and finish preparation together. We do not speak as we leave the room and head out to breakfast. I feel as though I understand Lenora better. Clearly I assumed wrongly. She did not despise me, for she does not despise. I myself cannot possess the feeling. I don't wonder whether I'd prefer to.

We reach the cafeteria and begin to peck through the pans. We are soon seated and consuming our meals solemnly. Lenora and I pass vacant glances occasionally but stay uninvolved in any conversations. I am not surprised when the bell rings overhead to usher us toward the first class of the day.

As the days progress my concept of time seems nonexistent, and the minutes, hours, and days pass vaguely. Routine is always there as my close friend, to keep me safe and secure. A trip to the garden used to be part of my routine, but I feel no need to leave the University.

I remember one moment quite clearly, although I can't connect it to its place in the past. It was a while ago, I believe. When I was at lunch, I saw Aurek's eyes upon me always. I understood his expression as though watching from behind a glass wall. He followed me into the hallway and clutched my arm. I was against the wall when he took what he wanted, a rough kiss that left my lip bleeding.

I saw a half-blood pass as Aurek walked away and I wiped the red from my broken lip. He looked at me and must have seen, but what shone in his eyes was indescribable. I stood there staring down at my reddened fingers.

These thoughts don't matter, I'm sure. Here beneath the lights, among the eyes, this is where I am needed. This is why I live, to serve, to do what is expected. It repeats in my head, an assurance to my actions. The voice was once foreign yet is no longer. It tells, and I oblige. It guides, and I follow. Without it, I would be no more than a useless mass of matter.

The memory replays in my head as I walk to my locker. I shake it away and focus on the books I need, the notes I take. The halls are becoming emptier as students file into class. I hurry to be on time.

A hand grabs me around my waist. I am pulled into a corner and behind a row of lockers. I struggle in vain but cannot think of a reason to resist. The arms around me pivot my body to see a face.

I stare, but my cry is muffled beneath the hand over my lips.

"Oriana, you've changed." His eyebrows are narrowed, his eyes a pale shade of blue.

The sight brings tears to my eyes from some feeling long ago that I have no memory of. It is as if the tears are the only things within me that can recall the past. I search but find no answer; in fact I do not wish to. Instead my body freezes up. My mind goes blank. Who is he, this half-blood?

I try to shout, "Let go!" but his hand muffles my words. His eyes are wide, and the pupils so large that the blue is a thin ring around the black. He looks back and forth frantically, clearly hoping no one has heard.

"What has happened to you?"

I try to speak once again, but his hand is covering my lips. He is apprehensive, but slowly he removes his hand.

"Nothing has happened. I feel perfectly well." I chuckle at this, hearing a distant voice coming from my mouth.

"Something has to have happened; you're not yourself. I saw you with him." As he says this, he releases his hold on me. I leap at the chance and escape from the corner. But as I am about to call out for a professor, I collapse, shivering, on the floor. I break into a cold sweat and can't move. My body feels as though it is repelling something, and my head is sick with nausea. This has happened once before. I reach for my bag, but I have left it at the half-blood's feet, and my groping hand can't seem to find it.

CHAPTER TEN

I feel a soft breeze against my cheek. It rustles my hair. And the sun, it must be the sun, has warmed the grass around me. My cheeks burn slightly. The air smells of flowers and grass and dirt and all that is natural.

I open my eyes, close them, and then squint until they adjust to the sunlight. I don't think I am dead. I can't be, because I recognize the smiling golden flowers of the garden. They all sit beside me, each with the same grin upon its petals.

"Hello," I say to them.

"Good morning," they answer, but I soon realize that the real greeter is Dorian, sitting across from me on the stone bench.

I press my hands into the grass to raise myself from the ground. My joints feel stiff, and I fight off dizziness as I struggle upon weak legs. Without a sound, Dorian is by my side. I use his arm to steady myself. What is wrong with me? I feel like an infant just learning to walk.

I hobble toward the bench with help from Dorian. A turn of my head leaves me retching behind the seat. I lower myself sideways onto the bench. I rest the side of my face on the cool stone. It eases my headache, and I sense Dorian beside me.

"I knew that stuff would be strong," Dorian says in a disgusted tone, "but at least you're finally waking up."

I open my eyes, and a throbbing begins behind them. "What …

what do you mean … stuff?" My voice vibrates in my skull, and I decide to talk as little as I can.

Dorian holds up a water bottle and shakes it to draw my attention to the liquid inside.

"What is …?"

"I found it in your bag, I think it has some sort of numbing drug in it—highly addictive. I admit I wasn't sure you'd make it …" He looks down and tosses the bottle into my bag, happy to be rid of it. I watch it as if it might escape to attack me. After I am sure it hasn't moved, I close my eyes to speak.

"I suppose they will come looking for us …" I wait for my head to calm down. "How long have I been here?"

Dorian gets up from the bench and paces in front of me. He avoids my gaze, and my stomach sinks, "We've spent the night here."

My eyes wide, I sit up too suddenly, but the terrible ache of my body is less important.

"A full night?!" There's no escaping this. My mind races with excuses but finds nothing substantial. I'm dead—no, my fate is far worse than death. I am cursed! Odon will punish me. This goes beyond the Odonian, beyond a drug to numb my brain.

"How could you let this happen? Has anyone *seen* us?"

He is silent as he crouches and wrings his hands. He seems to be in deep thought, staring at the flowers.

"Dorian …" I breathe, a comforting sound in the silence.

He looks up at me, and our eyes connect. I see the hurt in them. "Oriana, I had to. I couldn't let them win like that … There was no other way to free you. I'm certain of that."

Shaking with fear, I nod in agreement. "I know, but what am I going to do now? There is no escaping the Odonians. I wouldn't be surprised if Lenora reports me the moment she spots me. No one can be trusted, and the University is completely guarded. We should just leave. That is the best chance we have." I am forced to lie down once again on the bench as the pain becomes unbearable.

"We can't leave now; it isn't the right time. You must wait until the Rebirth. It won't be safe until then." Dorian's mind seems to be flipping through the past, present, and future like a thick novel. His hands fumble with an invisible object.

There's no time to get the whole story so I change the subject.

"Even if I can convince Lenora of some lie, how will I get in again without the guards detecting me or the Odonians seeing? I was lucky that one time …"

"I'm used to sneaking around, and I've discovered the one fault of all the many guards and Odonians. It's their schedules. They keep to them exactly." His face hints of pride. "I've figured out their patterns and can avoid them. That's how I brought you here."

I flash my eyes at him. "You've learned every guard's routine?"

"It's simpler than it sounds. A bit of math and counting, although it has taken a while to learn," he adds cleverly.

My doubt begins to diminish; maybe luck is on our side. Perhaps somewhere, someone is watching right now, watching and willing us to succeed, to survive. The thought is enough to heighten my spirits, and the pain in my head recedes.

"You're still very pale, Oriana," Dorian says, handing me another canteen of clear liquid. I hesitate at first, but feeling parched, I accept it anyway.

"It's normal water from beyond the University's walls," he assures me with a confident grin.

My eyebrow arches as I begin to sip the cooling liquid. It seems to slide through my veins, healing all the way. Another question to add to my list: Dorian has already been beyond the University walls?

I drain the canteen and slowly get to my feet, feeling rehydrated.

"You'll still need to take it easy." Dorian sits down on the bench and motions for me to rest beside him. An odd breeze picks up and dishevels our hair.

"You must return soon. The Rebirth is closer than you realize. You have to be there." His eyes go gray, and I'm weighted down with curiosity.

I dare the question, "Why?"

"You will stay safe. It's best that you remain until the ceremony."

"What do I tell Lenora?"

Dorian has a quick response, "You must lie so they believe you. Act as if …"

I laugh ruefully, "As if I'm still numb? Yeah, I'm used to that."

With regret he continues, "Tell her you lost the water and passed out. You don't know for how long, but someone found you and was able to revive you with some of theirs."

"I'll have to become *her* again," I say with complete disgust. I remember a time when she was all I knew, when I was one of them.

"It won't be for long," I wait for him to go on, but he remains quiet. I stand next to him awkwardly, and for a moment I wonder if I can trust him. Why is he so determined I should go back?

"Now listen carefully. I will tell you how to get past the guards."

The numbers replay over and over in my head as I approach the University with a sickening speed. The grass seems to blur beneath my feet, although I am walking as slowly as I can. My head is in a haze, a brewing cloud of memories and fear that pricks at my skin like a thousand needles. I stop short. Was it three counts or four? I search my memory frantically, and I chase any recollection until it disappears beneath a dark horizon deep within my brain. A single second of idleness could be the difference between life and death.

It was three. I take a deep breath. It was three counts. The second reassurance is as ineffective as the first, if not more so. My feet are moving again, my mind spinning. I reach the door and nearly walk into it, but the shadow of the building awakens me before I have a chance to.

I raise my eyes to the sky. The sun is almost completely hidden by the building. It's then that the counting begins. I reach for the slate that Dorian gave me to slip within the door, as he did that first night. The sun is a slit of an eye dozing above the horizon. I hold my breath as it disappears.

My hands fumble for a moment, and then I am slipping the slate into the doorframe and sliding until the click of the alarm. With my other hand I press the cool metal handle. A feather whisks down my back. I open the portal and step over the frame—hand still on the slate, slate still on the tripper. The door isn't open long, and still it is open for too much time. My spirit shivers as something seems to escape through, but I can't tell if it's from me or the University, maybe both. The feeling passes, and I close the door and remove the stone. Silence; the sterile halls are lifeless. I don't breathe, trying not to show I'm even living. Better to blend into the white. There is a grass stain on the hem of my gown. I've only noticed it when all the white returned. Focus. Still there is silence.

My heart is gagging. Where are the footsteps? I cannot start counting without the footsteps! Focus, breathe, listen ... silence.

CHAPTER ELEVEN

A slight gurgle escapes in my throat as I struggle in the silence. My ears seem to hear only the thumping of my heart, which sends me into a panic. The footsteps! I have to listen to the footsteps! My distress only causes my heart to beat harder and faster. It taunts me, my own heart the cause of such terror. The frustration nearly causes me to cry out. I look down each corridor frantically. *What did I do wrong?*

And then there is an off-step in my heart. An extra beat, it seems at first, but then my ears manage to discern the sound from another source. One … I say in my head, my heart slowing and the heat in my blood slowly cooling. Two … I close my eyes, preparing myself to spring with the final sound. I hesitate in between when I remember the inner conflict. Maybe it was actually four. What if I'm wrong? But it seems that my heart can't wait any longer. It has me taking off toward the hallway ahead, slightly to my left. As I run I manage a glance to my right, where the shadow of the guard plays upon the opposite wall as he makes his final steps into the hallway. I was right! But I don't hear the fourth step or any other for that matter. I'm already in the next hallway, and a new set of numbers begins to play in my mind.

I reach the corner of a hallway that's perpendicular to this one. In my mind I have reached ten. By twelve I will hear a new set of feet. Eleven, twelve … The echo of a guard entering and crossing through to another hallway can be heard. By the fifth step I cover the last part of the hallway to my room as quietly as possible. I reach the pale door.

I grab the handle and, before entering, allow myself a sigh of relief.

I made it. Now I have to convince Lenora. It won't be easy. I turn the knob. I open the door in complete silence. I force my breathing to be calm and even. From somewhere inside me, I find *her*, the other me. I thought she was completely gone. But somehow I do.

Cross-legged, Lenora's wraithlike form takes up less room than the four open books that surround her on her bed. She blends into the white, almost disappearing. Even her blond hair seems to have absorbed the paleness of her skin. She looks up with ghostly eyes that startle my breath away. They seem transparent, yet they see straight through me.

"Where have you been, Oriana?" Her voice is a rush of air, and the force behind it causes me to blink. My skin turns cold beneath her icy stare, and I can't disguise an uncontrollable shiver.

Without answering I begin to busy myself with something on my desk, not wanting to look back at the cold mask on Lenora's face.

The silence becomes unbearable. I attempt a response, "I …," I begin, but my mind goes blank. Finally, I gain control and take a breath, clearing myself of emotions. I realize it's the only way to survive. Lenora might be conveying anger, but she is in complete control of what her body conveys. I cough to maybe cover up the previous short-lived statement. My back is now facing Lenora so I will not have to experience her reaction; her body lies anyway.

"I was having another one of those fits. Luckily I managed to explain to a part-blood to get me the water from my bag." I glance at her from the corner of my eye. She is motionless. "Then I spent the night at the medical center." By saying it was a part-blood I will be excused from any explanation about who it was, and that will save me a lot of trouble. A pureblood is not expected to know a part-blood by name; most don't bother to learn or remember.

"Where is your bag?" Lenora asks, stone-faced.

"My … my bag?" I look around, holding my breath, hoping it has somehow sprouted legs and followed me here. "I must have left it at the medical center." I shrug, but it seems more of a cringe.

In a flash I see Lenora's demeanor change. There is a clever smirk curving at the edges of her lips.

"Oh," she replies with a fake surprise ringing in the word, "well, that's odd."

"What's the matter?" I ask, feigning nonchalance by slouching on my bed and writing some nonsense into a notebook.

"Oh, well." Lenora seems to act as though I had shocked her out of deep thought. Her reactions are flawless. I know she's really just waiting for my response so she can pounce. I hear a whisper of movement, and I look up. Our eyes meet squarely; she doesn't blink. "Oriana, the first place I looked was at the medical center. You weren't there the whole day."

I freeze. My hand stops writing, my muscles are too tense to move. Lenora is silent, letting it sink in. My mind is racing but not with ideas, only the instinct to run and escape. Yet my body is planted on my bed, fear cementing it there.

"Lenora, I ... passed out for a while ... I don't ..." My jaw is shaking, and my hands are fumbling with the pen and book. They finally drop to the floor lifeless. I look at them with envy.

Lenora gets up from her seat on the bed. "Excuse me for a moment, would you?" she says sweetly, sliding porcelain feet into white slippers.

"Where ... where are you going?" I try to act as though the answer doesn't interest me by staring into the words on my notebook, words whose meaning I can't seem to discern.

"Bathroom," Lenora states carelessly and slips out.

My brain is on fire. Should I leave? I think back to what Dorian said: "Just until the Rebirth." He said I'll be safe here; he said to wait. I take a breath and let it out slowly, hoping it will help keep my legs from carrying me straight out the door and back to the garden. There is a sinking in my stomach, a feeling that something is not right. I should leave ... I should ...

But time has run out. Lenora returns and shuts the door behind her carefully. I watch from the corner of my eye as she sits on her bed and lets her slippers drop neatly to the floor. I hold my breath as another silence takes hold of us. It seems to squeeze the life out of me.

"Oriana." Lenora's voice is a whisper, barely audible. "What really happened?"

"I told you ... I—"

Lenora doesn't waste any more time. "Oriana, don't play dumb. I know you're hiding something important from me. You've been acting so strange lately, ever since that night at the garden. That's when this all started. You never were out that late before a big test." Lenora is in turmoil and her face is flushed. She isn't exactly yelling, but it seems as though her words are stabbing me harder than if she were. She doesn't move or stand, just remains rigidly perched upon her bed.

I'm frozen in place, watching the storm that had taken over Lenora suddenly pass.

My eyes grow warm, and I recognize the tears. This is not a time to cry, but it's hard to stop, to think, to breathe, when the emotions are so layered inside me. I'm realizing what a disadvantage they are. If only I could escape them, somehow release them from my body. I wish to tear them from within. They quickly transform into a boiling rage. The anger of my weakness burns up any tears, and I face her: my roommate, my friend, my enemy.

"Lenora, let me leave," I reply calmly, steadying my voice. I'm almost impressed with myself.

Lenora, mouth gaping, shakes her head, "I can't. You must tell me … I need to know. Why won't you?"

Just then there is a knock on the door. I almost scream, "Who is that, Lenora?"

She doesn't look at me or the door. Just shakes her head, "I can't let you … you can't go … this is how it should be … I am pureblood … I am a Winglet … I love Odon … he is everything … he is—"

"Who did you tell? Lenora! What have you done?" I scream and scream without anywhere to go. I can't seem to find my way around the room, and the knock on the door has turned to a pounding in my ears. I can't breathe, yet my screaming continues. The white of the room blinds me. There is a crash and thud as the door is kicked down.

The white gets brighter and brighter. It suffocates me and then swallows me up, starting at the tips of my golden hair.

A crowd of figures surrounds me. They are a blur of shadows in the white. I can't make out their faces, but I don't need to recognize them to know who they are.

Lenora is yelling behind me, begging me for answers.

I kick and yell in fury mixed with fear. They grab my arms, and I can't move. Tears are streaming from my eyes and nose and choking me. There is a deafening thud as something cracks the back of my skull, and a sharp pain ushers me into darkness.

CHAPTER TWELVE

I feel myself surge into my body with an exhausting ache. My head throbs in my ears, and I don't move. I can't move. Not just because of the lashing fire in my neck and skull but because my wrists and ankles have been bound tightly, viciously, together. As I try to move them in sudden panic, I feel the burns that have grown beneath the ropes and realize that I have probably been tied up for some time.

My eyes open, and I witness the intensity of the darkness. I see nothing, and I scramble around on the floor in another attack of disorientation. My hands slip across the smooth damp floor as I try to maneuver myself to my knees, and my stomach smacks back down with a sickening slap that causes me to reel in pain and cradle my body. I moan in agony and hopelessness.

"Did you really think you were going to get somewhere?"

I gasp at the sound of a female voice somewhere to my right. I search in the dark for the source. As my eyes start to adjust, I see her leaning against the wall. I realize that there is a faint glow coming from behind me. It's a small illuminated window crossed by bars; I soon see it's been cut into a thick wooden door. The flickering light suggests that a flame is casting its dimness into the cell. I can faintly see the outline of the girl's face and the reflection of her eyes.

"Who ... who are you?" Other questions quickly come to mind, "Where am I? How did I get here?" My voice is a croak, and my questions trigger a coughing fit.

Once I stop, she answers me. "You ask too many questions. As to the first one, my name is Azura, and you are?" she asks dryly.

"I'm Oriana," I whisper. My words hang in the moisture of the room. I suddenly realize that my name seems foreign to me now.

"It's a pleasure," Azura replies with the same sarcastic tone. "As for the second, I'd rather not answer it. Not that I could put this place into words." I see her hands come up to gesture around her, at least the best she could. It seems hers are bound as well. "Your third question I can answer simply. They brought you here. Other than that, my only memory is a blow to the back of the head."

"Mine too," I breathe and begin again the task of raising myself to my knees. This time I take my time shifting my weight slowly to my hands so that I can slide my legs underneath. After accomplishing this I begin an inching movement imitating a worm as I slide across the floor toward Azura. She watches in silence as I reach the wall and collapse with my back against it facing the wooden door. My body is weak, and I realize it even more as I slowly recover from my journey from floor to wall. Finally my breathing returns to normal.

"So what happens now?" I ask, not wanting the answer but needing to know.

"You'll learn soon enough …" I hear a waver in Azura's voice for the first time. It makes me nervous.

"Have you been here long?"

"It's no use wasting your energy on silly questions!" she snaps, but her tone changes at once. "You'll discover for yourself, any time here is a long time."

I shiver where I lie. I'm grateful for the dark to hide my eyes filled with tears and my body that will not stop shaking. My empty stomach twists in a knot, and I hug my damp arms against myself. I ask no more questions, and we sit side by side in silence, sharing the light of a flickering window that casts shadows on our faces. My eyes feel heavy, and tears burn down my cheeks as I imagine an endless possibility of torture. Then the room grows darker than black; everything disappears.

I open my eyes and try to swallow but can't. Somehow I have drifted to my side on the floor. I push myself back into a sitting position. I sense that Azura has fallen asleep; her breathing has slowed, although she is still sitting up. My mouth is unbearably dry, and I can't resist pressing my tongue to the wet stone wall. It tastes like dirt, and I try to spit out some of the grit but swallow some anyway.

There is a noise from outside, and my body tenses. They are footsteps, coming closer, the sound splashes in the moisture of the air. I say nothing. Azura awakens next to me.

"They're here again ... Oriana, be strong." Her hand slides inside mine and tightens. I squeeze it in return, setting my jaw and barring any tears.

A shadow appears in the window. A large figure is looking in. "Take the pureblood," it commands in a heartless voice. My stomach drops, and I intensify my grip on Azura's hand. *Be strong, be strong.* The many shadows come toward me, and I wait till the last minute to release Azura's hand and allow them to take me. Their hands lock under my shoulders and I'm lifted off my feet and carried into the corridor.

They turn left, and we follow the lead man. He wears the white silky robe of a pureblood. The stone corridor is lined with torches. My head is too heavy to hold it up and watch where we are headed. Instead I watch the floor rush beneath me and see the feet of my captors. They step together in unison, and I begin to count them, attempting to concentrate on something other than the fate that lies before me. I feel my underarms begin to bruise, and I struggle to shift their hold, but this only encourages a more crushing grip. I grit my teeth and wait for the numbness.

I can't tell how much longer I'm dragged down the hallway, and I'm not positive that I've been conscious for most of it. It seems forever until we reach a dark room. The guide halts and whips around to reveal a man of tight skin. He is a pureblood without a doubt, but I can't look at him long. His skin is stretched across his face so that bulging blue veins are visible on his forehead, and his crystal blue eyes poke out from beneath his brow. His gaze is the piercing look of a corpse, and I hide my face with disgust.

With a lucid hand, he gestures at the men to enter the room. They obey, roughly shoving me in before them. As we pass through the doorway, a globe light at the center of the room ignites and nearly blinds me as I fall to the floor in a limp heap. My hair sprawls around me, capturing the light and reflecting it back into my eyes. I try to climb to my knees, my hands and ankles still bound. With the last of my energy I make it to my knees and rest, trying to catch my breath. I look down at my shadow; it is so small beneath me.

A sharp kick deep into my side instantly drives the air from me and sends me forcibly to the floor. I struggle in a fit of coughing. My head reels as I try to grasp the floor and stop the spinning room.

"Stay where you are, Oriana. There's no need to get up." A soothing voice ripples through the room. I catch my breath but stay on the floor, my hair hiding my eyes. It hides any sight of the man who speaks to me from somewhere in the room.

"I know what you have been up to, Oriana." The soothing voice seems to run up my back. My arms move to hold the last of my body's remaining warmth. I can't think. I close my eyes and see the garden. I see the moonlight and the boy with the dark hair and blue eyes.

"There are no secrets here. You need only tell the truth. Tell us what you know of the half-blood. Then you may return as if nothing has happened." Steps approach closer and closer across the floor. I swallow and shut my eyes tighter. They stop and I feel a presence standing over me. I don't move. My body grows rigid.

He kneels down beside me, and I feel his breath over my ear. It is cold like the floor beneath me. "Oriana, you are a pureblood. You are one of Odon's children. He will protect you, as long as you are faithful." A hand strokes my hair and clears it from my face. From beneath my lids I see the light coming through. "You need only tell me of his whereabouts, and then you may go."

I am not listening anymore; I won't think of the one he's talking about or what he asks of me. The light is so blinding. I tightly close my eyes. It's hard to forget where I am. It's hard to think of anything else but the fear.

The hand clamps down on my hair and lifts me by the neck in one sharp jerk. My eyes snap open and I find myself gazing into two pale eyes. His face seems to lack any features: his nose and lips are so white that they blend into the rest of his face. There are two black holes for nostrils, yet no shadows cast upon his face to define anything else. Is he another Odonian? I can't seem to identify him as anything, and his features are so smooth that if I tried to recognize him again, I would not be able to.

He grins, yet no wrinkles line his lips, if they can be called that. I can only identify the smile by the gleam of white teeth overlapped by flaps of bleached skin. The sight sickens me, and he chuckles. "My dear, do you hear what I am saying?" His face is close to mine, and I struggle to wrench my hair free but he snaps his hand, pulling at my scalp. I cry out, and two tears escape my eyes.

He stares at me in silence a moment longer. I say nothing. With a sigh he tosses me by the head to the floor. As I reach down to catch myself, my hands make an echoing slap on the floor.

"There's no use wasting any more energy." He takes a few casual steps to the edge of the room. "Administer the device."

The words have no meaning to me, but the hint of amusement in his voice frightens me. "What are you going to do to me?" My voice is trembling, and I sound like a rodent squeaking.

"Now you speak?" he replies with mild surprise, "Well, it doesn't matter now anyway. I don't have any more time for this."

A door opens, and I look up to see a woman, her face a pure white light. Yet my gaze is quickly captured by the glint of something held in her hands. My lungs constrict at the sight. It's a large needle.

I begin to scurry frantically away from her. I break into a sweat that makes my hands and legs slip upon the floor. There is a high-pitched hum in my head as the room grows brighter. I must still be trying to escape because the guards grab hold of me. One latches onto my head and offers it to the woman.

I yell in a rage, kicking and jerking, but I am not strong enough. I know my screams are loud; they echo through the corridor, but no one will be coming for me. Above all the noise, I can hear him speak.

"He will come for her. I am certain."

The needle enters my neck, and I feel something forced into an artery. It sends a chill throughout my body, so cold that it burns. My eyes swell with a pressure and feel as if they might burst. As I slip into an unconscious oblivion, the man's last words invade my ears.

"Now we wait …"

CHAPTER THIRTEEN

Where am I? There is complete darkness, except I begin to discern a flickering light coming from a barred window. I remember—there was a girl.

"Azura! Are you still here?" There is silence. Where is she? I can't be alone here! "Azu—!"

"I'm here, you don't have to panic." The sound of a voice with emotion behind it is reassuring, even though she is clearly irritated.

Silence returns. I try to recall what happened to me. I remember them taking me away, and then a bright room. At this moment my head begins to split. The pounding is unbearable, and I can't seem to form any thoughts. Why can't I remember what happened? The pain in my skull grows.

"You didn't say you were a pureblood." Azura's voice switches the prying headache from full force to nonexistent.

"What? What do you mean?"

"I mean, I heard what that man said. Are you really a pureblood?" Azura seems to despise the word. I feel the hatred emanating from her, and I hesitate before answering.

"Why does it matter?"

"Because you're the reason I'm down here! You're one of them!" Her shouting rips through me. "You've ruined my life and killed my friends! And when I thought I could at least escape your kind for a moment in between the constant torture—I find out there is one sharing the same cell!"

I feel a lead weight on my chest. How could someone I barely know make me feel so worthless?

"You act like you know me."

"I don't need to. I know what you are." There's no mistaking her distaste. "Just don't talk to me." I want to return her hatred, but I can only empathize with her anger toward me. *Could I blame her?* I was once that girl—the one she thinks I am. I followed Odon blindly. Now in all this darkness, far below the bright lights of the University, I can see clearly.

"Azura, I'm not ..." I begin to make peace but am hushed by the sound of approaching feet. "Do you hear that?"

"Shh!" she hisses. We wait in fear.

My eyes begin to water. I hold back a cry. Biting my lip, I taste the bitterness of my own blood. My stomach sinks as the footsteps halt behind the windowed door. I hear Azura's breathing falter. I press my back against the stone wall, despite the chill. Watching the window, I see the visitor is carrying a lit torch. Its flickering light illuminates the room. I look for Azura who is also making the futile effort to escape through the wall. She senses my gaze and turns to meet my eyes.

My muscles freeze as we share a moment stricken in terror, holding our breaths, and seeing the flames dance in each other's gaze. Somewhere in the sway of fire, we see the being behind the blood.

"Oriana." My whispered name scurries across the stone like many spiders. "Oriana? Are you there?"

My heart leaps. Is it possible I have heard him? Or is it another trick of the fire?

"Dorian?" The word is spoken by both of us. The tones clash, and the name is nearly lost to dissonance.

My eyes search out Azura's, and I see a blaze lit dangerously in hers. She knows Dorian? Somehow I am certain that the twinge of jealousy is caught in her throat as well.

I hear something scraping at the lock on the door. A hand thrusts through the opening, a burning torch in its grasp. I feel the warmth of the flames from where I'm sitting.

Azura cries out as a face appears behind the torch. Peering into the blackness is Dorian. For a moment he sees only me, and we exchange smiles of relief. I leap inside when the flame flickers and it seems his smile might disappear, as if he is not a solid form but a trick of the mind.

"Dorian! You've finally come," Azura whispers in a loud gasp of air. "I didn't think it was possible! " She is scrambling in vain to stand, seeming to forget about me altogether, heedless even that the first word Dorian spoke was my name and not hers.

Once the cell door has been fully pushed open, I notice that Dorian is not alone. Behind him stands the lean figure of a young man, yet no light falls upon his face, and what light exists, creates only a silhouette. Dorian casts a wary glance over his shoulder before hurrying to us, a blade gleaming in his other hand. The other figure remains in the hallway, his head turning to either direction, keeping watch.

Azura's face slowly fills with contempt as Dorian slices at my wrist bindings first. He turns to Azura next, periodically looking over as I undo the knots at my ankles. His final look, before getting to his feet, is frightening to me. It's as if he is studying me, trying to capture my image, as though I might vanish forever.

Then in one movement he lifts me to my feet and moves at once to help Azura. I notice that she is not putting weight on her right foot. She never showed she was so badly injured. I take the torch from Dorian's hand, painfully sore but able to walk on my own.

There's no time to question, no time to wonder if this is all a wishful dream. I head for the door. I pause there, torch raised forward and above my head, unsure if the man in front of me is just a trick of the shadows. The flame lights the hallway as well as the figure's face. He is young, perhaps a few years older than Dorian, and he seems to be a part-blood. In the torchlight his eyes and hair seem to be on fire, or perhaps that is their true color. He glares with judgment at me but says nothing. Despite his soft features, his gaze is unsettling, and I can see anger in the dancing firelight.

I look further down the hallway. A few lamps are lit along the wall, their soft glow telling of lives soon to end. Beside me, the metal sconce that once cast a dreary light into our chamber has already departed. Looks like it's time for us to leave.

I turn my back to the hallway, addressing Dorian who has already assisted Azura to the entrance. As he turns to close the heavy wooden door, the nameless man takes Azura's other side. She looks up at him, whispering something that could be a name but is muffled from behind his shoulder. I keep my distance, feeling out of place around strangers. Azura awaits Dorian's assistance and does not put any weight on her foot. Instead she holds it above the ground with a bent knee. I shudder to think what brutality could have caused such an injury.

Once Dorian fastens the lock, he resumes his hold on Azura's other side then begins down the right side of the corridor. I walk beside him, my breathing heavy in my ears and my joints aching. The lamps sweep toward us, seeming to grasp at us as we pass.

Dorian and the part-blood pause at the sound of footsteps somewhere ahead. I look behind us. We have not traveled far from the door. Perhaps we could make it back. But Dorian does not turn around. He tightens his grip on Azura, who steadies herself on both young men's arms. I'm not sure what to expect, but I brace myself.

"Ten ... nine ..." Dorian counts in a barely audible whisper. As if in a trance, he stares unwavering into the corridor. I see the confidence in his expression and say nothing, but as I begin to hear the men approaching, I reach for him and press my hand onto his arm. He does not react, but remains still. I try to detect the part-blood's expression, but his face is once again in shadows and indiscernible.

"Three ... two ..." Dorian's voice rises slightly so Azura and I can hear. He looks straight into my eyes. I realize what I must do when he reaches one.

"One," he states firmly, and we start a fast walk that turns into a jog as fast as Azura can manage between the two young men. They are mostly carrying her, her foot only skimming the stone floor while the injured is lifted completely. Their movements seem to have a calculated pace. I know it is important to stay in time with their feet, while staying as silent as possible. Dorian's face maintains its deep concentration.

We stop as we come to branching corridors. Dorian keeps counting, waiting, breathing, tapping his foot in time: "Three ... two ... one." Then we are jogging again into the right passage. We do this three more times, a right, a left, another left. We alternate between a fast walk and a jog, pausing and then taking off at a timed pace. I lose track of the next varied turns and hope Dorian is certain of his way.

My body is aching by the next waiting period, and I can hear that Azura is out of breath as well. Dorian and the young man seem to be steadied, their breathing in better condition.

They must notice our waning energy because we walk a short

distance and then start a slower jog. With each step I curse the ruthless rock floor that pounds on my body. Sweat forms on my brow aided by the burning torch in my hand. I want to ask how much longer it will be. But I don't want to break Dorian's concentration.

And then the path slopes upward. At the crest there is light ahead, except this light does not flicker like the one in my hand. It is solid and fresh and consistently pure. At the sight of it, we begin a quickened pace. I can hardly wait to escape the endless labyrinth of tunnels. The light grows brighter with every bound. In the final stretch I drop the torch, tossing it behind me onto the stone floor. We are almost there, outside, free.

CHAPTER FOURTEEN

I shade my eyes as they adjust to the light of the sun. It seems to burn more brightly than ever before. When I am able to fully see, I drop my hand, eyes wide, taking in colors I have never witnessed before. We're in a garden, except it is wild, untamed. The trees tower far above the trimmed foliage of the University. They are not set in a row but have instead sprouted at will. Along the ground grows an array of soft moss, some in deep emerald, some in blue tones, in a variety of textures.

I gasp at the sight of a small flower tucked beneath the shade of a stately pine. It is a beautiful tint of pink, the color of the setting sun. I kneel to examine it and notice that at its center is a deep crimson. I reach to graze its delicate petals but withdraw, not wanting to damage its purity.

"Come, it's not safe to rest here." Dorian calls to me, breaking some connection I was unaware of beforehand. I turn to respond and find that I am seeing him for the first time. The sun seems to make everything clearer. I've seen him only either in shadows or the intense glare of the University. I never saw him like this.

His hair is disarranged and intertwining like the branches of the forest canopy. His eyes are blue and sharp, nothing reflecting in them. Instead they have become deep wells absorbing the nature around them. His expression seems to have matured since I last saw him. Maybe it has been happening all along, yet now I see he is no longer the smiling boy I first met. Something is aging him faster than time.

I look past him to examine Azura, a girl whose unique features were hidden in the darkness of the cave and then distorted by the light of flames. She has slanted green eyes and long brown hair that curls into unruly ringlets. She presses her pink lips together and glares at me. Somehow I know this look will become familiar.

The young stranger beside her does not look back. I feel uneasy about his presence but decide to remain silent. He is after all one of my rescuers.

I get to my feet and hurry after them. We head into the woods, moving as quickly as we can manage, weaving in and out of branches and bushes. I marvel at the many different species of plants.

Above is a sharp cry that startles me, and I look up to find the silhouette of a bird, its wings are spread, allowing sunlight to glisten through. I yearn for its freedom, its beauty and mastery of the sky, yet I know it will never come to pass.

Soon we've put many layers of forest between us and the cave's exit. We start up a hill, determined to put it even deeper in the past. As we reach the crest, Dorian and the stranger together guide Azura to the base of a fruit tree and help her sit on a large boulder.

As the part-blood turns to face me, I see that his hair is a deep auburn. Not the brilliant red I saw in the cave's firelight, but the deep red of blood. He looks up at me, noticing my gaze and I see that his eyes hold the same color.

I realize how strained my muscles are as I take a seat on the mossy ground. I let out a sigh of relief. Leaning back against the trunk of the tree I gaze up into its fruit-laden branches. Red ripened spheres ornament the teardrop leaves, some still green in places where they have not reached their peak. Hidden among the green leaves are smaller orbs, healthy, fresh, and awaiting their time to drop.

"Would you like some?"

I notice Dorian kneeling beside me. He holds a plump fruit before me, offering a chance to taste its sweetness. I nod, and he grasps both ends of the fruit, twisting in opposite directions to split it open. Juice escapes down his wrist as he hands me one half, the white center gleaming temptingly on top. I take it gently, first watching Dorian take a large bite and then hazarding a taste myself. It is much richer than the bland, gritty foods I am used to. I've only read about the fruit of trees. As I swallow the sweet center, I feel as though I've been accepted by the forest. My white robes take on the white of the fruit, the white of blooming flowers or the birds singing to the sun.

"Are they going to meet us here?" Azura asks between bites of fruit, which she retrieved from a branch overhead. "They can't expect us to walk all the way back by ourselves; we're already exhausted."

Dorian stands to his full height and stretches his arms over his head before tossing the core of his fruit into the nearby foliage. "I was hoping they would be here already …"

Just then, Dorian's fruit core hurtles toward him from behind and hits the back of his skull. He flinches, rubbing the sore spot and turning to face the source. "I guess I spoke too soon."

Then he smiles as the branches part to reveal a man of great height whose face glows triumphantly. He is followed by a young boy and a girl, clearly chuckling over the recent jest. The tall man approaches Dorian, grabs his hand, and claps him on the back in welcome.

"I see you've made it in one piece," he says in a deep commanding tone. His rich chestnut eyes twinkle with humor. They are shadowed by sandy curled hair that reaches below his ears, and as he steps further into the light, I notice his wide grin displays two charismatic dimples. He is older than Dorian and I, but still fairly young.

My mind automatically labels him as a part-blood. In fact, the others are part-blooded as well, all with shades of brown hair. As they approach Azura and the other part-blood in greeting, I'm awkwardly drawn to Dorian's side, not sure where I belong among these new people. I wish to contact his arm and feel the warmth of his skin. I begin to realize that he is from this completely different world and just as much a stranger as the others. Instead I hover, one hand extended noncommittally from my side.

The tall part-blood's attention turns to me, and I fear I will be trapped in his gaze. But his look is comforting, and he regards me with compassion, something that will take a while to get used to.

"So this is the Winglet." He takes my hesitating hand into his darker one. It is warm like his eyes. Looking deeply into mine he kisses it. I pull it, as politely as possible, away and gain the courage to reach out and take Dorian's. A heat rises in my cheeks as I study the ground.

I smile and venture, "My name is Oriana; what might yours be?" meeting his eyes once my face cools.

"She speaks! Oriana? Yes I know, but until now I didn't realize how well it suits you. I am Tor." I have never met a part-blood like Tor before. He is so alive and confident in his skin.

I'm not sure what he means, but I smile at him, hoping he will accept it as my own attempt at friendship.

I see him give a wink to Dorian before addressing the entire group. "I suppose we should hurry home, before the dark settles."

There is a murmur of agreement as the young boy goes to assist Azura to her feet, the red-haired man already beside her and helping as well. The small girl makes her way to where Dorian and I are standing. She has large black eyes and wavy dark brown hair, not quite black.

I have never seen a part-blood Finlet before; in fact, I only once saw a pureblood Finlet, a young girl somehow lost in the Winglet playground. Our elementary schools contained both races, with only a thin barrier between us. Her skin was a deep shade of tan, and she had flowing, silky black hair and eyes that were as black as their pupils. I remember how she was teased, her hair pulled with distaste for something the children had never seen before. The poor girl was in tears before an Odonian had corrected things.

The girl before me resembles her in many ways but cannot be pureblood. The lighter aspects of Winglets have leaked out into her hair and skin, although her eyes could not be any darker. I am hoping my stare does not show judgment. She dares a glance in my direction before addressing Dorian.

"It is amazing what you did. I have to admit, I was worried you wouldn't make it." The girl smiles. I can tell she is much younger and wonder how she is not at the University, sitting in class. Then I realize I am absent as well; it's a strange feeling, knowing that everything there is continuing as always.

Has anyone asked where I am? Do they worry what has happened to me? Or do they act the same way they always have when someone disappears suddenly? I've never reacted when someone went missing. I can only remember being thankful it was not me.

Dorian gives a modest smile. "Anyone could have done it, if they spent as much time as I have. I only wish Azura could have been rescued sooner. It did make saving Oriana easier." He steps aside, forcing the young girl and me to face each other. I gaze at her blankly, as if she were a wild animal. "Oriana, this is Malise. She is a friend of mine."

I smile immediately, determined to make a good first impression. She looks sideways at me, as if I were a new species as well. "Nice to meet you," I interject. Malise nods in response and then hurries to catch up with Tor and the others who have already begun down the gradual slope, further into the forest. Watching them leave I feel pressure on the small of my back and realize Dorian remains beside me. I look up at him questioningly.

"Malise doesn't see many purebloods," Dorian explains, probably noticing my look of dismay.

"But how …," I begin. Wasn't Malise born and sent to school as all of us are? Is there any alternative?

"She was not raised in Odon's schools," Dorian answers and then begins to follow after the others.

I feel his hand slide from behind me, hanging back a moment to consider his answer. "Then where was she raised?" I finally ask.

Dorian stops and turns. There's a spark in his eyes. "Come, I'll show you."

CHAPTER FIFTEEN

Dorian's reply leaves me thirsty for answers. I move to follow but am jolted to a halt as pain stabs into the side of my neck. I gasp as my vision blackens. I clutch the spot convulsively and try to steady myself despite my blindness. I nearly fall to my knees but am able to catch myself as my sight returns and I grab onto the trunk of a nearby tree.

My hand slides over the spot. I hadn't noticed it was so sore. I feel the swollen lump of a fresh wound. I guide my fingers over it a second time to be sure I felt correctly, clenching my teeth to bear the pain. How did this happen? I search my memory for a fall or attack. I recall the bruised skull I received when I was captured from my room; was it from that? Or maybe from being dragged into my cell, or striking the stone when they threw me to the floor. I had been unconscious and unable to catch myself.

No, this is different. It's as if an object has penetrated into my neck, inserted through the skin. Not an aimed fist or a rough shove. My body is bruised enough from that already. This could not be from the handling of any guards.

I recall a white room, bright lights. The voice of a man. He is asking me questions, but I refuse to speak.

"He will come for her. I'm certain." The voice is chilling.

"Oriana? Are you all right?" I feel the warmth of Dorian's hand in mine. He looks into my eyes searching for the source of my unsettling expression.

Abruptly an icy coldness surfaces in my veins, so cold that it burns. Its intensity collects at the wound. It reaches up my neck like long needle fingers, enveloping my brain. My mind cries out as it is suffocated into submission. I grab my head with both hands, sucking air through my teeth, trying to fight the overpowering grip of an internal force. Then as soon as it began, it is over. I look up, unable to form a response. In fact, I've forgotten what Dorian even asked. I stare at him blankly.

"Oriana, what is it?" Dorian has dropped my hand now and is grasping me by the shoulders. My body feels unusually numb, but slowly returns to normal.

"I ... I don't know. I mean, I can't remember." I look into his face, which only increases my fright. Somehow I feel like my mind is wiped clean, or rather that something within has been coated with a smooth whiteness.

Dorian says nothing for a moment, his mouth gaping and that awful look in his eyes. Finally he says, "Let's keep moving. The farther we get from that place, the better."

He starts off again toward the others, this time lingering by my side. I look over my shoulder at where we came from and cannot avoid a shudder. As I turn my head to look forward, I notice Dorian staring at me—at the base of my neck.

"What is it?" I ask. I don't like the way his eyebrows have narrowed, or his lips have tightened. He has even grown pale.

He makes eye contact as if he has been caught at something and quickly turns to look ahead. "Nothing, nothing at all."

We catch up to the others, who have paused to wait for us. They all seem anxious to continue on and had been moving fairly quickly despite having to help Azura. She seems most willing to speed up, probably looking forward to reaching her home. She was in the caves longer than I was. Didn't Dorian say he'd been planning her rescue for a while? It must've been far more complicated than the University. He had to calculate every tunnel and guard to plan not only sneaking in but escaping as well, and that meant planning the amount of time it would take to retrieve us from within the cell.

Why was Azura brought there to begin with? I glance in her direction. She wears a robe that at one time must have been a light cream color. Now it is brown and darker in places that have stains of what looks like dried blood. There are no sandals on her feet, which have become almost black, possibly bruised. The rest is undoubtedly a buildup of grime. She flinches as if she senses my eyes upon her.

We take a break as the sun begins its descent. I'm grateful for the chance to rest upon a mossy patch of ground. The shade of an evergreen covers me, and my body cools slowly. Although we have been walking for a while, the land has been forgiving despite an occasional slope. Yet sitting on the ground I feel the rush of exhaustion weigh into my limbs. I watch in envy as Malise hands Azura a canteen of liquid. Absentmindedly, I run my tongue across parched lips. In a last attempt, I search around for Dorian but before I look far, my gaze locks on the brown eyes of the boy. His hand extends toward me, offering a canteen similar to Malise's. I accept it willingly.

"Thank you," I say after a large gulp. I pause after the second one, realizing I have not yet learned his name.

"Toby," he supplies tentatively.

I nod from behind the canteen and then lower it to add a smile. He seems to be accepting of me. Unlike Malise, perhaps he has lived within the University. Although he might not be so friendly if he had met other purebloods. I don't recognize him, but then again I wouldn't recognize most part-bloods from there, with the exception of Fisk—who I'd rather not remember.

Toby is a Winglet part-blood like Tor. His hair, a deep bronze, is cropped short and straight. His eyes are much darker than his hair, the color of the soil. He is smaller than Dorian, thinner and probably younger. His eyes show a timid quality of kindness that is a relief among so many strangers. Could those eyes have looked upon the University walls and still remain so forgiving? What does he see in my eyes?

"Are you from the University?" I ask, handing back the canteen.

He looks down, fumbling with the canteen as if unsure whether to answer. Then he says, "When I was younger—I don't remember much."

I'm not surprised. He is a gentle boy. Whatever memories he lost as a child seem not to have affected him.

I notice he is no longer looking in my direction. I follow his gaze and find the culprits, Azura and the other part-blood from the caves. Their eyes are disapproving and directed at Toby. He is already getting to his feet to join the others.

"Thank you again, Toby, I feel much better now."

He turns as if my voice were at a distance instead of directly beside him. It takes a moment for him to understand, "Oh … yes, you're welcome." He hurries away toward the others.

They must be planning to isolate me. I've become the enemy to them, the evil pureblood. It doesn't matter; my attention is drawn to where Dorian and Tor are talking.

They have turned their backs to me and hushed their voices. Their words are lost in the vibrations of the forest. Dorian runs one hand through his hair while the other gestures earnestly. He looks at me, notices I am watching, and quickly turns back to Tor. It isn't the first time; I've noticed his eyes upon me before. Should I continue to trust them? I have no choice, no home to return to. My life is in their hands. I feel less liberated all of a sudden, and maybe even trapped.

Dorian approaches, taking a seat beside me he rests his elbows on his knees. "We should be there by sunset, there's not much farther to travel." So he is going to keep secrets, I frown. "Will you be all right?" His voice shows honest concern, and I stare at him in confusion.

"Of course, why wouldn't I be?" Too late, I hear the harshness in my tone.

"It's just that we've noticed you look weaker, possibly … ill."

At this I get to my feet, partially still hurt that he would discuss things about me without me knowing, and partially because he's accusing me of being weak and incapable.

"You mean you and Tor?" I snap, "Is that what you were talking about?" I feel anger rising and yet my voice doesn't seem to carry.

"I'm sorry, I didn't mean to hurt you. I was just worried …"

"I'll be fine." His words strike a nerve. I've become a person that others worry about, someone who is dependent, unable to make it through without help. I know I need to prove something, show that I'm strong. To propel my frail body forward by sheer will. Maybe the others are watching me right now, but I don't care. Let them see that I'm no longer the Oriana I once was.

As we set off once more, I follow directly behind Tor who has been leading the way. His long strides are difficult to keep up with, but I gain a rhythm that I refuse to slacken. The blood in my ears pounds harder and a flush rises to my cheeks, but with a set jaw and a stubborn gaze I press on. I sense Dorian behind me, as stubbornly determined to stay near me as I am to stay ahead. As I stumble, my legs turning to rubber, I hear him let out a sigh. I break into a trot, and now my legs go numb. Why am I so tired? The thought frustrates me, and I increase my pace to reach Tor's side before slowing to a fast walk. Tor slows as well, which irritates me, but I say nothing. He hands me a fruit once I am beside him and I realize my stomach is still fairly empty. He grabs another off a nearby tree in midstride and takes a bite.

"Thanks," I comment before taking a bite myself.

"You seem different. Is something wrong?"

I look up at him, but he is still watching the land ahead of him. "I ..." I hide my face behind the fruit as my cheeks flush further. The warmth in his voice gives me reason to trust him. "I feel as though the others are expecting me to fail. They've already labeled me, and Dorian acting as my caretaker isn't helping ..."

Tor grins at me. "Those two?" He chuckles, referring to Azura and the other part-blood. "Don't let them bother you; they'll judge a morning before waking up." He flings the center of his fruit into the foliage beside him.

Looking down, I kick a rock, feeling foolish for caring what two people I barely know think of me.

"As for Dorian," Tor whispers close to me—he smells of fresh pine needles—"I've never seen him so ... dedicated to another person before, other than himself." Tor laughs at this as if at a distant memory then turns serious again, "But he was young then. I can tell he's grown, matured even."

I turn away, smiling secretly to myself.

"Oriana?" I look back up at him. Tor is staring ahead once more. "It's true you are the only Winglet among us, but that's because you're special. Probably the only one in that *place*,"—he stresses the word with contempt—"who could have done what you did. They'll see that in time, and I have a feeling Dorian already sees what they cannot."

His words revive my fears. Is it possible that this man would think of me as *special*? I hadn't thought of being the only pureblood as an admirable thing. Has Dorian seen that difference in me from the start? When we passed in the hallway of the University? The thought makes me sulk even more.

Tor is far ahead of me. Three of the others pass, followed by Malise, who glances back at me curiously before hurrying on. I've slackened my pace while in thought, but it doesn't seem to matter anymore. I have let others cause me to lose control of my anger and lashed out at the person who was there for me all along. The more I live with them, the more complicated emotions become.

"Oriana …"

I stop in my tracks. I have lost pace with the others, and Dorian has slowed as well. He has remained silent, and I didn't realize he was still behind me. He stops beside me. I can't stop staring at the ground, unable to look him in the eye.

"Oriana, I'm sorry … I shouldn't have …"

I look up at him and laugh. He can probably see the tears welling in my eyes. I won't let them fall, although they are not really in sadness. "Will you stop apologizing!"

His eyebrow rises.

I start walking away from him. "I'm not mad anymore. You can relax; my tantrum is over."

He catches up to me and scratches the back of his head, "I thought you …"

For some reason I can't bring myself to admit I was completely wrong. "I realized something. I'm okay now."

I catch Dorian watching me, but he says nothing as we walk faster to join the others.

CHAPTER SIXTEEN

Their spirits have lightened when the sun touches the horizon, and I can tell we're almost there. We climb a short hill surmounted by an imposing oak. It sits upon the land, a giant among men. There is a small clearing around its base in which a layer of moss covers the limbs of a massive root system that has erupted from the ground. It stretches out far beyond the clearing, its fingers growing thinner the further it snakes along the land. It is a magnificent tree, larger in width than any I have seen. Its gnarled branches twist in stunning elegance, as if each turn were planned over the ages. I don't even try to turn my head upward to glimpse the top, but rather marvel at its trunk.

Beyond the oak I finally notice that the hill's opposite side descends sharply into a deep valley. Expansive trees file along the hillside blanketing it in a lush green. Far in the distance past the rolling hills of forest sits the falling sun. It's reflecting brightly off a line of silver. I shadow my eyes to get a better look. Am I seeing correctly?

"It is the ocean." Dorian stands beside me, admiring the scenery as if it were his first time as well.

"The ... ocean?" I search my memory for the word. The trees I knew from within the University's walls. I have studied whatever information was given about the outer boundaries of Odon's land, but an ocean? The word is foreign yet intriguing. I await Dorian's explanation, eager to hear of what lies beyond Odon's territory.

"Yes." Dorian seems to be searching within his head for the right explanation. "It's like a vast water-filled land. I have only ever been there once as a child, but I wish to return someday."

I smile in sincerity and turn back to the horizon, straining my eyes to try and get a better view of the silver lining. How had I never heard of such a place? Where land ends and water begins? I stare a moment longer, trying to imagine how large this world is, how many things I do not know about it. I feel so small. I restrain an urge to run full speed into the horizon. Instead I turn back and face the others, who have come to a stop.

Tor has halted at the base of the large oak and peers up through its network of branches.

He is a tall man, yet is dwarfed in comparison. He stands a moment longer, focusing above. The sun has moved to the base of the hilltop, and a shaft of light shines through to strike Tor with an orange glow. My curiosity grows as he removes a mirror from his pocket and angles it so that the rays of sunlight hit the mirror and reflect in a golden beam, straight up the trunk of the tree to the air beyond.

His hand drops to his side once a light from above lands upon his face. His eyes squinting, he raises his other arm to shield his face.

Following this, a rope ladder drops abruptly, very nearly hitting him in the face. He dodges it in time. This is followed by a ripple of laughter from above, which he returns with a glare. Dorian chuckles from beside me, yet I am far too much in awe to find anything laughable.

Tor gestures to the others who are waiting behind him. "Malise, you first. I'll bring Azura up." He turns to take her weight from the part-blood boy. Malise starts up the ladder. She quickly reaches a breathtaking height, but it doesn't seem to bother her, and she continues upward with an unchanging speed. When she is lost from view behind a bough that must be twice as thick as my body, I return my attention to those still on firm ground. Toby is the next to head up.

The other part-blood helps Azura onto Tor's back. She wraps her arms tightly around his neck and then encircles her legs around his waist, supporting her bad ankle with the other one as he pulls himself onto the first rung. The part-blood glances at Dorian and me before following close behind, wary of Azura and aiding the best he can. I turn away, and the thought of falling from that height leaves a painful pit in my stomach. When I look again, they have disappeared with the others into the arms of the oak.

"Are you ready?" Dorian stands by the ladder, one hand steadying it, the other reaching toward me.

I laugh nervously without meaning to. "Not really."

He shrugs. "It's safe enough." He tugs on the ladder firmly.

"Oh *good*," I chuckle, holding back a small shriek.

I take a large breath that is more like a gulp and fasten my hands around the highest rung of the ladder that I can reach from the ground. I step up, unwilling to leave the solid ground; the ladder is unsteady with my weight. I think of the others. They weren't afraid. Even young Malise had made it in no time. I keep taking steps, refusing to look below, concentrating on the rope in front of me. I feel Dorian latch on below me, and the ladder swings dangerously. I hold my breath and close my eyes, gripping the ladder till my hands turn white. The ladder regains a decent steadiness, and I start upward again, anxious now to reach the top, wherever that may be. I start off slow now that Dorian's weight is shuddering the ropes with each pull. Somehow I manage to find a rhythm, and my speed increases.

I only realize I've made it to the top when hands grab my arms and hoist me onto a platform. I had not expected there to be a solid surface so far above actual land. The platform of wood is wedged between two thick branches and strapped down securely. I sit, attempting to recover from the treacherous climb. Once upon the firmness of the platform, I take in my surroundings. The platform is bordered with a rope fence made of woven fabric and vines for protection. I still prefer to remain near the trunk. Above I notice that the canopy is full of layers of platforms, rope ladders hanging from each one. It's like a vertical city rising high into the oak's branches.

Dorian reaches the top soon after and pulls himself over the ledge and onto the platform. The surrounding company approaches to greet him with playful shoves and smacks upon his back. I notice that they all seem to be of a similar age, not much older or younger than myself.

"I can't believe you actually did it!" a dark-haired boy shouts, shaking Dorian's hand roughly.

Dorian looks downward modestly, not saying much other than "Anyone could've done it" as others come to congratulate him.

Two young girls standing behind me whisper to each other, "He really *is* a half-blood."

"He *must* be, only a half-blood could have done what he did and live to tell about it," the other chimes in. I glance behind me, but the girls have disappeared into the crowd.

Two hands grasp me from behind and hoist me to my feet. I steady myself and turn to face Tor, displaying his dimpled grin. "So you've made it. You were becoming quite pale last time I saw you. I'm glad you decided to join us anyway."

I smile. "I've been through worse."

"I'm sure you have."

"Is Azura all right?" I ask, not finding her among the others. Toby and Malise linger around Dorian as he tells the intrigued crowd of his courageous rescue.

"She has been brought to the healers; they'll fix her up, and she'll be as good as new fairly soon. Liam has gone to look after her as well."

Liam must be the other part-blood.

My questions will not stop there. I have a multitude buzzing inside my head. The first: "What is this place?"

Tor looks at me as if expecting the question. "This is our home, the Great Oak. Our only refuge from Odon, established by rebels a generation ago when Odon was first rising into power."

"Odon doesn't know about it?" I've been told that Odon knows everything. He sees all; there is no escaping him.

"If he did, I don't think we would still be here," Tor answers.

I nod. I'm sure that Odon enjoys his power. He wouldn't want it to be threatened by anyone, specifically a group of rebellious part-bloods.

I have another question. "There was a time when Odon was not in power?"

"When I was a child, the rebels were still attempting a complete revolution." He shakes his head to clear the memory. "Odon is strong, but his power only reaches those who let it, remember that." He gives a wink. Then he strides toward Dorian, the others taking notice as Tor approaches.

"I think Dorian has had enough praise for one day," Tor shouts addressing the crowd. "Trust me, his ego doesn't need it." The group ignites with laughter and a few nods of regretful agreement. "How about we have an early dinner?"

There are no retorts of any kind as the youths hurry toward the opposite end of the platform. As they pass me, some shoot looks of suspicion. I focus on the ground, knowing that my hair remains just as brightly yellow as ever. I'm grateful as they disappear around the platform's corner where it curves against the trunk of the tree.

"Sorry about that." Dorian is beside me, watching the others hurry away. I jump slightly, thinking he has seen the others look at me. Then he jabs his thumb over his shoulder, and I realize he is talking of their excitement over him.

I relax slightly and shake my head. "No, don't apologize, you deserve it."

He concentrates on the branches above, unable to look at me while accepting the compliment. "Thanks. Are you hungry?"

I laugh. "Of course."

I follow him as he makes his way down the platform, taking the same path around the trunk that the others had. As we turn the corner, we come across a building lying firmly upon the platform. I was not sure what to expect as shelter, but the wooden construction is impressive and fits snugly within the oak's branches. The rounded roof is made of a single bending branch as its sole support, surrounded by smaller branches gathered and neatly laid along the curve of the main branch. The building hugs the trunk of the tree, wrapping around it and out of sight. It's impossible to see its true extent.

The building glows slightly, and the smell of something sweet drifts past us from within. As I stare from the entranceway, an opening sheltered by a slanted awning, I notice the approaching night has darkened everything. I blink a few times to be able to see Dorian's form as he hurries forward. A cool breeze kicks up and encircles us. I walk close to him, hugging myself to keep warm. There is a new life in the forest, sounds I have never heard before, coming from creatures I cannot see. It is a peaceful song that grows as the sun's light shrinks. As I look out, past the ropes into the canopy of leaves, I see a small yellow light wink on and off. I approach the edge, stopping to get a better look. The light is gone from where I last saw it, but appears again a short distance away, glowing for only a moment before disappearing once again. To my surprise I notice many others, and they begin to fill the shadows like many moving stars.

"They're fireflies," Dorian whispers. His voice joins the chorus of the night.

I glance toward him as he grabs hold of the ropes at the edge of the platform. His face is barely visible in the darkness, and the building's light silhouettes him from behind.

I nod, looking back out into the treetops. There is so much I have not experienced. I sigh, frustrated at feeling left out of this other world. I will have to continue one day at a time, one moment after the other, learning what I can. The fireflies have found their light in a world of darkness and confusion. I can find my own.

CHAPTER SEVENTEEN

Dorian and I enter the building as any trace of light is lost from the day. He holds the flap door open for me to duck into a large, warm room full of people. There is a pleasant hum of conversation, broken occasionally by scattered bouts of laughter. It is far from the monotone hush of the dining hall at the University. The activity is overwhelming.

The others are sitting along a wooden table that stretches all the way to a substantial fire fixed at the center. I have never seen a flame so large and powerful. The light seems to be alive, dancing back and forth, meticulously trapped within a circle of large stones. The others seem not to notice as its fingers lick toward them, wavering far from its encased circle. It snaps as if in fury, but is barely heard among the many voices. A thick gray cloud of smoke billows up through a shaft in the roof. The fumes give off the familiar sweet odor from outside.

Dorian shows me a way around the table and benches of people. I notice Malise reprimanding a young boy who is practically an exact copy of her, although smaller and with his black hair cut short. She looks up and notices me walking past. I smile and give a hesitant wave, yet she shows no reaction. Finally she nods before turning back to what can only be her younger brother.

I feel the intensity of its heat as we pass by the fire. I remain still for a moment, waiting to see if the fireflies are born from its flying sparks.

Once past, I notice that another table begins and curves down the center of the building. Every seat seems to be filled, yet Dorian doesn't seem fazed. As we turn the corner, I notice an empty space beside the tall figure of Tor. He's smiling and engaged in a conversation with some others across from him. I follow his gaze to those he's adamantly talking with. My stomach drops, it's Azura, and she's sitting beside Liam.

As Dorian and I approach, Azura is the first to notice us. She smiles at Dorian but can't hide a glare at me as I come to sit next to him.

"Ah, just in time. The food is just starting to be passed out. You might have missed your share if you were a second later." Tor is as jovial as ever as he passes a pitcher to Dorian, who grabs the carved wooden mug in front of me and fills it. I thank him when he hands it to me, and he fills his own.

"Tor, your talk increases, and yet the Rebirth is almost upon us, and our plan is still not in order." Azura speaks across the table sternly. A glance in my direction tells me she's pleased I have no idea what she's talking about. It does, however; spark my attention, and I lean in to hear better. What plans do they have for the Rebirth? It's foreign information to me.

Dorian has stopped pouring his drink and sets it down with an unsteady hand. "Azura, this is not the time—"

Liam cuts in. "Then when is a good time? I for one am not willing to follow anyone blindly, and neither will the others. Without a plan all your ideas and aspirations are useless." His chestnut eyes seem to hold a secret. The light of the fire dances on the walls and ceiling, giving his hair a redder glow than its usual auburn. His eyebrows are set in a frustration that goes beyond the issue at hand. He stares across the table toward Dorian with clear contempt.

The discussion halts as smooth wooden bowls are passed down the table. The procession stops once everyone has received their share. I hold my own gently between my hands. It's warm, and the smell of the steamy contents wafts over me. The others have grown quiet as they dive into their food, and I allow myself the first savory sip. Lifting the bowl to my lips, I taste a thick stew, a creamy vegetable broth. I place the almost empty bowl on the table and reach for a piece of grain bread from the row laid out along the center of the table. After one bite, I find it to be both flavorful and sweet. The scents and tastes are so new, unlike the bland grit I am used to. I see Dorian cleaning the last of his bowl with a piece of bread and follow his example.

"I am not denying the situation," Tor begins again, taking a gulp from his glass to clear his throat. Conversation has begun to pick up throughout the room. "A plan must be decided upon, yet there is much that still needs to be discussed. I have no intentions of rushing into this."

"But we do not have the time to continue discussing at the speed of growing trees!" Azura speaks up and then lowers her voice. "We need to act quickly. Dorian is the only half-blood we've got, and I don't see any in our future. If we miss this chance, it's the end of us." Azura struggles to drive her point home, and Tor nods gravely in agreement.

"If he even is a half-blood as we think …" Liam mutters under his breath, loud enough for us to hear. Azura rolls her eyes in exasperation.

I glance at Dorian to see his reaction and notice that he seems to be used to this accusation. He nods, "You're right, we can't be sure; but there's only one way to find out. It's a chance we must take."

Tor sighs heavily. "We'll discuss this more tomorrow. It's been a busy day, and I'm sure you're all as tired as I am." As he stands, I notice that others along the table have begun to leave as well, and the place has emptied and grown quieter. Tor addresses the passing people, wishing them a good night and pleasant sleep.

Finally he turns to us. "Sleep well friends. There is nothing to worry about. I am certain we will find a way." He grins sleepily before heading off toward an exit at the opposite side of the structure.

Dorian and the others linger a moment in silence before standing as well. He glances at Azura with irritation that she smugly accepts blame for. I stand beside him, feeling the pull of my muscles as they reluctantly come into action once again. I'm extremely tired and ready to put the new issues aside until I am better rested. The discussion was disquieting, and I'm still not sure what they are planning. Still, I feel that danger is close at hand, though for what purpose or in what form, I do not know.

I begin to head past Dorian toward the exit, checking to make sure he is following. He is all too eager to leave. I notice Azura and Liam heading in our direction as well. I reach the doorway first, and Dorian and Azura come face to face. They pause, making eye contact for a moment long enough to make my blood heat. Her eyes tell me I'm not simply overreacting, and her hand tentatively brushes his arm.

At that I swipe the flap aside and rush into the night. The frigid air striking me in the face like a cold damp hand. A fury rises within me, though not of my hatred of Odon or the University. It's not the disappointment or betrayal of Lenora, or the disgust at Aurek's rough grip. This anger is completely different from the others, one I have never felt before.

Dorian bursts from the tent behind me, his eyes searching the night. My white robe and light hair betray me, and he settles at the sight of me. Azura is not far behind, and her contorted face reveals everything she is feeling. She's followed by Liam, who scuffs the ground and strides quickly away grumbling beneath his breath. He doesn't even look at me as he sweeps past, nearly hitting me in the shoulder. His form slowly blends into the darkness as he leaves the light of the building and is lost to sight around the bend of the tree.

Azura does not seem to notice him at all. "How could you betray us? Our home? Us!" The tears in her eyes reflect the glow of the dying flames from within the building. I can see her ankle has been bandaged and now notice that she leans upon a wooden crutch tucked under her arm. She refuses to show any weakness in her stride.

Dorian shakes his head. "You betray yourself when you blame others for your hatred." She falters, and he reaches toward her to help her regain balance. I back away, my heart leaping, and hide my twisted expression in the shadows. At his touch Azura softens. She gives him that look, the one from before, a look that can mean nothing else but love.

He steps back, retrieving his hand as if he has made a mistake. I see Azura lose control.

"I realized a while back that you and I would never come to pass." She trembles, taking a shaky breath. "But I can't stand to see you with someone like *her*!" She points at me, and every word bristles with the power of her pent-up rage. I flinch at the sound.

Gripping her staff tightly Azura rushes away at a speed that must be causing her a great deal of pain, although she does not show it. Once she is around the edge of the platform and out of sight, Dorian turns to me with a sigh.

"I never meant for you to hear that." He walks toward me, letting his black hair fall over his eyes, "She has ... a lot of anger. I don't think she'll ever get over it." He reaches up to clasp his forehead in his palm and collapses against the side of the tree.

"I wish she could see how much we are alike, Azura and I." I place my fingers against the oak, running them along its textured surface, feeling its complexity and letting it guide me through its crevices.

I see half of Dorian's face, which is still illuminated by the distant fire. He looks over to me solemnly. "No, Oriana, you are not the same." He struggles for words, "Her hatred for purebloods runs deep. That's no better than everyone at the University. Oriana, you don't complete the circle of hatred. I think instead you seek to change yourself, to grow by seeing both sides of the story."

I realize there is truth in what he says, yet I wonder if it is really the best way to live. Am I growing, or refusing to face my true feelings by compromising for everyone else?

He speaks no more as we head down the platform. I follow closely, not enjoying the utter blackness and the feeling that my foot may step past the edge at any moment. My eyes eventually become accustomed to the dark, and I'm able to see that we have reached a rope ladder leading upward to another platform. Grateful that I can see how far I must climb, I start ascending without objection. Upon this next platform sit a row of cottages of thatch and wood, some glowing from fires lit within.

Dorian walks past these and to another ladder, which takes us further into the limbs of the Great Oak. The next two platforms, reached by way of two more ladders, contain similar cottages, situated sideways so that they hug the tree as the dining structure had. I notice the trees branches have thinned to about half the size of the lower ones, though still too massive to wrap my arms around. By the third ladder and platform I am more exhausted than I've ever imagined I could be. I'm relieved when Dorian stops in front of a cottage to open its flap door and guide me inside.

It's even darker within, and I stand frozen for a moment to let my eyes adjust. Dorian walks to the corner of the room, rustling some items in search of something in the dark. There is a snap and then a buzz as fire bursts into life within his hands, and the room brightens to an orange glow. Dorian reaches for a square box that appears to be a paper lamp. He extends the fire, which is lit upon a dried stick, into the lamp and lights the center. The fire sits placidly inside the lamp, and Dorian extinguishes the stick with a sharp gesture. He turns back to me. "This will be your room. It's not much, but it can become home."

Now that my eyes have adjusted to the light, I look around. There's a bed laid out on the floor, different than what I am used to. The mattress is a rough cloth stuffed with what smells like soft grass, and there is a thicker cloth laid over as a blanket. I'm immediately taken by its humbleness and am pleased to call it my own.

"Do you like it?" Dorian asks doubtfully.

I laugh. How can I not love a place beneath the stars, held in the arms of nature herself, far away from the white of the University walls? I have only been within it barely a moment, and it feels more like home than the University ever did. "Of course, I love it."

Dorian grins. "Good, I'll be just in the next cottage, if you need anything. The flame should burn out in a short while." He begins to head for the door.

I hurry toward him before he can leave. "Dorian?"

He stops immediately to face me.

"I wanted to thank you for what you've given me." I want him to stay with me.

Dorian doesn't say anything. He takes me in his arms, holding me in his warmth. Making it impossible for me to ever let go. His hand smoothes back my hair, and I think I might not be able to stand if he walks away. I nearly forget to ask him. I pull away slightly.

"What were they talking about? At dinner, the plans, and you—"

"Oriana." He kisses my forehead and then stares closely into my eyes. "That is for another time. For now, I need you to trust me." He pauses, taking a slow breath. "I need you to know that—" His jaw clenches on his words. Finally he whispers, "Good night," before slipping from the cottage.

I stand a moment in confusion and disappointment, watching the spot where he just stood. A chill creeps over me, and I seek the warmth of my bed. Once beneath the blankets, I find my troubles and the world seeping away. As the flame takes its last breath, I slip into darkness.

CHAPTER EIGHTEEN

I can't escape them, the blue piercing eyes. They follow me wherever I run, wherever I try to hide in this black abyss. They see my every movement, surrounding me, blocking my attempts to reach freedom. The eyes bore into me, not only looking at my face but cutting through me, seeing my soul.

They laugh, and the sound vibrates in my ears, causing me to fall. There is nothing beneath me, and I hurtle downward, the cackling clouding my thoughts and blocking any resistance. I reach out for something, anything to grab before I reach my death. Below I see them, watching me descend rapidly, those crystal eyes. They know there is no one to rescue me, no one to swoop down and snatch me from the air, to keep those eyes from swallowing me, taking control of my every thought and movement. I cry out, screaming to find a way to escape them.

My eyes snap open, and I sit up in bed. The sound of a scream is dying away, and I realize it has come from my own mouth. I'm breathing heavily, and cold sweat drips off my forehead onto my hand, which clutches the blanket. I look around, slowly remembering yesterday's events and why I'm here in a foreign place. I remember fear, trying to escape, but from what I can't recall. The more I try to, the more it seems to sink into my subconscious.

I turn my attention to the sunlight streaming in through the heavy cloth flap that is folded slightly inward. It moves slowly in and out with the breeze. Running my hand through my hair a few times, I get to my feet, slipping them into the sandals I kicked off sometime during the night. I stand in the doorway a moment soaking in the rays, but something spoils the moment, making it seem not quite real. I feel burdened still, despite finally getting a night's rest. In fact, I feel weaker than usual.

I start for Dorian's cottage, hoping to wipe the disturbing thought from my mind. I've almost reached his doorway when I notice Malise walking toward me. She holds the hand of her younger brother, and Toby follows behind. He notices me first.

"Good morning," he says cheerfully.

He looks away shyly as I smile back. "Hello."

Malise looks up at me as her brother waves.

"You're the pureblood Oriana," he states innocently. Malise tugs on his arm.

I approach, bending over to reach his level. "Yes, I am, and you might be …?"

"M' name's Aaron," he replies confidently, ignoring his sister's eagerness to continue away.

"Well, nice to meet you, Aaron. I suppose you're off to somewhere important, so I'll see you another time." With a quick wave, I start for Dorian's door again.

Before I reach it, Malise calls, "Dorian has already left. Tor held an early meeting."

I turn, sure disappointment is all over my face. "Oh …" The word escapes in a rush of air.

"If you'd like …" Toby begins, "you can come with us. We're going to help forage for food."

Malise hesitates for a moment. "Yes, you should join us. Who knows how long the meeting will last? They may talk for hours. We'll show you around."

Aaron nods in earnest.

I follow them across the platform and down the rope ladder. We continue downward until we reach the lowest platform, which holds the curved dining hall. The building's doors have been tied open so that a cool breeze rushes through it, and we can smell freshly baked breads. The others hurry toward it, and I follow willingly, the feeling of hunger striking me as well.

Once we're inside, the source of the smell is clear. The long wooden table has been adorned with wooden platters filled with fresh breads in all kinds of shapes. Some contain fresh berries that burst in my mouth with a warm tartness. I sample everything my stomach will allow: scones, twists, and breads filled with fruit and walnuts.

I'm relieved when we've reached the other side and the tables of food have come to an end. We reenter the sunlight filled to bursting. Malise leads the way to the final ladder. I grumble to myself. I was afraid foraging for food might mean climbing back down the ladder I painfully climbed only yesterday.

Malise reaches the ladder and instructs her brother to wait until she has made it a few rungs down. Aaron starts down once his sister calls to him. When he has gone a fair distance, I take a deep breath assuring myself that my second experience will be as successful as the first. I take my first steps and gain the confidence to move quickly. Before long my foot touches soft earth. I step away from the ladder, holding my breath to steady myself and stop my head from spinning. I find Malise and Aaron waiting not far behind me.

Once Toby joins us, we head down the hillside I climbed the day before. Soon Malise turns aside from the route I remember. We shortly reach a tumbling brook that snakes its way at an angle from us. Once reaching its mossy bank, Malise picks her way upon the large smooth stones that interrupt the rushing waters. Her brother hops playfully from stone to stone, humming a tune to himself. The rocks seem slippery in the morning sun, and I eye them warily. I place a foot upon the nearest stone, testing its reliability before putting my weight on it. My foot holds, and I continue on, my steps turning into light taps to the melody of Aaron's murmured song.

As we continue downward, Malise still in the lead and Toby following behind me, I notice that the woods on either side have become extremely dense. The brook is a clear-cut path through the brush, which is why stone hopping is the most practical way to travel. As the sun reaches its peak, the thick forest opens into a broad field full of blooming wildflowers. The water slices through it and continues on through the trees below. I maneuver my way to the grassy embankment and cross the water, taking a final leap from my rock island to land on the soft ground.

I notice others across the field. Some are collecting flowers and herbs, while others meander through the bordering forest gathering nuts and fruits. Malise begins to pick her way through the high brush, her hands searching through the stalks. Finally she plucks a purple flower upon a long stalk. She hands it to her brother, who runs over and presents it to me proudly.

"This is lavender. My sister says it's your job to get it," he states matter-of-factly.

I smile and take the flower by its stem. I inspect it closely, twirling it around to study its shape.

Aaron rummages in a side pocket of his oversized cloth shirt and pulls out a square sack made from the same tan material. He extends it toward me. "Here, use this."

"Thank you." I take the sack and, after memorizing the flower, place it delicately inside.

We head off in different directions. I turn to watch Toby head toward a group of other young part-bloods. My eyebrows rise as I notice that they've been distracted from their work. They stand pointing and laughing as two boys have decided to wrestle one another playfully down the slope of the field.

I smile to myself, feeling the sun on my cheeks and the buzz of bees whirring by. As I search the ground, my mind trails off into a series of questions. What exactly is Tor's early meeting about?

I find a cluster of lavender plants amid the grass. I decide to take a seat alongside them, laying them inside the cloth sack carefully.

What do their plans have to do with the Rebirth? More important, what do they have to do with Dorian being a half-blood? I had heard those two girls talking about it as well. Is there some reason that everyone is so concerned with him?

The frustration causes me to toss a yellow flower into the bag. I sigh, rummaging through the purple ones to pull it out.

"You must be Oriana." Two girls have come up to me before I noticed them. The speaker has a sweet smile, perhaps trying a little too hard to be nice. The other stands awkwardly behind her, fumbling with a cloth sack that is half-full.

I get to my feet to greet them. "Yes, I am, and you might be …?"

"Oh!" I can't tell if she is surprised that I'm actually speaking or that she has not introduced herself. "Well, I'm Lily, and this is Piper."

Piper smiles weakly and nods at the sound of her name, yet remains silent.

Lily grabs a strand of light brown hair and twists it around her finger. I can tell she is about to ask something of me from the way she hesitates.

"We were just wondering … a few of us were going to head to the river to freshen up." She looks back at Piper for reassurance and then turns. "Would you like to join us?"

I look back at the flowers forlornly, knowing that I'd be wise to take this opportunity to meet new people. It isn't just an obligation; I'm starting to enjoy making friends, at least the few I *have* made. I'm not too sure how Azura, Liam, or even Malise feels about me.

I turn to the girls expectantly. "Sure, I'll go." They both grin and seem to relax a little.

I follow them to one side of the pasture, toward the forest barrier. Piper and Lily are silent, glancing at one another occasionally. I decide to end the awkwardness.

"Have you lived in the Great Oak all your lives?"

It's Piper who answers. "Just about. We were born into Odon's lands, but were lucky enough to escape when we were children." She clamps her mouth shut as if she might have offended me. Do they actually think I still follow Odon? Or perhaps assume I'm jealous of their early freedom?

"Yes, you are lucky. It's great to be welcomed into such a place; I couldn't feel more fortunate." I think back to the others, Lenora and Aurek. Do they think of me? Do they even remember me? If only they could leave that place and see all this. Would they change as I have?

The girls slow down to walk beside me, one on either side. "What is it like there now?" Lily asks warily, yet eager to know.

"Are they as strict as Dorian says?" Piper chimes in.

I pause for a moment, unsure of how to describe it. "I—" I glance back and forth, looking into eyes that are still young and hopeful. "I would not wish it upon anyone."

Lily swallows. "I see."

I regret speaking so harshly when it causes another spell of silence to settle upon us. We enter the forest, and the air seems heavier, muffling any sound of wildlife.

"This way!" Piper shouts and begins to jog through the trees. Lily picks up the pace behind her.

I take a deep breath and urge my legs to move faster. They lurch into motion, feeling rusted and heavy. It isn't long before I'm out of breath and straining to keep up.

Once we're past a row of evergreens, a cool breeze picks up, rushing through my hair and nudging me toward the drop to my right. I can hear rushing water nearby, and I can discern the sound of shouts above the din.

The girls rush toward the end, stopping themselves by grabbing onto trees at the last minute, some of which grow outward into open air at a right angle, hanging on by merely their roots.

I approach from behind carefully, unsure how steep the drop actually is.

"How cold is it!?" Piper is calling down to someone as I walk to stand beside her. She is inching closer to the edge, both hands firmly grasping a sturdy tree trunk.

I look down. The drop is shorter than I expected but still frightful. It overlooks a magnificent waterfall directly to my left, which is near deafening at this distance. Its spray reaches my cheeks, overlaying the beads of sweat that have accumulated from the run. The waterfall cascades in a spray of colors, thrusting into a deep river that sweeps off into the distance and out of sight. At the base of the falls I see the source of shouting, clearly the ones Piper was attempting to contact. A dark-haired boy stands beneath the thundering water, waving his arms for us to join them.

The girls do not wait for an answer. They are already picking their way toward the falls by the near vertical stairway of flat rocks. I watch from a distance, trembling slightly as they find a ledge jutting out over the falls. The boy has swum to a group of other boys further down the river, leaving the space beneath Piper and Lily open. Lily steps to the edge first, slipping off her sandals and curling her toes over the side of the rock to remain balanced. Her arms over her head, she dives over the side. I wish to close my eyes, but instead find myself moving closer to see if she's survived. The water barely splashes as she enters fingers first. I hold my breath until she reaches the surface waving her arms as the boys cheer and Piper claps, giggling to herself. I can't hold back a sigh of relief.

"Oriana, c'mon, it's safe. We do this all the time. Just aim straight down. You don't have to dive; just jump." My stomach drops. Piper turns to me again, and I wish I could disappear within the trees. She reaches out to me, beckoning me to join her upon the rock ledge. I look down toward the others. Lily is shouting something and gesturing me to join her, which I'd gladly do, if only they'd show me a safe side path around the falls.

I feel myself shaking, and it isn't because of the cool breeze or the spray of water. I get low to the ground, sliding myself slowly down the natural rock stairs. Piper has her hands out to catch me, yet I can picture myself slipping and her going straight down with me. I close my eyes for a moment, erasing the image from my mind. Then in a short time I'm once again on a flat surface.

Piper laughs. "I guess they don't have anything like this at the University."

I shake my head. I thought nothing would be scarier than that place, which causes me to reconsider my circumstances. I have been through a lot, feared things much worse than death, so what makes this so much scarier? I get to my feet slowly, still trembling. Shouts rise from below, which I think are words of encouragement. I look over the edge. *Let go, Oriana.* I gulp at the thought. *Let go of your fears, and trust yourself.* I judge the center of the river, testing my footing and the bounce in my legs. I slowly take off my shoes, feeling the sun-warmed stone beneath bare feet. I close my eyes, and jump.

CHAPTER NINETEEN

I'm falling, the air sweeping past me, the spray of water striking my face. My eyes shoot open, and I see the river hurtling toward me. I close my eyes, holding my breath as I plunge into the icy water. Then my arms are straining to pull me to the surface. I feel awkward trying to find some kind of coordination in my strokes. The current is strong, and I fight off panic. Which way is up? I gave no thought to how ready I was to swim. I haven't tried it since I was a child when a small pond outside the playground walls became a place to escape. They took it away from us once the Odonians noticed the children running back with wet robes. They locked the gates and shortened play time; then it was forgotten altogether.

My lungs are burning, and my strokes are not doing anything but tiring me out. Has this all been worth it? Trying to face my fears, to look danger in the eyes? I feel foolish as my tense body relaxes and I let the current take me. I lose track of how long I've been under. A last fighting urge rises in me, and I reach upward. My hand breaks the surface, and another grabs hold of it, wrenching me against the pull of the river. A second hand takes me around the waist and hauls me out. I burst through the surface gasping and coughing, swallowing the fresh air frantically. The young man's eyes show a tinge of fear as he brings me to shore where the others are waiting. Piper swims up after us, breathing hard and hurrying to reach me.

"That was a close call. You nearly didn't make it." The man has calmed and wipes the wet hair back from my face as I lean back against a tree. Something glints in his eyes as he looks me over. "Well, now …"

"Is she all right? Why didn't you tell me you couldn't swim?" Piper grabs my arm, and Lily comes up behind her.

"We thought you were gone for sure!" Lily hands me a dry cloth, and I bury my face in it. It is warm from being left in the sun.

My breathing has slowed, but I still hold back from answering. How can they understand my embarrassment at nearly drowning in front of everyone? I look down at my feet. They are slightly blue from the cold, and I pull them closer to my body. "I … I underestimated the current …" Then in my own defense, "I never swam in a river before."

Piper and Lily sigh as if they've been holding their breaths this whole time. "Well, I suppose we should've asked first," Piper replies.

"As long as you're all right," Lily adds.

"You're lucky I was there to grab you," the young man chimes in from behind the two girls.

Lily rolls her eyes, "Yeah, you better thank Finley now, or he'll be bragging about it forever."

Finley pushes the girls aside. "Don't listen to them." His bare torso shows he is a broad shouldered man. His dark brown hair is wet and plastered back from matching brown eyes. His tanned skin and a scar running down his right cheek give him a weathered look. He kneels beside me, studying me with a grin.

"Thank you," I state, trying to avoid eye contact without being rude, and unsure how to respond to his frank gaze. He seems a bit older than me and is missing that naivety that the others have. He has the look of someone who has been through a lot.

"Oriana, I would save you again in a heartbeat." He smiles, reaching out to take my hand and help me to my feet. Before letting it go he kisses it, giving me another long look with his daring eyes. The other boys I had seen from the ledge have gathered around us, and I hear them chuckle to one another and comment on their friend's advances.

"Finn!" Piper shoves him in the side with an elbow. "Are you crazy? This is Oriana, the pureblood."

Finley turns to her, shrugging. "I can see that." He scratches the side of his hair, sending a spray of droplets.

I begin drying my own hair with the cloth, acting as though I'm not actually noticing the conversation.

"Well, she's taken," Lily explains.

A guy from behind adds, "Dorian's girl!" in a teasing voice.

I can't hide the blush that rises to my cheeks, though I act like I'm looking at something in the distance.

Recognition lights Finley's face, and he laughs. "Yeah, I get it, the half-let boy's pureblood." He looks sideways at me. "But how was I supposed to know she'd be so … what's the word … beautiful?" The other boys burst out laughing. One even smacks Finley on the back playfully.

Lily comes to loop her arm around mine, probably noting the look of complete humiliation on my face. "Don't worry, he has an endless infatuation with pretty girls, and no amount seems to suffice.

"Hey, Finn, aren't ya goin' to introduce us to the lady?" a blond-haired boy to his right responds.

"Oh yeah, where are my manners? Let me introduce the guys." Finley points to the boy on his right, short yet sturdy and taking the pose of a boy twice his height. "This is Jagger, he's Dugan, that's Buck, and the little one's Weasel."

I nod to each one, Dugan being a boy about my age with his long black hair tied at the base of his neck. He gives a half grin, his eyes heavy lidded and calm. Buck is the tallest; strongly built and with chestnut colored hair and eyes, he appears powerful, but his smile proves he's harmless. He places his large hand on top of Weasel's head, nearly swallowing it entirely. The smaller boy peeks out at me to grin and give a floppy wave. His mop of mousy brown hair covers two wide round eyes.

"Nice to meet you all," I reply politely. It's hard not to giggle at the motley bunch.

"Well, now that everyone knows one another, we should probably get back to work," says Lily whose arm is still wrapped around mine protectively. She begins to lead me away. Piper starts to follow.

"Strange that you weren't invited to Tor's early meeting, don't you think?" Finley comments while rubbing at the short growth of beard on the side of his face.

We stop, and I slip my arm from Lily's to face him. She remains still.

"I mean, you've got to be wondering what he's hiding from you," Finley adds, knowing he has caught my interest. I notice that even the guys behind him have become nervous about the subject.

"Finley, you shouldn't …" Piper starts, but I cut her off.

"Do you know what it's about? What they're discussing?" I watch his face eagerly.

He shrugs. "Only what they've been telling the rest of us, which is probably more than he's telling you."

I can't help but feel his words hold truth. After all, Dorian left me without any explanation. How could he have known that I would meet up with Malise? I might have been wandering for hours! Not to mention keeping me in the dark about last night's conversation. The thought is striking a nerve.

"Finley, you *really* shouldn't …" Lily stands beside me now, deciding whether or not she should take my arm once more or let me be. "She's probably worried about him as it is …"

"Worried? About Dorian?" I turn to her, trying to read the look of shock on her face.

"Lily!" Piper shouts.

"You mean she doesn't—"

"Shh!!"

I nearly explode with frustration. "Is anyone going to tell me what is going on and why I should be worried?!" The others just stare at me silently. Even Finley is watching me guiltily.

"Oriana!" Malise bursts through the woods followed by Aaron and a relieved-looking Toby. "We've been looking for you everywhere!" She holds up my discarded cloth bag with a stern look.

"Toby found this, and we thought you were …"

"We thought you had been taken!" Aaron states emphatically.

"Taken?" I ask quizzically, unsure of what he means.

"Never mind. Let's just head back; it's nearly lunchtime." Malise begins to hand the bag back to me. "Oriana?" She looks at me oddly. "What's wrong with your neck? Did something happen?"

I reach up to stroke the skin and feel a tender lump. I gasp at the sudden pain. I try to remember how I got it, not from the jump—and then a memory flashes in my mind. The whiteness, the stinging pain. My brain feels as though it's being crushed, my skull is on fire, and I cannot think at all. Something is strangling me, keeping me from remembering that moment. What they put into me. I struggle to hang onto it, to keep the images alive. But it is too strong, and I've grown so weak. I expend the last of my energy and collapse to the ground.

CHAPTER TWENTY

A cool cloth is pressed against my forehead, and I open my eyes. Tor stares down at me, a smile pressing his lips and a look of relief in his eyes.

"She's waking up …" someone whispers at my side.

I prop myself up on my elbows. The cloth drops to the ground, and Tor lifts it back to my face. For some reason I'm lying on the forest floor. I begin to remember … Piper and Lily, the river, Finley rescuing me and then Malise. But why did I pass out?

"What happened?" I ask, taking the cloth from Tor's hand as I sit upright and then wipe the back of my neck.

No one answers, and I stop to glance at their faces. Piper and Lily are watching Tor nervously, and Finley has wandered to the back of the group.

"You passed out suddenly, and Toby ran to get me." Tor gestures to Toby who stands at his side, still breathing heavily from the long run. "Piper told me what happened. I think maybe you had a little too much water." He grins, patting me on the arm.

I nod but can't help being suspicious as Finley walks away muttering something beneath his breath. Tor looks back at him and then turns to me giving a small shake of his head.

"Well, I think it's time you all headed back for lunch …"

"Where's Dorian?" I ask, wondering why Tor has come instead of him.

Tor looks at me for a moment as if buying time for his mind to work. "He couldn't …"

"Can we go back now? I'm starving!" Aaron shouts from beside Malise.

The thought causes my stomach to grumble, and Dorian's absence loses its importance for the moment. I begin getting to my feet, and Piper takes my arm to help me up.

"You'll feel much better after you eat something," she says, leading me away.

I can't help wondering why Tor came all the way from the Great Oak to make sure I was all right. If all I needed was a cold compress, what was Tor there for? Not only that, if the situation was so serious that Tor was sent for, why hadn't Dorian thought to come? Maybe I'm thinking too much.

I sigh as we reach the base of the Great Oak. I hang back as the others begin to climb the ladder. I watch as Malise and her brother disappear behind the large bough. Why does it feel like there are even more secrets *outside* of the University? I thought I had solved everything by leaving, and yet this world is still a mystery. It's hard not to question everything when the others keep carrying on silent conversations with their eyes.

"Questioning your 'friends'?" I jump, not having noticed Finley standing beside me. I can't find the right answer, so he continues. "I recognized that look of suspicion on your face."

His smirk annoys me; his demeanor is too self-confident. I shake my head. "You're mistaken." I walk past him toward the ladder, not wanting to look back. I know he doesn't believe me. It doesn't matter. I need to get to lunch. But first, I need to find Dorian and clear my mind. I'll ask him what the truth is and force him to tell me why I should be worrying about him.

Climbing the ladder, I fail to notice the heights, and my determination to reach Dorian has me arriving at the platform before I know it. I look up when my hand is grasping solid wood instead of another rung. This time I pull myself up and to my feet. Finley swings onto the platform next to me. He doesn't say anything else.

The others are anxious for a meal and are starting down the platform toward the dining structure. Piper and Lily hang back to check up on me.

"You're going to sit with us, right?" Lily asks sweetly. Piper nods in agreement. I can tell they have honest intentions, and I reply with an equally honest smile.

"Of course I will. I just need to find Dorian first."

"Right, okay then," Lily answers. We walk the rest of the way in silence that I don't have the energy to break. I'm concentrating too hard on finding Dorian. If I can just see him, things will be back to normal.

The food has already been laid out as I enter the platform shelter. Flaps on the side of the structure that faces away from the Oaks' trunk have been opened to let in a natural light, and a cool breeze sweeps down the table, sending a wave of sweet aromas. Piper and Lily follow me down the side of the table until they find their seats halfway from the door. I continue down, trying to see around the corner before I've actually turned it. As I round the bend, I see Azura and Liam sitting in the same places as last night. I notice that Tor has already made it to his seat, and again they are speaking animatedly across to one another. My stomach sinks; Dorian is nowhere in sight.

"Oriana, come sit." Tor smiles and gestures toward my seat. It is a larger space with Dorian missing.

I almost feel like wiping the kindness off his face. Doesn't he notice I'm disappointed? "Oh, actually I was just looking for …"

"Dorian couldn't make it," Azura supplies. I can see she's enjoying it. "He was too preoccupied to eat." She looks down to scoop up an assortment of berries from her plate, ignoring my look of irritation.

"You'll see him tonight, I'm sure," Tor adds gently.

I try a smile, but it feels awkward. Instead I give a nod, eager to head away from Azura's judgment. "I promised Piper and Lily I'd sit with them …" I don't wait for a response before heading back toward the others. I can't help wondering what Dorian is so preoccupied about. Why couldn't I just ask? Demand some answers? No, I'm a guest here, a pureblood at that, and how can I possibly accuse them of hiding things from me? They've welcomed me, fed me, given me shelter. How can I be so ungrateful by doubting their intentions? If I could just see Dorian, then he would explain everything to me. Tonight he will tell me why their meetings are discussed in private and why even Finley and the others are kept in the dark about the details.

I lose track of my food as well as the others talking around me.

Jagger is teasing Lily about something, but I don't bother to figure out what. The others laugh, and I look up from my plate. I haven't really eaten anything.

"Oriana are you all right?" Dugan asks as he leans back against the wall and folds his arms.

I look from him to Finley, who has also looked up from his plate. I notice the others are watching me as well. "I ... I think I need to get some fresh air." I get up quickly, leaving them in silence, and head for the door. Bursting through the entryway, I run face first into a tall warm figure.

Tor turns to face me. "Oriana, are you feeling better?"

I give him a questioning look.

"Anyone could tell you were extremely uncomfortable in there. What's bothering you?"

I go to speak, but he stops me. "Actually, I think I know what it is." He begins to walk away, taking a route along the outside of the dining hall. He turns when he realizes I am still standing in silence. "Follow me."

Curiosity compels me toward him. I follow him around the platform and up a series of ladders. We pass my cottage and Dorian's as well. I look for a light within Dorian's but see only darkness. A voice in the back of my head whispers, *Is he avoiding me?* I shake the thought away.

Tor stops in front of a building larger than the other cottages. Moving forward, he unties some straps securing the flap with one hand and guides it open to let both of us through. Once inside, I wait by the doorway as Tor works his way around the side of the room, opening the side hatches to let in light and moving air.

In front of me sits a heavy wooden table, its surface clear of any objects. The building curves slightly like the dining hall as it hugs the tree. On this wall are a series of bookshelves, which to my surprise are filled with many volumes, all of which are different and do not repeat.

Tor moves toward a set of shelves. "Please take a seat." I find a spot on the table's bench, one closest to the light of a window. In front of me, Tor is rustling through a bundle of rolled parchments stacked on one of the upper shelves. He extends his long arms to reach them.

He pulls one from the bundle and turns to me. "Oriana, have you ever seen Odon's Lands? Beyond them?"

I look at him in wonder. Is it possible to actually see it all? Is there really anything beyond them? "No ..." I say hesitantly, unsure what he is hinting at.

He places the scroll upon the table and unrolls it, stretching it far across the table. I hold an edge down to keep it from curling up again.

"This is a map, the area of Odon's current lands, as well as the outer region," Tor explains, although I have assumed as much.

"I never imagined one existed. How—?"

"It was made before Odon had finalized his enforcement. You will not find the University, but it would exist somewhere in this region." Tor circles an area with his finger that has been drawn in as a tall forest hill. The map contains mostly forest terrain with blank canvas beyond a black line surrounding it. This is labeled simply: "Outer Regions." Yet what is most apparent is the large sketch of the Great Oak, labeled and detailed. Showing a complete outline of its platforms and structures, our current location being one of the higher ones.

Tor points out the thick line running around both the outside of the University's hill as well as the Great Oak. "This is Odon's territory. The border was drawn in later on."

My eyes widen, shocked to see a limit to Odon's power. Yet I cannot wrap my mind around the full meaning of this. "Then what actually is outside of all of this? Are there others ...?"

Tor nods and my excitement grows. "But"—I hold my breath for him to continue—"this only means that they are under the control of another ruler. Outside of Odon's lands is a world very similar to our own. So you'll understand why we still remain within his borders."

The situation is not as I imagined. Tor goes on, "Yes, if you were to escape Odon, it would mean falling under the restrictions of another tyrant. One that we are not familiar with."

I sigh, feeling even more trapped than before. When Odon was the only danger, it was easier to imagine a way of escaping. Now it seems hopeless. "And on this side?" I point to the opposite border.

Tor replies grimly, "The same matter, the map does not show all lands, but we can assume that others are existing in similar circumstances."

"But how did this happen?" I ask, frustration rising in my voice. "If there was a time when Odon did not rule, then how did he and these other rulers take over?"

He sighs. "It is a story others can tell better than I." I am sure he has seen the look of disappointment on my face because he quickly adds, "But I do know the one person who can share it with you."

My gaze alights with intrigue, "Who might that be?"

"Falda," Tor replies with confidence.

My eyebrows rise. "Who?"

"Falda," he repeats. "My mother."

CHAPTER TWENTY-ONE

"Your mother? She lives here?" I ask incredulously. Am I hearing correctly? A woman from an earlier generation, one who might have lived before Odon's rule and can explain to me how things got to this point?

"Yes, I'll arrange for you to meet with her tomorrow," Tor affirms. "I think it is important that you speak with her."

I nod emphatically. I have many questions to ask.

"Now I would like to discuss the matter that I am able to explain quite well." Tor settles himself upon the bench opposite me and rests his elbows over the map and tabletop. I lean forward, prepared to absorb every word he says. "I have noticed your frustration, and I can understand it. Especially since I have explained nothing of the conversation you overheard at last night's dinner."

I watch him, feeling slightly guilty at making him divulge the community's secret, while only living within it for little over a day. Yet my curiosity prevents me from protesting, and I keep silent, eager to learn more.

"I guess the best place to start would be at the basis of the problem. This is no secret. Odon has taken over our homes and families. Every day we cower in his powerful grip. The Great Oak and its people represent a final hope. We are the last chance for Odon to be defeated and our freedom regained." Tor's eyes brighten with anticipation.

The idea is heartening, yet I remain doubtful. It's difficult to imagine someone as powerful as Odon being taken down by a group of young rebels.

Tor must recognize the look of skepticism in my eyes because he continues with added vigor and assurance, "Odon is powerful, yes, but we have a secret weapon as well. Someone he will not be expecting."

A cloudy realization slowly creeps into my mind.

"The only one of us who will have the power to defeat him." Tor's voice is strong and determined, as if nothing could convince him otherwise. He waits for my response, knowing I have figured it out on my own.

"Dorian," I whisper, not actually understanding why he is the one.

"Yes," Tor replies with a sigh. "I'm afraid you, Oriana, will play a much greater role in all this than you know."

This catches me even more off guard, and I glare at him, demanding to know more.

"Yet you cannot fully understand much of it until tomorrow." Tor starts to get to his feet while rolling the large map. "You must first learn the time before. Then you can begin to make sense of everything."

"But what effect could I possibly have on … all this?" I stand, hoping to get his attention as he turns to set the map back in place. "I've been here for such a short time."

Tor glances back. "You will come to understand." He begins to leave. "Tomorrow I will find you when it is time for your visit with Falda." He has reached the doorway.

"Wait." I have one more question for the moment. He pauses to hear me. "What does the Rebirth have to do with this?"

Tor grasps the top of the doorway. Facing me, he leans in to reply. "The Rebirth is Odon's weakest point and the only time that Dorian will be strong enough to defeat him. If the moment passes, then it is likely we will never have another chance."

I nod gravely, almost wishing I had not asked the question at all after receiving such a daunting response. Tor leaves, and I sit back down, trying to figure things out. I have more information, but I feel worse. I almost wish I were still ignorant of the situation. Tor is probably not prepared to explain the details to everyone. The burden of carrying the knowledge alone must be tiring, to say nothing of having to carry out the plan.

I recall Lily's remark, which makes sense to me now. I should be worried about Dorian. If he does not succeed in destroying Odon, then Odon will destroy him. It's odd trying to imagine Odon as just a man.

Yet a burning question that I now fear to ask is why Dorian? What makes him so different? A possible reason comes to mind. He is a half-blood. Just as the other from before had said when I made it to the first platform of the Great Oak. The day he saved Azura and me. She said that him being a half-blood was the cause of his success. But what does that mean? What does his being a half-blood have to do with it?

I get up from my seat and find myself perusing the shelves of books. An old tattered volume catches my eye, its binding worn and cracked, evidence it has been opened many times. Lifting it up, I realize it is not a book but a journal. I open the cover, hearing the crunch as the binding breaks further. Signed on the inside page is the name Narena. I can tell from the messy handwriting within that the words were written quickly. Still they are legible, and I slip it protectively into the soft pocket at the front of my robes.

Leaving the structure, I decide to head for Dorian's quarters. I hope that finding him there will give me some relief. I discover that a soft drizzle has begun, and the heavy clouds I glimpse through the Oak's foliage tell of impending rain. As I take my time down the slippery platforms and ladders, my mind mulls over my secret find and what I might discover within its pages. As the rain begins, I have reached the cottages, and I slip inside Dorian's without thinking to knock. Wringing any loose water out of my dress, I look around, allowing my eyes to adjust. To my dismay, it is empty of any life. That familiar worry creeps over me. Dorian's room is in an upheaval, and not the result of negligence, but the ransacked havoc of someone in frustration. Baskets filled with personal items have been turned over, and his bedding is splayed in all directions. A canteen of water is dropped on the floor, its contents creeping across the ground. Even the lantern set atop a wooden dresser is on its side, staring at me in dismay. The room is unsettling to look at, much less live in, and I decide to devote the following time to tidying it properly. If this is the only way I can help Dorian, then I'll do my best. Once finished, I leave the room, satisfied and assured that he will be pleased.

I dash from Dorian's to my cottage eager to get out of the rain, and light the lantern for warmth. I fall into my bed, feeling the exhaustion of my efforts. My mind is active, however, and I look at the ceiling, trying to focus my thoughts on something definite. Then I remember the journal I found. I feel for it inside my pocket and slide it out holding it above me to run my fingers along its rough surface. I sit up in my bed, reaching for the lantern to allow for better lighting. Flipping open the cover I finger through the pages, realizing that many have been torn out. The first pages have been removed but I find one that is readable.

They've separated us from our families and put us into classes based on our ages. I just can't understand how our own people could do this to us. Pearl says that it's not their fault and that he's controlling their minds, but I can't believe that. I'd never do what they've done. I'd never let Odon take over me. Our only hope is in defying him any way we can.

I skip through to the last passage. I notice that it has been frantically scribbled.

I thought that all hope was lost, but maybe he can save us. We're leaving the Great Oak now, it's safer that way. If Odon ever found out he would surely die. I cannot believe that this was all for nothing, that his fate is no better than my own. I think this will be the last time I write. It is too dangerous to bring this book back with me, and I do not think it is wise to write down my thoughts anymore. I am hoping he will find this and maybe see who I was and became. I am sorry we must leave, but please understand there is no other way ...

A small section of the bottom page has been peeled away, and I can't read the end of the sentence. With a sigh I close the cover and shut my eyes. I feel the sadness in their words, and it pains me to think that in some unknown way this person has sacrificed themselves. Although the story is not clear, I can't help the tear that escapes down my check. I can taste that same entrapment of some uncontrollable destiny.

My stomach grumbles, signaling it's time for another meal. The sky is darkening quickly, meaning dinner can't be far off. A knock at the entrance to my room startles me, and I set the journal aside to approach the entrance. I lift the flap back and discover Dorian standing drenched in my doorway. I guide him inside to dry and warm up. There is a grim look on his face that frightens me. How could he have changed so quickly since the last time I saw him?

"Is there something you—"

"You didn't have to do that," Dorian snaps. His words leave my heart pounding.

I hesitate, "What ... what do you mean?"

"I can tell you were in my room. You didn't have to do that. I didn't want you to." He avoids my gaze, and I notice the corners of his mouth twitching.

"I'm sorry, I only meant to ..."

"It's okay, it doesn't matter." He looks at me for the first time, and his face relaxes. "Have you been all right?"

I smile, feeling that the Dorian I know is returning. "Yes, I was only worried about you. I wanted to tell you that ..."

His eyes have wandered around the room and settle on the journal that I had left on my bed. "Where did you find this?" Dorian asks. His tone causes me to struggle to answer.

"I ... I ... Tor showed me the hall on the platform above. There was a bookcase, and ..."

"Tor gave this to you?" There is bitterness in his words. He seems hurt.

"No, I ... I found it, and I wanted to—"

"You have no right to look through other people's things." He shakes the book in my face. "This is not yours to take, Oriana ..." His jaw tightens, and he looks down at me. "Just stay out of this!" Still clutching the book, Dorian rushes out into the storm, heading toward his own room.

I realize my body has stiffened, and I relax my muscles, which only results in an irrepressible tremble. I didn't mean to cause him so much grief. Several retorts come to mind, but I sigh, recognizing that they mean nothing now that Dorian has left. I try to sympathize with his situation and the stress he must be under but my boiling anger remains. I hadn't seen him since yesterday, and his only reason for approaching me was to tell me off? I clench my fists in frustration. Any drop of sympathy for him is wiped away, and I head out into the rain, dashing in the opposite direction toward the dining hall.

CHAPTER TWENTY-TWO

My feet slip as I hurry down the last ladder, and my knee scrapes against the wooden rung. I jump down the last distance, my hair plastered against my head and my dress heavy with water. When I round the bend of the platform, I see that I'm not the only one prepared for dinner. Piper and Lily along with Finley and the others are seated beneath the awning of the dining hall's entrance. Finn leans against one of the stoop's supports watching as I run toward them. My sandaled feet splash on the wooden surface with each bound. The glow escaping through the doorway proves that it is late evening, and I feel its warmth as I step up onto the porch and out of the rain.

"Oriana, you're soaked!" Lily says in dismay. She sits upon a wooden bench situated on one side of the door.

"Well it's raining," Piper smirks. She stands upon the edge of the porch and stares into the downpour.

Lily gives her a look and shakes her head in exasperation. "I'll get you a towel." She disappears behind the door flap.

"Here." Finn drapes a heavy brown cape over my shoulders.

"You should really get some better clothes than that University silk," Piper adds. "Me and Lily will find you something better."

Dugan and Jagger make room on another short wooden bench pressed against the face of the building, and I take a seat, pulling the cape beneath my chin and allowing a wave of shivers to pass over me.

People are still filing into the dining hall in groups. Malise and her brother rush out of the storm, hugging similar cloaks to themselves.

I don't realize who they are until they have pulled back their heavy hoods, and join us beneath the protection of the awning. I nod with recognition, and Aaron waves emphatically. Malise responds with a soft smile. Toby appears shortly after, and he sheepishly grins before hurrying inside.

Lily returns with a thick cloth, and I reluctantly reach out from within the warmth of the cloak to begin drying my hair. Lily remains standing over me, staring hard at my face. I avoid her gaze by hiding behind my hair.

"Oriana … is there something wrong?"

I gaze up at her, knowing that there will be a visible redness in my eyes. Knowing that her look of concern may cause me to lose control of myself.

"What happened?" she exclaims, kneeling down to my level. Now everyone is looking at me, except Finn, who stares out into the storm.

"Lily … maybe she doesn't …" Piper begins.

"I'm fine, I just … Dorian is acting … different." I'm not sure how to explain the way he snapped at me. I'm not even sure whether to feel angry or upset.

Weasel shows up beside my knee, an oversized leather cap on his head has two bent-up flaps that give the appearance of ears. His large eyes watch me with concern. "It's because of his destiny," he squeaks—and then jumps as Buck's large hand clamps down on his shirt at the back of his neck, pulling him off his feet and backward to Buck's side at the edge of the porch.

"Wease, hold your tongue!" Jagger hisses from beside me.

Another wave of cloaked people rush inside and out of the rain. We remain silent a moment longer after they've passed.

"It's all right," I sigh. "I know about Dorian. Tor told me the big secret." I finish drying my hair. The towel now damp, I lay it next to my feet and lean back with a sigh.

Dugan follows my example, resting his hands behind his head as he settles upon the face of the building. "Then you understand the pressure he is under." Dugan's smooth voice is calm and confident. He looks at me with serene black eyes.

"Yes …" I say slowly.

"Most of the others have taken their seats," Piper remarks while leaning in through the doorway.

Jagger is already to his feet and beside Piper. "Good, I'm starving," he says. In a moment of brightness the building's light floods the stoop and he has vanished behind the flap.

Piper follows, and the others are quick to stand and head inside. I hang back to hand Finley his cloak, give a quick "Thanks," and then enter the building.

Once inside, I am struck with the warmth of the blazing fire at the center of the building. It causes me to realize how cool my skin is, and I rub my arms in response. Lily is in front of me as we pass down the side of the table. The room hums with a pleasant murmur of voices. Above is the pounding of the rainfall in a steady rhythm, which almost completely drowns out the talking. I see the fire in front of me hiss as droplets that have entered through the smoke hole dive into the hungry flames.

Dorian's empty bench space halts me, and I break away from the others to take a seat. Finley watches me for a moment but says nothing and continues forward. The area to my right is bare; neither Tor nor Dorian has arrived. I grasp for the mug in front of me and am grateful for the taste of cool water.

"He's not coming tonight."

I look up from my mug. Azura stares at me across the table. Placing the cup back on the table, I notice that Liam is not beside her.

"Tor and Liam are taking their meals inside their cottages," Azura continues. "Today was overwhelming for us all."

"Then why have you come?" I ask. The tension between us is strong. My intentions were otherwise, but I've grown to dislike Azura.

"For me, being around others takes my mind off everything." She looks down the table into the line of faces, as though our conversation bores her. "I thought you might wait for him. Especially after Tor had filled you with false hopes at lunch." Azura looks sideways at me. "It's a good thing I came; you would've been waiting here all night." She gives a short laugh.

I'm not sure whether to smile or be offended. Instead I stare into my mug, feeling hopeless and, despite the company, very much alone.

"Listen," Azura begins. "It's nothing for you to feel upset about. He's just going through a lot."

I glance up at her, surprised. Is she really trying to cheer me up? "I know that, but he's different. Something has changed inside him."

Azura leans toward me, her face serious. "He has a lot to deal with. I can't imagine it not changing him."

"No … I mean … I know, it's just …" I look off into the distance, remembering the moment. "If you saw the way he spoke to me. I don't know what I did to make him so angry, but …" At that I feel myself break a little. I lower my face, trying to conceal my reaction.

I know Azura sees it anyway, because her lips flinch to the side and she watches me intently. There is a moment of silence, and I sense that Azura is thinking of something to say. I avoid her eyes.

"Oriana." She is trying to sound soothing, but I can tell it is hard for her to find sympathy for me. Finally she sighs, and it is as if the tension breaks at last. "I haven't made it easy for us to get along, but I think that I understand how you feel." Now it's her turn to stare into her cup. I watch her, thinking that somehow a small victory is occurring for both of us. "It's different for you though. Dorian …" She swallows, and her voice gets stern as she forces the words out. "Dorian cares for you, I can tell. I'm sure whatever he said, he didn't mean."

I lose my breath in surprise as Azura finishes. I hadn't expected her to say anything like that, and I feel a twinge of guilt at having stolen him from her. After all, she has known him for much longer than I have. "Thank you." I say with sincerity, trying to hide any awkwardness. I wonder for a moment if we might ever form a friendship.

Azura takes a drink from her cup in an attempt to cover the following silence. When she sets it down, I decide to attempt a conversation. One that is separate from our connection to Dorian.

"May I ask you a question?"

She brightens at the prospect of a different subject and nods.

"How were you captured if you live here at the Great Oak?"

Azura settles, and any awkwardness dispels. It's as if we have been close our entire lives, and nothing is between us. "I lived in the University, for most of my life. I've only recently settled into a new life here." She gestures to the area around her.

"I never knew my mother or father, only those prison white walls. Still, I never bought into their teachings, and I cursed Odon every chance I had. My temper got me into a few fights"—she pauses, and her eyes shift uneasily—"with purebloods, girls who thought they were too good to breathe the same air as me. Of course I was caught and sent to the Odonian, their usual punishments are mind distortions. It was cruel, but I remained hopeful that they were wrong about part-bloods. I just couldn't understand what made us so much worse." Azura sighs. "But that was when I was still young and attending the elementary levels. Things were different even then."

"What do you mean?" I lean toward her, knowing that her willingness to share will not be frequent.

"Odon was only just getting settled into his stronghold and as children we were the least of his worries. That has changed as the years went on. I suppose he realized our minds are best molded when we are young."

I nod, remembering how the boundaries were less strict and the races not so forcibly separated.

"I wouldn't have lived very long if I'd been any older. I learned that soon enough. A few of my friends disappeared. At first harsh discipline meant a trip to the Odonian, where they would hammer the teachings into us and then return us to classes. Slowly the part-bloods were taken away, but never returned. The rest of us quickly fell in line, we were all so afraid …" Azura's brow clenches, and she is not looking through her eyes but in her mind, reliving that time long ago.

I think of Lenora and the boy so young and innocent, and it causes me to shudder. I was there the whole time but never realized how barbaric Odon was, still is. I wanted to believe I could trust them, believe that what they were doing was the right thing. Now I know there is nothing right about it. "I'm sorry," I say, knowing it gives no comfort.

She shakes her head waving the apology away with her hand, "It's not your fault, you were just another victim, like me." I know she only half believes the statement but am grateful she is at least trying to believe it.

"No, I was there, I just let it happen. I was one of their pawns. Doing nothing is the same as helping their cause." The words flow out of my mouth, and as I hear them, I realize that I have been saying them inside of my head for a while.

Hearing them, Azura pauses, and her gaze falters. We are interrupted as food is being passed down in front of us. I can't think of eating, so when I receive my plate, I lay it to one side. Azura does the same, although her mind is elsewhere as she maintains her changed expression.

"I once thought that to be true, but now I can't bring myself to blame you. We were all young; there was no way any of us could have stopped them. Being angry at you would only serve Odon." Azura notices her food and plucks a steaming vegetable from her plate and in a final act of satisfaction takes a bite.

I give a small laugh, and she smiles at me, a new aura of peace surrounding her. "So then how did you wind up below ground?" I inquire, now finding my appetite and picking from my own plate.

Azura nods, finishing the bite in her mouth and washing it down with a gulp of water. "That was after I met Tor, which was while I attended the University. He was one of the rebels who first established the Great Oak. When he was younger he would sneak into the University with other part-bloods and free as many as he could. This became more and more dangerous as the years went on. I was lucky. They brought me here and told me the truth about Odon and their plan to stop him. That's how I met Dorian ..." She looks away. "I thought he was the bravest boy I'd ever met, and still so young. He carried his burden well—even now when we're so close."

She's right. I never met anyone like Dorian. All it took was his smile that day when I was still just Oriana the pureblood, and I was completely changed.

"More guards appeared and it became impossible to sneak in. Getting caught meant certain death, but Dorian insisted on returning. It was for personal reasons. He could never let the past die. He wanted to know everything he could about his parents."

"His parents? He never spoke of them to me."

"It's a difficult subject for him. They died when he was very young." Azura shifts in her seat. "It's a terrible story to even think of."

"Oh." I feel uncomfortable after asking and am grateful when she continues her story.

"It made me nervous to know he was still over there. Risking his life and the future of us all by snooping around the University. Tor didn't like it either, and after a period of time when he didn't return, I decided to go in myself and bring him back to safety." Azura runs a hand through her hair as if trying to stop her past self from making the mistake again. "I should have known it was too dangerous and I was still inexperienced. Dorian had always been the best at fooling the guards. I think he liked the idea that he had found a way to beat Odon inside his own domain."

She shakes her head. "But I made things worse by getting caught. I knew he would come to save me. He was the only one who could do it, but it was still so risky, and I didn't want to be the cause of his demise. I guess it all worked out in the end," Azura says, plainly trying to reassure herself that the past is over. "I think I earned my punishment for my mistake." She visibly trembles and then reaches for another morsel of food.

"Has your ankle healed?"

"Yes, well enough for me to walk properly." She gives a half smile.

Something flickers in my mind, and I find myself asking, "Do you remember everything that happened down there?"

Azura shoots me a look that frightens me and answers hurriedly, "It's all a blur, I don't think I want to remember."

I nod and shift my attention back to the food on my plate. Talking to Azura allows me to forget about Dorian's confrontation earlier. Knowing some more pieces of the past settles me as well and by the time we have finished discussing earlier times our plates are empty and I am ready for sleep. Azura and I leave the dining hall together and separate on the fourth landing. Once inside I gratefully fall into the blankets and am instantly asleep.

CHAPTER TWENTY-THREE

At dawn I wake with a start, feeling much as I had the previous morning. I know I have dreamed something terrible, yet I can't remember any part of it. As I wipe the dampness from my brow, I can hear two voices approaching. One is high and fluttering like birdsong, which can only be Lily. The other is smoother and steady: Piper. They enter my room with smiles and early greetings.

"Here, just as we promised!" Lily grins, extending her arms laden in clothes toward me.

"They should fit you just fine," Piper adds. Her long brown hair has been tied back in a braid that is draped over her shoulder.

I slide my sheets back and lean forward to pick up the first article of clothing, which is a fresh cloth dress the color of the morning sky. My own robes once a crisp white, have been stained along the hem a yellowish green by the grass. The rest is darkened from dirt.

"We had the weavers dye them light blue," Lily points out.

I nod in awe at the beautiful hue and the smell of ripe berries that the material still retains. "I hope it wasn't too much trouble."

"Nah, they were itching to show off their craftsmanship," Piper assures me.

"Well, thank you very much." I reach out to grab the second piece of clothing, which is a long dark cloak, similar to Finley's, yet sewn to my size.

Piper and Lily exit the room for a moment as I slip into the clean clothing. It's a heavier material than my old robes, but I feel like these suit me better. I call for Piper and Lily to return.

"It fits perfectly!" Lily remarks, walking through the doorway.

"I wonder if they could make one in green ..." Piper thinks out loud to herself.

"How do they turn clothing this color?" I ask while smoothing away any creases along the skirt.

"Oh berries and such things," Piper explains. "It's funny to think they have time for that sort of thing. It wasn't long ago that we were all struggling just to survive."

"It seems like you've come a long way putting a place like this together, it must have taken a lot of work. Are there many newcomers still?"

"Very few. Dangerous times are approaching, and we wouldn't want to draw attention to ourselves," Piper replies. "Our time to rest is just the lull before the storm. If their plans carry through, that would mean the release of everyone under Odon's control."

"Which is hard to say will actually work," Lily sighs. "Finley even says he wants to break away from the Oak, but that would be a major setback."

Piper gives her an uneasy look, but agrees. "Tor needs him; he's one of the few who is familiar with the University and the guards' movements."

"So why would he leave?" I can't fathom why he wouldn't want to end Odon's reign for good.

"I've never known him and Tor to get along very well," Lily replies. "On top of that, we don't get the impression that he actually thinks it will work."

I realize my muscles have tensed, and I relax them as I breathe out. I had never imagined this would be so complicated. Who's to say that Finley doesn't have a legitimate reason for not helping? Maybe Dorian really can't defeat Odon, and if that happens, how many lives will be lost? If only I could understand the reasoning behind these plans, then I could decide for myself who is worth believing in.

"Do you know what the plans are?" I venture the question.

They both shake their heads. "We aren't meant to be there or participate, only a select few, mostly the older part-bloods," Piper supplies.

I nod. At least I'm not the only one who is in the dark. Still, I can't help wanting the whole truth, and my mind touches upon my meeting with Falda today. I will have many questions for her.

"Well, we should be leaving to help the others. They're out getting supplies, and it couldn't hurt to pick some berries and fruit for the cooks."

After a quick meal, I follow them down from the Great Oak and to the large field I saw yesterday. Others from the community have already begun harvesting herbs and what other goods are needed back home. We walk past them into the surrounding forest where a row of berry bushes are thickly ornamented with blue ripened fruit. I select a plant that sits nearest to the edge so that when I'm seated in front of it, the warmth of the sun is not blocked by the tall trees.

Piper hands me a basket that she has retrieved from a group of children seated in a circle. They are weaving more with thin strips of bark. At the center sit more of the finished products. They laugh and talk as their fingers deftly work. Piper takes one basket for herself and Lily from the growing pile before finding her own place beside the bushes.

Laughter and shouts coming from the field cause me to look over my shoulder. Some of the others have begun some kind of game with a stuffed cloth ball. Part-bloods large and small run after one another, trying to steal the ball from the opposite team. I watch the game in fascination, noticing that Toby is one of the children taking part. He looks happier than I have ever seen him.

I turn back to fill my basket with more berries and notice a shadow cross the top of my arms. I look toward the sky, shielding my eyes from the glare of the sun to get a good look. There is something flying at a far height, higher than a normal bird. As I study the sky further, I notice that there are others.

"Piper …" I call, still staring at the figures.

She looks at me and follows my gaze. In an instant she is on her feet, pressing her fingers to her lips and giving an ear-piercing whistle. I watch as the children stop their game immediately. Piper's whistle is taken up by the others around her, and youths from all across the field run for cover.

Finley appears beside me, takes me roughly by the arm, and forces me into the forest foliage and to a kneeling position behind the line of bushes. Once the last part-blood escapes the field, the group is completely silent. Piper and Lily have taken shelter beside me, and we all try to slow our heavy breathing. After what seems like an hour, an unusual birdcall is heard from the forest at the opposite end of the field. Piper imitates the call, slowly rising from the ground and heading toward the field.

Once her call is answered, Piper turns. "Okay I think it's safe, but no more games, everyone should be working and watching the skies. There's no telling if they'll return."

A few of the younger children groan or kick the dirt but comply as they walk back into the field. Others inch out slowly, glancing upward every few seconds.

I stand addressing Finley and Lily in confusion. "What exactly did I see up there?"

"They're members of Odon's army," Lily states as if the answer is obvious and without need of explanation.

"Army? I didn't know—" I begin.

Finley speaks gravely. "The real question is why they were passing over now. They've changed their flight pattern, which is not a good sign."

"It could mean anything." Tor appears standing behind Finley. He winks at me from over his shoulder.

Finley shakes his head. "You know as well as I do that Odon rules in orders, and the only way those brainwashed followers will stay loyal is if he's consistent. He doesn't take risks easily."

"Warning taken." Tor puts his hand up in defense. "But I doubt that Odon will be taking much of anything after long."

At this Finley rolls his eyes and strides heavily away. I can't help but worry that Finley's words might have some truth to them.

Tor watches him leave and runs his hand through the curls of his hair. Finally he turns to me. "Oriana, I came for you. My mother is ready to meet with you now."

I nod expectantly. I'm hoping many of my questions are about to be answered.

I follow Tor back to the Great Oak, where the long ladder is waiting for us. Each climb becomes less terrifying. In fact, as I step higher up, I venture a glance below me and gasp at the height. I can see the tops of many of the other trees which have sprouted in the shadow of the Great Oak. It truly is an ancient and magnificent tree.

Once we've cleared the first platform, Tor brings me up successive ladders to the uppermost level. There are small cabins here as well, home to the Oak's many residents. I follow him to the very end of the platform where a cottage sits slightly set back from the others. Its windows have been propped open to let in the sun. Tor reaches the entrance and knocks upon the shelter's front wall. A soft voice from within calls, "Come in."

Tor looks over his shoulder at me. "You may enter; don't be shy. She's the only other pureblood you'll meet in the Great Oak."

My eyes widen, and I find my feet propelling me forward. "But you said I was the only pureblood," I whisper as if I ought to hide the conversation from the woman inside.

"I said *Winglet* …" Tor gives a wink and then heads away, leaving me to face the doorway alone and wonder what the difference is.

I take a deep breath and duck inside. The room is dark but cool, smelling sweetly of fresh flowers that I notice are set in vases upon every surface. There are different projects set in every corner. A partially complete, intricately woven basket lies upon a set of shelves. Another area holds cloth supplies and the workings of various dresses, one dyed the color of lavender. Next to it is a beautiful wreath made of dried flowers and leaves. Amid it all sits Falda.

Her impressively long hair is a bright white and has been crafted into braids of all sizes; one wraps around her head like a crown. Her eyes, which must once have been a sparkling blue, have been drained of some of their color, but still retain a youthful shine. As she smiles, her age is further shown by the fan of creases streaking from the corners of her eyes. The two dimples that form at her cheeks are an immediate giveaway that she is Tor's mother.

It causes me to smile in return and I give a respectful bow with my head.

"What a charming young girl," Falda exclaims. She rocks back in her chair which is constructed of smooth wood and a basket weave seat and back. The legs of it are unusually long and curved which allow Falda to glide forward and backward in place. "And that color suits you nicely," she winks, reminding me again of Tor.

"Thank you," I reply, fumbling with the skirts absentmindedly.

"Please take a seat. I'm sure you have many questions, and my story is a long one. In my old age I'm afraid I might not have the energy to tell it all at once." She smiles regretfully.

I find a nearby wooden chair. It doesn't move like Falda's, yet is still comfortable. "I'm grateful for whatever time you may give me."

At this, Falda laughs. "I can tell you are hungry for answers. You will not settle for less than everything I can tell you."

Heat rises to my cheeks, and I look away having been read very accurately. It's true. My expectations are already set at having all my questions answered.

"Don't worry, curiosity is nothing to be ashamed of. I will tell you all I can, if you have the patience to wait for an old woman."

"That I can promise you. I've learned patience well."

Falda chuckles and nods. "I am sure you have. Now—" She pulls at a large blanket that has been draped over the back of the chair and over her shoulders, adjusting it so that it better covers her. "I believe the best place to start is at the beginning, or at least the beginning as far as I'm concerned. I'd like to explain to you who we really are. The Winglets, the Finlets, and eventually everyone in between, but in the beginning, only the former two existed." Falda is about to continue but stops herself. "First things first ..." She grasps at the sides of the blanket hiding her small form and begins to slowly pull them aside. The blanket falls to the floor behind her, revealing two arcs of feathery white wings.

CHAPTER TWENTY-FOUR

Falda watches my expression solemnly. She slowly extends her wings to their full span, which reaches far past her shoulders, the curved tips nearly touching the floor. I marvel at their beauty, covered in smooth white feathers that reflect the light of the sun shining in through an open window.

She folds them delicately back behind her, resting them against the chair and holds up her palm to me. "Now before you say anything, let me explain." It's easy to do since I'm utterly speechless. "When I was your age, the passage into adulthood and the arrival of one's wings were common knowledge. Like my parents and theirs before them, every Winglet reaches the stage in their life when they transform into a full-grown Winglarion, which as you can judge means that you gain the ability to fly."

"You mean … you can actually … and one day I will …?" The stream of possibilities floods my mind, and I can't form any meaningful sentences.

"I have grown old, and flying requires energy that I am unable to bring forth easily. However, for most Winglarions their feet hardly ever touched the ground." Falda smiles in what appears to be reminiscence. "Now as a Winglet yourself, Oriana, my answer is yes. You will one day change and evolve into a Winglarion."

She seems to be waiting for me to fully understand, but I've already figured it out. "Is that the Rebirth? The one from the University?"

"You are correct, but that is a silly name created by Odon to keep his people from knowing too much." Falda casts aside the title with a wave of her hand, "I'd rather discuss a time when Odon had nothing to do with our people." She relaxes in her chair and sets her fingers together upon her lap.

"Now, as I have already said, in the beginning there were the Winglets and Finlets. Together they lived upon our planet, which we once called Valkyrie, although the name has slowly become obsolete. For many years the two races were unaware of each other. The Finlets tended to inhabit Valkyrie's shores and beaches, while Winglets remained within the forest. Of course in a limited amount of space and the growing populations, the two were bound to meet up eventually. When this happened, they embraced each other, learning of their different customs as well as each other's special abilities, which they received upon reaching adulthood. It was at this stage that the two races were forced to separate. Winglets, now Winglarions, became keepers of the sky while the ocean became the domain of the Finlarions. This separation was inevitable and while they returned to land for the sake of their young ones, their fates lay in opposite realms."

Falda's description of the interaction between Winglets and Finlets comes as a shock. The thought of living harmoniously with one another seems like an impossible dream.

"But then problems arose between the two groups."

I sink in my chair, knowing that this story does not have a happy ending.

"The Winglets and Finlets began to do something unspeakable. Something that caused major turmoil between the elders." She pauses, waiting to see if I am able to supply an answer.

I have already thought of one, yet hesitate at stating it.

"You know what I'm about to say, don't you?" she chides.

"They fell in love?"

Falda sighs with satisfaction. "Yes, although it was never thought to be possible. Winglets and Finlets, as youths often do, began to relate to one another. It wasn't long before the first half-blooded child was born, an outcast to the society of both the Winglarion and Finlarion elders. They heard about the child and very nearly sent it away from the community. However, other children were born, and you can presume what this led to."

"Part-bloods."

"Eventually, yes and those terms thus became a vile part of everyone's vocabulary."

"May I ask a question?"

"Of course," Falda replies.

"I now know what happens at the Rebirth, I mean, transformation, for the Winglets and Finlets. But what happens to the others?"

Falda's wings tremble. "Yes I knew you would ask this." She takes a breath. "Returning to the first half-blood child, which was a girl, many wondered the same thing. What would happen to her when she reached that stage in her life? Her parents were forced to leave her, separating from each other as well after their transformations, one to the air and the other to the sea, and she was left to discover for herself. On that day, when the purebloods grew their wings and the Finlets their fins, the only half-blood gained neither.

"Instead, something extraordinary happened. She was given so much more, abilities beyond what anyone could have imagined. So much power was very dangerous for such a young girl, but she had been well loved, and she had no desire to use this power against her people. Her promises were not enough for the others. The elders foresaw great destruction and devastation. Despite her reassurances, the purebloods would not believe a word of it. The girl escaped death by the pleas of her loving parents, but she could not escape exile. Along with her went the other half-bloods. The part-bloods, who did not receive any abilities following their adulthood, were sent away as well. The purebloods refused to take any chances. However, their decision became a grave error. The half-bloods left in sorrow and hatred toward their families. They became outcasts and many longed for revenge. As they separated, many conquered lands individually.

"Thus began the tyranny of the half-blood's, though not all were corrupt. Some half-bloods even attempted to stop the others of their kind, but there were too many of them. Their hunger for more power led to quarrels, and they were determined to conquer more land and more of their people, no matter what blood ran through their veins. Any fellow half-bloods they came upon were killed, and they separated all Winglets and Finlets, a strategy to prevent further competition for control of our world. Which leads us to today and Odon's lands. As we speak he is forming an army of purebloods, determined to defeat his fellow tyrants and take over the planet."

"Which is where Dorian comes in!" I exclaim. I have never imagined that Odon would be a half-blood. After all, our teachings tell us that purebloods were best. But it all makes sense now: Odon would want us believing our race was most important because he would need the Finlets and Winglets as followers to attack his enemies. The part-bloods are of no great use to him other than to reiterate his teachings, as they do not transform. Odon tells the purebloods that we are the supreme race and therefore earns our further devotion.

"Yes, Dorian is the last one, a half-blood who has escaped death and is loyal to our cause." Falda nods but then looks down. "That is … as far as we know."

I study her with worry, sensing the grave doubt in her voice. "What do you mean? Dorian is loyal; I know he is."

"Do you? Are you so certain that when he gains that power he won't do exactly what those before him have done?" She stares out the window. "Dorian may care for others now, but he has a lot of hate, especially after what happened to his parents. That hate is a dangerous weakness." Falda turns to me. Her face is serious and her eyes bore deep into my own. "Oriana, you may be the only one able to hold back that hate inside him. If he cannot do this, than we are all doomed."

Suddenly everything has taken a different turn. I swallow, feeling lost. I was so close to thinking I could understand everything. That I could actually feel steady on my feet. Yet the ground seems to drop away from beneath me. "How could Dorian ever turn against us? It can't be possible." I shake my head, wanting to believe that nothing can change him.

"Unfortunately it has happened before—another half-blood, a failed attempt." Her words stop my breath. "But child, it grows late, and I am weary. You shall return another time, and we will discuss more. You must not speak of this to anyone, especially Dorian."

"I … you must tell me more …"

"You have enough to think about. Go, join your friends for your midday meal, and leave your worries here. I will send Tor for you soon enough."

My eyes plead with her, but I already can tell she will speak no more. I leave with a sigh, my hands trembling. At first I was in awe of her wings and delighted at the thought of gaining my own. I have always dreamed of flying away, feeling that freedom. But knowing now what lies ahead dampens my expectations for the future. I feel an ache inside, and I keep replaying my confrontation with Dorian just the other day. He was so different, in a way I had never expected. Could he really turn on us? Become another Odon?

I head down the ladders of platforms thinking of how badly I want to tell Dorian of everything Falda has warned me of. Yet she specifically told me not too. I can't break her trust. I believe that she is telling the truth. It would only cause him more grief anyway. If Dorian must not know, then it is up to me to take responsibility. Maybe I do have a role in all of this, even though I can't imagine what good I could do. Many others here at the Great Oak have known Dorian for a much longer time than I have. Wouldn't they have a greater influence on him than I?

My body is sore as I reach the landing where my quarters are located. I decide to rest for a moment inside my room before I continue on. So many thoughts are running through my head that I don't notice Dorian waiting for me on my bed until he speaks.

"Oriana, are you all right?" He gets to his feet, and I turn to him, an uncontrollable terror rising to my face. Am I actually afraid of him now? He doesn't yet have his power, and yet I instinctively take a step backward. He looks hurt but continues as if he hasn't noticed, "You look pale; did something happen?"

I take a deep breath, seeing in his eyes the person I have grown to love. It is a relief, and a genuine smile eases his stance. "I'm fine, I only felt tired and needed a rest." To prove my point I take a seat on my bed, smoothing my dress over my thighs.

Dorian sits beside me. "You should take it easy, you've grown so … thin." He takes my hand, and I feel like nothing has changed between us, like I never saw that other person inside him. I wish I could tell him all that I have learned, but I hold back.

"I'll be fine," I assure him once again.

Dorian gives an unconvinced nod and glances toward the floor, releasing my hand. "I wanted to explain the way I acted before."

I turn to face him, pulling my legs sideways onto the bed to look directly at him.

"Tor told me you met with Falda." This surprises me, but I keep silent. I thought our meeting was a private one, but I'm sure he doesn't know all that was discussed. "I haven't been completely honest with you, but I think she was probably the best person to explain everything."

"Yes, she told me quite a bit," I reply shakily.

"So then, you understand my situation and what I must do." Dorian has been looking away, but now we make eye contact, and I see a young boy looking back at me. I can see a fear in his eyes, yet also a determination to carry through.

I take his hand in both of mine. "I'll be there with you …"

"No." Dorian gets up, pulling his hand away, and strides across the room. "That can't happen. This is my fight. Just me and Odon. There is no reason for you to be there."

My mouth drops open. "How can you say that? You're not alone in this; we all are affected by him. I have every right to come."

"Only I can defeat him. Don't you understand? I'm the one who will kill him."

His words frighten me. "Kill him? Is that all you can think of? This is a revolution, not revenge. Your thoughts should not be of anger, but of hope."

"You don't understand. Odon must die, after all the pain he's caused. After what he's done to my parents. Oriana, you haven't seen all that; you've only been in your little world of perfection. You were always one of Odon's prized possessions."

Tears well in my eyes as his words rip through me.

"I lost my childhood, any chance of happiness, and to you it's all some mystery you have to solve. That book that you so casually sat down to read? It was my mother's. The last shred of proof that she ever existed!"

I get to my feet, fists clenched. A feeling of complete fury rises from within and rushes forth. "You think my life was easy? You think all I had to do was walk around with a big smile on my face and everyone would adore me? You are greatly mistaken." Dorian's face reveals his shock, but I have only begun.

"While you were able to think and feel whatever you liked, I was trapped in a place where there were no thoughts for the future, no hope, only the constant stare of every Odon's Eye. Knowing that one mistake, one twitch, and I would be ripped apart. It took every fiber of strength I possessed to keep going."

My voice remains steady and stern, my eyes level. The words flow easily and without hesitation. It feels as though I'm not just telling Dorian; I'm releasing it to the world. "Do you think it has been easy, knowing I've been betrayed by the only person I thought was my friend? I don't want to ruin your display of pity, but I don't even know my parents and probably never will."

There is a moment of silence before Dorian clears the distance between us and takes me in his arms. The anger leaves me, and I embrace him as well.

"I'm sorry, I shouldn't have said any of that," Dorian whispers in my ear. "You're right, this has been hard for everyone. I don't want to be the one to hurt you."

I pull back to look at him. "This is going to change our lives, and Odon is just the beginning. If we turn on each other, we lose any chance of surviving."

CHAPTER TWENTY-FIVE

Dorian turns from me to pull something from his pocket.

"Your mother's journal," I remark as he weighs it in his hand.

"I used to read it every day, hoping that maybe I could get to know her better," he explains. He smoothes the binding. "I even tore out my favorite pages to keep hidden. They were about the better times, the happiness. What's left in here"—he waves the book at me—"are the worst memories. I didn't want to look at it anymore, but I couldn't just dispose of it. So Tor kept it in the private library, never to be touched again."

"I'm sorry. If I'd known, I would never have …"

"I know, you don't have to explain." He tosses the book onto the bed. "I wish I could just forget about it! But every time I'm reminded of my parents, I want to make Odon pay for what he did!" He clenches his fists; his body shuddering.

I place my hand on his back to console him, and his shoulders sag under a heavy weight. Whatever Odon did to them must have been truly terrible for Dorian to feel so much anger. I decide not to ask for the details. Instead I ask, "That was the reason you remained in the University?"

"I found a way of volunteering in the medical wing, which gave me some access to their records. It wasn't just personal; I needed some proof that I was a half-blood." Dorian shakes his head. "I don't know what I was thinking. It was a dangerous move, and I didn't even find much of anything." He gives me a look and grins. "Well, that is, except for you."

"Which brings up another question that's been on my mind," I say with a start. "Why did you smile at me? Didn't you know how much you were risking? Especially since you're so valuable to everyone else."

Dorian shrugs, rubbing at the side of his face where the growth of a short beard makes a scratching noise. "I really can't answer that for sure." He looks downward. "I saw something different about you, an inner turmoil."

"Was I that readable?" Even now that I'm far away from the University, I still feel that fear of being transparent; of being found out.

"You know how the others are. How could you *not* stand out around them?" He kisses my forehead and then my lips.

When he releases me, words flood from my mouth. "I'm going with you. I can't let you just risk your life and not be there to help."

Dorian's face is grim as he turns away and heads for the door. "I should leave now. I have a lot to think about." He doesn't turn to look at me as he exits the room.

It feels cold without him close, and I regret speaking so suddenly. I know I must be there, and Falda's words make sense after the short time I've spent with Dorian. He may be trying to shelter me, but he doesn't realize what's at stake. His hatred for Odon can turn dangerous when he gains his power.

I fall onto my bed, landing on a hard object that I discover to be Narena's journal. I pick it up carefully, as if the words within are as fraught with peril as the young woman's life who wrote them. Even though I'm curious about the story that unfolds in these pages, I decide not to read them for the time being, afraid I may cause its contents to spill out into reality.

A rap at the entrance startles me, and I squeak a response. "Who's there?"

Piper pulls aside the door flap to peer within, "Are you coming to dinner?" she asks with a stiff politeness.

"Dinner? Is it that late already?" I must've left Falda's later than I thought.

Seeing that I'm my ordinary self, Piper hurries inside, a cape drawn close around her shoulders. She is followed by Lily who, adorned in a beige cape and new yellow dress, half-skips through the doorway.

"Yes! Can't you tell by how hungry you are? You never showed for lunch. Tor said not to worry, that you were speaking with Falda, but we eventually had to find you. We missed you too much!" Lily gives me a quick hug.

I laugh, knowing that Lily and Piper could actually be considered my friends. The word takes on a new meaning. "Well. I'm glad you found me. I would've been hungry all night."

"You probably would've withered and blown away!" Piper chides. "Come on, let's get some food in you."

Lily reaches for my cape and places it over my shoulders. "Here, the air has chilled. You may get cold."

"Thanks." I nod and button the front closed with a wood toggle and leather loop. The material feels heavy at first, but I soon adapt to its weight.

Once outside, I feel the temperature has indeed dropped. It has begun to grow darker as we make our way to the dining hall. My stomach pains are more apparent the closer we get to a potential meal.

The night has swallowed up the sky as we enter the building. Here it is warm, and I push the sides of the cape to my back. Piper leads the way as we head down the line of benches, which are practically all filled. I wave at Azura, who watches us approach. She gives a half smile and returns to her meal. Liam is back at his ordinary seat beside her, looking worn and tired, even pale. Tor sits across from them. He seems stressed as well, and it is a trait I never thought to see him bear. Still, when he follows Azura's brief gaze to me, he manages a warm grin, and I see the shine has not left his eyes. As I pass by, he grasps my wrist.

"You're feeling well?" he whispers so only I can hear.

I nod to assure myself more than him. He pats my hand and then releases it so I may continue forward.

Further down Finley and the others sit, and Jagger is explaining the occurrences of the day. He keeps his voice low, although I see those around him sneaking glances to listen secretly, impelled by the urgency in his voice.

"Isn't that strange? Odon's Winglarions flying over the field with everyone there? And us thinking we had the schedules figured out."

"We did," Finley declares, his elbows resting on the table and a mug in one hand.

Dugan takes a bite of his bread. "So then they changed," he says smoothly.

"Is it such a surprise?" Buck adds in his deep voice. "Odon has plans of his own. The schedules only work so long as they suit him."

"Why did he have them to begin with?" Piper asks as the three of us take seats across from the guys.

Buck, Weasel, and Jagger turn to Dugan to explain. Finley glances at me and then looks away.

"It's simple to explain," he begins in an even tone as his hand smoothes the side of his slick black hair. "Odon likes his followers better when they're brainless. They take orders easily and don't ask questions. The downside is they also don't have the ability to think for themselves. They need structure, and a simple one at that. Thus came the schedules." Dugan shrugs and continues to eat as if all this were obvious.

"But us not knowing the schedule? It don't sound good," Weasel says, half hiding his face behind the collar of his shirt. His large eyes peek out from beneath his hat.

Finley smirks. "Of course it's not good, which is what I've been saying from the start. They think we can easily beat Odon at his own game?" Finley gives a laugh that quiets people further down the table. Weasel tries to hush him, but he presses on. "Odon's not a fool. He has eyes everywhere, and now that he's changed his schedules, maybe some of these part-bloods around here won't be acting so cocky."

Whispers erupt from close around us and I catch parts of the conversations.

"Finn's right, we have no idea what we're up against," a young boy says to his friend next to me.

"But Tor says plans are already under way," his friend replies.

I hear an older part-blood speak from across the table to a separate group. "We don't stand a chance! Not if we can't even tell when the guards are above us."

"Yeah, they could sneak right up on us in the night, and we'd never know," a girl puts in.

"If Dorian is willing to risk his life for this, then I'll support them till the end," comments a third.

I turn back to the others who are silently eating their meals. I can tell that their thoughts most likely reflect the discussions occurring around us.

It's late as our plates are being passed back and the others get to their feet.

"Oriana, you're joining us at the fire tonight, right?" Jagger asks.

"What do you mean?" I had expected everyone to go their separate ways afterward.

"We sit outside sometimes, on clear nights," Piper explains from beside me. "Come stay with us. It'll be fun."

I shrug. "Okay."

We head out the front of the building, which is opposite from the end Piper, Lily, and I entered. Upon the platform, a few other part-bloods have formed a large fire and laid out some benches and sit staring into the flames.

The night is cold, and I tug my cape tighter around my body. Once I'm near the fire, the heat melts away my tension. Piper and Lily beckon me to a bench where they take a seat. I'm grateful it is on the side of the fire that is closest to the trunk of the tree. I have still not grown comfortable with the platform's edge.

Jagger stands up, the fire's glint in his eyes, and begins to tell a story. The others watch him intently as his voice grows deep and enchanting. "The story of the lovers' demise is the most tragic and frightening tale ever told. It occurred not long ago, and not far from this very spot they were forever lost."

Jagger continues his tale, stopping once when Dugan intervenes.

"Jagger, you got it mixed up, it wasn't a pond, it was a garden," Dugan states coolly.

Jagger nods and continues.

I look away, judging by the content of the story that it will only cause me greater distress. Across from me, sitting alone and staring into the night air, is Finley. He is not listening to Jagger but thinking deeply, his eyebrows knotted in concentration.

Seeing that the others are still focused on Jagger's tragic story, I make my way around the benches to Finley. He startles as I take a seat beside him.

"Oriana" is his only response.

"I've been meaning to speak with you." I wrap my fingers around the edge of my cape. "There's so much to think about, and I'm just … lost."

The scar upon Finley's cheek takes on a glow in the firelight as he stares at me with surprised brown eyes. "Speak with me? How do you think I can help you?"

"You think differently from everyone else. Like you know something they don't, something they're not telling me."

He smiles at this. "You don't say much, but you're more aware of things than I thought." He looks into the flames. "You remind me of someone. A girl I knew. She was smart like you, but it didn't matter. It never matters." Finley turns his gaze back to me. His hand reaches to grasp my hair. "You're still so young, and yet somehow you've managed better than any of us."

I shake my head, staring downward, feeling the heat rush into my cheeks. "I haven't … I'm not really …"

"The mere fact that you're the only pureblood from the University living here is proof enough." Finley lifts my chin. "And so beautiful. You probably don't even know it." He gives a wan smile as he studies my face, leaning toward me.

I pull slowly away. All I can think of is Dorian. Despite everything, I still care for him. "Please, I only came to hear what you know. If Odon is to be defeated, then I must …" He has already released me and crossed his arms, turning back to watch the fire.

"Defeated? Very doubtful; it's been tried before, and probably before that. Yet still everyone believes that this time it will work." Finley's face is serious.

"But Tor seems to think—"

"I know what Tor believes. He is an honest man; I know that, we grew up together. We were practically brothers," he explains.

This surprises me, after seeing the conflict between them. "Brothers? But you seem so … at odds."

"We have our differences. Unfortunately it has to do with this, and what's at stake is life and death." Finley shakes his head, "There's so much to lose, and Tor's ultimate faith lies in you."

"Me?" I knew I played a large part in all this, but *ultimate faith*?

"You have learned of your role, haven't you?" Finley conjectures.

I nod. "But—"

"I'm assuming you don't know what happened last time."

I remember Falda's words, *"It has happened before, another half-blood, a failed attempt."* Yet I wasn't sure what she meant. "No, what happened?"

CHAPTER TWENTY-SIX

"Dorian wasn't the only half-blood to be willing to go against Odon. There was another, and it was only a few years ago that the attempt occurred."

Finley's face is grim. "His name was Kadin. We were all friends while living at the University. Tor, Kadin, and later the guys." He nods in the direction of Jagger, Dugan, Buck, and Weasel. "We had this plan to help all part-bloods escape. Our meeting place was the Great Oak. It was successful to a point, until Odon became stricter and a few others were caught. By then Azura, Liam, Piper, and Lily had been rescued, and the young ones like Toby came later on and sparingly.

"It just became near impossible to rescue many others, and this idea of an actual attack began circling in our minds. We all knew that Odon was a half-blood and that the half-blood abilities came at the Rebirth. We figured if we could find a way to sneak Kadin in, then he could use his new powers to attack Odon."

"But why must it be exactly at the Rebirth?"

"We were certain that Odon would be inside the University at the time. But it's not just that. At the moment when the Winglets and Finlets change, Odon must be there in order to direct his power toward them and grab hold of their minds. They are in a weakened state, yet so is he because of the concentration needed to gain control of so many in one moment. Even though Kadin might not be as powerful as Odon when he first transformed, Odon's weakened state should give him an advantage."

Finley sighs. "The plan seemed flawless at the time, but it wasn't just Kadin's lack of experience that caused it to fail. Instead of following the plan to distract Odon so that we could work together to overpower him, Kadin attacked to kill. He turned on us and even started trying to take over the others. That only made him weaker, giving Odon the advantage. Not many of us managed to escape safely. Others were trapped between the dueling half-bloods. We're not sure if Kadin survived or not, but we think he somehow left to conquer his own territory and form an army of his own." I see the anguish in his eyes, the fear and sorrow as he relives the moment. He smoothes back his dark hair with both palms.

I place my hand on his for comfort, "I understand why you're unwilling to support Dorian."

"It's not for my sake, it's the others. If anyone were to die because they trusted me to lead them to salvation …" He shakes his head. "At the time I thought it was the right thing to do. But now? I could never forgive myself if the past repeated itself. It's not worth the risk to me. And the younger ones like Piper and Lily—they don't even know of our previous attempt."

I find myself agreeing with his logic. They tried to defeat Odon and failed, so why should they attempt the same plan over again? Granted, we can't live under Odon's rule forever, but there must be some other way. "Why is Tor so determined to make this idea work? He already knows what happened last time."

Finley glances at me. "Tor believes this time will be different."

"It's Dorian, isn't it? He's different than Kadin, right?"

At this Finley smirks but shakes his head. "No, I've already told you. Dorian is like a brother to Tor; he practically raised Dorian since his parents left. But there's no way to trust a half-blood. After all, we trusted Kadin; he was our friend, and now you've learned what that led to. Tor is not foolish enough to think that no added variables would change the outcome of our plan."

"Then the only main variable … is me," I say with a sigh.

Finley nods. "Tor wanted to wait for you to settle in. To slowly learn the situation, past and present, before knowing your final purpose. He thought you would agree with the plan once you gathered all the information at a bearable speed."

"And you've been planning this for how long? Is that why Dorian talked to me in the first place? Is that how I got here?"

"Not at all!" Finley replies. "This wasn't a long-term idea. You came to us, not the other way around. Dorian has no idea what role you play. In fact, he's been trying to protect you and keep you out of it."

"He has?"

"It's a difficult task trying to persuade Dorian to allow you to come. One that I won't have anything to do with." Finley turns back to gaze at the fire. "Personally I agree with him: it's too dangerous for a girl like you to come along. Someone who is not used to sneaking around Odon's guards. It's bad enough Azura insists on coming."

"Well, I appreciate your concern, but it's going to be my decision, and as far as I know"—I take a deep breath, and I feel a courage bloom within me—"if facing danger is what it takes to bring Odon down, then I'm not being left behind."

"That's very brave of you." Finley smiles and places a large hand on my shoulder. "But when it comes time, you'll be facing a formidable fear like the rest of us."

I sigh. "So be it, but at least let me know what exactly you expect me to do."

"Yes, I knew you were waiting to ask." Finley pauses and thinks the question over. "It's better if Falda tells you the rest. I've said enough already, and Falda has a calming way with words." He laughs as the disappointment forms on my face.

"Fine, I understand, I already feel like my mind is about to explode." I stand, brushing my dress downward with my hands. "I guess I can wait until tomorrow."

"Wait, one more thing." Finley stands and leans close. "Don't tell anyone what I told you. Not even Dorian." He glares at me sternly.

"Yes, I know, I got the same speech from Falda," I retort sorely. I begin to head away.

"Where are you going?" Finley calls after me.

"To bed. Don't worry, I'm not heading to confess anything," I reply brusquely over my shoulder. I hear the snort of his dry laugh and continue forward into the night.

I hear him run toward me. "Maybe I'd better walk you back."

I stop, pivoting to reply, "Why's that? You don't trust me?" He begins to walk next to me. The others seem to be too involved in Jagger's tale to notice us leaving.

"Not entirely, you may decide to throw yourself over the edge in a bout of insanity." He grins, and I see the glint of his teeth in the diminishing firelight.

"You wouldn't want your last savior to die," I remark sourly.

Finley stops abruptly. "Is that all you think you are to us? We're all worried about you, especially since you came back from the underground of the University with that injury …" His voice trails off, and he tries to casually study my face to discern if I have been listening.

"What do you mean, injury?" I retort.

"Listen … it's better if you didn't know. In fact, forget I even said anything." Finley tries to walk faster and avoid any response.

"Forget it? But if everyone is so worried, how can I just forget it?"

He grabs me by the shoulders and looks hard into my eyes. "I can't explain this to you, but for some reason it's been having effects. Just trust that we're discussing it."

"Wait a second. You mean something's wrong with me, and no one knows what?" I fall to my knees and clutch my head. It has suddenly exploded in light and pain. I'm able to recover, and Finley helps me to my feet. His eyes are wide with concern. Is that what he meant by having effects? Fear keeps me from saying anything more. I decide to trust the others to figure it out for now.

We pass the rest of the way in silence as I try to forget what I've heard and concentrate on getting to sleep. Maybe by tomorrow this will all seem simpler; maybe I'll become stronger or discover it was all some strange dream. Perhaps I'll wake up in the University—Lenora awake and ready for classes, sitting upright in her bed beside mine. For a moment I will imagine I have dreamt something but then lose interest and begin to dress for class. My concentration directed toward a test or the proper behavior of a pureblood.

We make it to my shelter, and Finley wishes me a good night. I return the favor, giving him a slight wave as he heads further down the platform. As I step into my room, it becomes darker, and I immediately notice a firefly is caught within. It winks on and off, floating above my head and landing on the wall behind me. When I move to reach it, it takes off again, letting its light be seen every other moment, when it appears slightly further from its previous glow as it continues its flight.

    Finally I cup my hands around it and bring it close. I feel its soft wings as it flies against my palm, and my hands light up briefly. I pass through the flap door, set it free into the night, watching it disappear among the surrounding trees, and turn my head upward. The stars above are distinct and bright; they hold their illumination in permanence. Alone they are small pinpoints in the sky, but together they could outshine the full moon.

    Letting the flap fall behind me, I climb into bed and fall asleep in a final moment of calm. I wake several times throughout the night, only to fall back into a light sleep, tossing from side to side and reaching out at every corner of my bed.

    I wake to find it is early morning. Although my eyes are open, staring up at the ceiling of branches, I do not move. Something seems to weigh me down, and my body does not fight it. Instead, I let it push me farther into the mattress beneath. I feel as though I'm sinking, first at my stomach, followed by my numb limbs and next my head.

    I have been dozing slightly when Piper and Lily pass my cottage. I hear their chatter halt when they are at my doorway; perhaps they are listening for any movement. They do not peer inside but continue on, whether at an inkling that my energy is failing me or because they were warned against disturbing my sleep.

    I sigh once they are out of range, grateful to be left in peace. Yet serenity is not completely easing its way inside me. The quiet isn't entirely welcoming. It only makes it easier to focus on what feels like my impending doom. I don't have the will to address this thought, and before I know it, I've already entered another superficial slumber.

    I wake with a start, sensing that I have heard something but cannot remember what, and there is no sign of it within my room. The sun sheds an orange glow on the thick cloth that covers my door, telling me it is midday. I feel overly rested, and it makes me sluggish as I sit up and slide my legs over the side of my mattress. I hear the sound of approaching footsteps.

    There is a knock on the side of my doorway, and I beckon for whoever calls to enter. Tor slides inside, his head nearly reaching the top of the doorframe and a disrupted curl just brushing it. "How are you feeling?" he asks with a hopeful grin.

"Not myself," I reply.

At this, I notice a frown, but it vanishes quickly and is soon forgotten, "Falda was hoping to meet with you today. But if you are not well …"

In an instant I am to my feet and heading toward him. No manner of illness could hold me back from finding out more. "Please, I would still like to go if that's all right."

"As you wish," Tor answers with his accustomed wink. His long strides carry him out the door, and I struggle to keep up with him, my feet feeling like heavy weights.

By the time we reach Falda's cottage, my spirits have lightened. The sunlight, although it disappears every few moments behind a large white cloud, has given me some much-needed energy. I notice that the biting of hunger has risen in my stomach, and it rumbles softly. As if hearing it, Tor turns and says, "You must be hungry. My mother will have something for you." I grin in thanks, and he flicks my hair as he passes me and heads away.

When I enter, the scene before me is much like the one witnessed yesterday. I notice that the lavender dress, in its last stages, is now laid across Falda's lap as she rocks slowly in her chair. She smiles at me warmly. I nod and say, "Good afternoon."

"Indeed we have, although I believe tomorrow may bring another storm. The winds have been guiding large clouds our way." This does not seem to bother her though, and she merely shrugs at the thought and continues stitching a line of the dress with shaky hands. I wait, watching her, trying not to feel the impatience rising at the back of my throat. She reaches the end of the line of fabric, gathers it up, and puts it on a side table that is woven like a basket. Reaching further past, she lifts a cloth-lined basket and beckons me to her. "Here, dear, have some." I get up from my seat to peer over the edge of the basket at a cluster of fruit scones. I reach in and pull out two the size of my palms. Returning to my seat, I begin to gradually pick at them, feeling the hunger fade but a pit of anxiety remain.

With a sigh, Falda replaces the basket and rests deeply into the cushions of her chair. She nestles softly in to them like a bird, a plume floating from the side of her chair to glide neatly to the floor. She doesn't notice. Her blue eyes have focused on me, and her eyebrows have drawn together like a stitching pulled too tight, "What is the matter, dear? I only just saw you yesterday, and yet you look very different."

"One can learn a lot in a short time, and the knowledge may be heavy." I know she can hear the irritation in my voice.

"Tell me what you have heard." Falda rests her fingers together in her lap, and there is a soft forbearance in her tone. It's in this moment that I think to myself, this must be what having a mother is like. Her desire to listen eases my frustration, and I tell her of my talk with Finley last night: explained the previous attempt to defeat Odon and finally the discovery that I play a part in the Great Oak's future, yet he would not tell me exactly what it is.

She says nothing until I am finished and then nods her head. "It is all true."

"Then you can tell me? What is expected of me?" My demeanor brightens, and I move to the edge of my seat.

Falda's mouth opens, but no words escape, the breath she has taken slides out between her teeth in a low hiss. Looking down, she shakes her head. "I believe it is best that you figure that out for yourself." She pauses as if deciding whether or not to agree with herself; then with a nod she continues, "If I were to tell you, it might affect your reaction in the moment of need. You will know when the time is right."

I lean back in my chair, somehow realizing that I knew all along I was not ready for the information. Still, I am not satisfied with the answer.

"Oriana, I know you must be upset, but your visit is not for nothing." Falda presses her lips together. "It should gladden you to learn I knew your mother."

CHAPTER TWENTY-SEVEN

"You knew my mother!?" I nearly leap from my seat but hold back, only just catching myself and maintaining a level of composure.

Falda nods solemnly, and I fear the story will not leave me so elated.

"What was her name? What was she like?" I fall silent, my attention solely fixed on absorbing everything Falda has to say about her.

"Her name was Sonya, a brave young woman indeed. You resemble her strongly, which is probably why the memory of her comes back to me so clearly. She had just received her wings and shortly later given birth when I met her. Both are turning points in a female Winglet's life, yet she seemed to carry the responsibilities well. We were from separate clans of Winglets, yet the danger of Odon had been causing what Winglarions were still alive and free to gather together. We were all sharing information of neighboring areas and searching for news of family members.

"She came to me as many others did at that time. I was a well-known member of the rebels. Word had spread of a sanctuary in the forest that was being slowly built within the arms of a magnificently ancient tree. Sonya was one of many seeking my help. She was desperate but not without direction. I could see the determination burning in her eyes. She was one of the few purebloods who had come to me that day, asking for a way of escape. In her arms she held two baby girls. Both from the same birth and crowned with similar gold sweeps of hair on their small plump heads. Yet I noticed clearly they were not exact copies, and I could see the differences of their souls from within their large blue eyes."

"Two babies …" I whisper. I have a sister? But instead I ask, "Did she mention my father?"

Falda shakes her head, "I assumed he had already been captured, as many young Winglarion men had been at that point. Odon's first goal was to form an army, as well as create his elite soldiers, which you know as Odonians, who are most closely bonded to Odon's will.

"Now Tor was just a young boy then, but he and I led the people of the Great Oak to rebellion. Part of which began as secret guidance and escape, for anyone willing, to the protection of the Great Oak. We would leave in groups, spreading word of our encampment and offering passage there. You said you met Finley?"

I give a short nod.

"Then you've met his band of ruffians as well. They are never far behind him." The corner of her mouth lifts, displaying a single dimple. "They helped as well, Tor and he being of the same age, and of course Kadin was right beside them. They were all such close friends back then." Her eyebrows rise, her abstracted gaze shifting to other memories. "Amazing how quickly we are swallowed by time, pulled from people we once knew so well. Perhaps this ancient Oak truly suits us. It will live to see many generations, growing new branches with each year, adding to its girth. I only hope the young ones rise with it to greater heights. It is our intention that, if not in our lifetime, then a future generation will bring freedom to all our people, no matter their lineage."

Falda brushes at a silver thread of hair by her eye, but I see she is actually wiping at a tear.

"Excuse my ranting; my old mind wanders into digression."

I wave a hand, dismissing any need for apology, and she bows her head in return before her pale irises rise toward her furrowing brow.

"Now where did I falter? Still at the beginning of the tale, I believe. When your mother Sonya sought me in hopes of reaching the Great Oak, I was only too willing to supply her with the meeting time and place, which was to be that night at the edge of the forest. I had one final word of warning to offer her: 'Dear girl, please heed my words with severity. No matter what threatening situation you find yourself in, do not take flight. Remain on the ground.'

"My words were swept away by the wind, and we were forced to part quickly as others moved around us. Odon's spies were growing in numbers, and it was never certain when one could be watching. It was probably for the best that our conversation was brief, as it was never safe to talk openly anymore, and we did not want to be seen together for long. However, I believed she'd heard my crucial words, as she gave a short nod before disappearing among the others.

"That night, many part-bloods arrived at the cover of the forest's edge. They were all young, none older than Tor and most younger. I tried not to think of how many fathers and mothers had sacrificed their lives or freedom to allow their children to escape. The future of the Great Oak relied on the survival of these children. Although they did not realize it, their parents' lives had not ended in vain. I would not allow them to.

"No purebloods had showed. It became a common occurrence for myself and the other rebels. We might speak with a few, tell them of the meeting place, but never had they made it there. Somehow Odon's men were always able to intervene in their escape. There was no telling what happened to the Winglarions who never showed, whether they lived on or were terminated. It was Odon who made decisions on who best suited his purposes.

"That night I didn't turn away, that night I was certain at least one Winglarion would arrive. It was late, but I refused to lose faith. I thought for certain Sonya would be seen any minute making her way through the clearing to the protection of the forest. Her silhouette in the glow of the moon revealing two young girls held firmly in her lean arms.

"I tried to keep the younger ones quiet, as they were getting impatient and the waiting only brought thoughts of their lost loved ones. Yet although the hour was now well past the appointed time, I was certain that young Sonya would make it. I had seen the force behind her blue eyes. It was a refusal to fail, if not for her own sake, then for her offspring.

"Finally, just when I thought my hope would fail me, I saw her running desperately toward us. Her daughters were caught snugly, one in each arm. One wailed at the top of her delicate lungs while the other remained silent, her eyes wide in anticipation. Sonya held her wings folded behind her, I could see they were weighing her down.

Like birds, Winglarions are made for the air and face a disadvantage on the ground. Despite this, Sonya hurtled forward, the sweat dripping off her porcelain brow and her cloth skirts soiled with dirt.

"Not far behind her, I gasped to discover, was a group of guards running at top speed. They did not shout or show any expression but focused their blank gaze on Sonya. It was this lack of any soul that was most frightening about them. As the guards closed in on the frail form of Sonya and her two children, she did what a Winglarion knows to do best. In a state of panic, Sonya's wings spread and, despite my warning earlier, lifted her into the sky with the elegance of a swan."

I clasp my hands together, palms going hot as I try to prevent the impending danger that I know has already occurred and been buried in time.

"My stomach sank, and I closed my eyes as I heard the thud of an arrow into flesh. I looked up to watch Sonya's fast but graceful descent. Her wings extended and her body curled into a protective circle around her two most precious treasures. A second arrow found its mark in her wing, embedding itself among silken feathers. Her body struck the ground in a sickening crunch of feather and bone, and only once she had ended her fall did her tense figure open to reveal two lovely infants. They were terrified and wailing but unharmed."

I cry out, quickly muffling the noise with a burning palm. Closing my eyes, I try to tear myself away from the image of my mother, in all her beauty, felled by the bite of two wooden shafts. But the scene remains, like the light of the sun burned into my eyelids.

Falda continues, "I motioned in earnest for the children around me to remain as still as stars, but they were already frozen in shock anyway. Once the guards had hauled away the babies and the young woman's lifeless form, I led the part-bloods away. Unable to look anywhere but forward, above the tree line and into the night sky."

My eyes are hot and wet when she has finished the story, and Falda does not pass judgment as I heave long whimpers as if I were once again only an infant. It is only after I've run out of tears that the anger comes. "Why did you just stand there? Why didn't you try to help her?" My fingers grab at my hair until some strands pull free with a snap.

"Oriana, no selfish intent kept me from saving your mother. I was afraid, yes, but more importantly, I had a duty to the young ones around me. If I was captured, what good would I have been to them? Or the ones who followed? I had a responsibility to their survival."

I bite my lip and hang my head in shame. Falda is right, and furthermore there's no use venting anger for past events which have no hope of being changed. "I'm sorry, I only wish … that I could've known her."

"I sense she is still with you, a part of your spirit now." Falda's warm words seem to be truth more than shallow comfort.

I look up suddenly, compelled by a question. "Falda, how do you know that Sonya was in fact my mother?"

"Well, other than your near identical features, she had told me your name. Had even stitched it with care into the collar of your tunic," Falda explains.

"Then you would know the name of the other child, my sister?" I ask with new anticipation.

Falda nods putting a finger to her lips. "Of course, you would want to know such a thing …" She looks up, her eyes shifting back and forth as if searching through a thick novel. "Her daughters were Oriana … and … Lenora."

"Lenora," I repeat in a daze. This distant idea has suddenly been revealed as fact. Despite the gravity of this new information, I feel as though I have been considering the possibility for a long time. Lenora and I share similar features, and we were placed in the same room. I have also thought of her as a sister and now know it to be true.

Still, the thought of having shared the same womb with Lenora brings about a different feeling. Any previous disdain for her actions is wiped clean. Suddenly I have an undeniable need to see her again. Maybe once she learns what I know, Lenora will join me and see that our bond goes far deeper than the one with Odon ever could.

Then another voice takes over. It will never happen. Lenora is in the University, and I am out here. I will have to wait until the Rebirth. If Odon is defeated, then Lenora and I can start anew. I cannot let our mother's sacrifice be in vain. I cannot bear her to see that I have let my only sister remain alone in the walls of the University.

"I can see that Lenora is familiar to you."

I jump, having forgotten that I was not alone, "Yes, we shared a room together at the University. I should've known all along, but I guess Odon wouldn't have wanted us to be closer to each other than we were to him."

"It must please you to know you have family." Falda smiles. She seems to see into the depths of my thoughts, compelling me to respond as I've already begun to.

"Yes, but it pains me to think she is still in the University. I wish I could help her."

Falda nods. "I presumed as much, but Oriana, you must listen to me. You're most helpful here at the Great Oak. You must not attempt to sew too many threads into one piece of fabric; that will cause it to fray." She puts a finger against her chin as if pleased with her analogy and decides to add to it, "One focused stitch can connect many materials, eventually creating something useful."

I press my lips together in a faint smile letting her know I understand the deeper meaning of her words. Still, the yearning to reach my sister and make some connection is hard to subdue. Falda is correct: so much is going on here, it would be too difficult to attempt to meet with Lenora. Besides, the Rebirth is swiftly approaching. I must be patient and have faith that our plans will not fail.

A tall form barrels through the doorway, and I can sense an urgency swirling into knots around him. Tor stands before us, his sandy hair in disarray. He rubs his forehead sourly; he did not duck quickly enough and collided with the doorframe. Unfortunately it's slightly too short for a man of his stature. His eyes turn from me to Falda and back again; there is no trace of a dimple on his stern features.

"Oriana." His voice lacks warmth, and it causes me to tense further. I simply gulp in reply. "I'm sorry to interrupt, but there is an urgent gathering at the meeting hall. I think you might want to be present for this one."

I'm on my feet in a moment. Turning to Falda, I ask, "Are you joining us?"

"No, dear, my ancient limbs no longer carry me up those insufferable ladders. And furthermore, I am of no use to the council now. I am but a link to the past." She reaches for the dress on the table beside her and searches for the needle.

"Then I am sorry to be leaving like this." I bow my head slightly.

"Child, I am not the least bit offended. My son speaks in earnest. You must leave. Hurry now; we will meet at another time." Falda sends me off with a wave of her hand; her wings even flutter forward, propelling air currents to push me out the door.

Without further response, I follow Tor out. He bends down much further than necessary to pass through the doorway this time. I don't find much humor in it at the moment. I'm too nervous about what discussions await at the meeting hall. The prospect has Tor taking giant strides that cause me to trot beside him. I hope he will notice my struggle without me having to complain. We are halfway around the uppermost platform when I decide to make my presence known again; perhaps it will remind him of my short legs.

"Tor, can you please tell me what is so urgent?" I cannot hide the breathlessness in my voice.

He stops short, looking down at me as if shocked out of deep thought. The expression gives way to a smile of understanding as he answers, "I'm sorry." He starts walking again at a slower yet still brisk pace. "I guess I'd better just tell you outright," he says, half to himself.

I quicken my pace to walk ahead of him and get a clear view of his face. I can tell it is difficult for him to speak.

Finally he stops again, and I see we have reached the ladder to the next level below. I turn to face him, blocking his way so that he is forced to give an answer. The anticipation is too much. I need him to tell me.

He falters and then sighs, submitting to my penetrating gaze, "It's Malise and Aaron. They were captured by Odon's Winglarions."

CHAPTER TWENTY-EIGHT

I waste no more time for explanation and tackle the ladder, skipping rungs as I hurry down it. I burn the back of my forearm on the rope, but it doesn't faze me. The thought of Malise and Aaron facing the torment of Odon's guards is too much for me. They are so young, and I have envied their innocence. Neither has witnessed the cruelty of University life. I can't bear to let Odon hurt more of those I care about. He has taken too much already.

Tor and I reach the meeting hall. I feel light-headed, and I try to slow my breath to something softer than gasps. Inside, many others have already arrived, and judging by their faces, the cause for council is no mystery. To my left, Azura and Liam sit side by side toward the center of the long table. She gives a nod of acknowledgment that I've returned. Following them and filing around the back of the table are Finley and his rough-looking followers, Dugan, Jagger, Buck, and Weasel.

Piper and Lily are here as well, squeezing between Weasel and Dugan. They are whispering softly yet so rapidly I don't see them take a breath. When they notice I have entered, they stop, gazing at me with wide eyes. I press my lips together, trying to appear comforting, but they make no movement.

Tor has pushed past me to take a seat at the head of the table, and I search for an empty spot. There is warmth on my arm, and I look downward to see Dorian, his soothing eyes focused on mine. He is seated to the right of Tor. I take the empty space beside him. Weasel sits to my right. Dorian must sense my anxiety, because once I am beside him, he curls my stray hair behind my ear and presses his lips to my cheek. I am startled by his gesture, but move closer. My fears ease at his affection. His hand rests upon my knee so that only I know it's there.

My eyes move to the other side of the table, and I see an unfamiliar face. It is a young boy with blond hair and brown eyes and a cascade of freckles upon his cheeks. Tor speaks to him in a low voice, trying to comfort the clearly frazzled child. His eyes are red and swollen, irritated by a recent onslaught of crying. When the boy finally begins to respond to Tor's prodding, his words rush out of him in between gasping breaths. The talking of others around me drowns out his words, but I see Tor react with a nod and eventually a small pat to the youngster's back. The boy wipes at his eyes, already flooding once again, and gulps back a sob.

Tor gets to his feet, suddenly taking on a commanding air. His height and squared shoulders reflect the part perfectly, and this brief movement causes the others to fall silent. They face him respectfully, awaiting what information is to be given. Tor, however; does not speak and instead turns to gesture to the small boy, inviting him to stand beside him. He leans over to speak kindly to the boy who is obviously frightened of the attention of so many people. Hesitantly he stands but looks down, studying the smooth wooden table.

Once the boy is standing, Tor straightens to his full height once again, which might be intimidating if not for the softness in his hazel eyes. "As you all know, Malise and Aaron were taken not long ago. There were only two witnesses to the capture, Toby and"—he places a large hand on the boy's shoulder—"Damek."

If Toby saw it, why isn't he the one standing here, telling the story? He is much older and could've saved Damek from the task. I fear the answer is soon to be revealed.

"Damek, will you please tell the others what you saw? Do not be afraid; you are among friends. We need to know in order to help the others." I see the true extent of Tor's skills as a leader. Not only can he gain the attention and regard of a large room of peers, he is able to earn someone's trust, giving them the strength to overcome their oppressive fears. He has my trust as well, having made me feel welcome when I felt alone and confused.

Damek's eyes are focused on his fumbling hands when he begins to speak. "We were at the bottom of the meadow." His voice comes out as a squeak, and he clears his throat to continue. He begins to forget the many avid listeners as he relives his story. "That's where all the wheat grass was, and Malise said the cooks were running low and that we *had* to get wheat grass. Me and Toby were on one side, and then Malise and Aaron went to the other side.

"Everything was okay until I heard Malise yelling, and I saw her trying to pull Aaron away from one of the bad wingers!" Damek trembles at the thought; he shakes his head. "She wouldn't let go, and another one of them picked her up, and then they started to fly away!"

"And Toby? What happened to him?" Azura asks calmly, her hands folded on the table. Damek glances at her, and she nods for him to continue.

"Toby, he ... he ran after them! I didn't know what to do! He just started running through the woods!"

"In which direction?" Liam presses, his eyes focused on Damek's round face. "Where were they headed?"

"I don't ..." Damek struggles to remember and describe it. "They ... were headed toward the sunset," he finally answers and draws a steadying breath.

Tor nods as if he had already assumed so. He glances at Azura, who returns an expression of grave agreement.

"Thank you, Damek; you did well. You may leave. You've been through enough for one day and are ready for some dinner." Tor grins with a new idea. "Tell the cook I said you can have something extra for dessert."

Damek beams and scurries out the door with a newfound hopefulness.

When Damek is gone, Tor's face grows grim, and he lowers himself into his seat, suddenly under a visible strain.

"So they've been taken to the University caves," Dorian comments, looking around as if speaking for the others.

Tor looks up and nods. "So it would seem." He shakes his head, "Odon has been changing the courses of his army. We can't let anyone else leave the Great Oak until we figure out the new time slots of safety."

"I knew it; I knew something like this would happen. You wouldn't listen to me!" Finley's voice betrays his struggle to restrain himself. "We may be planning Odon's downfall within our tiny walls, but out there he's still doing just as much damage. You're so focused on Dorian's great destiny that you don't even realize what's happening around you!" He shakes his head. "I knew something seemed suspicious. He may already know of our plans …"

Tor maintains composure. "Finley, what goes on in this room is no small thing. We need to concentrate on our original decision. If we can picture our success, then we can make it happen. Guards, schedules—they'll have no meaning anymore. Odon will no longer have an effect on our lives."

"And if it doesn't work?" Finley asks, his gaze boring deep into Tor, forcing him to remember that time not long ago when failure caused innocent deaths.

"I cannot believe that will happen, we are too well prepared." Tor's head moves slowly back and forth, fending off Finley's words. Could Finley's pessimism be based on solid grounds? Or is he simply unable to let go of past mistakes that will soon be righted? *I hope so, despite my doubts.*

"Then why are we even here?" Finn asks. "To discuss something we're not doing anything about? Because I know you're not planning to form a rescue party. After all," he adds, an edge in his tone, "Odon will soon be gone anyway."

"The rescue party is already formed and in front of you. Whether Malise and Aaron are freed from Odon here or there makes no difference. We must not risk losing any more. Taking on too many tasks will only lead to our own demise. You have to think of the greater good."

Tor speaks stiffly, but I can tell he will not waver. I can't blame him. It is the strategy of a leader who must consider the many still standing around him, trusting him to save them. If one or two are sacrificed to ensure the survival of the majority, then maybe that is something we all must accept. I know it pains Tor to leave Malise and Aaron in Odon's clutches, but he must focus on the future and the others of the Great Oak. He cannot afford to lose anyone else.

Still, my heart is not as strong as his, and I was never born to lead. I can't leave them to be killed, or worse, in the dungeons of the

University—and who knows what has become of Toby? There must be a way to get them back, and if there is, I'll find it.

I feel Dorian beside me shifting nervously in his seat. Tor's words make him uneasy, and no doubt he is feeling the pressure of it all on his shoulders. I squeeze his hand in reassurance, and he leans into me.

Azura is the one to break the silence. "Tor, your words are painful to hear, but I know you speak truly. We all must be strong and use this situation as further motivation to be ready when the Rebirth arrives. I survived in the caves for a long time. Although it was a terrible place, I am able to move past my time there. As I'm sure Malise and Aaron will, they are both strong."

"But what reason could Odon have to keep them alive?" I ask. It is unlikely that Odon would have any use for two children part-bloods. I find it odd that Azura survived so long. The others look at me awkwardly. "I'm sorry, I was just wondering what Odon's motives would be for keeping prisoners."

Azura decides to explain. " If the Odonians learn that they were picked up in the middle of the forest, then he will want to keep them for questioning. He will value them for information on any rebellious activity." I see a shudder pass through her from some internal chill. Azura's expression is of someone who has stood facing the sheer drop at a cliff's edge, expecting to fall but being pulled to safety at the last second.

"So you believe the Odonians will keep Aaron and Malise alive to get information out of them? To learn of any other rebels?" I press, waiting for a definite answer.

"We can only hope that they can wait for us to end this," Tor says.

"So that's how we're leaving this? With a hope?" Piper's voice is strained. I can tell it does not feel right to her either, but I believe she trusts the others. After all, Tor is several years older and has dealt with such matters before.

Silence follows Piper's query, except for an audible snort from Finley, and the answer is understood. It tears at my insides. How can they leave two children who were born outside the University walls, pure and innocent? They may survive the experience, but will they ever be the same? Will they ever know happiness the same way? Or will they forever carry that scar within them? The same damage that dwells within Azura, that I can only presume marks my own soul. The thought wrenches me from my seat, and I find myself standing at a table surrounded by mourning faces.

My hand smacks the tabletop as I state my resolve. "I will go, I will find Malise and Aaron … and if Toby has been captured, I'll save him too."

Tor moves to protest but lets Dorian instead. "Oriana, no." He is pleading with his eyes, and he reaches for my hand as if to keep me by his side forever. "You don't know how to get past the guards."

"You can teach me. I'm a fast enough learner." I stare into his eyes, ready to dispel any other excuses he throws at me.

But it is Tor who speaks next. "We need you here …" He looks at me, trying to remind me with his eyes of my importance. Yet I hold an advantage, Dorian cannot know that I am needed at the Rebirth. He expects me not to go at all. I argue, knowing the others can't accuse me of being involved in Tor's plans.

"There are enough people without me. After all, if Dorian had never met me, you would've gone ahead anyway," I say, avoiding the stress of Tor's gaze.

"You're not going to the Rebirth," Dorian declares with a tone of finality.

"Exactly, that's why I'm just the person to go to the caves." An awkward silence follows, and I feel a bit guilty for arguing for my departure, even though I know I'm needed. Yet there's nothing they can say at the moment. Dorian does not know the underlying situation and I'm sure the others—Tor, Azura, and Finley—want to keep it that way. As far as I know, Piper, Lily, and the guys are still unaware.

But I know there is something about my words that keeps them from making further protest. As if they are hoping someone would step up and take action despite their plans otherwise. Perhaps it's the confidence in my voice, as if the task has already been accomplished successfully. I've even somehow convinced myself that there is no possibility of failure.

"You'll need to pick the lock … that could take weeks to teach." Dorian bursts through the silence triumphantly, knowing my ability to counter ends there. I have no idea how to pick a lock, especially under the pressure of urgency. I would need to be capable of succeeding in one try, and Dorian is right, that would take far too long to learn.

I shake my head, trying to fight through the setback. "I can pick a lock. I will go." I search the group and find Azura's green eyes upon me.

I cannot hide my appreciation, and I grin in spite of myself. "You don't have to do that. I'm sure Tor could use your help at the Rebirth."

Azura smiles blithely. "If you're willing to take the risk, then so am I. Together we will have Malise and Aaron back in no time. Tor won't have to worry; I will find someone to take my place just in case."

I look at her curiously. I nod assuredly, "Then I am thankful for your help."

"Tomorrow Dorian will teach us the guards' movements until we are ready. The following day we will leave at dusk." Azura takes charge, setting the time and place for the three of us to meet. Dorian's replies are far from submissive, but he offers no protest. Finley insists that he accompany us on the trip there—meaning that Jagger, Weasel, Dugan, and Buck are coming along as well. Piper and Lily plead to join us, but are sent to dinner by Tor who tells them they are needed here.

Once Piper and Lily have gone, Tor turns to the rest of us. "I can't agree with any of you leaving tomorrow, but I must insist that some of you men remain here. The more eyes to watch the skies tomorrow, the better." With that he exits somberly, and I wonder if maybe my actions have betrayed him. I still refuse to carry out his bidding and remain here. I could never forgive myself for denying Malise and Aaron rescue as soon as possible.

"Weasel and Buck, you two stay here. I have to agree with Tor, cautious actions must be taken at the meadow. We can't afford to go running back and forth trying to save more captured children."

Buck wraps a burly arm around Weasel's neck. "Me 'n' Weasey will keep watch. He's got the sight of a hawk with them big eyes of his." Buck lets out a rumbling laugh while Weasel shakes his head and grins, still caught by Buck's forearm.

We begin to stand, an air of apprehension settling upon us despite a definite course of action. I notice Liam still sitting beside Azura. I haven't spoken to him since my first dinner at the Great Oak. My first impressions were not entirely warm, but I did sense there was more to him than his harsh words. I watch him staring forlornly at Azura's slender figure, her chin tilted upward, her tangle of curls cascading over her shoulders. I admire her cunning, her ability to turn proposition into action. I can tell Liam is seeing the same in her, yet he finds it frightening. He grasps her with his dark ruby eyes, like fingers into water. Azura is unaware, or is she? Does she see his devoted glances?

I know Liam doubts both Dorian's abilities to perform as well as the solidity of Tor's plans. Yet he knows Azura trusts Dorian, maybe even that she loves him. Despite it all, Liam remains at Azura's side. Somehow I see this in his eyes. Somehow I can tell he's ready to follow Azura into the depths of Odon's caves, no matter what he believes.

He looks tired as he gets to his feet to follow her out of the meeting hall. I wish she would turn to see him, but Azura is deep in conversation with Finley about the safest actions tomorrow at the open field.

The weight of Dorian's hand in mine reminds me of his presence still beside me. We follow the others out of the room side by side. It has already gotten dark, and I shiver in the night air having left my cloak in my room. Dorian's arm is around me at once, and I am drawn into a moment of peace. I look up into his eyes, dark blue as the twilight's sky, making me think he could never turn against us. That he is as steady as the cycling moon, as grounded as the roots of the Oak beneath us.

"I need to talk to you alone," he whispers into my ear. I wrap my arms around his waist, our bodies pressed together. I am so fragile within his arms, and I sigh at the feeling of protection, safe from anything outside them. Dorian's hand strokes my hair down my back. I know what he wants to tell me. He wants me to stay here, safe, if not in his arms, then in the arms of the Great Oak where nothing can harm me. But I am not a child, I have a will of my own, and I can no longer let another decide for me. I will give him his moment to try and convince me, but nothing he can say will change my decision to go.

I tilt my head upward. "All right, but not here. We can go to my room."

CHAPTER TWENTY-NINE

Dorian and I face each other in the center of the room, neither of us eager for this talk that could lead to another argument. I light the lamp sitting on the dresser nearby, and its flickering light casts ominous shadows across our faces, the secrets and hidden emotions between us. I can see Dorian's eyes clearly. They have taken on a distant look. His eyebrows are narrowed as if he is in pain.

I extend my fingers to brush against his unshaven cheek. He has changed since the time we first met. His hair is disheveled, his skin darkened by the sun. He has fallen further into wildness. Has he been tormented by the task that lies ahead of him? I wish I could take away the desperation in his eyes, but his destiny was prescribed long before I was ever born, and it will remain to be fulfilled.

He reaches up and takes my hand. My touch awakens him from his thoughts. His smile warms me, and I smile back.

"Oriana, I sense the approach of the Rebirth. I can feel it within me. Not just the nearing event or my responsibilities, but the rise of something else, something powerful. It's as if I'm being slowly drowned, that it might overcome me, take control."

He shakes his head. "I don't know if I'm making any sense. So many things are happening at once. It's getting hard to find peace"—he reaches for my other hand—"except with you, Oriana. You make me see things the way they truly are. You take away the jumble of emotions inside me and leave me with one …"

I look at him oddly unable to hold back. "You've been so distant lately. I hardly ever see you, and when I do, you mostly have harsh words to say." The statement comes easily, and yet it sounds as if another person is saying it.

Dorian's eyelids fall as if struck by a heavy blow. I think at first he will not answer me, but at last he sighs. "I have certain reasons for that, not good reasons, but reasons nonetheless."

I raise my eyebrows. "Are you going to explain them to me?"

"I… there's no excuse for my anger; for that I blame only my own weaknesses. But for our time spent apart? The truth is … my own motives were to keep you from following me to the Rebirth." Dorian releases my hands, approaches the bed, and collapses onto it, rubbing his forehead with probing fingers. "Perhaps that was part of the reason why I caused you pain, to keep you away. I'm too dangerous now, and I fear what might happen to you if you were to become a part of the plans. I know I would completely lose control if anything happened to you."

My features soften. I take my place next to him on the bed. "That is the reason? You are worried about me?" I run my fingers through his hair, blacker than the shadows of the room.

"I can tell it hasn't worked, I just can't keep myself away from you." He smiles, catching my hand in his and kissing it, a glint of mischief in his eye. Yet he falters, and our hands slowly settle onto the space of bed between us. "I'd be lying if I said that's the only reason."

I feel a twinge of foreboding in my stomach and a lump in my throat. What else could possibly go wrong?

He notices my concern and waves a hand trying to wipe it away. "It's nothing we can be certain about … but Tor believes something happened to you when you were inside Odon's caves." He pauses. "It's probably better not to speak of …"

I remember Finley's mention of an injury I had gotten. He was reluctant as well to explain it to me. "But what does that have to do with us?"

"Tor thinks we might be a danger to each other …" Suddenly Dorian fumes with anger, and his hand clenches. "If Odon has hurt you in any way … I swear I'll—"

"To each other? You mean I might be harmful to you?"

"Never!" Dorian's hand cups my cheek, "We only thought it better to let you heal on your own, to keep you from worrying about my obligations. Yet it hasn't seemed to work, Oriana, you appear to be growing ill, becoming weaker."

His words worry me. What if Tor knows something I don't? What if somehow I am a danger to Dorian? He is right: I have lost my usual energy, and despite my days in the sunlight, my skin is paler, my hair without its luster. "Dorian … what if I'm a threat to you? It could be possible … if Odon—"

Dorian pulls me close to him. "No, you could never; If anything, I have been causing you harm. I've left you alone in a place that is still new to you, and now you're sick and leaving, and I can't even go with you to protect you!"

I look up at him. "I'll be fine. Somehow I know I will return." I want to say, *My role in this life has not yet been achieved* or *I must be by your side at the Rebirth*, but Dorian can't know of all that.

We forget about dinner lying beside one another. Dorian's arm creates a shield around me, his breath against my neck. His familiar smell of evergreens and everything natural lulls me into darkness.

Deep in my consciousness, I feel *him* there. He seems closer than ever, and in my weakness I know I can no longer run and escape his gaze. My legs are heavy, my heart beats on the verge of bursting. There is endless blackness, and yet I know I am trapped—unable to move, to run, to scream for help. I feel the whiteness start to well up. It fills my eyes. I am vulnerable, stripped, naked, and cold. It freezes my skin, which has turned as white as this light, a light that emanates no heat. He is searching my mind, clearing a pathway to all my secrets, my private thoughts. I realize it is not the lack of clothes that causes my nakedness, for I have no body in this place, but the lack of boundaries. As if a door has been opened into my skull for those eyes to violate. It probes with needled fingers, attempting to cast my final resistance aside and begin sifting through memories. I find myself pushing against the invisible force, straining to protect my mind, to keep from melding with his.

But it's no use. I've lost my usual energy. I've been drained from fighting night after night. I realize that even in waking I struggle, although it is easier to find myself when I am attached to my physical form. It's the nights when I become weak, and it's then that he strikes with utmost urgency. In my final efforts I feel the cold of his gaze numb what barriers remain. He smiles, yet I do not see it; there is no seeing, only sensing. There is no more resisting. I await the moment when he shatters the glasslike surface of my mind with one crushing blow. I tremble in place, bracing myself for the piercing pain.

The cold is so fierce that it turns hot, spreading through me in translucent veins. I realize suddenly that it isn't the cold but in fact a separate warmth. I sense him still near, confusion building in a cloud around him. He backs away, cringing from the heat as an eye from the sun. A new energy pulses through me, but it is not my own. The white shrinks away, receding back into those penetrating eyes, bleeding into their irises. I burn with a new strength, and the laughter that follows is my own, a triumphant cry as he moves back, fleeing from this fresh and foreign power.

I slowly surge into the space behind my eyes, feeling as though I have finished a pleasantly fulfilling dream, one far from memory but nonetheless satisfying. I open my eyes to find myself in Dorian's warm embrace; his steady breathing and stillness tell me he is still asleep. There is something moving about his touch. Watching his peacefulness slowly draws my eyelids downwards, and when I finally fall into a light doze, my dreams are of birds and fireflies soaring among the branches of an ancient tree in a time that is neither night nor day yet both.

When I awaken again, I feel more rested than ever before. I find that my cheek is pressed against Dorian's chest, while my arm drapes across his stomach. I sit up, my eyes easily opening, and my body moves with a refreshed strength. I notice Dorian is awake as well, as I stretch my arms over my head. We make eye contact, and he grins, unable to keep from snatching me into his arms and kissing me swiftly. When we finally separate, Dorian's eyes study me curiously.

He runs a finger along my jawline. "You seem different."

I laugh, "I feel different."

With a new lightness in my step, I walk with Dorian. The platforms are damp and cool, the roof of each cottage holds pools of water that display the result of a late-night rainfall. Apparitions of fog float in the notches of the Great Oak's arms, looking like great webs of glittering orbs. I pull my cloak further up my neck. The sun's rays are still unable to penetrate the veil of clouds and gathered moisture. The canopy has erupted with birdsong, proving that nature sees every day as one worth singing about.

I dare a glance at Dorian to find him lost in his own thoughts. I wonder if I somehow fit into them. It is in this moment that he turns to find me watching him and quickly takes my hand, as if I might dissolve into the air like one of the many wraiths of mist.

We make it to the lower level heavily dampened by the thick air. I can't wait to remove my cape, which now bears down on my shoulders. As we approach the dining hall's entrance, I see Liam and Azura attempting to speak in hushed tones that sound more like restrained hisses. Clearly they are having a disagreement of some kind. Neither has noticed us as Dorian and I come within range of their discussion.

"Azura, if you will not stay, then I am coming with you," Liam presses. His face is half hidden beneath a mahogany cape and bent close to Azura, whose frustration is clearly framed by an emerald hood.

"That's ridiculous! Finley has already elected to go; there's no need for you to come as well." She makes to enter the building, but he grabs her by the arm.

"What's ridiculous is … is …" Liam's grip seems firmer than he may have intended, and Azura yanks her arm away, her face aghast. The movement causes her hood to fall back, revealing a mass of curls that have formed more magnificently than ever in the humidity. Liam shakes his head, reaching toward her. "I'm sorry, I didn't mean to—"

"It doesn't matter." She lets her face fall. "This is something I have to go through with. I don't care about the danger, I can't let …" Then she sees Dorian and me emerge from the mist. Liam, following her look, turns to greet us with a nod, guiding his hood back to fall at his shoulders.

Azura smiles, taking on a formal air. "Good, I'm glad to see you both. The sooner Oriana and I start learning the counts, the better. I want us both to be well schooled."

If Dorian heard that bit of conversation as I did, he makes no apparent sign of it. "I agree, I want both of you to be well prepared."

I squeeze Dorian's hand, realizing that he does not like my decision to leave but has accepted it. Perhaps in a way he too wishes he could rescue Malise and her brother, but for him that is impossible. Dorian is too valuable to risk going. It surprises me that he entered the caves for Azura and me. Did Tor realize then that he needed me? That somehow I would become a key element in Dorian's success against Odon? Or maybe Dorian insisted on going, just as I am set on leaving now.

Liam follows us in silence. I know what he is thinking, what he really wanted to say to Azura but could not manage to. His worry seemed to come out as anger, criticism. In reality, Liam cannot bear to see Azura injured or worse. Watching him, I see the fear behind his melancholy eyes, fear that he could lose her forever. I begin thinking of ways to convince Azura to let him come. Somehow I feel it will help ease his concerns.

Before finding our seats, I follow Dorian to the fire where we each place our capes to dry upon a pegged rack situated nearby. I see that others have already settled their own cloaks upon most of the wooden pegs. I already feel more spirited. The blazes keep the building warm, drawing away the air's moisture and adding light to awaken heavy eyes. We take our seats, and Dorian begins to explain the basics of our plans.

Azura pulls out a pencil and parchment from her dress pocket and readies her hand.

"That won't help once you're inside the cave," Dorian points out. "It'll be too dark, and you'll waste too much time trying to read it by torchlight."

"I realize that!" she snaps. "It just helps me remember." She gives a shrug and then proceeds to write.

Dorian begins with the first tunnel, the number of guards, and how often they pass based on the number of steps heard at the entranceway.

"You must wait until they pass and the sound of their footsteps dies away. Then count to three and run twenty paces past three caves, two on your right and one on your left." Dorian recites the numbers with a concentrated stare, yet the calculations flow from him easily. He must have been working for some time on the plans. How did he figure them out?

By the fifth tunnel, when I've already forgotten most of what the first few tunnels contained and have mixed up the numbers of the rest, I am compelled to ask, "How did you possibly figure these calculations out?"

He stops abruptly. "It took time, lots of it."

Azura crosses her arms, leaning her elbows on the tabletop across from us. "I can assure you it was a very long time."

My eyes narrow, and Dorian can tell I'm not entirely convinced. I need more information.

"…but also some clever thinking," he adds, giving in to my inquiry.

I raise an eyebrow, intending him to continue.

"Well …" He scratches the back of his head, unsure where to begin. "I began by using the same methods as when I was at the University. Counting footsteps always worked for me. In the case of the tunnel, it was not so easy. I had to not only avoid the guards, but find the right passages. I camped out in the caves, memorizing how far I had gone and which tunnels I had taken. I went over and over them in my mind to make sure I had it right so that I could still leave them safely. After many days I had no choice but to find my way out. I had run out of supplies. I returned to the Great Oak to discuss plans with Tor."

"He allowed you to go in there on your own?" I ask, still wondering why he was the one, even though he is our last half-blood.

Dorian chuckles. "Uh … no, not really. But he let me make the final decision. I think I was still a bit overconfident at that point, having been sneaking around the University, and also meeting you." My cheeks redden, and I notice Azura's eyes upon me.

He continues, "Plus, I was concerned about Azura, and at that point I was the best person to go. I wasn't really thinking about anything else. I was certain I could do it, and no one else dared to enter Odon's caves. Many of the others believed that once someone entered, they never came out, at least not alive."

"So then how did you do it?" My eyes widen and I sound a bit like a small child hearing the tale of a great hero.

Dorian smiles at my eagerness. "When I finally returned to the Great Oak, I began revisiting the University. I had gone to seek anything I could find about my parents and then to see you." His hand secretly finds mine beneath the table.

"Basically, he completely forgot about me," Azura says, her green eyes flashing.

"Of course I didn't!" Dorian insists. "When I wasn't researching at the University, I was at the Great Oak discussing plans with Tor. We knew there had to be a way of figuring out Odon's maze." Dorian's eyes light suddenly. "Then it occurred to me that it might be simpler than I thought. I realized that Odon's guards were not actually there to keep people from coming in but from escaping. The whole time I had tried avoiding the guards, but I actually needed to use them to my advantage. My next trip to the caves, Liam accompanied me."

At the mention of his name, Liam looks up from his plate and nods, acting as though the conversation bores him. Yet somehow I sense he is honored by the recognition.

"Together we simply began following the guards, which was not difficult, seeing as they carried torches, and began to figure out that many of the caves connected. After finding the most direct route, we planned a day when Liam and I would make the trip. The others would wait outside the caves as reinforcements. By then you had been captured as well and had been placed with Azura, making the rescue more of a success." Dorian takes a drink of water with an air of finality.

"It also made Dorian some kind of champion," Liam mumbles around a bite of bread.

Dorian looks down humbly. "It's Tor that puts those thoughts in their heads. I couldn't have gotten far without your help." Liam catches Dorian's grin but makes no response, pushing food around on his plate.

An idea comes to me, and I can't restrain a mischievous smile. I force it away before it draws anyone's attention. "Liam, are you coming with us then? To get Aaron and Malise?"

This immediately rouses Liam's interest, and I settle back, satisfied. Unfortunately, Azura also hears my suggestion, and she is less pleased. "Certainly not, we already have enough people going," she says imperiously. "You and I will accomplish this ourselves, once we learn Dorian's plans."

"I only thought it would be wise to bring someone who has actually done it before. I think it would be to our benefit," I add, to make my intentions clear.

Azura glances at Liam waiting, for him to support my proposal, but he says nothing, although I can tell he is listening closely.

Dorian clears his throat. "Oriana makes a very good point. Liam is more experienced than anyone else you could bring." Without knowing it, he's helping achieve my goal.

"Only the two of us are entering those caves. That's how it must be." Azura's lips are tight.

"Fair enough, but Liam might help us before entering." I shrug offhandedly. "In case we were to forget something."

Azura thoughtfully shifts her gaze between us. "Fine then, I suppose you've made a good point. Although I doubt that we will forget anything. I plan on making this a well-organized operation."

I nod in complete agreement, grateful that Azura has submitted to Liam's attendance a day from now.

It is as this conversation concludes that Tor strides toward us at a speed only his long legs could withstand. We look up in alarm, awaiting his urgent message.

"Toby has returned."

CHAPTER THIRTY

Toby sits at the head of the meeting hall's long table, in front of the group that will be leaving tomorrow for the caves along with Dorian and Tor. A cup of water and plate of food have been placed in front of the boy, and he chews slowly, seeming to have little appetite despite an empty stomach. He takes heavy gulps from the cup, undoubtedly exhausted from his long run through the forest.

The rest of us watch him patiently but eager to hear his news. After all, we've only surmised that Malise and Aaron were taken to the caves. If they aren't there now, that means a complete change of plans, or maybe even a total resignation.

Toby finally takes a breath, and I can hardly breathe awaiting his words.

"I followed them all the way there," he sighs. "I thought maybe I could stop them, or at least keep them from harm, but I could only look on from below." He shakes his head. "Once they were inside, I turned back, knowing I had failed."

"Then they were brought to Odon's caves?" Finley is the first to speak.

Toby lowers his gaze to the food now growing cold. He pokes at it listlessly. "Yes, deep into the darkness," he says with a shudder.

"Toby"—Azura reaches across the table, placing a hand on his arm—"you did well. This is actually good news to Oriana and me."

Toby looks up at her with curiosity.

"We're going tomorrow to rescue them," I add, resolving the confusion on his face.

He looks at me in disbelief brimming on hope. "But … how can you? We are so close to the Rebirth, it would be too dangerous to—"

"I know we can make it. Dorian is going to teach us how," I explain with the same confidence as before.

Toby brightens. "Then I will come with you."

Tor places a large hand on his shoulder. "No Toby, you are to stay here. I think the others will agree. You've had enough running about for a while. You'll rest today, and tomorrow you can help here."

Azura nods. "We already have plenty of volunteers."

"You should rest and get your strength back," I put in.

Toby sags as he gives in to his weariness. "I suppose you're right …"

"Don't worry, kid, we'll get them both back safe and sound." Finley gives a wink and rises to leave, gesturing to Jagger and Dugan seated beside him. "C'mon, guys. We'll be heading to the fields to help out; there's still time before lunch."

Azura grins. "By that you mean diving into that river? One day you won't swim to the surface."

Finley has clearly heard because he pauses, trying his best to look wounded. "I'll have you know we've put a lot of time and effort into our work."

"That's right, breaking our backs!" Jagger adds with mock offense. He glances over to Dugan, who looks on coolly at his other side. When he says nothing, Jagger jabs him in the side.

"Uh … yeah, sure, slaves almost," Dugan finally states in his normal indifferent tone.

Azura laughs and shakes her head as they file out the door. I can't help but grin after them. I'm glad they will be coming with us tomorrow. Their light spirits will be well appreciated.

I notice Tor watching, standing at the corner of the room. He seems to be deep in thought, his face drawn with worry. It pains me to see him so distressed. His usual charm has been waning, understandably so during such hard times. I wish to see him back to his old self soon. Remembering the brilliancy of his usual glow, I have to believe it will not be long before it outshines his concerns.

He addresses us. "Now that you have the room to yourself, I think you should go over the steps for tomorrow. From what I understand, it is a complicated procedure." He studies each of us like a commanding father before leaving us to our work.

"He's right." Azura gives a nod. "We'll need the time and practice." She pulls out her piece of parchment scribbled with notes, and gestures for Dorian to begin.

Dorian starts to outline the steps, beginning with the first tunnel. I sit quietly, trying not to let my mind wander into all the things that could happen if I don't remember every single thing he says. Azura stops every now and then to repeat what he has said or to ask him a question.

"Then the last turn is a left," Dorian concludes.

"It's a right," Liam mutters. It is the first thing he has said since we came here.

"What?"

"A right."

"Oh yeah, that's it." Dorian shakes his head. "There are lines of cells. You should have enough time to find which one they're in."

"Okay." Azura sits back, lifts the piece of paper, and begins to reread what she wrote. "So it's …"

Hearing Azura restate it, I am able to fine-tune my memory. Finally she finishes, with only a few corrections from Dorian.

"This is going to take a bit of studying." Azura looks over her notes. "How are you doing, Oriana?"

I look up, not sure I should admit that I've already set it into my memory. Perhaps my memorizing skills are better trained, having been pressured to learn things quickly at the University for so long. In many cases I was asked to know lines of the text word for word and repeat it either orally or in writing. Yet I hesitate to explain this, unwilling to offend Azura by being ahead of her. She herself should understand the strict teaching in Odon's schools, but maybe since she escaped earlier than I, she's lacking in the same skill. I don't dare remind her that she made a mistake at her last attempt, which was why they captured her.

"More time would be helpful," I finally reply, trying to sound convincing.

Azura dismisses Dorian and Liam. After several protests, they eventually comply.

"We'll bring you two lunch in a little while," Dorian calls over his shoulder before following Liam out of sight.

"Good, now that they're gone, we can concentrate." Azura goes over the list out loud several more times. My mind begins to wander through the last few times. I can't help but wonder if maybe I should be listening more closely; best not to grow overconfident. I listen to her last words and am able to recite them word for word inside my head.

"I think I've got it, how 'bout you?" She looks up and I simply smile. "I think we can do this! I mean I'm really certain now." Azura folds up the paper and slips it inside a pocket within her robes.

"Of course we can." I get to my feet, feeling the hunger for midday meal.

"You finished yet?" Dorian peeks through the door warily, as if expecting an outburst from Azura at having interrupted. The more I get to know her, the more I see that Azura is actually harmless. Together, she and Dorian are like quarreling siblings.

I speak up before any altercation can occur. "Yes, and starving, I might add!" I notice that Dorian is holding a tray of covered plates and two filled tumblers. As he walks in, Liam follows. His eyes immediately seek out Azura, but she is too busy snatching the food and cup off the tray to notice.

"Are you certain you've memorized it?" Liam asks once we are finishing up the last bit of crumbs on our plates.

Azura shoots a glance at him, probably about to vent her impatience. But before she does, I see her eyes soften at Liam's honest concern. The earnestness in his eyes says everything. She shakes her head in assurance. "We're both ready."

Once outside the meeting hall, I see that evening has fallen. The clouds above are fairly heavy still. Apparently the sun's work must wait until tomorrow. Dorian waits at my side as Azura departs to the fields, explaining she will catch Finley and his rogues slacking off at the river. Liam follows after her solemnly. I wave good-bye to him, but he has been too deep in thought to notice.

Now I stand struggling with a sudden idea. "Dorian, I think I'm going to see Falda." Hearing her words always gives me guidance and calm; it feels like the right thing to do before our journey. She seems so frail, and yet she has accomplished so many great things in her life. The thought is inspirational.

Dorian's visible disappointment causes me to reconsider, but he says, "I understand, I'll meet up with you at dinner." His hand pushes through my hair to settle behind my neck.

"Thanks," I sigh, relieved by his response. I steal a kiss from his lips before he can say anything else and dash away toward Falda's cottage.

Facing her door, I call from outside. When there is no answer, I hesitantly knock on the cottage's side. I am uncertain how she will react to my unannounced visit. I have never come here on my own; Tor has always escorted me.

"Come in." Her voice is a soft murmur from within.

I enter, seeing Falda in her usual position, this time layered in a few more heavy blankets. One is draped across her shoulders, completely concealing the beauty of her wings. It is darker in the room than I've ever seen it, and I stop for a moment, regretful that I might have interrupted a time of rest.

Falda motions me forward, her hand peeking from between two of the woven shawls and then slipping back out of sight.

I grope forward and take a seat across from her, squinting till my eyes have adjusted to the dimness.

"Forgive me," Falda murmurs as her hands appear once again to light a candle on the wicker stand. As the flame lights up her face, I am forced to hold back a gasp. Dark circles shadow her eyes, and the lines of her face seem to have deepened. Her lips are surrounded by deep black niches. Even her pallor is a ghostly gray, despite the candlelight. I wonder for a moment if the change was occurring all along, or if it's emerged all at once. Have I not noticed it on my previous visits until now that it's unmistakable? I divert my gaze of obvious concern, not wanting her to see that her increasing age is becoming apparent.

"Tor has told me of your decision to leave," Falda states levelly, erasing any opinion from her tone.

I look down at my feet, recognizing the hollow in my stomach as guilt. After all, she recently told me that I was most needed at the Great Oak and should refrain from taking too many responsibilities at once. I had even made a point of agreeing with her logic. At the time, it was a correspondence easily made. Now I know it cannot be kept.

"Yes, I had to follow my heart." They are the first words of explanation that come to mind.

Falda's nod is grim. "I was once young and determined like you. In my old age I see the wisdom in staying safe, but having once been in your position I understand the passion for invincibility. Death does not become an option."

Her reaction is a shock. It is neither a definite approval of my actions nor the reprimand I've been expecting. "Do you believe I will succeed?"

Falda smiles. "I do not think you will allow anything less."

I can't hold back a triumphant grin. These are the words I needed, the guidance I wished to receive by coming here.

My lips tense as I watch Falda's face stiffen. "Still … there are many lessons to be learned by someone who begins to tempt fate. I can only warn you, they will come, and you will have to face them."

I study her, not sure how to take her words. They seem to limit her original reassurance. She seems a mystery to me.

"Falda, what was your life like? I've visited you several times now, and yet I still do not know your story."

She settles in her chair, sinking deeper into the mound of warmth so that the upper blanket sits just below her chin. "I will gladly tell you, my child," she replies. "I believe the old have a duty to tell of the past. Every life is significant, every life can teach a lesson to those just beginning their own. Mine is no different."

CHAPTER THIRTY-ONE

"I'll begin when I was about your age. Now this was a time before chaos, before Odon and the half-blooded tyrants. Life was relatively simple. Of course there were half-bloods and part-bloods by then, but there was no real danger to consider.

"It was during this time that I fell in love. It didn't matter to me that he was a part-blood and that my family disapproved. I thought of no one but him. I was still a Winglet, so my parents assumed that our bond was a mere infatuation that would vanish once I gained my wings and took to the sky. He and I would be of two different worlds then; we would have no choice but to separate. But as fate would have it, shortly after I became a Winglarion, I discovered I was pregnant with a part-blood child." Falda beams as she recalls this part of her life.

"Tor," I state with a grin, trying to picture him as a newborn babe.

Falda nods. "Yes, I told my parents and older brothers of the child within me, hoping that maybe it would prove to them my love for—" She pauses at the mention of his name, as if it is too painful to say. She draws a breath. "My love for Taurin, Tor's father."

She seems relieved once the name is spoken and continues on unwavering. "Of course the knowledge of my baby only fueled my family's anger, and they disowned me as their daughter. It was hurtful, of course. They would not acknowledge me or even act as though I had ever been their daughter. The hatred for those 'un-pure' was strong within everyone during that time. I suppose it never really went away."

"It will." I conjure this from little besides hope, and I have no proof that my words might one day be true. I fall silent, feeling foolish for having interrupted.

"I truly hope so, and for some reason I believe it as well," Falda responds, before going on. "I was able to deal with the separation from my family because I had begun to form one of my own. Despite my urge for the sky, for flight, I remained on the ground caring for Tor and sharing my love with Taurin. Soon any doubts of my rightful place were gone, I knew I had made the best decision, and things were peaceful for a while.

"It was when Tor turned ten that we started to hear of the half-bloods—at first little more than rumors that had traveled through so many ears and mouths that it was not certain they could be trusted. But then talk grew. About a year later we began to see the effects. Taurin and I found safety with our son in the forest, where we came upon the Great Oak." In her tone I can hear an affection for this great tree as for an old friend.

"The three of us began working on a place of refuge within its branches. Taurin would leave to seek others of the land, part-bloods who had managed to escape Odon's soldiers, and of course purebloods were welcome as well. Another year went by, and our community had grown. Tor was twelve, and despite my objections, he accompanied his father on trips to find others in need of protection. Sadly, most of those who came back were part-bloods, as I have told you before, and none were much older than Tor."

"What happened to their parents? Did any of them make it to the Great Oak?"

"Some did, but I'm afraid the generation was lost in other instances. I will explain soon enough," Falda hastens to add, seeing my grim face. It is disheartening to know that Odon was able to wipe out a whole generation. Could that be why the others are missing their parents?

"One day Tor returned with a group of young ones, but Taurin was not at his side. I immediately panicked, expecting to hear the worst from my son. His explanation was not far from it. Taurin was never the type to fight battles passively. I suppose he believed our efforts were not enough. Odon's power was increasing, and our secret group of rebels was doing nothing aggressive to stop him. So Taurin remained behind, fighting off what soldiers he could.

"You must understand that those soldiers were our own people who had been taken over by Odon; no one wanted to kill other part-bloods. It was why we reacted as we did for so long. Taurin felt he had to react in some other way. He led a group of fellow part-bloods, some parents, some not much older than you are now. Many were killed, unskilled as fighters and unequipped with suitable weapons. The following generation that remained at the Great Oak, too young to fight, began a tragic story of their own. Malise and Aaron?"

I nod unsteadily, not sure I am ready to hear her tale.

"They were born at the Great Oak, the first of a pure generation. Their parents loved them very much. Perhaps they acted foolishly, as the young often do, but they risked their lives as well, hoping to make the future better for their children. I suppose I don't have to tell you they lost their lives for it." Falda's head drops.

"Then they fought alongside Taurin?"

"No, not beside, but for an equal cause. They were among those lost during Kadin's attempt, but it was only a few years or so after Taurin's battle that it occurred."

I hold back tears. So many had risked their lives, many not far from my own age. I wonder if I will ever have the bravery that they did, knowing the numbers against them were so great. "Is that how Dorian's parents died? Helping Kadin?"

Falda shakes her head. "Oh no, their story is quite a different tale entirely. One with mysteries even I do not have answers for."

I realize I am leaning forward in my chair, and I settle back, offering to sum up. "So then they all died … or else were turned into Odon's slaves?"

Falda does not respond; she does not have to. "Taurin was the only one to return. He was near death when one of the children found him. He had dragged himself as far into the woods as he was able. He did not last the night …" Falda's voice catches in her throat, and she nearly loses the calm she has maintained since I met her.

"I'll never forget the look in his eyes. He died in this room, his head upon my lap. He had the most charming features: dark brown hair and eyes like the depths of the rich soil, and so tall. I thought nothing would ever bring him down, but that look in his eyes … it told of defeat, failure to protect his family, to triumph over evil. We were still so young, we never thought that good could not prevail. I only wish he could have died with a sense of hope …"

"But he must have!" I cry out as if the dead might hear my words. "He had Tor, Tor was his hope! The next generation, the Great Oak, you had found the Great Oak!"

"Perhaps you are right; I'd like to think so, but when I close my eyes," her lids fasten shut, "and I see his face …" She presses her lips together as if concentrating on the image, trying to find something more. She releases the hold with a sigh and shakes her head. "I just don't know, it is so long ago. Sometimes I can't forgive myself for staying behind. Sometimes I wish I had died with the rest of them. They were my peers, and now it's as if I am stuck somewhere between this life and their deaths."

"You did what you had to. The children needed someone to take care of them." I move toward her and kneel beside her seat, my hand upon her knee, "You became the key, the connection into the future. Your presence reminds us all of the past, of what never was, but of what is to come."

She nods as if the words are familiar to her, spoken perhaps by her own voice within her head. "Yes, I believe you are right." It seems that is not the end of her statement, but she says nothing more.

There is a moment of silence in which we retreat to our own thoughts and the invisible link between us is broken. I withdraw to my chair across from her, staring at my hands fumbling with the folds of my dress.

Finally Falda begins again. "Either way, my time here is soon to close."

I glance up at her. It is true she is advanced in years, but the tone of her voice seems much more certain, more an affirmation than something considered. "What do you mean? You have more years yet."

Falda attempts a frail smile. "I'm afraid it is not to be. The sky calls to me; it is a voice I have heard for many years. I do not have the strength to resist it much longer."

I am still confused and remain quiet, unsure of what she is describing, yet certain it will be painful to accept.

"If you had been raised among Winglarions, my words would not sound so foreign. There comes a time for all Winglarions when we must leave our homes to travel the distance into the world beyond. I have held off too long, perhaps in the belief that my presence was needed for a bit longer. You have proved that idea to be true, but now that my work is completed, I must depart soon, before my wings lose there abilities completely."

"But what about Tor? He needs you ... you can't just leave."

"Tor already knows of my plans. He understands I was never meant for the ground. As you will learn when you hear the call."

The idea still hurts, and for a moment I lose my compassion and speak in selfishness. "But you can't. That would be like giving up! Don't you want to see us succeed?"

"I will be watching you always, from the stars—much better view than in this old shack." She smiles. "I must fly to *him*, I must meet Taurin in the sky. I know he is waiting for me there. I gave up the sky to be with him, and now I must seek it to finally reach him in the end."

I hang my head in sadness in guilt at having placed Falda's wishes behind my own.

She raises her hands, indicating the air above. "It is where we all must eventually go; we lose our blood, our hair and eyes. We all eventually meet in the same place, no matter what or who we are by birth."

I think about this for a moment, the idea brightening my spirits. If we are all destined to the same place in the end, then maybe one day my family will be together again. Maybe once we have been stripped of our physical forms, then there will be no fighting, no more judgments and pain. Children can be with their parents and love whomever they choose. "When will you leave? I wish to say good-bye to you," I whisper, finally accepting her decision.

"I will not go when you are away. I will wait for you to return," Falda states, a relief in her voice. Perhaps she was nervous I might not forgive her for leaving.

"Thank you." I bow my head before getting to my feet. It is near dinner, and I sense that our conversation is at a close. "For all your guidance."

She nods, her eyes drooping, and I see she is holding back a yawn. "My wishes go with you on your journey tomorrow."

At dinner I sit beside Dorian, deep in thought. I sense the tension of the others around me. All are aware of our journey tomorrow. Even Azura is far quieter than usual, and the page of notes lies beside her plate of food, allowing her to glance at it between bites. Yet my own thoughts are on past events, not the future. I think of all the broken families, the ruined childhoods. Everyone seems to have their own story of sadness and loss. Falda's final statements repeat the most inside my mind. Her fateful flight, and her quest into the stars to join her kin. Are there really no distinctions up there? Is it possible that everyone can live in harmony? If there is a chance for us up there, then there may be one here as well. That night I watch the fireflies float above Dorian, and I am not certain of anything.

CHAPTER THIRTY-TWO

The next morning begins early. Azura is through my door before Dorian and I have a chance to compose ourselves. We sit up immediately, still dazed from sleep but clearly having shared a bed as well as each other's arms. Azura halts in the doorway, and a heavy sack in either hand drops to the floor.

My face growing hot, I leap away from Dorian and out of the bed. Smoothing my hair, I try to appear nonchalant about the whole incident. It would do no good to explain that Dorian and I were chaste companions the entire night. When I glance at him still beneath the blankets, he tries to hide a roguish grin by rubbing his hand against his unshaven chin—a gesture he repeats whenever he is nervous.

"What's going …?" Liam walks through the flap door. He need only glance from my red face to Dorian in my bed to draw a conclusion. He can't help a smile before striding back out again, only too willing to let Azura handle the situation.

"Oriana …" she finally begins, regaining her voice, "once you are"—she searches for the right word—"decent, then we'll be meeting at the dining hall. I've asked the cook to prepare an early meal for us." She snatches up one of the packs in confusion, as if unable to recall dropping it. "The other bag is yours; don't forget it." With that she dashes out after Liam. I have to give her credit for not losing her temper.

Dorian chuckles. "Well that was awkward." He gets to his feet and slips into his sandals and stretches his arms overhead. "Good, I could use some breakfast."

Even though I am shaking my head in disapproval, I can't melt the smile from my lips.

A few moments later, I have gathered my cape and satchel and am heading to the dining hall with Dorian at my side. I'm hoping it will be enough time for Azura to have forgotten her earlier interruption. When I see her standing at the doorway, hands posed on her hips and her foot tapping impatiently, I think otherwise. I hope it has not ruined our growing friendship. After all, it was only days ago that we were at odds with one another.

"Sorry … I didn't mean to make you wait." I speak first, hoping to be the one to diffuse the tension.

Azura's green eyes are piercing. "It's not you I'm waiting for." Her response brings instant relief. "It's that lazy Finn and those two slugs he has for friends."

I laugh to myself, heading past her into the dining hall where a basket of freshly baked breads awaits. Mixed fruits and nuts, along with boiled eggs, are also laid out for us.

"Dorian! You don't expect to eat, do you? You're not even going anywhere!" Dorian and I turn to find Azura peering in through the doorway at us.

"C'mon, there's plenty here!" He helps himself to a bit of everything, ignoring whatever else Azura has to say. Eventually she gives an exasperated sigh and lets the flap fall shut with a smack. A few minutes later, we hear her again in a series of reprimands, announcing the arrival of Dugan, Finley, and Jagger.

Dorian and I have taken seats on one of the benches halfway down the table. "I'm so glad I'm not them right now," he mutters. He then pops a whole egg into his mouth.

Finley emerges from the door first, looking even messier than usual. Jagger follows, making no attempt to conceal an expansive yawn. Behind him is Dugan, his sleek black hair neatly pulled back as usual, not a strand out of place. Somehow he manages to ignore Azura, close behind him and still scolding.

"Do you realize how late you three are? I can't believe you can sleep at a time like this! I don't know why I even bother letting you come! I'd better see your plates cleaned in under five seconds!" Azura is clearly stressed and makes no efforts to hide it.

The three seem not the least bit fazed about the situation, but I can't help feeling sorry for them. It is surprising that they have kept silent for so long. Finley gives me a grin as he sits across from Dorian and me with a plate full of food. Azura's ranting has finally come to an end; she either ran out of things to say or lost her voice.

I return Finn's smile, but it is also a reaction to my recent thought. Thankfully Azura cannot read minds.

Of their own accord, they finish their meals in moments, picking at any leftover crumbs. Together we deposit the empty dishes at the corner of the room where a tray has been left out. Luckily, Azura finds nothing to disapprove of. As we are gathering our things, Liam walks in through the opposite entrance.

"It's best we leave now," he announces simply. We comply without a word, following him out the door and along the lower platform. As the others begin their climb down the main ladder, I hang back.

"Dorian …" I cannot think what to say. I want to make so many promises, but I can't help hesitating.

"Just—please be careful," he says.

This I can promise, and I nod assuredly, letting him pull me into a close embrace.

As I latch onto the ladder and start down, I take one more look at him, wondering if it is as hard for him as it is for me. Dorian smiles weakly, and I can tell that it is. I look back at the ladder, focusing on the rungs beneath and in front of me. I am trying to concentrate on each step instead of the great task that is still far ahead.

We set out through the forest, away from the shade of the Great Oak and away from the rising sun. As we descend the hill, familiar from when I first arrived, we lose sight of the Great Oak. Apprehension rises within me, surely within us all. It is probably what causes the others to be silent. Yet as our steps continue and the distance from home increases, I begin to relax. Accepting the decision that has brought me this far and visualizing the desperate innocents awaiting our help.

It is a clear morning, save for the occasional cluster of whipped clouds, the last remnants of yesterday's fog. The wind propels them across the sky, now and again pushing them in front of the bright sun and providing a moment of cool shade. I take a breath as the same wind whips through my hair, picking it up from my shoulders and sweeping it from my face before taking a turn and lashing it forward. The wind finally surges past me, settling my hair neatly upon my back.

I find myself walking beside Azura. She has taken a pace behind the others. Liam walks ahead, Finley, Dugan, and Jagger in step behind him. Azura surveys them with an approving eye. Her nerves have certainly eased now that we are well on our way. I watch her eyes focus on Liam and linger. I chance a question from my recent curiosities.

"I do not know him well, yet he seems so quiet ..."

She turns, startled, realizing I have noticed her gaze upon Liam. "Of late? Yes, he has not spoken much to me either. The thought of more deaths is more painful to him than most. It brings bad memories of the past, when he was only a few years old." Her voice is low, and it is clear that she too is haunted by his memories.

A bird shrieks as it flies overhead, and we are unsettled for a moment. I look back at Azura, who meets my gaze. "What happened to him?" I ask.

"During the time of chaos, many part-bloods were killed. There had come to be so many, and Odon didn't see value in them. He kept some alive, mainly the young ones to bend to his will. But as in the other bloodlines, he killed many adults. Liam's parents had heard of the sanctuary at the Great Oak and of Falda, the Winglarion who could show them the way. From what I've heard, they had already prepared to slip away to the location where Falda's son, Tor, would lead them to safety."

Azura lowers her head, burdened by the knowledge; she concentrates on the ground passing beneath her. "They came across a group of Odon's guards searching for stragglers and hid in the nearby foliage. You see, Liam was so young then, only just able to use his legs, he had no idea what the situation was. He ..." Her gaze finds Liam among the others, his gait forced, his feet barely lifting with each step. Her eyes soften for a moment, and I can see she yearns to relieve his pain.

"He cried out unexpectedly, giving away their location. His father diverted attention while his mother ran for the woods where she knew Tor was waiting. Liam's father did not make it far before he was downed by an arrow. His mother soon realized she and her son would not make it together. So, she urged Liam to walk forward into safety, shielding him so that he might escape. I suppose I don't have to explain that neither of his parents survived."

I feel the searing pain of compassion for the boy, now a young man still dealing with the losses and guilt of his past. "So they saved him ... he never went to the University?"

Azura presses her lips together ruefully. "I wish that were true. Unfortunately Liam's small legs did not carry him far. Perhaps the weight of guilt slowed him down the moment his voice escaped him. For whatever reason, Liam was captured and did live out many years at the University until he escaped just as I did. I think that only made the whole thing worse for him. He not only blames himself for their death, but also that their lives were taken in vain. They had sacrificed, and he failed them."

"But it wasn't his fault! He was too young to know! His parents would not want him to live the rest of his life in grief for a mistake made in infancy."

She raises a hand as if in defense, although I did not mean to attack. "Believe me, I know the truth of it, but he will not see. No matter what I say to him, he will never release the burden. See ..."—her eyes flicker toward him—"even now he carries it like a sack of stones." I watch Liam move slowly forward, fighting each step as I had seen before.

I nod gravely. "It is so sad. Odon has caused so many deaths, but what is far worse is the wreck he's made of the living."

"Yes." Azura sighs. "I don't know how, but Liam's managed to live on. I thought his lack of will might ultimately lead to his death, despite how I've tried to change him. Still, something keeps him in this life."

I glance at her, wondering if she truly cannot answer her own question. To me it seems clear that it is Azura herself who keeps him alive. Yet the expression of puzzlement upon her face tells me she still has not figured that out.

Our path leads us to a clearing. Liam heads toward its edge, choosing to use the bordering trees as cover from the open sky.

"Stay close," he calls back to Azura, and we comply willingly, now that our discussion has ended.

"Look! Up there!" It is Jagger who motions toward a patch of clouds, stepping back into the shade of the nearby trees and waving the rest of us after him.

At first I don't see anything, merely the burning reflection of the morning sun off the starkness of the cloud. Then as the wind sweeps it aside, I see them. They emerge from the white canvas onto the rich blue of the painted sky. Their billowing white robes and feathered wings blended perfectly into the cloud, rendering them practically invisible. Now they are in clear sight. I count ten Winglarions, specks in the sky but still discernible. They shift the angles of their wings nimbly, using the currents to lift them into greater heights. I gasp as in one motion, together as if one creature they angle into a dive against the wind. The magnificent dive propels them out of sight, behind the treetops that block our view.

"Odon's winged soldiers," Finley comments with distaste. "We should be extra careful; their level of activity concerns me. He could be at odds with an enemy half-blood."

The rest of our trip we remain within the shelter of the forest, avoiding open fields and staying low whenever we crest a hill. By midday we reach the final hilltop, the spot where Dorian and Liam brought Azura and me after escaping the cave. I take a seat beneath the familiar shade of the fruit tree, imagining Dorian beside me offering one of the red orbs. Looking up into its branches, so lean compared to the girth of the Great Oak's, I notice that there are no more green fruit. The ones that remain have reached their full ripeness, but many more lie rotting on the ground beneath.

There will not be much time to rest before Azura and I enter the caves. But we take some time to open our packs and replenish ourselves with food and drink. I gingerly chew at a slice of bread, spread thickly with a sour berry jam.

Azura sits in silence beside Liam on a mossy patch of ground. Both chew on their lunches, deep in thought. Not far are Finley, Jagger, and Dugan who converse in low tones. Judging by their gestures and occasional glances upward, they are discussing the reappearance of Winglarions.

Our time of refreshment is soon over, and I sense the familiar sting of apprehension. I put away what food I cannot force myself to swallow and lean my pack against the tree's base. I discard my cloak as well, shrugging it off my shoulders. I know it will slow me down. Azura lays her own beside her pack. Both will be a burden to us once we are within.

Liam leaves our campsite, heading sideways into the woods. When he returns shortly after, he carries a foot-long branch that is thick enough to wrap a hand around comfortably. He coats the top with an oily wax that he has brought inside his satchel. Handing it to Azura, he says, "When you are past the first few guards you will reach a series of black tunnels. You can use this as a torch by lighting it on one of the lamps before then."

Azura nods; we are both familiar with the set of tunnels that contain no lamps. I make a mental note of the number of tunnels preceding them and then go over the guards, visualizing their stations and counting them inside my mental picture.

"And the Winglarions?" Azura asks hesitantly.

Finley approaches from behind Liam, flanked by Dugan and Jagger. "We'll keep our eyes upward. You just worry about getting in and out as fast as possible."

Together, Azura and I give a short nod, perhaps agreeing that it is the only goal our minds can comprehend at the moment. There are too many numbers, steps, and tunnels rolling through my head for me to be able to worry about something else.

The others follow Azura and me to the edge of the forest where the land slopes toward the black opening of the cave. Looking down at it, I cannot decide if it more resembles the pupil of an eye—or a gaping mouth prepared to swallow us.

I realize now more than ever how grateful I am that Azura is beside me, prepared to accompany me the entire distance. I steal a nervous glance in her direction. Her own eyes are turned toward the sky, noting our vulnerability once we leave the forest. I imitate her, scanning the blue expanse splattered with white. As far as I can tell it is clear.

Azura seems satisfied as well, and together we start down the hill. We walk at a brisk pace, unwilling to take the chance that someone is watching us from behind the clouds. Still, it is not solely the fear from above that plagues us, but the approaching hole—the entrance into Odon's caves.

There is no time to think or change our minds; once the entrance to the abyss looms over us, we have no choice but to enter. The danger from the skies outweighs the danger from within. As I step out of view of the sun's heated gaze, I'm jolted by the numbing chill of the cave's eerie breath.

CHAPTER THIRTY-THREE

"One, two, three ..." I hear Azura counting footsteps under her breath. It is the only way I can tell she is still standing beside me. The darkness of the cave we are traversing leaves me virtually blind. As she reaches three I hear her stop to move forward. I react quickly, grasping for her arm in the black emptiness. I find a fold of her clothing and hold her still.

"It's six," I whisper, counting the last three steps before starting forward and pulling her along with me. There's no time for wounded pride in here. We have to get the counts right, or it could mean not just our lives, but Malise's and Aaron's as well.

We take a turn into a lighted hallway. The guards have just turned the corner at the far end. Here we will light our torch and take the last few turns toward the cells. Azura wastes no time and reaches up at one of the flickering lamps. It is square shaped like a small house with a hinged door on the front. Azura opens it and thrusts the torch inside it. Flames engulf the tip in seconds. I turn my gaze away until it settles to a steady burning. With the glowing fire holding us at the center of a globe of light, we descend into the final corridor.

Azura and I are breathing heavily as we set off at a fast jog down the last tunnel. On either side it opens up to other turns that seem to beckon us into endless mazes of darkness. We pay them no heed, keeping our eyes straight ahead. As the tunnel bends, we slow our pace. I feel my muscles tensing from the strain. The long walk had affected me more than I expected; now I can feel its toll on my body.

Still I push forward, gaining a burst of new energy at the prospect of reaching our destination. After a final turn, a row of lanterns appears on the stone walls. We have reached the cells.

On either side, embedded into the rock, are heavy wooden doors. A sight that is not new to my eyes. To my left I spot the one most familiar, the doorway into the cell I had shared with Azura. I veer clear of it, moving past it to the doors further down.

Azura starts toward the far end opposite from me, raising the torch above her head so that she can peer on tiptoe through the door's barred window. In one hand I see she has already retrieved the thin stone from the folds of her dress. She must use it to pick the lock once we find Malise and Aaron.

I situate myself in front of one of the doors, raising myself as high as I can to see through the window. The room within is devoid of light, and without a torch of my own, I have no way of seeing in. "Malise?" I call, my voice bouncing off the stones like flecks of glass. There is no response. I move to the next door, repeating my previous actions; nothing. I continue down the corridor, calling into each barred window, holding my breath for some kind of sound. For a moment I think I have heard a reply, but I soon realize it is my own voice reverberating in the corridor.

This is taking too much time. I hear a whisper that startles me, but soon realize it is Azura, her torch above her head, searching the empty cells on the opposite wall. We should be leaving by now, and still we have not found either Malise or her brother. I didn't expect them to be so far into the tunnel of cells.

I force myself to increase my speed, taking less time to wait for an answer before continuing on to another doorway. The lamps around me flicker as I pass, their trembling reflecting my own inner fear. I notice Azura has quickened her pace, but the cells stretch on before us, and not one seems to contain our captive friends.

Finally I step to the center of the tunnel, positioning myself so that I face toward the doorways still before us. If they aren't here, we need to know, and we need to know now before it is too late for us as well. I take a breath, thinking through once more the need to take this step. If we don't find them soon, then we will be found.

I force a long call, "Maa-lise!" It is not as loud as I hoped, but still it echoes down the tunnel, scattering into many voices.

"Why did you do *that*?" Azura hisses. I see her eyes wide in the flickering torchlight.

"I had to. If we don't find them soon, we'll be caught anyway …" My voice trails off into a mumble. I'm almost sure I heard another one, not just an echo of my own.

Azura watches me. "I heard it too." She starts down the tunnel, the flames of the lamps reaching toward her like begging prisoners. "Malise?" she beckons softly.

First nothing, and then a sigh that seems to float to the floor: "Help …"

We run farther down the tunnel, and then we see a pale finger slid between the bars of the door.

"Hold this." Azura shoves the burning torch at me, and I snatch it away so she may set to work on the lock. I hold it above her to give light. Her hands are shaking, and we both sense the urgency in her work. Despite her nerves, they are well trained.

When I hear the click of the lock opening, I release my breath, using my free hand to help her open the door. Unexpectedly, Malise collapses onto the floor in front of us. Apparently she was resting her full weight upon the door.

Azura helps her to her feet. "Where's Aaron?" she whispers soothingly, trying to hide how frantic we are to be leaving. Her eyes search the cell, and I lift the torch higher to illuminate its depths. Aaron is nowhere in sight.

Malise finally gains control of herself. "They … they took him." Her voice is dry, and the light of the flames reveals purple circles beneath her black eyes. I wonder if she has slept at all since she was taken here. I'm certain she has had no food or drink.

"Do you know where?" I ask doubtfully. Malise may not even know where *she* is.

As I expected she shakes her head. She manages to get to her feet, using Azura's arm for support.

I look up at Azura, hoping she has some plan of action in mind. We can't just leave without Aaron. But one glance tells me she is as helpless as I feel.

"Could he be in another cell?" Azura ventures, taking a glance backward.

Malise shrugs, and the gesture seems to exhaust her. Have they already done their worst? Or is her weakness due to lack of nourishment? "I don't know, but I think they took him to the room ... the one for interrogation."

This makes Azura turn gray, and her face is too grim to look at for long. "Then we need only wait; they'll bring him back." Azura moves to heave the door closed. I offer my aid to Malise with my free hand.

"We should find a place to ..." My voice is caught in my throat. My gaze reaches past Azura as she shoves her weight against the heavy door. Her eyes meet mine, and she whirls around, a cry escaping her lips at the sight that has riveted my feet in place.

The Odonian's piercing blue eyes wash over us, showing a surprise that is soon overtaken by rage. Behind him two guards surround Aaron, each gripping one arm in a relentless fist. His head lolls forward below his shoulders, and a dark liquid leaks from beneath his hair. I can only assume it is blood.

There is a moment in which time stops. The fire freezes, I am not breathing, and no one is moving. I simply stare, the realization of my worst fears coming true, paralyzing every muscle in my body. We've been caught, and there's no escape. Odon will come for us, and we will never again see the Great Oak. Tor was right. I have betrayed Dorian. *How could I have been so foolish?*

The Odonian's mouth opens; then his jaw is moving, but no words are coming out. He was not expecting our presence either. His eyes keep me in place, familiar eyes that bore into my skull. Have I seen them before? They are focused solely on me, in—could it be recognition? Does this man know me? He is the first to move. He lunges towards me, his grasping fingers bent like talons.

Azura is the first to react. To my surprise she rushes behind the Odonian and forcibly shoves him into the cell. It is fortunate she had not yet closed the door. The remaining gap allows the Odonian to fall right through. Malise finds the energy to slam against the door, joining Azura in using their full weight to push it closed.

Then Malise grabs at Aaron, who is slowly gaining awareness. The guards holding him stand in bewilderment, unsure how to react without direct orders from their leader, the Odonian. Luckily no sound can be heard from within the cell; perhaps his head striking the stone floor rendered him unconscious. Just as Aaron is safely in

Malise's hands, Azura clicks the lock of the door shut, withdrawing her hand that still holds the smooth stone pick.

They hurry toward me. I suppose they haven't noticed that I still have not moved. I can't; something more than my own fear is keeping me in place. My vision is slowly fading, and a pain is rising from the base of my neck into my skull. A memory flashes, a white room, those blue eyes, and a voice. I try to fight it, the ice of grasping hands keeping me from escaping. They don't want me to leave, they want me here … they want me. My forearm burns, the flames of the torch still clutched in my hands, licking at exposed skin. When I drop it, the clatter on the floor sounds like a whisper far in the distance. It is the last thing I hear before I slip into darkness and silence.

I wake with what would have been a gasp if there wasn't a hand clasped over my mouth. I can't see anything. The cold damp of a stone floor beneath me shocks me more fully awake.

Malise speaks near to me. "She's awake."

"Where … what happened?" I struggle to orient myself in the blackness.

"Shh! There's no time for that now." That is Azura. "We have to get out of here."

I sit up, and the memories of the past few hours return in an onslaught—the journey through the tunnel, finding Malise and then the Odonian. I push that last memory away forcibly. "Where are we? Which tunnel?" There are no lit lamps on the walls. I dropped the torch among the cells. Did they pick it up?

"I … I'm not sure …," Azura says shakily. "When you passed out, you dropped the torch, and it went out. There was no time to get it; Malise and I had to pull you and Aaron out of there. Everything happened so quickly. We were just moving as fast as we could. There was no way of keeping track of where we were going."

"Aaron! Is he okay?" I recall the sight of him bleeding, hanging like a limp doll between the two guards.

"He is able to walk on his own, but we must get him out quickly. He is badly injured." Malise is the one to answer, her voice edged with panic.

"The question is can *you* walk? Those guards could come looking for us at any second. The only way we're getting out of here anytime soon is if we work together." I feel the warmth of Azura's hand on my arm, and I slowly rise to my feet, shaking off the lingering dizziness. Why has it happened again? What thoughts were going through my mind? The last question can wait. I fear that its answer will cause another collapse.

"I'm fine, which way did you enter from?"

"We came in from your left, and the tunnel continues down on the right," Azura explains, relief audible in her voice now that I am able to help.

"Okay, I guess we better continue down. Dorian mentioned that many of the tunnels are connected to each other. Perhaps we'll find someplace familiar if we keep going."

I realize that the situation is not as simple as I have made it sound. True, many of the tunnels connect, but many others are surely dead ends. We may get lucky and be in one of the joined tunnels, but then again we could be stuck down here for much longer, blindly groping for a way out or, worse, running into more of Odon's men.

"Let's link hands," I say, grabbing hold of Azura's. "We don't want to lose each other down here." Once everyone is accounted for, I start down the tunnel at a fast walk, hoping the pace is not too taxing for Aaron. I hope he has not lost much blood.

I extend my free hand, trying to keep from colliding with anything. It hits the rock wall faster than I would have liked. I'm grateful my hand reached it first. Feeling along the wall, I realize that the tunnel bends. "We're at a curve," I call softly to the others.

I feel back along the wall to see if there is another passage. Then it occurs to me that we may have missed several openings; without the torch there is no way of knowing. My confidence drops, but I say nothing. Instead I start along the turn of the tunnel, hoping my determined strides will hide my uncertainty.

My legs are aching when I reach a dead end. I wonder how Malise and Aaron are holding up. I only wish I could apologize for all the trouble I'm putting them through. They deserve a better rescue than a girl blindly running through the tunnels as their guide. I really messed things up by passing out unexpectedly. How could I have been so weak? I take a breath. Now is not the time to be doubting myself, not when we still haven't found a way out.

"This tunnel ends here; we need to go back and search the walls for a connecting tunnel. Don't wander too far." I hold back any anxiety as we release hands and separate. I focus instead on feeling my way along the far wall. I hear echoing footsteps around me, and there is comfort in their company. I continue along the stone wall, reaching out along its surface. I'm grateful for one thing about the darkness. The others cannot see I am near tears. The sound of my own breathing grows louder, muffling the others' steps.

 I stretch my hands farther, but the wall continues as solid as before. The footsteps grow louder, a fast heavy pace. *Is someone coming toward me?* I pick up my pace sliding my hand along the slick stones, moving back down the tunnel. And then it falls through, my hand reaches nothing, and as I probe the air further, I'm sure I have found an opening, one that brings a chilling breeze against my body.

 Just at this moment, as the footsteps are at their loudest, they attack. Before I can cry out or dash to avoid them, I meet violently with a body. The collision knocks the wind from me, and I am unable to shout a warning to the others. I start to fall backward, but am halted by a firm grasp upon my arms. Once I can breathe again, I inhale, filling my lungs to capacity, and then begin screaming.

CHAPTER THIRTY-FOUR

"Run!! Get out of here—they've found us!!" I shout to the others, hoping they can escape before we are all taken. The guard has a strong hold on me. I struggle, but he keeps my arms locked at my sides. I kick blindly at his legs. Someone is beside me, trying to help me get free – it's Azura. She is foolish for not fleeing. It's too late for me, I've already been caught!

"Oriana? Is that you?" The guard ... no, the young man speaks.

"Liam!?" Suddenly my arms are free, and I steady myself against him.

"Yes, it's me."

"Liam, what are you doing here?" Azura's voice follows in relief.

"Azura, you were in here for so long ... I got worried and came in to look for you," he explains.

"Then you know the way out?" I hear the slide of Malise's tired feet and Aaron shuffling beside her.

"Yes, follow me. We must hurry."

Azura takes my hand, and I assume that Liam has already taken hers. He leads us down the corridor. I'm grateful for not having to concentrate on footsteps, I'm already drained both physically and mentally. It's nice to be the one being rescued.

We reach a corridor with lamps, and I blink in the sudden brightness. Dropping hands now that we can see each other, Liam reaches for a blunt branch that has been tied around his waist with a sash and lights it off one of the livelier lamps. Before we continue forward, I turn to inspect Aaron, knowing of his injury. I kneel in front of him, trying not to look as concerned as I feel so as not to frighten him further.

"Aaron, are you doing okay?" I ask.

Malise still holds his hand protectively, "Of course he's not." I look up to see her eyes welling with tears. I've forgotten how young she is herself.

"Then I'll carry him," Liam says, blocking Aaron's gaze on me for a moment as he moves between us. I focus back on Aaron, an odd look in his eyes as he observes me. I am taken aback when I realize he is not the same Aaron I met at the Great Oak; he has changed. They have already changed him. I bite my tongue to suppress a cry.

Azura accepts the lighted torch from Liam. "Here, Aaron, climb on my back; you need to rest." Aaron's small arms clasp around Liam's neck, and he lifts himself to his feet.

We press on through the lit corridor. The tunnels ahead are familiar to me, and I remember the counted steps that follow. With Liam as our guide we make good time and are soon traveling down the final passage that leads to the outside.

The day is brighter than I remember, and I shield my eyes for a moment. After extinguishing the torch in the sand, Azura hands it to Liam, who slings it back through his waistband and starts toward the hill. We must reach the cover of the trees. I allow Malise to walk in front of me so she can keep a close eye on Aaron, who still has his arms clasped around Liam's neck. Azura hangs back as well to walk beside me, stealing wary glances toward the cave's mouth as we leave it behind.

Liam is cresting the hill as Azura and I start our climb. With each step toward the trees I breathe easier. The hard part is over; now we must get Aaron back to the Great Oak so his wounds can be tended.

Seeing him and his sister safe leads me to believe I made the right decision. I've shown that I can accomplish something great. Yet the thought of losing consciousness within the cave irks me. I wanted to be the one in control, someone dependable and self-reliant. Instead I turned into a dead weight. It troubles me that something so uncontrollable can leave me so helpless.

I watch and openly release a sigh as the others crest the hill. Malise and Aaron are both safe and soon will be far away from the Odonian's clutches. Aaron ventures a glance backward from his perch upon Liam, his eyes focusing on Azura and me. He seems so different. Perhaps he's just tired.

My stomach drops as his gaze moves upward, toward the sky directly above us. It is the sight of his face, black eyes widened, mouth gaping, that tells me everything. Malise is shouting at the top of her lungs as I turn to look behind me, only to have my fears confirmed.

A male Winglarion is seconds away. His broad shoulders and the magnificence of his long golden hair and wings in the sunlight might have once been cause for admiration. However, in this moment I know too well his intentions. His wings pummel the air, sending shocks of wind that push Azura and me to our knees. Sand and debris become airborne, and it's impossible to see clearly.

Between gusts I see his strong arms clamp around Azura in one swift movement and begin lifting her from the ground. Quickly I throw myself at her, clutching her by the waist and trying to be heavier than I actually am. The Winglarion's wing beats falter but not for long. The astonishing span of them might manage to haul us both away. Azura is struggling, trying to keep him off balance and force him to release her arms.

My eyes and skin are burning from the constant whipping of sand all around me. I feel as though my arms might fall off, but I dare not release Azura. Without my weight, the Winglarion could easily fly away with her. I open my eyes for a moment, desperate to take in the scene around me.

My view is of the sky and a line of Winglarions diving directly toward us. One is a worthy opponent for both Azura and me; if the others reach us, we'll be gone in a heartbeat. I shut my eyes tightly, hoping it will end, that it is all a dream and I am still in the cave, passed out in the darkness of a corridor. Azura has given a final twist, hoping to wrench herself free, but the energy is wasted. I will not let her be taken alone, I got her into this mess, I will take whatever punishment she must.

In the whistling of wind past my ears I hear a voice. Is it a cry of triumph? Or one of despair? Am I imagining the sound of Dorian's voice when he discovers I will not be returning to him? No, the shout is real, from someone beside me. I strain my eyes open, squinting in the tornado of dust. Liam leaps through the air at an impossible height. His outstretched hand bears the weight of a wooden club, the torch. His arms are tensely corded as he strikes the back of the Winglarion's head, rendering him limp and dropping us to the ground.

I scramble free, letting Azura go and getting to my feet. We are not safe yet. Liam tears the winged man's grip off of Azura and hauls her to her feet in what seems like one movement. Her arms are already bruising from his damaging grip. She is still in shock as we bolt for the woods, forcing Liam to scoop her into his arms. From beside him I watch in awe. His speed never slows, his arms remaining strong and true, carrying this most precious burden. Finley is halfway up the hill, where he takes me by the hand and launches me forward, providing me with the help I need to scale the incline.

Once under cover of the forest, we continue with steady speed through the trees. Finley guides us, whipping past branches that seem to reach for us and score any exposed skin. He narrowly skirts growing obstacles, leaps over tumbling roots at the last second. Our breaths come in heavy bursts, louder than we would like but as quiet as our lungs will allow.

Finley leaps over a downed tree, its roots fanned upward in a network of lifeless shoots. I vault over its side, grateful for the extra lift that Finley's hand provides. Beyond the trunk I discover a drop much further than I had expected. I hold my breath as I make a crumpled landing, absorbing the shock through my knees. No time to recover; Finley pulls me back, into the shallow crevice beneath the tree's side.

Jagger and Dugan crouch beside me, pushing Aaron and Malise behind them, forming a protective shield for the two children. Finley pushes me behind him, further into the dampness of soft earth and decaying bark. Azura and Liam slip in beside me, side by side, their hands maintaining a tight grip.

We stay there for a long time, trying to breathe silently, tensing our muscles to avoid the slightest movement. It feels like hours later when Finley emerges from the crevice, easing himself into the sunlight, his face toward the sky. Jaggar and Dugan are next, flanking him. The rest of us follow soon after.

Azura separates from Liam to stand beside me. I feel as though our bond has flourished in a very short time. We have been through so much too quickly. The memory of everything sweeps over me in blurry images.

When I make my own assessment of the sky, I'm relieved to see no more than a distant cloud, innocently gliding toward the horizon. I notice the sun descending toward the west. A steady hike home will get us there in time for dinner.

I search the others for Aaron, remembering his injury and sensing his need for care. Malise supports his arm as he lowers himself to the ground. As I approach, Azura notices my movement and follows. I kneel beside him, trying to get a better look at the damage that had the dark brown hair upon his forehead soaked in blood.

"May I take a look, Aaron?" I ask reaching up to pull back the sweep of bangs and expose the injury.

Aaron nods, but with little energy; he is still losing blood.

Lifting away the plastered hair, I see the result of Aaron's time spent with the Odonian. A gash, starting from the side of his forehead and slicing through his eyebrow to the corner of his eye, is steadily oozing. Although his eye is presently swollen, I do not see any impairment to his vision as the gash stops abruptly above his lid.

Azura rips at the bottom of her skirt, tearing off a long stretch of fabric. "Are the packs nearby?" she asks anyone.

"Dugan and I grabbed as many as we could." Jagger walks up to us and raises two bags in one hand.

"Good, get out one of the canteens," Azura orders as she presses a folded piece of cloth against Aaron's injury.

Jagger hands her one of the filled canteens from within a pack, after undoing its cap.

Azura pours the contents onto the fabric and applies it to the wound, gently cleaning it. She then pours some slowly into his hair, washing out the layers of blood and grime. Aaron is still and silent, although every few moments his lips tighten in pain. Malise is beside him, holding his hand and remaining quiet even when he squeezes hers too tightly.

Watching them makes me think of my own sister. But Lenora is so far away, perhaps even further internally than physically. I try to picture her face, but I can only imagine parts of it. Her nose, slightly turned up, the gold of her hair ... traits that are easy to see because they are so similar to my own. I can only hope that someday it will be possible to put aside our differences, forget our past, and realize how valuable a sister can be.

As Azura is completing her work, I search through the remaining packs, four altogether, and find two relatively full canteens. I hand one to Malise and then the other to Aaron, who both accept them gratefully.

Despite our bodies' need for further rest, our desire to reach the Great Oak before nightfall soon has us hiking eastward at a quick pace. We take no more breaks, except a short stop to allow Aaron to climb onto Finley's back. It is sunset when we reach the base of the Great Oak. My lips are parched and my legs ache, but the sight of the magnificent tree is enough to forget all of it. The ladder has already been dropped, and I see two figures descending the many rungs with an urgent speed.

I squint my eyes, attempting to discern the person furthest down the ladder, "Dorian …?" I hurry to close the last distance between us. As Dorian reaches the ground, I see that the following figure is Tor, his height allowing him to look over Dorian to see I am all right. His evaluation is a short one, because I am soon enclosed in Dorian's strong frame, his arms holding me firmly, taking the weight of my own body away from my weary legs.

I pull away sooner than Dorian must have wished, as my thoughts return to Aaron and his sister. Both are in worse shape than I and need food and rest. Aaron, who had been sleeping upon Finley's back, his head lolling on one shoulder, is now awake and insistent to be on his own feet. Tor strides quickly to Malise and embraces her with a hug. His large shoulders, which once seemed immovable, collapse in relief at their safety.

"Food and drink have already been laid out for you both in your rooms," Tor says with a fatherly air.

Malise's eyes light, the child within shining through, and she heads for the ladder. Aaron follows behind, insisting that he is capable of walking on his own now. Yet I notice his skin has grown paler. Finley starts up the ladder behind them, his gaze steady on Aaron. Jagger and Dugan are right behind him.

The rest of us stay behind, forming a circular group. My stomach drops, for I'm certain that Tor will ask for a full report. He is probably already suspecting something since we arrived later than planned. Azura glances nervously my way but lifts her chin with dignity when Tor addresses her. Liam is at her side, his shoulders drooping with exhaustion. Does she notice his gaze upon her never falters?

"So you've made it back in one piece." Tor ruffles the mess of curls on his head and gives a quick nod, a grin spreading across his face.

Dorian is beside me, slipping his hand in mine and pulling me close so that we touch slightly at the hip.

Azura's head is still lifted as she replies. "Yes, we made it," she says simply.

Tor eyes her, trying to read the unwavering expression on her face. Yet Azura is too stubborn to let any evidence of our mishaps show. Tor develops a new strategy. He turns to me.

I feel my eyes widen. I know Dorian is directly beside me. He will be furious when he learns what we faced. He might never let me leave the Great Oak again. Despite my years at the University, I know I've never mastered the art of remaining expressionless. Now my eyes betray me once again.

"Oriana ... I know something delayed you; the sun has nearly set. What happened back there?" This time there is no humor in Tor's face. The dimples have vanished. He wants an answer, and fast.

My mouth opens, but no words come out. I know it was my fault that we got lost in the tunnel, which is bad enough. But to tell him that a Winglarion had nearly lifted Azura and me away? That was too near a miss. "We ..." I eventually manage.

"It was nothing we couldn't handle," Azura interrupts. "Tor, you need to have a little faith in us! We're not children anymore." With that she strides toward the ladder. I give a nod over my shoulder before moving after her, relieved that the pressure is no longer concentrated on me. Dorian releases my hand, hanging back to speak with Liam. I decide not to look back at them. Instead I concentrate on the rope ladder ahead.

A young girl's scream erupts in the sky above. Azura and I jump together in surprise and then turn our faces upward. I gasp, a small figure is hurtling downward through the branches. The body collides with thin growth as it falls, narrowly missing a large bough.

"Aaron!!" I scream, trying to halt him midair in an effort of willpower. Yet he continues to fall, his arms and legs limp, his head

bent backward. He must have passed out from the loss of blood. I try to estimate his landing spot, but it is impossible. From where I'm standing it seems the pathway of his fall is leading him directly into one of the Great Oak's mighty arms.

CHAPTER THIRTY-FIVE

I watch in horror as the small boy, once so close to safety, now approaches death. There is no one to save him; the Great Oak's arms were not meant for catching children. I expect the worst. How can he survive a landing at such speed?

He passes under a shadow as she is about to take him. The white wings maneuver through the air in graceful beats, speeding toward him, avoiding every branch with cunning. Her arms reach out to him, a stunning wraith, her white robes glowing within a golden aura of sunlight as he softly settles within her grasp.

She hovers for a moment before whisking forward once again, silver hair flowing past her and upward. Her body arcs in one fluid motion as she descends, the boy cradled in front of her, his head pressed gently against her shoulder. She spirals in bliss, the wind, every current a familiar companion more fitting than the ground beneath her feet. She extends her wings in the last distance, fighting the desire to pull upward once again, away from the land and further into the sky. Her feet meet the grass, toes touching first, and then she walks toward us.

Falda folds her wings behind her, subduing their urge to expand again as she has done for many years. Aaron stirs, still within the safety of her arms. Tor is at her side immediately, taking the boy from her, his eyes never leaving his mother's face.

I approach them, my legs feeling wobbly and unsteady. The shock of the situation still affects me; so many close calls in one day.

My gaze is upon Falda and how different she appears. Her hair has settled wildly upon her shoulders, many of the neat braids creeping apart. Her robes are misshaped, creased and pulled in all directions. But despite her disorder, despite the new look of fierceness in her eyes, she is radiating with a glow of pure beauty, pure joy. To see her standing on the ground, to recall her in the platform cottage, rocking upon a stationary chair … my only perspective of her seems utterly unnatural. Her wings seem not as graceful, folded awkwardly upon her back, her hair not as alive as it folds around her shoulders. Seeing her in the air, I understand what she gave up for the ones she loved—the sacrifice she made, regardless of whether it saved her from being captured. She was never meant for this realm, but for the one above. Where the canopy is not that of a forest's fingers, but the endless expanse of a starlit ceiling or a maze of nimbus pillows. Will my toes one day touch this soil for the last time to join her in the sky?

Falda's attention is drawn to me as I reach her side. "Oriana, my dear." Her growing weakness shows in her smile, and I see that the flame in her eyes will be short-lived. She smooths the hair down the side of my head. "I have waited for you to return."

I nod, the tears already threatening to escape and a lump forming at the back of my throat. I know if I answer in words, it will come as a sob.

Falda looks toward Aaron, who is safely held by Tor. He has turned a grayish color, with beads of sweat forming upon his brow. A grim expression masks his once innocent face. Tor glances from his mother to me before striding toward the ladder with the boy. Others are already upon the ground, having witnessed the event and brought supplies from above to improve Aaron's condition.

I turn back to Falda. "I am glad you did, for Aaron's sake as well." I can't hide the shakiness in my voice, and before I can react, my cheeks are wet.

"Oriana, do not cry, I leave you now, but we will meet again." She wipes a droplet from my cheek with her thumb.

"It's just that … I wish you could have been free"—I gasp, still trying to hold back the tears—"in the sky like the other Winglarions. Instead of having to give that up."

Falda smiles and looks upward, yet she is not concentrating on the sky, but the height of the Great Oak. "My life was exactly how I wanted it to be. It was my decision to remain with my son and Taurin.

I have no regrets about that or my time spent at the Great Oak. After all, it is where I was able to meet you." She looks sideways at me and then focuses once again on the tree, studying it like a close friend.

"I've grown to love this tree. We share the same stubbornness in our old age, but I'm afraid her body will remain long after we have all moved on. Yet that only makes me feel sorry for her; it must be a lonely existence to see so many die before you." Falda sighs and lets her gaze fall. "I, on the other hand, have seen enough deaths in my lifetime. I am ready to move on and reunite with them once again."

I am warmed by Falda's words and her compassion for the ancient tree. In all the Great Oak's magnificence there is a sorrow rooted deep within her body, something I believe all her inhabitants can sense. It is a heavy weight that we all carry with us, having faced countless deaths in our lifetimes. Perhaps together our shared sadness keeps us standing tall, refusing to be knocked down, and instead growing upward into the future with every new hopeful sprout upon the Great Oak's branches.

Falda has lived with this weight long enough. I can see she is ready to leave this world behind, to find Taurin and her family somewhere in the sky. Somewhere far from half-bloods, part-bloods, and purebloods. Where there is no distinction between Winglet or Finlet, where the sky, land, and ocean come together, and we are all one.

I do not say anything as I reach out to embrace her, my hands brushing the softness of her delicate feathers. I hide my tears. They are the result of my own selfish desires not being met. She kisses my forehead as we separate. I take a step backward, not realizing that Tor is beside me, taking my place as he hugs his mother. He embraces her tenderly, squeezing his eyes shut like a little boy.

A hand grasps my own, pulling me backward into a warm body. It is Dorian who holds me up, and his touch keeps me from crying out.

When Tor retreats with red eyes but his back straight, Falda spreads her wings. With a sigh of satisfaction she sweeps them downward, her heels lifting up, followed by her toes. She sweeps them downward again, the rush of air flowing over us, my hair blown back from my face. Falda rises into the air. Her wing beats increase with each stroke. Her pathway is along the Great Oak's side, as she lifts further into its branches. I am mesmerized once again by the beauty of her movements, how easily she slides through the currents. The sun strikes her wings before she passes behind a bough, the reflection virtually blinding, and then she is gone. Vanished into the canopy above.

It is today, in this moment, that I make a decision. One I cannot tell Tor, Azura, or my friends at the Great Oak, and one I can certainly not speak of to Dorian. The danger means nothing, the risk is worth taking, and failing to go through with it would mean wondering for the rest of my life. In Falda's absence I can feel it, the loss of knowing I will never see her in this world again. I loved her, and seeing her disappear has made me experience how fleeting life can be. So many words come to mind, things I should've said, confessions of my gratitude for sharing her wisdom with me. Yet time cannot reverse; what is lost is lost, and perhaps it is this helplessness that causes me to choose a certain path. I decide to return to the University to find my sister, Lenora.

Dorian's hand pressed in mine brings a wave of guilt. I know when he discovers me missing, it will cause him worry and pain. But he cannot go after me; no one can. It is days before the Rebirth, and they know as well as I do that there will be no more rescues. "How many days?" I speak the words softly and then clamp my lips together to prevent any more. I hope no one has heard or understood the meaning of my fragmented sentence.

"Three," Dorian answers, the shadows of the foliage above twisting across his face. Looking up at him, I see he thinks nothing of my outburst.

The sun is settling into the horizon as we climb the long stretch of ladder to the Great Oak's first platform. I wonder if Falda has found him yet, Taurin, and if they are flying among the stars with the others of their time. I pause a moment, looking out into the expanse of sky beyond, where the sun ignites the strip of ocean and the trees become one glowing blanket. Behind me, the night sky is a dark violet, deepening into black as it rises. I notice the first stars opening their eyes to each other, sharing their radiance. I shed a final tear, somehow certain that Falda has found her own place among them.

Dinner is silent, the day's events wearing on everyone. I sit beside Dorian, Tor, Azura, and Liam in their places around us. Three days; that gives me enough time. I will leave tomorrow evening and return that night, by early morning at the latest. If I remember the map correctly, the University is at a direct diagonal to the base of the Great

Oak. I will return to the meeting hall before I leave and borrow the most accurate map I can find.

For a moment I realize the true extent of what I'm planning—to betray my friends, to lie to them, and steal from them. Yet I know they would not let me go, and it is what I need to do. Lenora is in the University somewhere. She's still living in that environment. What if she is suffering as I did? I could never forgive myself for leaving my sister in such a place. If she only knew we are twins, then I'm sure she would change her mind. Maybe even come with me back to the Great Oak. I have to believe that she will, I at least have to try. She is the only family I have left. Right now, whether she realizes it or not, Lenora needs me, and despite whatever wrongs she's done, I need her too. My mind is settled; I will seek her out within the University walls.

The night is short. When we have finished eating, Dorian and I return to my room. I see the relief on his face. I'm back, safe and unharmed. I avoid his generous gaze, the admiration in his eyes and the small curve of the side of his mouth. Tomorrow I will be the one to take his ease away once again.

I say nothing as he gives in to the urge to take me in his arms. It feels true, honest, as we are always meant to be. I follow him to the bed, my aching body collapsing beside him on the soft mattress. With Dorian's hand upon the inward curve of my waist, I fall into a dreamless sleep.

I awake with a single thought: the Rebirth is in two days. I sit up. Tonight I must leave for Lenora. Dorian wakes next to me, pulling me back down to lie beside him. I shift to face him, sharing a comforting look. He strokes my hair, his eyes shifting back and forth to study each of my own individually.

"I worried about you ... I couldn't stop thinking that I might lose you forever," he says with a look of vulnerability.

"I thought of you too," I reply and then feel compelled to add, "But it was something I had to go through with."

He eyes me curiously for a moment. I am speaking of the past and yet I am confessing about the future. His face relaxes. "I'm just glad you've returned safely." He presses against me and shares a lingering kiss that makes it hard to even think of ever leaving him again. My spine is still tingling when he pulls away. My hand rests on his chest. I see only him and know only this moment.

I sit up quickly, shaking away my mesmerized state. He knows too well how to keep me from the rest of the world. It makes me smile to myself as I get to my feet, brushing my hair out with my fingers.

"You're leaving?" Dorian asks, lying sideways and propping his head on his hand.

"We can't stay in bed forever!" I remark, searching for where I discarded my sandals in the dark last night. I can't help but notice the way Dorian is grinning openly as he shifts onto his back, folding his arms above him. He chuckles to himself in a distant thought.

I can't resist throwing one of my discovered sandals at him. "Stop thinking so loudly!"

He jolts upright, rubbing his forearm where the sandal hit. I barely have time to react before he is chasing me out the door, one sandal upon my foot, and the other one in Dorian's threatening throwing arm. We dash past a blurred Piper and Lily on our way to the dining hall and barely see Toby, Malise, and Aaron on the lower platform. When we've reached the entrance, I am out of breath, and I have the feeling that Dorian has let me escape him for most of the way. When he catches up to me, I am backed against the wall, bracing myself for whatever revenge he has planned. Instead, he kneels before me, lifting my bare foot and slipping the sandal gently onto it. I watch from above, stunned.

He straightens up again and offers me his arm, which I graciously take, allowing him to escort me into our morning meal. At breakfast he is quick to cater to my every want, and he even joins the others and me in the field where together we gather a mixture of herbs and berries. At one point he beckons, and I follow him away from Piper and Lily who are picking through a bush of berries to find the most ripened ones.

He guides me through the trees, eventually taking my hand, reminding of a time not long ago when we were together in the garden. The foliage thins, and I see a small clearing centered by a lush fruit tree, its branches bearing the reddest, plumpest fruit I have ever seen. At its base, a large root erupts from the ground, providing a perfect seat for two. I gape in wonder at its quaint beauty.

Dorian leads me to the curved root, where I take a seat, and then steps away, only to return shortly with two of the tree's best offerings. He takes a seat beside me, handing me the redder of the two, and the scene reminds me of our shared moment just after we had escaped Odon's caves. Is the relation significant? Will this be my last day at the Great Oak, just as the previous occurrence had begun my first? Do I follow through with my plan? Is it really worth losing all this?

Dorian must notice the strain on my features. "Is something wrong?" I shake my head, smiling, and take a bite of the fruit, the taste bittersweet in my mouth.

As we walk back to the field, I see Malise and Aaron side by side searching through the tall grass. Would Malise have left her brother behind if we had not found him in time? Of course she would not. How then can I enjoy happiness here, knowing my sister is still experiencing that kind of life?

By midday Piper, Lily, Toby, Malise, and her brother as well as Dorian and I head to the river. Already diving from the rock cliff and swimming below we find Finley and the four others. Through the spray of falls I can see Dugan as he descends a smooth arc into the gorge of rushing water below. This time as we approach the river from the forest, just looking upon the height of the cliff makes me shiver.

Dorian lifts his shirt off over his head, his gaze focused on the ledge above. Piper and Lily slip off their dresses, revealing cotton undershirts and shorts underneath. I decide to sit out, knowing that in a short while I must think of some excuse to return to the Great Oak on my own.

Malise and her brother find a place upon the shore, sinking their feet slowly into the running water. Toby follows Dorian around to the incline that leads over the river and above the falls. I watch him ascend the hill and disappear behind a stretch of trees growing upon the angle of the ground beneath them. Moments later, he appears at the ledge, an impressive figure, squared shoulders, strong neck, the sweep of thick black hair. I know his features well, and yet the mental image does not satisfy my desire to have him near.

He walks to the edge, positioning himself for the dive. In one fluid movement he takes into the air, the leap taking him to a height level with the falls above. It seems he might never fall but instead take flight, remaining in the air, propelled by invisible wings. Yet with the ease of a bird of prey, Dorian curves his body downward, mirroring the streak of the cascade of liquid behind him. In his final moments above the river he transforms; taking on the swift agility of a fish and breaking through the river's surface as if returning home. He does not resurface until after several moments in which he has traveled a distance downstream. Dorian finds me upon the shore and swims toward me, his strokes propelling him against the current with ease.

"You're not coming in?" he queries slyly.

"No … the river and I have come to an agreement. I don't go in, and she doesn't drown me." I venture a glance at the tumbling current, and the foam that breaks upon the smooth river stone.

"You can stay by me; I won't let her take you." Dorian reaches out his arms toward me and starts to wade up the rocky shore.

I take a step backward. If I let him near me, I might not be able to tear myself away. That would cause me to miss my chance, and if I don't leave today, there will be no time before the Rebirth. To my shameful dismay, Dorian's kindness only seems to have grown throughout the day, making my plans harder and harder to carry through.

I shake my head. "Actually … I … Azura asked me to meet with her today. I promised I would … I should head back to the Oak … try to find her."

Dorian halts, letting his arms fall to his sides, and frowns. "Okay …" He thinks for a moment, "I will go with you then." He moves to take a step forward.

"No! I mean … I don't want to ruin your fun. It'll only take a short time." I am already stepping backward into the woods. "I'll see you soon after." The last I say over my shoulder, knowing I have lied to him and not able to stare him in the face any longer. Luckily Dorian respects my privacy and does not follow.

I make it back to the Great Oak with an hour or so till evening. The platforms are nearly empty, I do not pass anyone on my way to the meeting hall. They are all probably in the forest or meadow, enjoying the last half of the pleasant day. I on the other hand am already looking forward to the night, when I will have safely returned to the Great Oak, Lenora beside me.

I reach the meeting hall without interference. I enter slowly and peer into its depths, listening for any sign of occupants. I sigh, realizing it is completely empty.

I search among the shelves for one of the scrolled maps. I unroll the smallest, knowing it will be easiest to carry, I notice an odd difference about it. The drawing of the Great Oak is missing; instead, among the many sketches of forest trees, one stands out among the rest. A single tree has been drawn with circular fruit ornamenting its branches; at its base, a root is shown curving into a perfect seat. I roll the parchment back together and tie it with its twine strap.

My next stop is my room, where I grab the pack from my journey the previous day. I spot my university robes folded neatly upon my dresser. Piper and Lily have kindly had them cleaned to their original whiteness. I never thought I'd wear them again. Lifting them off my dresser, I notice a book revealed beneath them. The journal of Narena, Dorian's mother. Something compels me to grab it and I stuff it inside the bag with my old clothing beside an empty sack and drained canteen.

On the lower platform I slip inside the dining hall and find a basket of rolls that was left out from lunch. I remove the empty cloth sack from my back and fill it with as many rolls as it will hold. I tuck it back inside, hoist the straps over my shoulder, and head for the long ladder. I will fill the canteen with water from a stream in the forest. As my feet finally touch the solid ground, I whirl around to face away from the Great Oak. It has grown darker, and the setting sun has turned the forest a bright red and umber. Taking a deep breath, I start forward, concentrating on the steps directly in front of me and trying to picture Lenora's face in my mind.

CHAPTER THIRTY-SIX

I pause at the edge of a stream to fill my canteen and take a quick sip. My hands are trembling when I fasten it closed and replace it inside my bag. It will not be long before night arrives and I reach the University. It's as though I can sense its gaze upon me already, the watching eyes of Odon seeing into my head, observing my approach with a smirk of delight.

It takes all my energy to continue, the memories of my life there flooding back. I already hold my face blankly, hanging my arms directly beside me, taking steps parallel to my shoulders. I do not attempt to switch back. I must assume my previous habits if I am to walk among the others confidently.

In the shade of the forest wall that surrounds the University hillside, I change into my white clothing. Despite the silkiness of its fabric I find no comfort within it. I fold my blue dress into the pack. But before I leave it behind, I remove Narena's journal from inside and slip it into my pocket. The weight of the journal bangs against my thigh as I move forward. I press my palms to my hair, smoothing it to perfection and then straightening any folds in my robes. I clear my mind, not allowing myself to think of anything but the whiteness of my blouse and the importance of remaining perfect. The past disappears, the emotions are unimportant, I can only see the next step.

The sky is darkening, and I look up the grassy hillside. Past the wall of foliage surrounding the garden it stands. A square white building protruding from the ground, its sides lined with rows of black ovals, like the many eyes of an insect. The whiteness is nauseating, and the sun's dying rays hit it with rage. I pass the garden walls and entrance, refusing to glance at it and clearing my mind of any memories that it might trigger. I stare straight ahead. In moments my presence outside will be against the rules, it is growing late.

I step into the dead air of the University hallway. The lights have dimmed, but the white is as blinding as ever. My eyes take longer to adjust than I remember. It has been so long since they were forced to strain against the color. I remain still, trying to keep my eyes from snapping shut and my hands from trying to press the pain away. I stare downward until my vision clears enough so I can walk. I swallow, getting my bearings, and head down a corridor that feels as though I walked it just yesterday. It leads to a hallway perpendicular to my room.

I pass a group of other purebloods who are silently heading to their room. I hope my face does not reveal my shock. Their eyes are so empty, their faces so still. I am frightened by the paleness of their cheeks and the lifelessness wafting out of them. I walk past them, attempting a mindless nod of acknowledgment and trying to stiffen my shaking body.

Another turn leads me to the row of doors to each of my sector's dormitories. I have lived here for so many years, and yet it was never home. Not like my bed among the arms of the Great Oak, where Dorian's body keeps me warm and the walls become black after sunset. There is no night here, and the air is always still.

I halt beside my doorway, or what once was my doorway. The metal handle reflects the light of the ceiling orbs in a piercing spark. I hold my breath. No sound can be heard from within. This is it, the final moment when I tell Lenora the truth. When I tell her I forgive her, and everything that has happened within these walls means nothing to me now. It has all been Odon's doing, the result of his hold on our malleable childhood. I have to believe that there is still hope, that we are still young enough to change. Dorian gave me this chance, and now I wish to grant my sister the same opportunity. In honesty I cannot trust that we will win. That on the day of the Rebirth, Odon will fall. And if we fail, at least I will know that my sister is safe.

With this in mind, I seize the door handle, its metal chill causing me to lose my breath. I wrench it sideways and push the door open.

The light within escapes into the hallway, and I step inside, scanning the room. Lenora sits at her usual desk, a text laid open in front of her and a notebook splayed beside it with rows of neat handwriting filling its exposed page. Her gaze turns upon me as I enter. Yet my eyes do not dwell for long upon her. Beside her, at my desk, or at what once was my desk, a Winglet sits. This desk also displays a text and notebook. Together the two stare at me, uncertain how to react to my sudden arrival. Lenora is the first to respond.

"Are you lost?" she asks, irritation rising in her voice—a familiar tone.

"Lenora … I'm here to …" I begin, but there is something about the way she addresses me that causes my throat to tighten.

"How do you know my name?" Lenora replies stiffly, confirming the fear that is already growing inside me.

"It's me, Oriana … Lenora, don't you …?" I hear the waver in my voice, the hot tears that I withhold desperately by biting down on my lip.

"I think you are mistaken. I have never met you before in my life," she declares. I would think she was deceiving me if not for the honesty in her eyes.

My mouth gapes, opening and closing with no sound escaping. I am frozen for only a moment before recovering enough to escape through the door. Before I know it, I am staggering down the hallway, my palms pressed into my eyes as the tears pour from them uncontrollably. I wipe them away, but the flood continues. In a panic I start to run through the halls, finding my way back to the main entrance by a subconscious instinct.

Outside, I run down the hill, stopping short at the garden entrance. I hesitate for a moment before deciding to enter. Its comforting walls beckon me inside. I follow the stones, the sun still providing enough light for me to greet the rows of flowers. I think of Dorian, our first meeting, his hand in mine as he led me for the first time to the stone seat. Now I make my way toward it, desiring one quick rest upon its cool surface before I return to the Great Oak. I smile as I take a seat, remembering when Dorian first kissed me, when I first saw the love in his eyes.

My panic now under control, I rest my chin in my hands. How could I have been so foolish? I had completely forgotten the power of the University walls. It can control the minds of hundreds of students, set them against each other, take away their every emotion, and now I know it can make a girl forget her own sister. I do not feel relief at having carried out my plan, but there is something that settles inside me, a feeling that makes my journey worth the time it's taken.

Sitting here, I find my independence. I made a decision on my own, and my determination gave me the strength to go through with it. I have to give myself credit for accomplishing that much.

I press a hand against the seat beside me, and my thoughts flash to Dorian once again. He must be worried, and when I return, I must face him. I must tell him the truth and what I have done. I will tell him that I am satisfied and that I will never leave his side again. Not even at the Rebirth, and he will have no choice but to agree because he will want me with him forever after. I smile as he appears before my mind's eye. I even imagine I hear him call my name.

"Oriana."

I startle, looking toward the entrance of the garden. A dark figure stands, the flame of a candle in an outstretched hand. I did not imagine it. Someone did say my name, but it was not Dorian.

"Oriana … that is your name, I remember it." Aurek approaches me. I am on my feet, readying myself for an opening through which I can flee. But his large form blocks my only exit. He comes closer, and I try to move around him but his hand reaches out to grip my arm. It is strong, incredibly painful, and when I attempt to struggle, his grip tightens. He places the candle and holder upon the bench behind him and settles his eyes upon me smugly. "I saw you come out here. You must not have noticed me because you were running."

I look around, hoping to find something I can use to escape. Nothing catches my eye. Perhaps I can persuade him to let go instead.

"That is your name, isn't it? Oriana? Somehow I think I've known you …"

He reaches out and strokes my hair, sliding his hand down the back of my neck. I want to scream, cry out, but who would come to my rescue? It's when his hands move downward that I begin to retch. His palms explore the curves of my body, sliding up my stomach toward my chest. I let him go no further. I pull backward, struggling against his hand, and he reaches for my flailing arm. I don't give him the chance to take it. A new strength that I never knew existed emerges from within, and I deliver a swift kick. He doubles over in surprise, not having expected my initiative to fight back. A young pureblood girl would never be expected to do so.

I take advantage of his moment of confusion and thrust my elbow into his side. This causes the air to escape him and his fingers to loosen their grasp. I wrench my arm free as he topples backward. His weight and considerable height make the fall more forceful. His head sails backward and strikes the bench with a sickening crunch, followed by an eerie silence.

I stand over him, staring in horror. I pray he will make the slightest movement, that his chest might make one rise and fall. He is completely still. A black liquid oozes across the bench from beneath his head, it creeps across the smooth surface like a living creature.

I move to kneel beside him, to check his eyes, examine his injury, but I leap back as the ground behind him bursts into flames. Aurek's fall knocked the candle from the bench, causing it to set the grass alight. The fire spreads quickly, my vision blurs as I mindlessly try to put it out. If I don't, the entire garden will soon be ablaze and burn to the ground. I throw dirt upon it. Someone will notice the flames, and I will have no time to escape ... no time ... *I have no time.*

Aurek is still not moving, and my breath comes in terrified gasps. *Relax, Oriana, think ... think of something ...* I am not sure if I should run now or stop the flames, if only I can stop the flames from spreading! *Think!*

There is a voice behind me, a whimper. I whip around, leaving the fire for a second to search out the noise. Fisk stares at me in horror, his eyes discovering the still form of Aurek, not just still, dead. He starts to yell. A shrill shriek of rage echoes in my ears like thousands of alarming crickets enveloping the night. I hear my own scream and swallow it, searching behind me for something, someone. I only find the bench, dripping with black blood, and the raging fire that has now engulfed half the garden. I back away from it. *What have I done ... what ... what!?* My body lurches convulsively, my hands pull at my hair, sweat upon my brow from the intense heat of the fire. I watch as Aurek's body attracts the flames, the red fingers licking off his flesh and clothing. I shake my head trying to rid myself of the image, the image I had caused.

"NO!!!"

The hands of the guards fasten around my arms just as the Odonian instructs them. I am unable to fight, unable to find the sky, the stars, the ground beneath me. It all spins in one revolting daze. I feel a sharp pain in my neck that sends me hurtling toward unconsciousness, the echoing words of someone from above chase me downward into darkness.

"Bring her to Odon."

CHAPTER THIRTY-SEVEN

This nightmare, I remember now, I've had it before. The eyes have returned. I thought they were defeated, but they are back. They're stronger than ever, probing my mind, seeking out my memories, my secrets. I shrink from their touch, struggling against their power. Then the eyes break through, sifting through my earliest memories.

I'm an infant, clutched in my mother's arms, my sister beside me. The pounding of her feet upon the ground frightens me as she runs. My fingers clutch the air, trying to pull myself forward, away from the pursuers. Mother's heart hammers against my shoulder, her breath is warm upon my head and neck. I am hungry, and I wish to rest, but the jostling causes me more discomfort. Those behind us gain distance at a greater speed, they will soon grab Mother. Perhaps then we can rest, and Mother will feed my sister and me.

At last she takes flight, I love it when mother flies. Yet this time is different. We glide into the air, the up and down rattle of her run turns into the soothing motion of wings and the rush of air. Now I can close my eyes. Mother withdraws a large breath. Her wings halt and she curls around my sister and me.

We are falling, and mother remains still, her wings wrapped around us. Her heart is not hammering. No more breath escapes her. Why does she not move? I cry out, anxious to hear my mother's soothing voice, to feel her soft lips pressed upon my brow, to know that things will soon be all right. But she does not answer my cry. Lenora is screaming beside me as we drop, I watch her, eyes wide. Mother strikes the ground first, I clutch at her dress, my body colliding with hers. Tears fill my eyes as the strangers surround me and Lenora. Mother's arms no longer hug us close.

I fly forward through memories, the repetitive days of the University, the endless hours of classes and studying. I see Lenora and the part-blood, her first love. The way she changed afterward, lost what was left of the happiness in her eyes. Aurek and I alone, my first kiss.

The piercing blue eyes—his eyes—watch it all through mine. I try to fight it, attempting to stop reliving these experiences. His eyes do not just witness the event, but he sees my thoughts. He sees the doubts of Odon's teachings, my hatred for the Odonians and professors. He steals my thoughts, disregards my privacy, and then I see Dorian. No! I try to move away, to hold on to the past and keep from moving forward. But his eyes press further, and the images flow again.

Dorian walks toward me, smiles. I now recognize the emotions flowing through me, the attraction, the intrigue. Yet it is bittersweet, I am sharing these moments with *him*. He laughs at my torment, the way my cheeks grow hot when I think of Dorian, I tremble. It is all exposed, every thought and feeling, all of my love. We are in the garden, sharing a kiss. Then I am sneaking back inside, thoughts of our next meeting circling in my mind.

The memories shoot forward, the Odonian, my mindless state. Aurek's kiss. I shiver at the sight, although it seems it was not me who was actually there. Yet seeing myself, unmoving, body numb, the moment is confirmed. I notice Dorian watching from afar. I did not recognize him at the time. I was too blank, I had forgotten. Now it pains me to see the hurt in his eyes, the way his muscles tense at the sight of Aurek's touch.

I am propelled past this, the memories picking up speed and then slowing down for yet another painful event. I am in my room. Lenora is across from me. I am screaming at her, the flood of my panic, the intensity of my fear all returns. I know what is about to happen, and yet I am as powerless to stop it as I was in that moment. The guards storm in, knocking me into darkness.

I awake in the cell, noticing the shock of moving from the white of the University to the black caves. Time is moving quickly again, and it speeds through my first discussion with Azura and then the approach of the guards. It is here that my mind begins to close up and the eyes pry at my brain, bringing focus to the fading vision.

The guards haul me between them as the Odonian leads us to a white room. The scene instantly becomes familiar. The man interrogates me briefly. I remain silent, lying upon the cold floor. His voice evokes a returning hatred inside of me. I watch the scene, wanting to force myself to my feet and lurch toward him, doing as much damage as possible. Yet I remain still, listening as his voice slides in and out of my ears, the light burning through my closed lids.

I watch as the scene progresses: "Administer the device." I watch in horror as my past becomes clear. The woman enters, needle in hand. I struggle inside a body that is not under my control. I yell for myself to hear. *Oriana! Move! You can't let them!* It is too late, the needle plunges into my neck.

The eyes watch from inside my mind, bursting with laughter.

I hear the last words of the Odonian as the memory comes to an end, their meaning finally becoming clear. "He will come for her. I am certain. Now we wait ..."

NO!! I shove myself away, tearing at the bindings that have connected the eyes to my mind. My own eyes fly open, I draw my hand up immediately to shield them from the white room. Am I inside the University?

As my vision returns, I study my surroundings. It is a circular room; behind me is a curved wall of windows that look down a familiar hillside and out over the distant forest. It is daytime. The sun is already high in the sky. I am in the University, in a room at its highest level. I lie in a circular pit at the center of the floor, which has been littered with white cushions. The rest of the floor is slightly raised around me and reflects the smooth white surface of the University hallways. Further confirmation of my location lies on the ceiling where rows of familiar orb lamps glare down at me.

Beside me a darker color stands out upon the blank pillows. *My satchel!* They must have found it by the tree somehow. *How long have I been watched?* I grab and shove the flap open, searching for the food and drink. I sigh, discovering it has all been left within. I take a moment to swallow some water and fill my stomach with the bread. Then I remember: the map! It is missing from the depths of my satchel. In this moment I grasp for my pocket and feel the hard cover of Narena's Journal. I sigh, discovering it has been left within. But where is the—?

"Looking for this?"

I jump, whirling around, the piece of bread dropping from my hand, to discover I am not alone. The room's wall is smooth, breaking once for an oval door. I follow its surface with my eyes till I discover the source of the voice.

A man stands, strongly built, white robes draping stoically upon his shoulders, thick arms crossed in front of him. One of his hands grips the scroll of parchment, scrunching it together at its center.

"Don't worry, it was of no use to me. Your precious Great Oak is nowhere on the page. Useless thing." He throws it to the floor.

My gaze moves up to his black hair reaching to his shoulders in loose waves. The tone of his skin is somewhere between the pale of a Winglet and the darker tan of a Finlet. Yet these features are not what is most striking about this man. As if glowing from an inner light, the gaze of his eyes freezes me in place. The gaze of two piercing blue eyes.

"I can see you remember me."

Odon holds me in place, keeping me from answering. Somehow his inner control of me has strengthened, and I am powerless inside my own body, unable to move.

"So you've figured out my name as well. Impressive." He smirks and starts pacing around the room toward the windows to his left. As he walks in front of the light pouring through the windows, I can see it, the aura of his power coiling around his body. The power of a half-blood.

"But then I thought you would've figured it out long before now. After all, I've been following you for days. Have you been sleeping well?."

I cringe inwardly, and he chuckles. He is seeing straight into my thoughts!

"Yes ... although things didn't go exactly as planned. That half-blood ... he's more powerful than I expected. Nowhere near myself, of course, but powerful nonetheless. If he hadn't been so close to you ... I would've already discovered the whereabouts of the Great Oak."

Then he knows it exists, and he already knows of Dorian being a half-blood. I shut my mind off to it immediately, sensing his gaze upon me, not just from within the room, but inside my mind as well.

"You can try as much as you like. Now that I have you here, it will not be long before I have exposed your mind completely."

Without Dorian near to help shield me from Odon's power, I am helpless. But then how was I able to break free, to awaken myself just now? And if Odon could simply take what he wanted from me, why is he waiting? Why not extract it at once? Perhaps I still have some hidden advantage.

Odon turns his stare out the window and casually waves his hand backward in my direction. My body is released suddenly, and I am able to move once again.

"Why have you brought me here?" I rise to my feet, attempting to look confident, but my knees threaten to buckle beneath me. I, Oriana, am facing Odon, not only a man twice my size, but one who possesses the ripened powers of a transformed half-blood. Not long ago I would have bowed before him, pledged my devotion to his authority, but never again.

He eyes me with amusement. "I've been watching you, Oriana."

My eyebrow rises. "For how long …?"

"Since before you ever met that foolish half-blood. You must have known that you stand out among the others. You were never able to achieve the perfection of that blank look." He smiles to himself as if this is a humorous subject.

"Then you knew I was never devoted to you like the others. You knew all along I thought against the University."

"Oh please, it was obvious. Did you honestly think I wouldn't notice a Winglet girl making trips to the garden every evening? I could tell your mind was working beneath that rush of gold, behind those starlit eyes. You truly resemble your mother Sonya very much. It's a shame I had to end her life like that. If you weren't so amusing, I would've destroyed you from the start, but you never had the backbone to act upon your thoughts anyway. Even now you stand there, a fragile flower." Odon looks me up and down with a disgusted glint in his eyes.

"Then you were toying with me?" My fists tighten. My jaw is clenched. I am a fool; I knew it all along—a cowardly fool.

"Well, the rest of the bunch aren't very entertaining, are they?"

He pushes fingers through his slick black hair, laughing softly. "Yet there was a slight interference, though I couldn't have planned it better myself. Dorian, the last half-bloodlet, took an interest in you. You suddenly became the perfect ploy. I knew I was keeping you around for something. I still can't wait to watch him squirm."

"What do you mean?"

"Why, at the Rebirth, of course. I'm sure he wouldn't miss it, especially now that I have you here," Odon studies me as his words hit home.

Can he possibly know? That Dorian and the others are planning to sneak into the Rebirth and attempt to defeat him? But then why shouldn't he? Odon was there when Kadin carried out his attack. If Odon is aware of Dorian's age and lineage, then he could expect a similar assault from him.

"Your face confirms my assumptions. They will make an appearance at the Rebirth, but then I had already presumed. Doesn't matter anyway, I was suspecting a second attack, seeing how the last one went unsuccessfully." He shakes his head in pity. "The fool, turning on his own men, although I can't blame him. Who would want to share power like this? Do you think Dorian will be any different? You think somehow he will get past his hatred, his thirst for power? I guess that's what keeps you people hopeful, the idea of reachable dreams." Odon approaches the edge of the floor where I lie below. "It's useless. The true winners are the ones with the power. Once Dorian realizes that, once he feels it in his grasp"—Odon holds out his hand, staring into it as if it were a fountain of endless energy—"he'll forget all about you and his friends."

"You're wrong." I quake with anger from his words. "Dorian will succeed. He's going to be the most powerful of all, and he'll use it just to kill you!" I spit out the statement before considering my intentions. Is that really what I want? Is that really how I feel?

"The way you killed Aurek?" Odon's smile broadens as I am slowly brought to my knees. That's right, I killed him, in the garden last night. Aurek is dead, and I am the one who ended his life. Somehow I was capable of such an execution.

I shake my head, staring at my outstretched hands, the same ones that have caused destruction. How can I ever face the others again?

What will they think of me? What will Dorian think? "But it was only an accident! I didn't mean to …"

"Didn't you?" Odon's eyes blaze with innocence, as if he is simply providing the truth. "You hated Aurek from the beginning. I saw your memories … I heard your thoughts, felt those emotions of repulsion. You thought he'd be better off dead!"

"No! I never wanted it … *really*!" I sob into my hands, still resisting the truth of his words. I wished Aurek would disappear, leave forever, but death? "I didn't want this … never …" My tears form dark spots upon the white cushions below.

Odon is beside me, his hand upon my shoulder. "Little Winglet." His voice is soothing, his hand warm. I feel the pulse of the power reaching out through it and coursing beneath my skin. My body stills, my tears stop, I lose all emotion, all feeling. In fact I can hardly remember what I was crying about. "He deserved what he got."

Oh yes, Aurek … I was crying over Aurek.

"For what he did to you, any man would deserve the same fate."

I nod as he lifts my chin with fingers that cause my skin to flinch. Our gazes meet, his eyes so blue the color seems to pour right through me. His face that of a man with great force, a ruler's face.

"Oriana, now you must sleep, sleep and relax your mind." He is close to me now, our noses nearly touching. I feel his breath against my lips, but I want to back away, to keep him from moving toward me. His eyes flash with the slightest alarm. His eyebrow twitches slightly. "Oriana." His voice is sterner, more demanding. "You will sleep." Odon's eyes drive further into my own, and I plummet backward, submerging into my subconscious.

I am following Dorian through the forest. The path is so familiar, the forest a friendly acquaintance. I am nearly home, journeying back to the Great Oak. We pass the fruit trees, the clearing, swiftly sailing over the rise and fall of the lush landscape. I am eager to reach her, the Oak, to grasp onto the endless ladder that once frightened me. Now it is a welcome ascent, each rung bringing me further into the Great Oak's arms, pulling me upward toward the sky where I can scan the horizon of endless trees and the sun setting over the sliver of ocean. Dorian takes my hand and pulls me forward. I see the back of his head, the flow of hair blacker than the night. I notice a familiar opening in the trees ahead, and he guides me toward it.

I wish to slow down, to appreciate the beauty of the forest around us. To listen to the calls of the birds, it is so fulfilling to be back. To be back? Have I left? I remember leaving, but—

Dorian jerks at my arm, but he does not turn to see why my pace has slowed. Instead he shakes my attention back to the foliage ahead. Why doesn't he glance back at me?

We finally reach it, the base of the hill on which the Great Oak stands. Dorian has taken an even faster pace, and I move into a jog to keep up. It's all right. I am not tired; in fact, I do not feel a strain on my legs at all. We make it to the top, and I see her, the Great Oak. Rising up above the forest canopy, shadowing all other growth around her. She is truly a sight of greatness.

I search for Dorian, as we are no longer hand in hand. I find him standing a short distance away, standing by the base of the Great Oak, gazing up through the infinite branches above. Placing my hand against his shoulder I attempt to speak his name. No sound escapes me. I wrap my hands around my head, screaming for Dorian's help, feeling as though I am being suffocated by my own words. Dorian whirls around to face me, and I see that I have been terribly mistaken.

It is Odon I see, the malignant grin already formed upon his face. He begins to laugh, spreading his arms wide enough to encompass the entire tree. His laughter surrounds me, the image of the Great Oak shrinking away as his face fades until only his eyes remain, swallowing up the forest, slicing through the Oak's roots, and sending her crumbling to the ground. It is only when his eyes close into blackness that I hear my scream, my body wrenching in horror at what I have done. He has tricked me! Deceived me into showing him the way to the Great Oak!

I recoil inward, unable to hold onto my sanity. I feel as though I might die from grief and shame. A dark liquid rises around me, I swallow its thickness, it leaks into my eyes. I sink deeper and deeper, losing any desire to fight against it. My arms float above me, although I have no arms in this place. I have given up, when something grabs me ... hauls me upward and out of the pool.

"Dorian ..." I am somewhere else, a place of peace and tranquility. He stands before me, his hand still holding mine. I can see his face now, the sapphire eyes, his kind smile.

"Oriana, I thought I had lost you." He moves toward me, grasping my waist. "Somehow I found you … wherever we are …" He looks around at the endless darkness. Suddenly the world begins to change. Four walls of greenery rise around us, flowers sprout among flat stones that form a pathway. We are in the garden from the University, and yet this one, that Dorian has created for us alone, is far more beautiful.

I smile, wondering how I could've ever given up, and then I remember. Despite his glow of happiness overwhelming me, I remember. "Dorian, there is no time. I must tell you …" I feel something or someone approaching. I don't have much more time unwatched. "I can't tell you how sorry I am." Dorian searches my eyes with growing concern.

"Dorian … he … Odon knows where the Great Oak is! He's going to seek you out! You must tell the others, protect them!"

"But that's impossible … how could he …?"

"It was me, it was all my fault. I—" I feel myself sinking again, but this time Dorian brings me back. "I'm sorry. I'm so sorry. I didn't mean to." The image pulls away, Dorian's touch retreats, our bodies separate. I am rising back into my body, into consciousness. I only hope Dorian will heed my message. If anyone else were to die because of my mistakes … I open my eyes in time to feel the shudder pass over my physical form.

CHAPTER THIRTY-EIGHT

The orb lights above me glow dimly. It is late in the evening as I reposition myself on the white cushions. I can't get comfortable no matter how I try. My mind keeps returning to the Great Oak and the safety of everyone there. Did I actually speak with Dorian? Or was it merely a dream? Another of Odon's tricks? And if it wasn't, did Dorian believe me? Did he have enough time to warn the others?

Every inhaled breath brings a twisting pain in my stomach that refuses to go away. I hold my breath, tightening my stomach and then releasing the air slowly. The result is a moment of relief before the knot retightens within my gut and the memories replay in my mind.

I look up at the oval door across the room. I get to my feet and climb onto the upper floor, still eyeing the door. I glance backward. Could Odon be watching me? I wouldn't be surprised, and yet I have to try. I cover the distance to the door and press my hands against it. There is no handle and merely a narrow slit around its edges. After this waste of time, I retreat to the center of the room.

I fall back onto the cushions, sighing openly. The weight of something hard strikes me as I bounce against the pillows. I search my pocket, finding a small piece of bread and Narena's journal. I chew the bread, which crumbles in my mouth, but at least it fills my stomach.

I adjust my position and open the journal, hoping to find some strand of inspiration within it. My eyes rest upon a page addressed to Dorian.

My son, every day seems to bring further hardships, greater sorrows.

You have not yet entered this world, and sometimes I wonder if it is selfish of me to want you to. I feel your heartbeat inside me, the movement of your infant limbs. Your father is so proud. He wants to see you too, but I am frightened. I never thought I would admit that, but I am. Now that you're here, I am afraid for you, for the future of our world. They say you will be our only hope. I'd rather not say where that path has led others before you. I have lost many friends to this talk of destiny. Somehow I believe you will not follow the same path as those of the past, but I fear in time you may lose your way. It is why I have decided to write this journal, because one day I might not be by your side. One day the weight of fear and anger may overpower you. Dorian, you must admit your fears, your mistakes, it is what separates us from the corrupt. Whatever should happen to your father or me, remember this, if ever you should stray, your only way back is through the eyes of the one who truly loves you.

I shut the book, a shiver passing over me. There is something about those last words that lingers in my mind. Is this information some sort of key for the future? I close the book, feeling satisfied with the passage I have discovered. Placing it inside the satchel, I reach for the canteen that still contains some water. In a few minutes I have finished the rest of the loaf and half drained the canteen. As I am replacing my things inside the bag, the oval door opens. The Odonian enters, a snivel of recognition on his face as he eyes me.

"What do you want?" I ask.

"Master Odon has asked me to check on you. You appear in good health," he states, sizing me up with distaste.

"That's a matter of opinion." I snort.

"You'd be wise to hold your tongue and recognize your place." The Odonian moves to let the door shut behind him.

"Where might that be?"

The Odonian smirks, watching me from the upper level of flooring, "Below me."

I burn with rage.

"Control yourself!" he commands and then considers before explaining. "If that simple statement has brought such emotion, then you will most certainly be moved by my further bit of insight."

I take a breath, holding back my temper and returning to my instincts as a University student, "And what's that?"

"News of the Great Oak."

I am completely silent, straining for him to continue.

"Odon's men have already been sent. In fact, they have probably already done their damage. I wouldn't be surprise if the whole place is burning to the ground at this moment," he adds casually.

"You're lying!"

"You know it to be true. It was you who revealed its location. Foolish Winglet."

"I didn't know ... how could I ... it was a mis—"

"Mistake?" He shakes his head as if I were a misbehaving child. "You've been making a lot of those lately, haven't you?"

I clench my fists, a growl rising in my throat. It is all I can do to keep from lunging at his hideous form. The wraith of a body and featureless face, skeletal in every way save for the streak of blond hair upon his head. It hangs lifelessly to one side like a withered blossom.

I must not let my anger control me. Narena is right, and I've experienced it firsthand. I must not resort to anger and give him the upper hand. Yet I'm finding it increasingly difficult, given the situation.

"I can just picture your half-blood burning alive. His lasting memory of your betrayal. Now no one can save you, Odon will live on, and the University will prevail." His smile is the rictus of a feasting maggot.

"You'd rather Odon win? And I'm the one who's foolish? You're just a slave to him! You're too stupid to realize that! You're worse than I could ever be!" I jab my finger toward him. I await in pure delight the look of injury upon his face.

But it never shows. The Odonian's pale eyes look upon me slyly, that slimy smile still wriggling on his face. "Oh, but you are ... haven't you figured that out yet? I should think you might have surmised ..." His laugh hisses in my ears.

"What ... what did you say?"

"What do you think that scar on your neck is from?"

I reach to brush my fingers against it, recalling the memory of the painful injection. It is still sore to touch. "What is it?" I know I will regret asking.

"You're one of us now."

"One of—"

"Little Winglet, you are an Odonian." In the end he wins, exulting in my stunned stare and then turning and walking out of the room.

CHAPTER THIRTY-NINE

My first reaction is to deny it. How could I be one of them? One of Odon's mindless servants? I'm not an Odonian, my name is Oriana, I am myself! How can that be taken away?

Yet something did happen in Odon's cave, they put something in my neck. Not only that. I've seen Odon and witnessed his power firsthand. He was able to control my body and kept me from moving. What would stop him from making me a mindless servant?

I shudder. This whole time I thought I was free of him. I believed the Great Oak was a sanctuary, a place where I was safe, where no one was watching. It was never true. Odon was in my head even then, invading my mind. When Dorian came for me, he didn't save me at all. They had known he would come for me and bring me to the Great Oak. If it hadn't been for Dorian's power, Odon would have read my mind and found its location a long time ago. That must have been his original plan.

I look around the room helplessly. Would it matter if I'd never decided to find Lenora? Was I destined to end up in this room? If I had never left the Great Oak on my own, I would still be there living a fantasy. At least now I know the truth. That Odon is too powerful to defeat. He has taken over my mind. He has probably already destroyed the Great Oak, and if they've managed to survive, he is already aware of Dorian's arrival tomorrow. How can we possibly win? I'm useless to them now, and if anything, I've caused them even more grief. Now that I'm to become an Odonian, I will most likely lose all consciousness of who I was and any memory of the past. Why even worry about what is to become of the others? There's nothing I can do to help them now.

I immediately shake my head. Giving up is not an option. Not when all my friends are involved, not when Dorian is. At one time I might have been satisfied with letting Odon think for me, but not anymore. I have fought his powers once. I owe it to the others to keep trying. Tomorrow is the Rebirth, which means that Dorian will soon gain his powers. Maybe my situation is not completely hopeless. It could be beneficial for them to have an ally on the inside.

But Odon wouldn't be that foolish; he's too intelligent for that. If he believes I'm a possible threat, he won't take any chances. Is he keeping me near to watch me closer? Is he planning to use me as Dorian's weakness? Or maybe I have an advantage that he isn't aware of … or he is aware but he doesn't want me to know it!

I bury my face in my hands, and my head begins to hurt. What if Odon is listening to all my thoughts? Hearing me slowly drive myself crazy? He doesn't have to do anything at all. I will simply sit here, fueling my own insanity in this empty white room.

I get up again and walk toward the windows to distract my mind. It is nearly dark, this last day until the Rebirth. Tomorrow can start a new life—or end many. Meanwhile I remain here, unable to be with Dorian. He must be so afraid, and I won't even have the chance to see him one last time before he turns into someone else. Will I even know him after his transformation? Odon believes Dorian will become like all the other half-bloods, and why shouldn't he? Why should he be any different than the others, full of expectations and a flood of unruly emotions? That doesn't make him evil; Kadin was never evil. But is he capable of handling a sudden burst of power? I have no idea, or maybe I refuse to believe he isn't.

I wonder for a moment if maybe Odon was different at one point. He must've had a mother, a father, perhaps siblings. He was once a young man just like Dorian, and then in one moment, of one day in his life, an incredible burden was thrust upon him, and it changed him forever. Now all he has as company are the mindless subjects around him. Granted, he has a conscience, and he has the ability to change his situation. But perhaps his story runs deeper than I had assumed. Maybe Odon has his reasons for being who he is. I remember what Falda said, how the purebloods sent the half-blood children away and how this created hatred and caused the half-bloods to use their powers negatively. In a way, my own people have brought this upon themselves. It doesn't mean we should continue to suffer for it, but there is some justice to the situation.

I turn around suddenly as the door opens and Odon enters. I see him in a new light, no longer a tyrant, but a man. Someone who was once a child, someone who has his own emotions. Someone who can make mistakes.

"Why are you looking at me that way?" he snaps. He moves quickly around the room, pacing back and forth. Is he nervous? Has something gone wrong?

I blink, changing my expression to nonchalance. "What has you so troubled?" I ask, attempting to sound casual in hopes he will confess.

He stops, "Troubled? What would I have to be troubled about!?" He laughs as though it is ridiculous. "Child, I am Odon, these are my lands, *my* people!! I control it all!" Odon grasps the air in his hands. "So what would trouble me?"

Suddenly Odon seems unstable, someone possessing too much power, too many emotions. Something has caused him to lose control, unbalance his plans. "You tell me. I know something has happened … the Great Oak!" I shout before clamping a hand over my mouth.

Odon turns on me with fury. "What about it, girl? You think you know everything? What about it?!"

"Nothing … I don't know," I look around for some kind of support but fall backward against the window with a thump.

"Your Great Oak is gone! Do you hear me?" Odon raises a finger at me, and I'm unable to move. My body goes numb. He doesn't even allow me to breathe as he takes over my mind. "Whatever you told that half-blood was pointless! It didn't save them. It's gone. All of it!"

I stare at him, screaming inside but unable to show it and feeling as though I might faint.

Odon's hand lowers, and I fall to my knees, gasping for air. He watches me fight for composure. Is he waiting for my answer? I realize Dorian and I *have* really spoken to one another. That is what Odon is angry about! I was able to contact Dorian before Odon could do any real damage. If this is something Odon was not expecting, then maybe I really do have some kind of an advantage.

Finally I turn to him. "So I've surprised you?!" I allow myself a laugh. I, Oriana, have made Odon nervous! "Mighty Odon's plans were ruined by a Winglet girl!"

He speaks with a clenched jaw. "You realize you are making this worse for yourself."

"I might as well enjoy this moment then!"

Odon calms, which causes me to falter; his mind is working. "I think I'll have to pay more attention to you. If you are such a threat, perhaps it'd be better to keep a closer eye on you."

"But …" I suddenly feel light-headed. I take a step toward him, trying to think of something useful, something that will make him change his mind. I already know it's hopeless. I have given him the perfect reason to be suspicious of me. I can't take back what was already said. Instead I redirect the conversation, "Is it true that I'm an Odonian?"

At this Odon's eyebrows rise, yet he seems pleased. "You will be, at the Rebirth when all purebloods are in their weakened state."

"Weakened state? You mean because of the transformation."

He nods. "Yes, yes." He waves a hand impatiently. "I don't have time for your petty questions."

"At least I still have a mind to ask them. I deserve to know what you plan to do with me!"

"You continue to raise your voice when you know I have no problem taking more of your freedom away." Odon crosses his arms and begins to walk toward me. "Then again, if you prefer to sacrifice your mind to me sooner, I won't be the one to stop you."

I stand my ground, glaring at him in fury, which only seems to make his smirk broaden. He takes me by the wrist. I try to pull away but he holds me still, drawing back the hair on the side of my neck and running his fingers across the scar where I was injected. I flinch at the remaining soreness.

"What is it? What did you put in my neck?"

Odon turns his gaze to my eyes, staring down at me tenderly. "A sliver of stone. It will help me concentrate my energy."

"Why stone …?"

This is something Odon is willing to answer. "Every half-blood is different. We each use some natural item to focus our powers." He drops my wrist, recrosses his arms, and turns to stare out the window.

"For myself, this stone is most sensitive. In one aspect it is white, a powerful color,"

"And secondly?"

"A stone maintains its own coldness; it does not take on the temperature of its surroundings," he explains evenly.

These descriptions bring more clarity to the University as well as my recent experiences. Even now I feel his icy grip within my skull. If white is what Odon uses to concentrate energy, then it is obviously the reason why the University is flooded with it. The cold floors and metal are ways for Odon to make his power grow.

"You say that every half-blood is different. Then how did you figure out your individual source?" I ask, hoping that his answer may be of help when Dorian transforms.

Odon smiles. "It takes time, a half-blood does not simply figure it out. It develops, and slowly becomes clear as the power refines itself."

"Does that mean all half-bloods have different powers?"

"No, but there are different ways of using them." Odon pivots on his feet. "That's enough discussion for one night. Besides, by tomorrow this will all be insignificant to you, as it currently is for me now." He chuckles to himself. "Sleep well," he adds sarcastically over his shoulder. "Tomorrow is your big day."

The door shuts behind him, and I lethargically move toward the center of the cushions. I'm not tired. There is too much on my mind. Are the others all right? Has the Great Oak really burned down as Odon said? Is Dorian alive? I wonder for a moment whether I might be able to contact Dorian again in my sleep. Then I'd be able to find the answers to all my questions.

I recall Odon's words. He threatened to watch me more closely. If he means it, then it probably would be best if Dorian kept his distance from my mind. Odon is still the one in control for now.

The lights above have dimmed considerably. In a few minutes they will be completely out. I will be left in blackness. It won't make any difference. I already feel as though I've been left in the dark. I sigh, knowing this whole situation is my own fault. Falda warned me of taking too many responsibilities at once. Now not only have I ruined the plans for the Rebirth tomorrow, but Aurek is dead.

I struggle with the memory. It seems so unreal. As though it was some terrible nightmare. But I know it's true: Aurek is dead, and that too is my fault.

I slump into a ball, hugging myself tightly. It's true. I had a strong dislike for Aurek that intensified into pure contempt. I even thought of his absence favorably, but did I wish for his death? Odon said he deserved what he got, and for a moment I agreed with him. I thought, after everything that Aurek had done to me, after what he had tried to do there in the garden, maybe his fate was in fact fairly granted. But I know better. I realize more strongly than ever that his death has not made me happier. Contrarily, I feel worse. Aurek was unaware of the wrongs he had done. The University had made that happen. This whole system has changed everyone, so how could I completely blame Aurek for his actions? Maybe, if he had only been able to witness life outside this place, he would have been different. There is no way of knowing that now.

Perhaps in some way, his death has made something more clear. I understand why Kadin did what he did, but more importantly, I understand why Odon must not die. Why Dorian must not kill him.

Kadin's hatred for Odon overwhelmed him so much that he turned on his own friends. He was so bent on killing Odon that he couldn't see what was really important. Odon's death would not change the past. It would not bring loved ones back. It would only mean becoming like all the other half-bloods, letting their emotions make their decisions for them. We cannot expect to win against them if we become them. We cannot fight death with death. I didn't intend to kill Aurek, yet I hold it as my own mistake, something I will carry with me for the rest of my life. If I ever believed his death would alleviate my own pain, I know now it is false. Yet Dorian doesn't see this.

Dorian doesn't know of the failed attempt. He has never heard of Kadin and all that was lost. I owe it to Dorian to use this experience, this knowledge, to keep him from remaking the mistakes of the past, from seeking revenge. It's not in our hands to become gods, to decide who deserves to live or die. If Dorian cannot see the danger in this, then I must make him see. Otherwise he is destined to become his enemy.

In the dying illumination of the lamps, I reach once more for Narena's journal, flipping through the pages until I come across the significant passage, "*if ever you should stray, your only way back is through the eyes of the one who truly loves you."* Although it's meaning I cannot completely fathom yet, I reread the passage until I can see the words fully when I close my eyes. By then the lights have gone, and I settle further backward.

Tomorrow is the beginning and the end. Tomorrow we will all be tested, our strengths, our weaknesses, our greatest fears. I must not give in to Odon's powers. I must not lose myself. I am Oriana, I am a pureblood, a Winglet, and a daughter of the Great Oak. I sift through the memories of what I believe makes me who I am as I slowly slip into sleep. I am Oriana, pureblood, Winglet, daughter of the Great Oak …

That night I dream of flying beneath the stars, a pair of iridescent wings upon my back as I ascend through the endless expanse. I force them downward, feeling the air currents attempt to alter my course. At first I fight their advancement; soon tiring against their endless onslaught. Then I change my approach, embracing the wind instead of opposing it. Altering instead the angles of my wings so that their arcs break smoothly through the air. Ahead I see the horizon where the moon reflects on the surface of the ocean, still just a line of silver magnificence. I fly onward, my focus centered on reaching the mystery before me. Although the ground passes swiftly below, the distance remains the same, and the slice of ocean remains always at the far edge of the land.

CHAPTER FORTY

The morning comes, oblivious to the destiny of the day it brings. I wake, my dream falling away and the reality overcoming me at once. I find Narena's journal lying next to me, and I slip it back into the pocket within my white robes. My body feels heavy as I get to my feet, smoothing out my skirts absentmindedly.

I wonder what Dorian and the others are doing. Are they already awake? Are they heading here now? I walk to the window and look out into the forest. Wherever they are, let them be safe and protected.

In the distant sky I notice movement. Odon's Winglarions, and they are heading toward the University. I watch them approach, spread in an arc across the sky. There is no joy in their flight. It is merely an ordered movement, a mundane part of life. Perhaps today will change that. If not, I will become one of them, losing my identity. I take one last look at the rising sun striking the treetops.

Behind me someone enters the room. I turn to find an Odonian I haven't seen before, despite my difficulty in telling them apart. This one is a woman, and I look closely into her soulless eyes, the eyes that reflect my potential state.

"Odon wishes you to attend the Rebirth," she says in a monotone voice.

I sigh, partially grateful to see Dorian and the others, but afraid to witness the final outcome of the battle. I know I must be there, whether Odon realizes it or not. I now understand why my presence will change the outcome of this event. I know what I must tell Dorian.

As soon as I step into the hallway, I realize I have left my sandals within, and the smooth floor makes my toes go numb. The Odonian leads me through a series of hallways that I am unfamiliar with. I think for a moment of escaping, hoping that if I can lose the Odonian, I might somehow find my way through the hallways. Yet the moment my mind tries to focus on stepping away, I am unable to move or even think.

"Odon …" He is watching me, somewhere else, but still able to see me clearly by some vision beyond the restrictions of his eyes.

The Odonian leads me down a spiraling staircase, each white step glistening beneath the lights. At the base of the stairs, the Odonian quickens her pace down the hallway, stopping abruptly at a set of double doors.

She opens the doors and reveals an enormous domed auditorium. At its center is a large circular platform, which is surrounded by rows of seats radiating outward around the entire room. They are empty, but I can presume who is meant to occupy them. I am amazed that I've never seen such a large room located within the University. My gaze moves upward along the globe ceiling to its highest point where there is an opening to the azure sky.

The Odonian explains nothing as she leads me down the slope of an aisle through the seats. We reach the center platform, where she motions for me to climb a short stairway to the top. I halt for a moment, looking up at the elevated stage. The sun strikes its surface, sending a beam of light upward and through the ceiling's opening. The Odonian motions again, and I climb the stairs, unsure what awaits me. Is this where I am to see the Rebirth? The steps are even colder beneath my bare feet than the hallway. Odon's power must be strong here.

I reach the top, the platform's surface quite cold despite the brilliance of the sunlight. I look out around me, shading my eyes until they have somewhat adapted to the glare. In all directions are the seats; clusters of them separated by inclining aisles that lead to sets of double doors like the one through which I entered. Everything is white, the seats a smooth metal, all meant to concentrate Odon's power in this single location, the platform I am standing on.

I walk along the edge, noticing that the Odonian has disappeared up the walkway. It is then that my knees give out and I topple to the ground, striking the hard surface and unable to get to my feet again.

It is as if I am stuck to the floor, as though a weight holds me here. I clench my teeth, again feeling the frustration of losing control of my own body.

It is then that a commanding voice echos around me, *"All upperclassmen will now be led by the Odonians to the Rebirth,"* it rumbles from above. I now recognize it to be Odon himself speaking. Then it occurs to me: Was the voice within the room or within my head? Has Odon been communicating to us all through our minds without us knowing? It does not emit from some visible device.

The doorways open at all ends of the circular room, and students pour into the auditorium. Odonians lead them in lines to their seats. No questions are being asked, no comments made. They remain silent, following without protest. In one half of the room are the Winglets; the other half I see filling up with Finlets—a crowd with flowing black hair, sleek beneath the rays of sunlight, their skin of a darker tone as if in constant shadow. I now see the opposite of these two beings, one destined to live above, the other below. There are no part-bloods here. These are the two races, each in their pure state as they first began.

These children do not know their past, nor do they understand their present state. They have been separated by Odon to keep their races from mixing, to prevent more half-bloods and forestall competition. It's ironic that my ancestors also wanted to keep the races separated. What they didn't understand is the power available as they come together and embrace their differences. The power of the half-blood could have brought good if only they had accepted change. Instead they tried to rid themselves of this new race. In the end, it only caused their own demise and the enslavement of their children.

"Oriana ..." I look around, surprised at having heard my name spoken nearby. I realize I didn't hear it through my ears, and I settle quickly hoping no one has seen my change in demeanor. It's Dorian I heard speak within my mind somewhere nearby. I relax; he is all right, and he has made it to the University safely. I search the rows of seats but see no one familiar. He is well hidden too.

My eye stops on one particular seat. Lenora is there, sitting beside her roommate, my replacement. I linger on her face, but it is vacant, empty. *Lenora, soon we will be reunited. Soon you will remember me again.* I know she cannot hear my thoughts, but the words comfort me anyway.

I notice the many faces around me turn upward toward the center of the globe. I lift my own eyes to the opening above. For a moment the sun is too strong to see anything as it's nearly at its peak in the sky. Then we are overshadowed by three figures, followed by an arc of several others. Odon is held between two of his Winglarions as they float downward, wings outstretched to their fullest extent. Behind them in perfect formation are the other winged men, Odon's bodyguards most likely. The Winglarions place him on the platform beside me. He wears an assortment of white silks draped upon his torso. In addition, a long cape has been laid across his shoulders, held decorously by a smooth round stone, which clasps both ends together at his chest. However, I know these are not merely garments of vanity. Odon's adornment will add to his power, allowing him to bring forth and control it.

His eyes scan the filled seats. He glances in my direction, stopping my breath for added measure. Then finally his eyes turn upward. The sun has nearly reached midday, when it will be exactly overhead and centered in the ceiling's opening. I regain my breath and turn my own attention upward. I realize he is waiting, patiently watching as the sun moves into position. I feel something within myself begin to change, some power, some transformation ready to be released inside. It rises up my feet and through my legs, reaching all the way to my torso. It is when I sense it in my neck that it halts. My scar becomes cold and shatters it into a million pieces. I shiver physically, unsure what has just happened.

I follow Odon's gaze once again to the opening, and the sun is sliding into its center. All around me I see the students begin to glow as the light of the sun intensifies inside the room. Odon closes his eyes, spreading his arms and concentrating. I attempt to yell, to jump to my feet trying to distract him, but of course, he is not letting me move or speak.

All around me the purebloods are fading, their colors melding and becoming indistinct. It is difficult to see them from within the most concentrated point of sunlight. I search for Lenora, but she too is impossible to discern. My head whirls around trying to comprehend what is going on. In my final turn, when the light of the others has dimmed and the sun continues through the sky, I see him. Risen into the air and surrounded by a vibrant dome of golden light.

Dorian floats above the crowd. His black hair whips upward as his body burns with an inner flame. I cover my eyes as pain shoots through them and then chance a second look. For a moment I can see him, and upon his back I distinguish translucent wings folded neatly behind him. His legs have been replaced by a long aquatic fin covered in shimmering scales. I gasp in surprise. Yet it seems as soon as I see him, the light explodes outward and when it completely dissipates, Dorian is himself again standing within an aisle on two feet. It leaves me to question whether I just imagined it.

The other students soon attract my attention. The Winglets have sprouted arcs of bleached feathers, and they ascend from their seats, hovering just above the auditorium's floor.

I notice Odon has remained still, his eyes shut. He makes a movement with his hands, his lips moving silently, and the Winglets, now Winglarions, fly across the dome to where the Finlets sit. I notice Lenora among them. She looks beautiful with the currents brushing back her hair and her wings lifted behind her. For a moment I wish to join them, I flex my wings outward, attempting to get to my feet. I arc them upward, feeling suddenly as though I have been flying all my life. But I remain seated and glance backward to find the air empty, my body unburdened by any new appendages. *I have no wings? I am not a Winglarion? No*, I realize, *I am not, I can never be, Odon has made me an Odonian*. It did not occur to me that they are pureblood as I am, and they do not have wings. I wish to scream, to cry with rage, but Odon restrains me from that as well. Instead I remain still, tearing at myself from within.

I watch longingly as the Winglarions fly to the Finlets who are changed as well. Their legs once laid separately, have now become one fin of iridescent scales, large and powerful. They now appear completely out of place on land, unable to move from their seats. Yet the curve of their green lower half possesses a beauty I have never seen before, and I wonder what agility they must display in their true environment within the ocean.

To my surprise, the Winglarions swoop down, plucking the Finlarions from their seats and propelling them upward. I wish to call out as Lenora takes to the air following the others through the hole in the ceiling. I watch as the distance broadens between us until she disappears through the opening and is lost into the sky.

Odon's eyes open to watch the last of the students leave through the ceiling. He relaxes for a moment to scan the empty seats. Or is he searching them? I look around and notice Dorian has gone.

"Come out, half-blood. I know you're here. It's time to finish this." Odon raises his hand, and the Winglarion men who brought him here take to the air, circling the room from above.

"I'm right here, Odon." Dorian steps into the aisle, his stern gaze upon Odon. I have never seen him so full of anger. His hands tremble. I look closely at him. He has changed. Squinting through the glare of the sun's rays I notice the power that entwines itself around his limbs. He has transformed.

"Good," Odon mutters beneath his breath.

Dorian's face softens as he notices me.

"Glad to see her?" Odon remarks, turning to me. I see a minor shift in his vision. The Winglarions hurtle toward Dorian. They reveal gleaming weapons poised in their outstretched hands. Dorian does not seem to notice. His focus is centered on Odon and me. His eyes narrow with rage at the way Odon walks over to stroke my hair.

I am powerless, unable to warn Dorian of the peril diving toward him. I can't even move away from Odon's caress.

"Don't touch her!" Then as Dorian runs toward the central stage and down the walkway, a Winglarion is struck down, his wings crumpling around him as he plummets to the ground. An arrow protrudes from his shoulder.

Tor emerges from behind a seat, bow in hand and another arrow already strung. He is not the only one. Finley stands from among another row of seats. Azura, appears as well, followed by Dugan and Jagger. Yet I notice as more of them appear, more Winglarions come to triple the numbers. They string their bows, striking down Odon's soldiers with grim accuracy. Finley gives a call, and more part-bloods burst through the double doors to join in the battle.

Odon's laugh rises above the swell of fighting. "Is this what you've brought to defeat me?" He chuckles again raising his hand triumphantly and balling it into a fist. In a second the others freeze in place, halted in action. Azura is fitting her bow with an arrow. Tor raises an arm to block an advancing Winglarion. They are like so many statues, chiseled into a never-ending battle. "This will be easier than I thought." Odon releases his Winglarions, having them stand, long, thin-bladed weapons raised to bring down each of the helpless part-bloods.

I plead in my head, "Please, don't let them die. Please, Dorian, do something!"

Dorian eyes the scene, studying it closely. Beads of sweat form on his brow. He must act quickly. He must think of something fast. I swallow, a lump forming at the back of my throat.

The Winglarion's weapons waver before striking downward together in one smooth movement. Dorian's fingers snap closed, and he cries, "NOOO!" The part-bloods come to life, some dodging the attack, others unable to react quickly enough. I see Jagger take the blow in his leg as he rolls sideways to avoid a second.

Dorian has found a way to deflect Odon's hold on the others. I sense him in my own mind, trying to push aside the coldness. But Odon is too close, and his hold much stronger on me than on them. Dorian continues toward us. His eyes focus in and out as he tries to concentrate on the minds of the others as well as the scene before him. He is not as well trained as Odon. He pauses to concentrate again, his fingers reaching for his temples and his eyes closing. He takes another step forward. The next is more difficult. Then I realize he is fighting Odon. I turn to look at Odon, who is still beside me, one hand resting on my hair. I can feel his power flowing through that palm. His other hand extends toward Dorian. The corners of his lips turn upward.

Dorian stops, unable to take another step, his eyes clamped shut, the sweat now dripping down his jaw. I watch helplessly as he struggles against Odon's will. There is a moment where he gasps for air, trying to force himself to breathe. Out of the corner of my eye I notice a streak of white. Odon has sent a Winglarion after Dorian. He plunges toward him, lifting his weapon above his head to drive straight through Dorian's torso. I try to scream, wanting to fling myself at him, even merely close my eyes. But I am unable to do anything.

Beside him a figure appears. Her bow is raised as she reaches for an arrow. Azura uses her body as a shield, searching desperately for an arrow that does not exist. When she realizes there is nothing to grasp, she stands tall, tensing her muscles to stop them from trembling. Dorian stands beside her, unaware of her presence as he fights to hold back Odon.

I watch as the Winglarion approaches, unmoved by the scene

below, weapon willing to run through anything in its path. At last my breath escapes me, and I scream, a piercing note that somehow cuts through Odon's hold for one moment.

The Winglarion's blade thrusts into the body, stabbing through to the other side, releasing the life in a deep red liquid that stains the white floor. Liam sinks to the ground, the weapon still protruding from his chest as his eyes darken. He had thrown himself in front of Azura, protecting her at the last second from the Winglarion's sword.

Dorian comes to life at the sound of my voice. Knocking back the Winglarion with a wave of his hand, he continues toward Odon and me. There is a look upon his face that is frightening to witness.

Behind him, Azura rests Liam's head against her thigh, sobbing into his limp form.

CHAPTER FORTY-ONE

Inside I am ripping apart with sorrow, wishing I had been able to help in some way but still powerless to do so. Liam had loved Azura enough to give his life to save her. Now he will never share that love with her.

Dorian reaches the platform, glaring up at Odon with a full-fledged hatred. "Your life ends now Odon," he says, beginning to climb the steps, "Your reign of damage is over. I will see to that myself!"

Odon pulls me up, using me as a shield against Dorian. His hand grips my neck, but it is within that I am being strangled.

"Let her go, Odon!" Dorian shouts, there are tears trembling in his eyes and his body shakes in the grip of hostility.

"It's too late! She's already mine!" He pulls me backward to the end of the platform. I open my mouth, trying to draw in breath but powerless to do so. My lungs burn and writhe in pain. I wish to strike him, beat at his hold with my fists, but I still cannot move. Tears escape the corners of my eyes, running down my cheeks and flooding my open mouth.

Dorian watches me, I see the hurt in his eyes; the torture at seeing me struggle. Around us the fight continues. The part-bloods hold back the onslaught of Odon's Winglarions. Somewhere Azura holds Liam in her arms, somewhere Jagger limps to Dugan's aid. Somewhere Malise and Aaron wait staring at the sky wondering if today will bring freedom. Odon reaches the edge of the platform, Dorian now cornering him. "Release her now!"

"I think not!" Odon spits. From behind us Winglarions appear.

Two take Odon's arms and lift him upward. My breath returns as the last grabs my limp form and moves to take me away. "You've failed again!! Not only have you allowed me to increase my army, but you've handed me your precious pureblood." The Winglarions fly us toward the opening as Odon calls down, his voice gaining strength as our distance increases, "Foolish child, you are even weaker than the other! You didn't even have the courage to try to kill me!"

The Winglarions hover in midair, wings beating simultaneously. Odon grows quiet, but I cannot lift my head to see what he has planned. I notice that our height begins to decrease, the Winglarion descending to the central platform below.

The auditorium has grown quiet, the part-bloods and Winglarions no longer fighting. Instead they look to Dorian, their faces blank, as if awaiting orders. The scene makes my skin crawl as the Winglarions touch down on the smooth white floor and place me on my feet. I feel Dorian's warmth enveloping me, and I am able to stand. When I am released, I run to his side, grabbing hold of his arm and turning to face Odon in triumph.

The Winglarions hold him fast, but I see that Odon is incapable of moving on his own anyway.

"Thought you were going to get away?" Dorian says with a sneer. "Did you think I'd let you take Oriana?" He smirks, stepping toward Odon and freeing his arm from my grasp. I find myself rooted to the floor, but it is not Odon who holds my body in place.

Dorian paces in front of Odon's face; although Dorian is not as wide in girth, they share the same height. Odon blinks silently, the struggle in his eyes apparent. He is trying to wrench free of Dorian's grasp. It's not just Odon that Dorian holds prisoner. I look around at the many faces, each maintaining an expressionless gaze. Dorian has taken over the entire room, including myself.

I turn my attention back to Dorian, where Odon's face is slowly turning blue from lack of air. With a gesture from Dorian, the Winglarions step backward, allowing Odon to fall to his knees his fingers raking at his throat.

I move to stop him, to get Dorian's attention. He must not kill Odon. But it is Dorian now who stops me. I have become lost in the minds of the others he is keeping in place. I speak his name, trying to nudge at him from within. "Dorian."

He stops for a moment, has he heard me? Odon reels on the ground, his life fading fast.

"Dorian!" I shout louder in my mind, desperately fighting his hold.

He faces me, but I barely recognize him. His expression scares me. I can see he is consumed with power and revenge. When our eyes meet, I see him flicker within: the Dorian I know, the one who would not hold his friends as prisoners.

I search my mind now that I have his attention I must speak something that will bring him back. If I do not act quickly he may be lost forever, burned up by the force that now flows strongly within him.

"Dorian, please, you've done enough. It's okay now." I hear my voice in my head speak warmly, beckoning him to me. "Come with me, we can be together now."

He takes a step toward me, his face losing its anger as we make eye contact. I see Odon's tense body begin to relax.

"You must not kill Odon," I begin, but that is all wrong. The moment I mention Odon's name Dorian turns away from me, and I see Odon grasping at his neck once again. Dorian has always reacted against me when I've brought up Odon before. I have told him he must not seek revenge, and he reacted defensively. I search my brain. How can I make him realize what I have come to know?

The words come to me all at once in perfect clarity. Narena's words. *If ever you should stray, your only way back is through the eyes of the one who truly loves you.* I repeat the sentence in my mind, focusing on Dorian. I alter my struggle against him and instead allow his hold to completely enter my mind. He is pulled inward, his power too strong for him to withhold without practice. In an instant he is behind my eyes, the place where Odon had seen my memories through my mind, and he is feeling my emotions and remembering all my past experiences. Dorian sees himself through my eyes, he sees who he has become. The hatred in his eyes, the uncontrollable anger leading him to murder, to become the evil he has striven to defeat.

I sense him pull back in horror at his own image. His powers retreat to his mind, and I watch as the others blink into awareness. Even the Winglarions open their eyes with a new vision, experiencing the freedom of conscious thought.

Dorian backs away as Odon gets to his feet, eyes bloodshot and face a scarlet red. "You … you didn't kill me … you coward!!" Odon spasms, a look of panic on his face as he stumbles backward. His mind reaches out for mine, and I can feel him probing for an opening, but Dorian is beside me, and when his hand touches mine, Odon's power dissipates completely from my senses.

"What are we to do with him?" Tor stands beside Dorian on the platform watching the pitiful sight of Odon in a disordered outrage.

"He will not be a threat to us any longer," Dorian affirms.

"How can you be certain?" Finley joins us, looking down with distaste at the broken man.

"I can hold back his attacks. I can't explain it any more than that," Dorian explains.

I am suddenly struck with a memory, and I release Dorian's hand and rush down the platform steps to where Liam has fallen. Azura lies beside him, grasping his hand as Liam holds on to his last moments in life.

"You can't leave, Liam! This is all my fault … it was me you were trying to protect …" Azura's face is broken. So crippling is the sight that I nearly break down before even reaching her. I swallow any sobs and straighten my back. I must be strong for her.

I kneel beside her and Liam as he mutters her name. "Azura …"

"I'm here, Liam."

She does not notice me beside her until I place my hand on her shoulder. I look down at Liam. His wound cuts directly through his vitals. His life will not last much longer.

"Azura, I've wanted to tell you …"

"I know, Liam, I've always known," she whimpers, her hand reaching to caress his face. Her tears splatter upon his wound thick with blood.

"I need to tell you, I love you …" He gasps for air as the blood fills his lungs further.

Azura shakes, her weeping becoming uncontrollable so that she is almost unable to answer. "I love you too." Liam's face becomes peaceful as he looks upon her one last time before closing his eyes forever. It is then that Azura turns to me, wrapping her arms around me and releasing her sorrow into my shoulder. I remain silent, knowing my own tears will only make it harder for her.

I feel warmth beside me, and I turn to see Dorian and the others standing over us. Dugan holds Jagger up, but the others seem to have only minor injuries.

We begin to gather others who have departed during battle, pureblood and part-blood alike, working alongside the Winglarions, who appear to remain in a state of confusion. Do they remember when they were younger? Their families or old homes? Or have they always been under Odon's control and know nothing else.

One of the younger Winglarions approaches Dorian cautiously. Together we turn awaiting the words that he is having difficult producing.

"Where are we to go?" Other Winglarions join behind him, supporting his courage for speaking what had been on all their minds.

Dorian's mouth opens for a moment before any sound comes out. "I ... I don't know. Wherever you please, you are free now."

"But," the Winglarion begins.

"We do not know what to do, where to stay," a second finishes for him.

My thoughts move to Lenora and the other students who left not long ago. Are they facing the same situation?

"Your place is in the sky," Tor says soothingly, "as Winglarions. I believe you will feel most suited there."

The Winglarions look around at their fallen comrades. Some turn to glance at Odon, who remains upon the platform, muttering to himself.

"We will provide them with a proper burial," Tor continues and then jabs a thumb in Odon's direction. "And you do not have to worry about him anymore. You're safe as long as you remain in these lands. Outside them, Dorian cannot provide protection for you from others like him."

The Winglarions look toward Dorian, further uncertainty upon their faces, "How will we know," the first one asks, "if we leave?"

Dorian's expression takes on a certainty. "You will know." It is then that I feel his presence, not that of an icy grip, but the shield of his power in the air surrounding us. I wonder if the others feel it as I do.

The Winglarions nod, still unsure whether to believe him and proving that they do not feel what I can. Their faces turn upward, and they rise into the air with the first stroke of powerful wings. Wings that I long to possess as well. I find Dorian's hand resting in mine, and a soothing energy flows over me. I smile slyly at him, "Get out of my head!" I say mentally.

He gives me a grin, his eyes sparking as he answers me without speaking, "You're the one who let me in." I realize he's right, when I had forced him to see through my eyes, I had opened my mind to him. Now his presence will forever remain.

"Tor! We have found the remaining students and professors, but none of the Odonians." A part-blood boy leads the stray students toward us. There are so many young faces, not just of the eldest grades but those below. Their numbers stretch backward up the aisle and past the doorway, probably stretching even farther.

Glancing at Tor, I can see he is overwhelmed, unsure how to accommodate so many. I notice the professors moving toward us, meandering around the frightened children. One of them I recognize as a teacher from long ago. He does not recognize me as he approaches, a part-blood female following close behind him.

"What has happened?" he asks. I can tell he is struggling with memories that do not seem real. Dorian and I keep our distance as Tor boldly explains the occurrences of recent years. The look on the faces of those listening tells that his words are reaffirming hazy visions of their past. When their attention is drawn to Odon, Tor's words take on a stronger clarity.

It is evening before arrangements can be made for those of the University. The remaining adults are left in charge until further organization can be put into effect. Tor makes the final decision to stay behind, where he will be able to assist the professors in their task. There are so many children, and so much has changed in such a short time. Several part-bloods from the Great Oak volunteer to remain with Tor and help the others settle into their newfound freedom. The rest of us depart for the Great Oak, eager to be home once again and share the good news with friends left behind.

The sun's red eye watches us as we carry those lost to us from the University. I watch the sky, hoping to see any of the purebloods returning, hoping Lenora might be among them, but the sky is empty. Behind us, Odon is being led by two of our strongest part-bloods. Although Dorian insists he will remain harmless, Finley is adamant about the extra precaution. I notice that Buck is not one of the two.

"Where is Buck?" I ask, walking beside Dorian.

He glances at me and then turns to the forest ahead of us. "Buck was lost at the Great Oak when Odon's men came."

My stomach sinks, "Then Odon *did* attack?" I've been hoping that my communication with Dorian prevented any damage. I was wrong.

"Were there others?" I ask hesitantly.

"Yes, some other part-bloods, but no one very young. It might've been worse if I hadn't spoken to you." He forces a smile, trying to hide how much Odon's actions had hurt him.

"Dorian, it was all my fault. Odon found the way to the Great Oak by using my memories! If I hadn't ..."

Dorian nods grimly, "I suspected as much, but we can't think of our mistakes. It wasn't your fault." His second attempt at a smile is more genuine. "Think of how many you have saved today."

I nod, deciding to let those in the past rest and focus on the future instead. There are so many freed now who need us—our guidance and care. Today is merely the beginning of our hard work. It's going to take everyone's effort to find order in a now chaotic world. I think of the other half-blood realms where many more children are still enslaved. Our triumph today is small compared to what we are about to face. I glance at Dorian. He was so powerful today, standing against Odon, the tyrant I once thought indestructible. But Dorian is just one, and there are other half-bloods out there, including some that may be stronger than even Odon.

I decide to push the thoughts aside. Tonight we will honor those lost. Tonight we will celebrate the freedom of many and the prospect of many more.

We reach the Great Oak as the moon appears in the night sky, dancing among its many glittering children. Our celebration is bittersweet as we share our story and speak of those that will not return. As I look around me at the many faces of the living, I see the hope resurging that had once escaped me.

That night, before I fall into bed beside Dorian, I feel the weight of something from within my robes. Reaching inside the hidden pocket I find the burden, Narena's journal. With a sigh I place it upon my dresser, now finding the needed ease to reach sleep.

CHAPTER FORTY-TWO

I wake to find Dorian at the entrance to my cottage speaking softly to someone on the outside. He gives a nod and turns to face me, letting the flap close behind him.

"There is a meeting to attend," he announces, "Tor has returned to discuss Odon."

When we arrived at the Great Oak last night, Odon was placed in a well-guarded structure upon one of the platforms. It was announced that the next day his fate would be decided.

Today is that day. I slip out of bed and slide on my sandals. This meeting is sure to be a long one, as there will be many alternating opinions of what will become of the tyrant. My emotions wish him only death, but my head knows it would be a reckless act.

Dorian and I grab our cloaks; the morning is cold, and the cloud cover seems to forebode a chilling day. They sweep behind us as we rush along the platform. A wind howls overhead, pushing us backward, keeping us from our destination. My own uneasiness holds me back as well. I'll be glad when the event is over and we can concentrate on burying our loved ones. Dorian's arm helps me as I fight against the wind, clutching my hood to keep it from flying backward.

By the time we reach the meeting hall, it is a welcome sight. We slip in, the whistling wind heralding our arrival. As we are taking our seats, the last of the others enter, and last of all Azura. She hides her swollen face beneath the shadows of her hood. Liam's death is still fresh on all our minds. Finley, Dugan, and Jagger take their seats, I notice Weasel is not among them. I bite my lip in distress. He must still be mourning Buck. There are other part-bloods of our generation here as well, sitting against the wall, where stools have been brought to accommodate them. This decision must involve many.

I take my seat next to Dorian, uncomfortable with the eerie silence. I realize that the others stare at the far corner at the head of the room, where a lone figure sits. Beside him are two part-bloods, their hands wrapped around each of his arms. Odon's face is covered in shadow as he hangs his head. His wrists have been tied with twine as well as his ankles. Around his shoulders, a black cloak has been draped. I give my head a slight shake, thinking to myself, "Those types of bindings will not keep his power at bay." It is in fact Dorian who is keeping him from entering all our minds and taking over. He is only as powerful as those who follow him. Alone, he is as mortal as the rest of us.

Tor takes his place at the head of the room, and there is a shift of attention onto his tall form. "Let us begin," he states curtly. "We are here to discuss the fate of this man." Tor gestures to Odon as though he were just another being and not the once powerful dictator who caused uncountable deaths within his lifetime.

Finley is the first to stand and speak out. "I understand my words might sound heinous, but I think it only wise to execute this man. If he is left alive, we risk the past repeating itself." There are murmurs of agreement from among the crowd.

"He does not deserve such an easy escape," Azura mutters from within her cape. I watch her with compassion. She is truly suffering.

I am surprised when Dorian speaks next. "I understand your hatred as much as anyone here, maybe more ..." he murmurs to himself and then raises his voice again. "But if we were to kill Odon, it would be murder. This man is not a threat to us now. He is unarmed and unable to cause more destruction. We cannot kill him in this manner; we would be no better than he."

"Doesn't he deserve the same fate he would deal another?" Finley continues, certain that his decision is the right one. If I did not know him so well, I would think he was a cruel young man. Yet I know why he reacts this way. Finley was alive when the others died. He watched his friends fall beneath Odon's hand. His own family was lost to this man. Now that we have him in our grasp, we would have ourselves to blame if he ever harmed another again.

The hum of the rooms settles again as Tor stands to speak. "Finley, we cannot kill this man." He raises a palm to his friend of many years. "Dorian is right, look at his state. He is unable to defend himself; killing him would be cold-blooded murder. Could you live with yourself after something like that?"

Finley sighs, as if he can see no other way. "I could live with myself if it was him."

I hear the others around us muttering. There is a variety of opinions among them. This meeting will last for a time longer if I do not think of something. There must be some way to satisfy all parties.

"What if we could place Odon where he will be safe, yet no longer a danger to anyone else?" I suggest.

"We cannot guard this man for the rest of his life," Tor answers. "His natural death will not come for several years, are we to watch over him until then?"

I pause for a moment, trying to come up with something worth our time. It is Azura who answers.

"The caves," she says softly, and then louder: "The caves!" She stands, her hood falling back to reveal her reddened eyes and lips. "We can put Odon in a cell of the caves. If we supply him with food and water occasionally, then he could live out his life and never be a burden to anyone." Of course, Azura is likely to think of the plan. She herself spent time within its darkness. Odon is well deserving of such a place.

"He will be a safe distance, yet still within the lands." Tor slowly nods his head as he works out the construct of the decision. "Dorian's powers will reach him as necessary. We would merely have to monitor him every few months. Can you agree with this, Finn?"

Finley looks from Tor to Azura. All other eyes are on him. This new idea appears suitable. For Azura to see her captor sent to live out his life in the place where she was meant to live out hers is more than she could have imagined. I understand her desire to see him thrown away for all eternity. Finley needs no more convincing. He nods.

Tor calls for a vote among the crowd, but it is clear that Azura's suggestion has won them over. It is agreed that Odon will be brought to live out the rest of his days within his own dark prison. He will be given food and water when needed, but no more accommodations will be made.

The guards pull Odon to his feet and guide him through the

meeting hall's door. We follow him out. I turn to find Dorian, his face focusing on Odon with unusual pressure. "Dorian … what is it …?"

A yell erupts among those around us. I turn to see Odon tear away from the guards. Tor reaches out for him but Odon dodges backward avoiding his grasp. Then he flings himself backward, over the edge of the platform, descending into the shadows below at a breathtaking speed. Tor and Finley are the first to rush to the edge, peering into the abyss below.

"We have to see if he is still alive down there!" Finley shouts, starting to head down the ladder.

"He is already dead," Dorian calls to Finley with a bitter confidence.

"There is no way he could've survived that fall," Tor adds in the same tone of certainty.

"We can't take that chance. We would never be definitely sure …" Finley starts to protest.

"I am positive." Dorian states again, raising his voice for all to hear. "I felt his mind blink shut. He is in blackness now."

There are whispers among the crowd as they slowly move down the platform and out of sight. Finley and Tor speak quietly as they follow.

Odon had chosen to use the last of his energy to kill himself. He knew he would be driven mad in a cell within his own caves. He had chosen an easy escape.

"Odon won in the end, didn't he?" Azura stands beside me, the wind pulling at the curls of her hair.

"No, he didn't." I take her hand. It is so cold. "We are alive and free. Odon pays for what he's done, no matter where he is. It will torment him for eternity."

"You really believe that?" Azura asks. Her tone says she is willing it to be true.

"I do." We walk together, Dorian, Azura, and I, heading to the lowest platform where the others will be preparing to bury those gone. Odon will not be mourned. Now the wind compels us downward, willing us toward the final good-byes.

When we arrive on the lower platform before the longest ladder, we meet up with Piper and Lily. Toby, Malise, and Aaron are there as well. They welcome us, holding back tears. Word of Odon's demise has already spread, but thoughts are elsewhere.

In a long procession, we descend the ladder, the rhythm of our steps as one. I try to remain strong, knowing how delicate Azura is in this moment. I wipe at tears that refuse to recognize my stubborn will. Azura touches the ground beneath me, and I lick my lips before facing her. Dorian is behind me, offering soothing thoughts, and I am able to stand straight.

The others seek the graves of their dearest friends. Azura seeks a group of part-bloods burying Liam. His youthful form is wrapped in clean rough cloth. Azura grips my hand tightly, lifting her hood over her head and retreating slightly from the grave. When he is fully covered, his resting place beneath the shade of the Great Oak's protective branches, Azura kneels to place a single yellow flower upon the ground. In its simplicity I see its beauty, its delicate petals representing life and love. A thought occurs to me, and I leave Azura's side to dash into the forest.

I run along the familiar stream whose simple tune tells of a continuing circle of death and rebirth. I splash through it at its shallowest point, the cold water reminding me of pain that comes and goes. Past these rows of bushes, I reach the clearing where the fruit tree stands. Some things have not changed. I climb upon its root that forms a seat and reach into its branches to retrieve a ripened fruit. I hurry back to the others, cradling the fruit in my arm like a newborn infant.

When I've reached Azura and Dorian, who have been joined by Tor, they look at me quizzically. I kneel between Azura and Dorian and place the fruit beside Azura's flower. We all stand.

Azura clasps my wrist for a moment. "Thank you," she says before heading away.

One day the fruit will bring new life, a tree like its mother. Liam will live through the soil, through the tree above him, living forever through the endless life of this world. Dorian takes my hand as I begin to shed tears. I look up into his eyes, trying to console myself that with death comes life, with enslavement comes freedom. But when I see that Dorian sheds tears silently as well, I feel no shame in releasing my own upon his shoulder.

When we part, Tor shares low words with Dorian, and I find

myself drawn to another. Finley stands alone beside a grave. When I reach his side, he turns to me and simply says, "Buck."

"I'm so ..."

"I think Weasel feels the worst of it. He was there. Buck saved his life before losing his own. Even though Odon is gone, the pain remains." I am grateful that Finley does not blame me for Buck's death, although I still blame myself.

"It will take time to heal, but the days will pass. Weasel will realize that Buck can never die. He will live on with all of us, as will the others." I gesture toward the fresh graves, arranged neatly in a circle. I feel as though no words can justify our feelings, although I try to see the reason in it all.

"We succeeded." Finley pushes a hand through his hair with a rueful grin. "And with every great accomplishment comes great loss."

That night Dorian and I sit upon the platform outside our shelters. I look up into the night sky, searching through the stars to find one familiar. They are all alike, yet beautiful individually.

"Dorian, do you know what happened to the others? The purebloods who transformed during the Rebirth yesterday?" I can't help but wonder if Lenora is all right.

"I sense their minds, but there are so many. It is difficult to tell what they are thinking or feeling." Dorian closes his eyes for a moment, and I sense his mind reaching out into the lands beyond. I am already beginning to perceive his thoughts. Nothing distinct; instead I feel the essence that they emit.

"During the Rebirth I watched the Winglarions carry the Finlarions away." I ask the question I've pondered ever since. "Where did they take them?" .

"They brought them to the ocean. If they had not, the Finlarions would've died without water."

I look out to where the moon casts its glow on the ocean's surface, still only a thin line to me. I strain my eyes, trying to get a better look, but there is no improvement.

"Don't worry, I will stand by my promise. One day I will show it to you myself."

I smile, Dorian finishes my thoughts often now.

"Oriana—"

I turn to him, trying to grasp his thoughts.

"I know you have been thinking of Lenora lately, your sister. There must be some way you could …"

"See her again?" I shake my head. "I tried that. She doesn't remember me. Now that she's gained her wings, she belongs to another world. We must be separate from now on, isn't that how it works?"

Dorian presses his lips together, "Odon prevented your transformation; that cannot be reversed … but now that he's gone, your sister could be a completely different person! You could start all over again, become reacquainted."

I eye him for a moment, believing for a second that it might be true. I shake my head, "You didn't see the way she looked at me. It is better if we stay in our separate worlds. I can't go through that again."

Dorian sighs but says nothing more of my sister for the rest of the night. We retire to bed as the moon reaches its peak in the night sky.

CHAPTER FORTY-THREE

Each new day brings some comfort, and I awake feeling refreshed. It was Odon's hold that had caused my illness. My physical form outwardly reflects the struggle against what threatened within. Now, with Odon gone, I feel as though time is making me younger.

Dorian has already gone, leaving me to rest further on my own. Hurrying out the door, I notice the platforms are quiet. I head to the lower platform where the dining hall is situated. Despite the empty seats, their occupants offering time at the University, it is bustling with movement as youths chatter between bites of food. From their heightened excitement, I can tell something is brewing.

I find Dorian in his usual seat, deep in thought. The seats directly across and next to him are empty. I sit beside him, startling him from deep thought.

"Good morning," he says, recovering.

I nod with a smile, taking a moment to glance at the part-bloods to my left who are talking at an accelerated pace.

"Where's Tor?" I ask. "Has he left for the University?" His work there is far from over. After his return to decide Odon's fate and bury those lost, I presumed he would leave again.

Dorian affirms my assumption, "Yes, but he is to return later today."

"Return?"

He nods. "And not alone either. He has sent word that we are to begin building immediately. He is bringing the others."

"Building? Where?"

He smiles. "At the Great Oak, and the hill below if we have to. We will need a great deal of housing for all those young ones."

After the morning meal, the Great Oak's inhabitants waste no time in beginning their labor. Below, youths gather whatever useful wood they can find. Branches and bark are hauled up the ladder in a steady stream of lifting arms and ropes. The weavers work steadily on new clothing. Others gather the fluffy seeds that yield the thread. Still more are needed at the field, where extra food is collected for the extra mouths. Although there seemed to be a large community at the Great Oak, the amount of work is overwhelming, and despite our determined drive, more hands are needed.

My time is spent gathering straight sticks and brush to roof the new housing. The twigs are bundled together and pulled up by ropes into the canopy above where they are deposited on newly built platforms. After placing an armful of branches on the pile to be wrapped, I head back toward the woods. I stop short when I hear my name being called, a call that only I can hear.

"Dorian?" I turn as he approaches, Finley following close behind. I watch them curiously; they seem eager to speak with me.

"I've found your sister," Dorian states bluntly, this time out loud.

I study him, unsure what this means. "Then she is well. I am glad to hear it." I kneel to continue my gathering.

"That's not all," Dorian adds nervously. He glances at Finley, who nods.

I shoot Dorian a glare, already perceiving the emotion that is emitting from him.

"I have sent for her to come. She will reach the Great Oak by midday."

"You what? But how did you ...?"

"I located her mind, it took a lot of concentration, but I managed." Dorian's eyes light with a pride that quickly dims at the lack of amusement in my stare. He continues with less vigor, "Then I simply sent her a mental image of you and the Great Oak. I wasn't sure she'd react to it. But she immediately changed course and is heading this way!"

From my knees I fall backward sighing as I sit upon the ground. "I guess I can't be angry with you. Your intentions were good." The idea of facing my sister again is unappealing. Yet I suppose now I have no choice. "Tell me when she gets here. I will speak with her."

Tor arrives near noon. The forest behind him is crowded with those from the University. I notice the professors. No, they aren't professors anymore. The elders carry infants in their arms. And when I spot the part-bloods who stayed behind, they carry infants as well. Tor separates from the others, and I follow, hoping for some explanation of what is to happen.

When I reach him, he is speaking with a part-blood. "Make sure they are fed and the infants are taken care of. Then those who are able will join the others and continue building the new shelters." The part-blood gives a nod before running off as Finley and Dorian approach from different directions.

As Tor turns to me, I notice the strain in his face. These events have tired him, and I hesitate to speak.

Finley wastes no time. "Do you expect us to build housing for all these people? How will the Great Oak withstand so many new platforms?"

"We will do our best," Tor states, his patience taxed. "And if need be, we will build upon the ground. They will work as well, and with so many hands the work will go quickly."

Finley nods, although he is thinking what we all are: How long until our lives go back to normal?

"Tor, the infants ... where did you find them?" I ask.

"They are all pureblood. We are unsure of their parents, but apparently Odon's University housed an infirmary as well." Tor sees that more explanation is needed. "The University had been divided into levels, separating the youths by age. You must remember being moved from one section to the other as you grew older."

"Yes, I do." The nursery is my earliest memory, when I was about four years old. I was unsure where the facilities were. Yet I do remember being brought from one place to the other. But where are the parents?

"Odon must have taken them from their parents," Dorian says, although it seems he is speaking to himself. "If he controlled the purebloods completely, then he could take their children without protest."

"He was truly evil," Finley mutters before leaving us.

"I must leave as well. I'm long overdue for some rest," Tor adds before striding toward the Great Oak.

I turn to Dorian, still by my side. "This is going to take time, even after everything is built. There are so many who have to rebuild their whole lives."

Dorian brushes my hair back gently. "It may take longer, but at least now they are able to begin healing." I nod, glancing back at the many faces of confusion and wonderment. The Great Oak will help them; we all will. They will learn, as I have learned, to think for themselves, to see the world with not just their eyes but their hearts. I will share their past, as Falda shared mine with me. I have seen what they've seen and lived among them. If any good came from my time within the University, it is the compassion and understanding I have for these others.

Glancing back at Dorian, I notice his eyes are closed, his forehead stitched with concentration. I feel his mind reaching out, providing hope and healing, thoughts of endless possibilities for the future. Yet his power pushes past me, flows up the Great Oak's trunk, and cascades down the hillsides reaching over all that inhabit this forest. I recall Odon's words after I asked him if each half-blood has a different power. He'd answered, "No, but there are different ways of using them." Now I can see what he meant by this. Dorian turned on us while at the University. He used his powers to control our minds, keeping us from moving. Turned Odon's own guards against him. Dorian's ability to defeat Odon means he must be more powerful, but still he relies on the same abilities: to enter the minds of others. Now he is using that power for good, spreading the needed consolation that will keep us working toward the future.

He opens his eyes suddenly as if discovering something unexpected. He looks down at me. "Lenora is here."

I try to keep up with his long strides as he heads for the Great Oak. We climb the base ladder quickly. My hands shake whenever I release my grip to reach for the rung above. I wonder what to expect. Will she be the Lenora I know? It's hard to want her to be the same, even if it means not knowing her at all.

Now all of it is gone, there is no more Odon, and the University is nothing more than a white shell, hollow at its center. There is nothing more to keep us apart—except our own destinies. Lenora is a Winglarion now, and I'm still meant for the ground. We will not be able to be together from now on. She will leave for the sky, and I will remain behind. Odon kept me from transforming so that I would become one of his Odonians. Even after he is gone, I remain as I am now—a Winglarion with no wings, no ability to fly. I can never go back; the moment of the Rebirth is over. I was right there, and yet I missed it completely.

Dorian leads me higher as we climb each ladder of the layered platforms. We reach our cottages, two thatch shelters side by side. Halting, he turns to face me and looks up into the branches surrounding us. I search as well, finding only the familiar network of limbs.

"She is here ..." Dorian speaks, his voice fading. His eyes move along the canopy. He looks back down at me, "You must call to her."

I watch him for a moment before looking upward again, "Lenora?" The name is caught in my throat, and I lift my head higher to call again. "Lenora!"

There is a rustle from above, followed by more movement along a neighboring branch. I hold my breath waiting for any sight of my sister.

Then several figures emerge from the tree, gliding softly in spirals downward to stand upon the platform. They are a young man and two girls, one of whom I recognize as my replacement, the girl I saw in the University inside my old room. Lenora is the other, with her wings folded delicately behind her and an expression growing on her face.

"Oriana," she whispers, approaching me with caution.

"You—you remember me?" are the first words that come to mind. Even that small recognition brings a rising relief.

Lenora nods. "Yes, I do. I remember other things as well, things I will remain shameful of." Her face is different now. Her features are softer, more relaxed and serene. Despite the sadness in her eyes, she radiates a peaceful beauty.

This surprises me. I was unsure what Lenora might recall, but I did not expect specific events. "I forgive you," I reply with certainty. It feels good to speak to her without fear, without thinking that I am saying too much, or without holding a blank stare.

"I don't think it will be that easy," she says, looking away.

"Lenora, we cannot blame ourselves. It was our environment that made us who we were." It's hard to believe that the girl I'm speaking to is the same Lenora. The cold, emotionless Lenora who showed no love in her heart. Now it seems she has a conscience, and the feelings of guilt and regret that were missing have returned decisively.

"It's hard to explain how I'm feeling now," she begins, "I remember some of it"—she looks up at me—"but I feel as though another person was doing them. We all feel this way." Lenora gestures to those around her.

"It is Odon's power that took your past away from you, but he is gone now. Odon is dead, and as long as you stay in these lands, Dorian will protect you." I find my place beside him.

"Then it was you that saved us?" Lenora asks, bowing her head to him as the others mirror her gratitude.

"We are forever in your debt," the young man states.

"Very grateful," the other girl adds.

Dorian reddens, waving away the compliments as though it was nothing at all.

I address Lenora once again. "I have something I've wished to tell you for a while now."

Lenora turns to me with curiosity. "Yes, I believe it is what brought me here. I remember thinking of you and then seeing this large oak. It was like a dream, and yet it became true. It sounds crazy, I know."

I glance slyly at Dorian who tries to ignore me. "It's not crazy, I believe you," I begin with a smile and take a deep breath. "Lenora, I have come to discover that you and I are more than just friends or roommates. We are twin sisters."

Lenora's eyes widen, and I can see the similarities in our features. "How do you know this?"

We sit upon the platform, leaning against the Oak, and I explain our story. How our mother Sonya had tried to escape to right here, to the Great Oak. When I speak of her death and our mother's love for us, Lenora begins to cry, something I thought I would never see. Lenora is not used to it, and she tries to choke back the tears at first, before embracing her sadness and allowing them to flow.

When I have finished our tale, I feel as though we are bonded by the shared experience of long ago. Although we were so young at the time, it is the knowledge that we came into this world together that brings us closer. We share an embrace, one that is genuine and honest. I find my own cheeks wet when we separate.

"Oriana, why don't you have wings?" Lenora asks, a look of true concern upon her face.

"Odon took away the lives of many, he took away emotions and years of freedom. He took away my wings." This seems to sadden Lenora more than ever. Tears flow from her eyes as if she is imagining herself without wings and finding the thought unbearable. I wipe the dampness from her cheeks and force a smile.

"You must fly for both of us."

Lenora nods. Behind her, the other Winglarions spread their wings. They are anxious to be in the sky, as are all Winglarions when they have been on their feet for too long. Glancing backward, she begins to extend her own wings, eyeing the air above with expectation.

"I will see you again?" I ask, and she looks back downward.

Lenora smiles. "Yes, sister, this will not be our last meeting." She lifts into the sky gracefully, only having her wings for a few days yet appearing to have been born with them. She gives a wave as she tilts her body upward, scooping her wings in swift strokes.

I wave back although her back is turned. "Good-bye sister," I murmur, watching her lift into the realm above, a place I will never come to know.

As she disappears among the branches, I realize something Falda accepted long ago. There is nothing definite in this world. Not all birds were meant to fly, not all flowers meant for sunlight, and even among Winglarions these exceptions exist. My place is with Dorian and my friends. My home will always be within the arms of the Great Oak.

EPILOGUE

I sit upon a large root at the base of the Great Oak. In front of me, the forest floor is filled with many faces belonging to children of all ages, arrays of colors, and races. Their eyes are upon me, enwrapped in the story of the half-blood who saved his people from tyranny. It is a story they are familiar with as well. They have lived beneath the ruler, the antagonist of my story, a story that begins well in the past when generations before us were fighting against his oppression.

The children grasp for each other as I tell of the final moments, when the half-blood was faced with his own hatred for his enemy and the swell of new power threatened to overtake him. The ending of this story is fresh in my mind, although it has been several months since it occurred. Many suns since the land around me was void of the buildings of this community, and the hillside held nothing more than the shade of the Great Oak herself.

Much has changed since then. More smiles can be seen, even among the adults, and there is never a time when laughter does not echo through the forest canopy. There is never any distinction between bloods anymore, as we all refer to each other as the people of the Great Oak, a title we are all proud to carry. For those who are still burdened by the past, each new day brings new healing. And who wouldn't be healed by the sight of children playing among the Great Oak's roots, or the sounds of the forest as the wind whispers through its branches? There is joy all around, the joys of new life and continuation of the old. We live with the memories of our past, and yet they make us grateful for each new day."

I complete the story and then stand up, brushing my skirts and trying to withhold a smile as the children groan in protest.

"One more, Oriana!" A small girl tugs at the hem of my skirts, grinning sweetly.

"Please!" the boy behind her begs with clasped hands.

"Tell us of the first half-blood again!" I hear from deeper among the crowd.

I hold my hands up in defense of the growing onslaught. "There will be time for more stories later," I remind them assuredly, and I need time to relax and regain my voice. "Until then, I think it's time you all got back to work. There is still plenty of gathering to be done before the sun sets." I look up at its peaked position in the sky.

A new wave of complaints follows. "But Oriana, we're so hungry!"

"We haven't eaten in ages!'"

I sigh, unable to turn away their pleading. "All right, go get something extra from the kitchens, and tell the cooks I said you can each have something special. But that means you have to get to work directly afterward!" I wag a finger at all of them, sounding as stern as I can.

They each give me a reassuring nod before running toward the hillside's dining hall. Somehow I'm not completely convinced.

"You let them get away with far too much." I look up to see Azura, her belly showing signs of the child within. She still refuses to speak of the matter, yet for some reason I believe the infant will be born with a sprout of auburn hair.

"Yes, I know; it's a weakness of mine." I give a rueful smile before following her back toward the Great Oak. I have work of my own to do at the meeting hall where Azura and I have been discussing the compilation of new maps. Now that most of the work has been completed at the Great Oak, our plans have been to explore the land and gain more information about the territories surrounding us. There is still the possibility of danger, so, it's important that we become familiar with our lands.

"Oriana!"

I stop abruptly, turning to face Dorian, who is breathing heavily from a brisk pace.

"I've been trying to get a moment's rest to talk to you," he says, covering the distance between us. "I was hoping to ask you something, a fulfillment of a promise …" I look down at his hands that he's trying to conceal behind his back. Both possess a burdened pack.

"A promise?" I ask, trying to make sense of his excitement.

"I would like to show you the ocean," he confesses. "If you'll join me."

I say nothing. Instead, I snatch the pack from his hand and start for the western horizon. I only glance backward to wave good-bye to Azura.

"I guess that was a yes," Dorian says with an amused expression, as he catches up to my side.

By the following evening, our travels have brought us to the end of the forest. The landscape opens up into soft soil that swallows my sandaled feet in warmth as I tread upon it. Dorian explains it as sand. Yet my attention is drawn onward into the expanse beyond. The endless blue of the ocean reaches far into the distance, where the sun slowly sinks into its surface. I place my pack upon the banks of sand before I approach it cautiously, watching as it flows up the land and then retreats backward of its own will. Dorian rushes past me, splashing upon the wet sand and diving beneath the murky currents.

I startle when the ocean reaches my feet, my attention having been on Dorian. The sensation is cool and welcoming, and it seems to draw me further into it as it pulls back again in its repetitive rhythm. I walk further in, concentrating on my feet as they begin to disappear at the ankles, and then my knees. A wave flows toward me, striking at my thighs and pushing me backward with startling force. I slip beneath the surface, hitting the ground below and fighting to reach the air.

A hand pulls me upward, Dorian brings me back above, I swallow the fresh air. Together we pass the evening among the waves, his grasp always there to bring me to the surface as I learn to maneuver against the roiling tide.

When night approaches we emerge from the sea, returning to our packs and gathering dry beach wood. Around the heat of a towering fire we dry ourselves and our clothing. The sky above is clear of any clouds, and the rush of the never tiring ocean prolongs its soothing song in the distance.

When I reach into my pack to pull out food and drink, my fingers touch a familiar surface. I pull out Narena's journal, and my eyes find Dorian, whose attention is already upon me. I look at him questioningly.

"I found it on your dresser, and something told me to bring it." He shrugs and takes a long drink from a canteen filled with water.

"This small book has been a great help," I say, feeling as though my words were meant not only for Dorian but for Narena herself.

I open it to discover the center now holds a grouping of folded pages, the missing entries that Dorian removed. I pull out the pages, unfolding them to discover the final passage laid on top. The ending to the first passage I had read from her journal.

I read the words out loud, "*I am hoping he will find this and maybe see who I was and became. I am sorry we must leave, but understand there is no other way. Know that we love you, my son, my Dorian—neither Finlet nor Winglet, yet equally both. Only when we are joined together, those born of the air and of the sea, in a place between, does our true power blossom.*

In faith and hope, Narena."

I look up at Dorian, seeing the effect the words have on him. "It came true for her, didn't it? The purpose of her book, the messages she was trying to bring? It all came true. Your mother and father are proud of you, I know they are."

"I thought for so long that what they wanted was to see him die. I thought if he was gone, then all the pain of losing them would go away. But that never happened, that isn't what she wanted, she never wanted me to hate or blame Odon. That was something I did all on my own. Even after reading her words over and over again."

He watches the flames, lost in thought, and then looks over at me. "Oriana, if you hadn't been there, I would've become him. I would've taken over everyone's minds, yours included. I'm just as weak as Odon. Sometimes I fear that I'm not free of it, that I might become someone else—the person I saw through your eyes at the Rebirth, out of control, unable to harness my anger."

"That's why I and the others who care about you will be here." I look down at the journal, feeling as though Narena knew better than anyone the importance of loving another. "You aren't like Odon, you may share the same abilities, but I've seen you use yours for good. That's something Odon never did."

"But there is a thin line between good and evil. With my power"—he looks at his hands as though they were foreign—"I can heal great damage, but just as quickly I can cause it, and I believe I would if anything ever happened to you again. There are others out there, half-bloods like Odon who are thirsty for power, who desire the minds of the innocent. Defeating Odon was just the beginning; the war is not yet won."

Dorian's words frighten me; I know they are true. He was able to overcome Odon's power, but that was just one adversary. There are others who could be even more powerful. There is no way of knowing. "We must be grateful for what we have and take each day as it comes. We can only do our best as those of the past were able to do. Who knows, it may be countless generations to come before we are all free. But I fear that evil can never truly be banished from this world. That is why there must always be good to counter it."

Dorian nods. He gets to his feet and approaches me. He takes the book from my hand, kissing me gently upon the lips and then drawing back. "I think I can let go now." He speaks to the book rather to me, smoothing his thumb along the binding. "I think that I must lay the past to rest, so that we can open the door of the future."

He draws a deep breath and tosses the pages into the flames. The paper immediately catches fire, bits of it drifting upward with the ash. We watch as the wind carries it away, into the sky, beyond the stars, to a place—the place where we are all one.

Manufactured By: RR Donnelley
Breinigsville, PA USA
January, 2011